KAUA'I
STORM

OTHER TITLES BY TORI ELDRIDGE

Lily Wong Thriller Series

The Ninja Daughter

The Ninja's Blade

The Ninja Betrayed

The Ninja's Oath

Stand-Alone

Dance Among the Flames

KAUA'I STORM

A RANGER MAKALANI PAHUKULA MYSTERY

TORI ELDRIDGE

Published by Thomas & Mercer, Seattle

www.apub.com

Amazon, the Amazon logo, and Thomas & Mercer are trademarks of Amazon.com, Inc., or its affiliates.

EU product safety contact:
Amazon Media EU S. à r.l.
38, avenue John F. Kennedy, L-1855 Luxembourg
amazonpublishing-gpsr@amazon.com

ISBN-13: 9781662525247 (paperback)
ISBN-13: 9781662525230 (digital)

Cover design by Ploy Siripant
Cover image: © G. Brad Lewis / Alamy Stock

Printed in the United States of America

For my darling moʻopuna, Moana and Nahele. Aloha nui ʻo Tūtū iā ʻolua!

PREFACE

Welcome to *Kaua'i Storm*. Welina mai iā kākou! I was born and raised in Honolulu of Hawaiian, Chinese, and Norwegian descent, but Kaua'i has always been my favorite island, rich in beauty and old Hawaiian ways. The rugged tropical forests and Hawaiian Home Lands issues made it the perfect setting for Ranger Makalani Pahukula and her multigenerational, multiethnic 'ohana. I have included a full genealogy of her family along with locations, characters, and words and phrases from 'ōlelo Hawai'i and Hawaiian Pidgin English as used in my book. As always, I have woven actual locations, history, and facts into my fiction and taken liberties where needed to tell an exciting story I hope you will enjoy.

PAHUKULA FAMILY TREE
FROM KAʻAHUMANU'S RECORDS

H—Husband
w—Wife

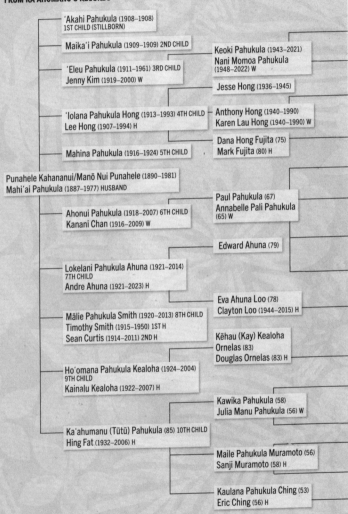

ʻAkahi Pahukula (1908–1908)
1ST CHILD (STILLBORN)

Maikaʻi Pahukula (1909–1909) 2ND CHILD

ʻEleu Pahukula (1911–1961) 3RD CHILD
Jenny Kim (1919–2000) W

Keoki Pahukula (1943–2021)
Nani Momoa Pahukula
(1948–2022) W

Jesse Hong (1936–1945)

ʻIolana Pahukula Hong (1913–1993) 4TH CHILD
Lee Hong (1907–1994) H

Anthony Hong (1940–1990)
Karen Lau Hong (1940–1990) W

Dana Hong Fujita (75)
Mark Fujita (80) H

Mahina Pahukula (1916–1924) 5TH CHILD

Punahele Kahananui/Manō Nui Punahele (1890–1981)
Mahiʻai Pahukula (1887–1977) HUSBAND

Paul Pahukula (67)
Annabelle Pali Pahukula
(65) W

Ahonui Pahukula (1918–2007) 6TH CHILD
Kanani Chan (1916–2009) W

Edward Ahuna (79)

Lokelani Pahukula Ahuna (1921–2014)
7TH CHILD
Andre Ahuna (1921–2023) H

Eva Ahuna Loo (78)
Clayton Loo (1944–2015) H

Mālie Pahukula Smith (1920–2013) 8TH CHILD
Timothy Smith (1915–1950) 1ST H
Sean Curtis (1914–2011) 2ND H

Kēhau (Kay) Kealoha
Ornelas (83)
Douglas Ornelas (83) H

Hoʻomana Pahukula Kealoha (1924–2004)
9TH CHILD
Kainalu Kealoha (1922–2007) H

Kawika Pahukula (58)
Julia Manu Pahukula (56) W

Kaʻahumanu (Tūtū) Pahukula (85) 10TH CHILD
Hing Fat (1932–2006) H

Maile Pahukula Muramoto (56)
Sanji Muramoto (58) H

Kaulana Pahukula Ching (53)
Eric Ching (56) H

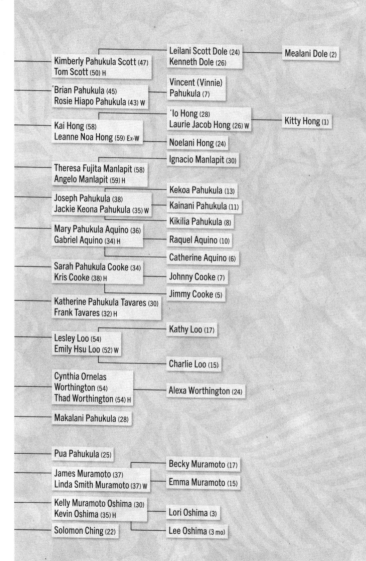

Kimberly Pahukula Scott (47)
Tom Scott (50) H

Leilani Scott Dole (24)
Kenneth Dole (26)

Mealani Dole (2)

'Brian Pahukula (45)
Rosie Hiapo Pahukula (43) w

Vincent (Vinnie)
Pahukula (7)

Kai Hong (58)
Leanne Noa Hong (59) Ex-W

'Io Hong (28)
Laurie Jacob Hong (26) w

Kitty Hong (1)

Noelani Hong (24)

Ignacio Manlapit (30)

Theresa Fujita Manlapit (58)
Angelo Manlapit (59) H

Joseph Pahukula (38)
Jackie Keona Pahukula (35) w

Kekoa Pahukula (13)

Kainani Pahukula (11)

Mary Pahukula Aquino (36)
Gabriel Aquino (34) H

Kikilia Pahukula (8)

Raquel Aquino (10)

Sarah Pahukula Cooke (34)
Kris Cooke (38) H

Catherine Aquino (6)

Johnny Cooke (7)

Jimmy Cooke (5)

Katherine Pahukula Tavares (30)
Frank Tavares (32) H

Lesley Loo (54)
Emily Hsu Loo (52) w

Kathy Loo (17)

Charlie Loo (15)

Cynthia Ornelas
Worthington (54)
Thad Worthington (54) H

Alexa Worthington (24)

Makalani Pahukula (28)

Pua Pahukula (25)

James Muramoto (37)
Linda Smith Muramoto (37) w

Becky Muramoto (17)

Emma Muramoto (15)

Kelly Muramoto Oshima (30)
Kevin Oshima (35) H

Lori Oshima (3)

Solomon Ching (22)

Lee Oshima (3 mo)

CHAPTER ONE

Giant fronds of hāpuʻu ferns whipped Makalani's face as she plowed through the Kauaʻi rainforest away from the men. They had emerged from the jungle like a pack of wild dogs, barking commands to find, catch, kill.

"Ovah dea," a man yelled, then pumped his shotgun with a distinctive *ka-chunk*.

Makalani dived into the red-spotted ʻamaʻu ferns seconds before pellets shredded the leaves.

A centipede crept toward her nose. She blew it away. She wasn't dead yet.

The pistol holstered inside her waistband dug into her ribs, but as she rolled onto her hip, another blast peppered the fronds overhead. She left the weapon in place and scurried through the plants. Even an armed ranger needed better cover for a firefight than ferns.

"You get um?" a man yelled.

Makalani didn't wait for the reply.

Staying as low as her near-six-foot frame would allow, she barreled through the undergrowth toward the darker shadows beneath the thick canopy of ʻōhiʻa lehua and koa trees. Because of her size, her pursuers had mistaken her for a man. That same size made it harder to slip between bushes without rustling the leaves. Not for the first time, she wished she had inherited her mother's slender grace.

Who am I kidding? If I were more like Māmā, I wouldn't be in this mess.

Recriminations assaulted her with every lumbering step—if she had stayed in the islands, if she had tried to belong, if she had honored her responsibility to her family and their land . . . If she had not gone to the mainland, she would have known what was happening with her 'ohana before it all went to hell.

Stop it, Makalani. You're a federal officer. You know better than this.

She shoved down the "ifs" and focused on the facts. Five people had been at the camp. At least four had pursued. Aside from the shotgun and probably machetes, she didn't know what weapons they had. She needed more distance and the cover of high ground before she could even consider engaging in a fight. Although trained in firearms, Makalani had never drawn her weapon against a person before. Her peace officer duties at Crater Lake National Park mostly consisted of traffic violations, theft, or the occasional brawl. The adjacent village where park employees lived and visitors lodged was almost as sleepy as her hometown in Kaua'i—or rather, as sleepy as she had always believed her hometown to be. The weeklong reunion for Tūtū's birthday had obliterated that belief.

"I see shaking by da big tree," a new voice yelled, followed by hoots of encouragement and hacking through brush.

Makalani charged through the foliage, knees jarring as she landed unexpectedly on the unfamiliar terrain.

I am kanaka maoli, she reminded herself. *This is my 'āina, no matter how long I've been gone.*

Despite her years on the mainland, the blood of her Hawaiian ancestors ran through her veins. Her kūpuna had thrived in these forests from the mountains to the sea. Makalani had done the same, returning to the forest whenever her discomfort with people became too much to bear. Although she cared for, policed, and sometimes rescued the two-legged visitors in her national park, her primary kuleana was to the natural resources, the animals, and the land. She had accepted this sacred responsibility. Whether in Oregon or Hawai'i, the forests were her home.

Tears of regret rolled down her cheeks.

If only I had placed my kuleana to family above all.

She bolted ahead, sank her boot into a hole, and pitched forward into a tree. She froze, hands on bark, a hairbreadth from having broken her shin. Behind her, the men argued about where she had gone. In open sunlight, her trail would have been as obvious as a road. With dark clouds above the canopy, she might still have a chance.

She dislodged her boot and cut through a sparser patch of shrubs. She moved even faster through the grove of invasive strawberry guava trees. Swinging her arms from one trunk to the next, she jogged, ran, and slid like a pinball, bouncing off obstacles as she careened down the hill. Clawing at the mud to straighten her slide, she plunged, feetfirst, through the wood rot of a decaying fallen tree.

Air left her in a whoosh.

Makalani twisted her head and checked up the slope. No signs of pursuit. She inhaled deeply and sighed.

As she brushed the bugs from her pants and pulled out her boot, the rotted stump crumbled, and she slid into the swelling stream. The treacherous Oregon wilderness wasn't as slippery as the Keālia Forest Reserve. It also wasn't as prone to deadly flash floods. The storm must have broken over Makaleha Peak. She needed to hike out of this gully before the rains reached her and turned the already slick hillside into waterfalls of mud.

Makalani opened her arms to the darkening sky and appealed to the Hawaiian god of agriculture, fertility, and peace. "Aloha mai, Lono. I know this is the last month of the Makahiki and the farmers are praying to you for rain, but would you *please* ease your blessings for a few hours until I get out of this mess?"

Lono roared from the mountain and shook the rock beneath her feet. The overabundance of his blessings was rushing down the canyon to wash her away.

Makalani scrambled out of the gully, seconds before the incoming rapids ripped the stump off the bank. Chunks of the hillside collapsed with every dig of her boot. The noise, like jets on a tarmac, swallowed her cries.

"E kala mai ia'u. Please forgive me. I love you, my family. I didn't mean to leave you and die."

CHAPTER TWO

One Week Earlier

Humidity hit Makalani the moment she stepped off the plane and enveloped her in the sticky, sweet scent of home. After the surprise cold snap in Portland, she welcomed the heat.

She rolled down the rental car's window and waited for a rooster to strut out of the road. The feral chickens ruled the island of Kaua'i with prideful indifference. This one was no exception. Crowned in red, caped in gold, this bird's brilliant teal plumes arched up and over from its rump like a cresting wave. It cocked its head toward Makalani, pecked twice at the asphalt, and moved on its way.

Hawaiian time.

One of many reasons Makalani had flown the coop before the ink on her high school diploma had dried. She had too much energy for the islands. Not the ambitious kind. More like an insatiable drive to work.

Makalani didn't flit from one fantastical experience to the next, sucked into drama or chasing the trends. Her social media accounts—on which she hadn't posted in a month—featured scenic shots from Crater Lake National Park, the ranger town where she lived, and the adorable critters she spotted on the job. Boring stuff for a twenty-eight-year-old woman, whose generation could make anything seem like such a big deal. She hadn't fit in with her peers as a child. Why would she feel comfortable with them as an adult?

She sighed at her foolishness.

Now who's making a big deal?

Although, if she was being honest, she had always felt emotions more acutely than most. Her yearning for friendship had pushed other kids away. So she channeled the rejection and loneliness into work. Even as a teenager, she had never kicked back with friends on a beach. The awkwardness made it impossible to relax. Instead, she stayed productive every minute of the day. Helping others gave Makalani the connection she craved and guided her to a park ranger career. What worked for her exhausted everyone else.

You're in Hawai'i, she reminded herself. *It's time to chill out.*

When she moved to the mainland, Aunty Kaulana had told her the island breathed a sigh of relief.

Or maybe Aunty Kaulana just didn't want me to make her lazy husband look bad.

Makalani chuckled. Uncle Eric had turned laziness into an art.

She leaned her head out the window and let the wind dry her unexpected tears. She couldn't wait to hug every member of her precious 'ohana. Even him.

As she drove up Kūhiō Highway—a generous classification for a two-lane road—she passed the Ko'olau Hui'ia Protestant Church, where her family worshipped. How long had it been since she prayed in a hale pule? A year ago Christmas? Christmas before that? Guilt tugged at her heart. Although she communed with God in the mountains every day, she would have felt more connected with her Anahola community if she had returned more frequently and worshipped with them. She had so many fond memories of community gatherings over the years. The best kālua pig she'd ever eaten had come from an imu dug into that sacred earth.

Would someone dig a pit at the homestead for Tūtū's birthday lū'au?

If not, I'll dig it myself.

6

She could almost feel the shovel in her hands as she cut through the ground, the weight of the earth, the sweat on her brow. Hard labor would feel wonderful after sitting for hours on a plane. The barren yards along the highway told her not everyone would agree. Bitter grass on hard red dirt. No crops. No flowers. Only the same Habitat for Humanity stilt houses she had helped to build, testaments to the poverty in which so many Native Hawaiians lived.

A belly growl chased away her somber thoughts. Like Pavlov's dog, her mouth salivated every time she glimpsed the orange walls of Kalalea Juice Hale peeking through the trees. If she wasn't so eager to get home, she'd stop. Instead, she rounded the bend and turned onto a narrow road where tall clumps of pili grass pressed in from the berm. Monkeypod and kukui nut trees older than her parents entwined their branches overhead.

She peered through the jungle on either side of the road for a glimpse of homes and domesticated land. The rain-soaked vines had grown too thick among the trees. If not for the gap in the foliage, she might have missed the open cattle gate to her grandmother's homestead.

Makalani followed the dirt road down the slope and parked beside the majestic banyan tree. How she loved walking along the high branches when she was a child. Now Uncle Eric lounged on a beach chair wedged between the roots. He jutted his head in recognition, slipped off a rubber zori, nudged the cooler with his foot, and retrieved a fresh can of beer.

"Ho," he said. "Look what da trade winds blew in."

Makalani turned off the engine and hung out the open window. "Howzit, Uncle."

"Eh, Makalani. You back for Tūtū's birthday?"

"That's the plan. Solomon around?"

"Nah. Not since yesterday. Try wait, tho. Bumbai, he come back." He nodded toward the cooler. "If fo' not'ing else, fo' da beer."

Makalani frowned. Solomon had been an active and bright child—scholastically challenged, to be sure, but intelligent all the same. If he hadn't blown out his knee, he might have thrived at UH. Without the football scholarship, he couldn't stay, and sank into depression.

Makalani shook her head. She knew better than to buy in to family judgment. That said, Uncle Eric had less ambition than the breadfruit hanging from her grandmother's trees. If not for the extra rooms her father had added to the house on Tūtū's land, Uncle Eric and Aunty Kaulana would be living under hala branches on the beach.

"Your cousin stay on da Muramoto side of da house now, you know dat? Dey get more room ovah dea since James moved his family into town."

"I heard. You think Aunty Maile and Uncle Sanji will ever join them?"

"Nah. Maile stay holding out fo' dis land in case your tūtū change her mind 'bout your dad."

"Yeah, but . . ." Makalani held out her hands. "He and Māmā do most of the work."

"Dass what I tell her. But she married a Muramoto so, you know, little bit entitled li'dat."

Makalani chuckled. He wasn't wrong.

Her uncle-in-law's ancestor had immigrated with the early wave of Japanese contract workers. When his plantation time was done, he married a young Issei woman and opened a store. The first- and second-generation Muramotos had been an integral part of the Japanese community on Kaua'i. Their status changed when Uncle Sanji married Makalani's Hawaiian Chinese aunt and eventually lost his family's store. Although their hapa-Japanese son, James, opened a new market, the Muramotos' standing in the Japanese community was never the same.

Uncle Eric swept his beer in front of him to encompass the jungle paradise in which he sat. "No can blame, tho. Dis homestead nō ka 'oi." He bumped the cooler with his toe. "Me and your aunty Kaulana get everyt'ing we need right hea."

Makalani felt bad for Solomon. He might have a better chance in life if his father applied for his own land.

Let it go, Makalani.

She took a deep breath. If she let her frustration with Uncle Eric grow, the emotions would trigger the stomach pains of her youth. Besides, there was nothing she could do to change him or anyone else. She knew this because she had already tried. Her laid-back uncle fit in with island life better than her. Makalani was the one who didn't belong.

She considered the rest of her family, many of whom would fly in for Tūtū's birthday at the end of the week. Like the majestic banyan under which Uncle Eric so casually sat, the roots of her family dug deep into the ʻāina with Tūtū as the trunk, Makalani's father and aunties as the limbs, and all the spouses and cousins stretched across the islands and mainland states like the leaves.

How many people are blessed with an ʻohana like mine?

Uncle Eric was fortunate that he could bask in their shade whenever he chose.

"James them good?" she asked about her cousins, feeling bad for not keeping in touch.

Uncle Eric shrugged. "I stay out of it."

"Out of what?"

"Everyt'ing." He leaned back and closed his eyes, as if he couldn't care less.

CHAPTER THREE

Makalani restarted the engine and followed the red-dirt treads down the gentle slope where her grandparents had planted fruit- and nut-bearing trees. Rather than align in neat agricultural rows, the trees covered the land in plentiful harmony, giving each enough space and sunlight to thrive.

During mango season, from May to October, the family would use long poles with hooks and sacks at the end to pluck and catch the fruit. They baked mango into bread, cakes, and pudding. They blended it into smoothies and added it to salsa, salads, and fish. If any were still green, they dipped them in soy sauce, dried them with li hing spice, or simmered them into chutney with Hawaiian chili peppers, ginger, vinegar, garlic, sugar, raisins, and salt. When the family couldn't eat, sell, or share any more, Tūtū sliced them up and froze them on foil plates. When the avocados ripened from September through May, Makalani's mother and aunties changed their recipes to fit. The overlapping months when the fruits ripened together were the best.

She drove past the ʻulu trees, heavy with spiky green breadfruit. Her mainland friends hadn't liked it when she bought it in the store, but the ʻulu grown on Tūtū's land tasted like home. Even the papaya and banana tasted different when ripened on the trees.

If Makalani had ventured down the grassy lanes, she would have found macadamia nuts littering the ground and the mountain apple trees she and her father had planted when she was a kid. Pāpā had chosen the wettest, shadiest hillside on the farm so the trees would remember the mountains and grow well. Makalani checked every week until the tiny gourd-shaped fruit finally appeared, their pale-green color brightening into shiny red. The memory of their crisp, watery sweetness made her smile. As tempting as it was to see if any still remained on the ʻōhiʻa ʻai trees, she would wait until she had greeted her ʻohana and given everyone a hug.

Warmed by these memories, Makalani continued down the grassy road. Later, she would check on the vegetable gardens and visit the kalo patch near the stream. All this, combined with Pāpāʻs fishing and Tūtūʻs pigs, chickens, and the ʻōkolehao she fermented behind the shed, made the Pahukula homestead a self-sustaining farm. If they wanted something else, they either bartered or bought it with the proceeds from their crops. The biggest challenge was labor.

Has that improved now that Solomon's come home?

Makalani parked under a shade tree and gazed at the plantation house, its wide-hipped roofs the color of soaked red dirt. The house had begun as a simple structure built with the help of Tūtūʻs parents and her husband's brothers before they moved back to China. Grandpa Hing had stayed in Anahola after the pineapple plantations shut down and lived with Tūtū on the homestead leased in her name. After Makalaniʻs father and aunties were born, Grandpa Hing and Tūtū added more bedrooms to the house and surrounded it with a wood-deck lānai. When the keiki grew up and married, they added new wings on either side. The entire compound sat on a raised foundation that protected it from floods. Despite its piecemeal construction, the house blended together with harmony and love.

Makalani hefted her camping backpack onto her shoulders and headed down the gravel path toward the steps as her two aunties—one large and one small—stormed out the front door and onto the lānai.

Tūtūʻs younger and larger daughter whirled on the elder, hands on hips and nostrils flared. "Shame on you, Maile. How you let your son spread dis junk about mine? Solomon would nevah hurt one child. Nevah."

"Oh, yeah?" Aunty Maile said, challenging her younger sister the way a terrier nips at a boar. "The police say otherwise. Your precious Solomon is a drunk and a degenerate."

"No throw big words at me, tita. Your Japanee husband and haole daughter-in-law no make you bettah dan us. Your moʻopuna barely got any Hawaiian left in her. She jus' one skinny, stuck-up slut."

"Whoa," Makalani said, hurrying up the steps. "What's going on?" Aunty Kaulana swatted her hand in the air. "You nevah heard? Dis one's granddaughter wen missing. Run away, mo' like."

"Or taken by your son," Aunty Maile said.

Makalani gasped. "Solomon? What are you saying, Aunty? The police think he abducted her? That's crazy. Solomon adores Becky."

Aunty Maile scoffed. "Exactly my point."

"You lōlō, or what?" Aunty Kaulana said. "Everybody knows your granddaughter stay crushing on my son. Been li'dat since junior high. Every time she come fo' one visit, she stick on his skin like sweat."

Aunty Maile crossed her arms as though her sister had proven her point. "And now dey gone."

"Not together. My Solomon is twenty-two and full grown. He can go where he like. Dis trouble 'bout your Becky."

Makalani's father yelled, "Knock it off, already." He walked up the slope on the makai-side—oceanside—of the house, carrying fishing gear and a string of pāpio. The jackfish looked tiny and pale swinging alongside Pāpā's powerful, sun-blackened legs.

The sisters turned their backs on one another and marched across the lānai to their respective sides of the house: Aunty Kaulana toward the mountain, Aunty Maile toward the sea. Makalani dropped her backpack on the deck and jumped down the steps.

Her father laughed. "Eh, little girl. When you get home?"

"Just now." She reached her arms around his massive chest for a hug. Although she was tall and sturdy, Makalani felt tiny in her father's arms. She could smell the ocean on his skin, baked into his pores by the sun, but his true warmth radiated from the love in his heart. She breathed in the comforting presence of *him* and knew she had truly come home.

"Good to have you back. Been crazy here li'dat."

"I noticed. What's going on with Solomon and Becky? Aunty Maile said something about the police."

"Auwē. T'ings so messed up. Dem kids been gone since yesterday."

"Together?"

Pāpā shrugged. "Nobody knows. But your aunties not da only ones fighting. People talking stink about Solomon all ovah town. Becky, too. She already stay grounded fo' staying out past curfew Sunday night. When she nevah come home aftah school on Monday, James and Linda figured she was acting out. Dey get plenny mad when she nevah come home at all."

"So they filed a missing person's report?"

"Not officially. Dey called Kimo Tagaloa. You remembah him, right? Beat cop. Played football wit' Solomon back in high school."

Makalani nodded. The officer and her cousin hadn't really been friends. "So they called Kimo because he knows our family?"

Pāpā shrugged. "You know how James and Linda are. Always concerned 'bout what everybody t'ink." He held up the fish. "I gotta clean da pāpio. Go inside and say hello. Māmā and Tūtū tell you all 'bout it fo' sure."

"You want help?"

"No need. But tanks fo' offering, yeah?" He squeezed her shoulder. "It's good to have you home."

She watched with envy as he headed for the working side of the property where he butchered and cleaned pigs, chicken, and fish. Makalani would have preferred those endeavors to a bickering 'ohana.

With a last look toward the trees, she headed up the steps and took off the hiking boots she had worn on the plane to save space in her bag. Her toes rejoiced to be free. She tucked the boots under a bench and ignored the inviting lānai chairs and pūne'e, a daybed-style couch where she often took naps. She had stalled long enough. Time to see how the rest of the family fared—a decision she regretted as soon as she stepped into the house.

Although the great room was empty, angry voices invaded from the kitchen beyond.

She left her pack at the entrance and padded across the hardwood floor, past bamboo furniture with hand-stitched pillows and quilts. Vibrant paintings from local artists hung on the walls. A cool river breeze blew in from the open rear lānai doors. Makalani breathed in sweet plumeria mixed with the spicy scent of mosquito-repelling plants her mother grew in planters on the rear deck. If not for the angry voices coming from the kitchen, she would have enjoyed the tranquil view.

Makalani dodged behind a potted palm to watch.

James's wife, Linda, paced in the stovetop aisle, her pale skin lobster red like the haole tourists who fell asleep on the beach. "Why are you defending him, Julia? He's not even your blood. You married into this family same as me. You should be sticking up for Becky, not Solomon."

Māmā struck the macadamia nut with a hammer and popped the broken shell out of an electric-pink slice of pool-noodle foam. The hollow inside the tube was perfectly sized for a nut. "Becky's my grandniece, Solomon's my nephew, both 'ohana to me. What's the difference?" She swept the brown shells aside and placed the white nut on the food dehydrator tray.

Across the butcher-block island, Makalani's majestic grandmother kneaded dough. Ka'ahumanu Pahukula towered above the other women, thick, silver hair braided around her koa-brown face. She looked like an ancient Hawaiian chiefess. Not the kind who would have ordered others to do her will, but an ali'i wahine who would have worked and fought alongside the men. The set of Tūtū's jaw and the resigned look in Māmā's warm, brown eyes told Makalani how long they had been under Linda's assault.

Linda curled her idle hands into fists. "The difference is blood."

Makalani winced at the familiar complaint, the wedge driven into her ʻohana by laws that shouldn't exist. No wonder Tūtū's jaw looked ready to crack.

Linda was referring to the blood quantum required to inherit Tūtū's homestead. Although the Hawaiian Homes Commission Act of 1920 still required a minimum of 50 percent to apply for the dollar-per-year ninety-nine-year lease, current lessees could now pass their family land on to children, grandchildren, and siblings as long as they had at least 25 percent. With luck and time, the United States Congress would finally pass the state's bill that reduced the successor blood quantum to 3.13 percent. Until that time, Makalani; her sister, Pua; and Solomon were the only descendants after their parents' generation who were eligible.

It was this rule—not Linda's insinuation of bigotry—that set the Muramoto cousins apart from the rest of the ʻohana. Not only had Aunty Maile married a full-blooded Japanese husband, her son, James, had married a pure haole wife. That made Becky less than 10 percent Hawaiian. Although the government considered that too little, the family knew any amount was enough. All of them were hapa in the truest sense of the word—part Hawaiian and part something else.

Tūtū threw up her hands and sent a puff of ʻulu flour into the air. "Enough already. Both kids Pahukula to me. I no like fight in our ʻohana. We need come together, find Becky, and bring her home safe."

Makalani walked into view. "Hey, everyone, I'm home."

Tūtū sighed with happiness. "E komo mai, moʻopuna." She clasped Makalani's cheeks with her floury hands, touched foreheads, and shared a welcoming breath.

Māmā waited impatiently, then descended with a hug.

Linda stood apart and muttered, "The favorite child."

"You just get in?" Māmā smoothed Makalani's unruly mane, which had tripled in volume from the salty, humid air. Short of tying it into a knot on top of her head, nothing would contain Makalani's explosion of waves.

"I came straight from the airport. Glad to be home but sorry about all this trouble." She glanced at her cousin's wife. "Any more news about Becky?"

Linda huffed. Her blond hair and pale skin stuck out in this family like a puka shell on a black sand beach. "I'm sure your 'ohana will fill you in," she said bitterly, and left.

"Nevah mind her," Tūtū said. "How you stay?"

"I'm good. But what's going on with Solomon?"

Tūtū sighed. "Auwē. Same as usual—'o ia mau nō. Drink too much, do too little. No one happy wit' him dese days."

"Did he really run off with Becky?"

"Of course not," Māmā interrupted. "Probably drinking with his old high school football buddies, talking story about the old times, and sleeping off a keg of beer."

When Makalani had seen Solomon just over a year ago, he had been relatively sober and only mildly depressed. They had talked deeply. Makalani had hoped he would turn his life around.

"He and Becky were always close."

Māmā frowned. "Closer since he came home from UH."

"You think there's something going on?"

"No. I'm just explaining how things might look from the outside. It didn't help when James and Linda brought Kimo into the mix." She hammered another nut, plucked it from the ring, and brushed the shells aside. "He and Solomon have a rocky past. Best friends as kids, rivals in high school. Kimo was always so jealous. I think he's happy to see Solomon brought low."

"Did he make James and Linda file an official report?"

"Not sure. But the questions he asked made them feel like they had done something wrong. I think blaming Solomon for corrupting Becky was easier than blaming themselves."

Tūtū muttered in 'ōlelo Hawai'i about kuleana as she pounded the 'ulu dough with her fist.

Although Makalani had forgotten much of the Hawaiian language during her years on the mainland, the concept of a reciprocal responsibility was deeply ingrained. Living off the land was a prime example of this reciprocity. The Pahukula family cared for and protected the 'āina, which, in turn, provided food, water, and shelter for them. The same applied to people. Without kuleana, there could be no harmony, balance, or respect.

As the eldest daughter of Tūtū's eldest son, Makalani felt responsible for her cousins' safety and reputation. The kuleana was hers. She would find them both and restore the peace.

CHAPTER FOUR

Kay Ornelas wiped the coffee mess off her pristine granite counter with a huff. Her relaxing afternoon decaf had ended with her daughter's news. The bulging veins on her wrinkled hands made her feel worse. She hated anything that marked the passage of time.

Douglas sat across the counter, thumbing through the *Honolulu Star-Advertiser*, more distinguished in his older years but as handsome as before. God had a cruel sense of humor to make women peak early and then fade. Although Douglas would never divorce her, she sometimes wished he didn't look like he could.

She folded the rag and smoothed her wavy, white hair, chicly cut and styled around her face like the rich Kahala wives. Decades of avoiding the sun had lightened her skin, making her look part haole instead of five-eighths Hawaiian and three-eighths Chinese. Kay had worked hard to shed her homesteading origins and fit into Douglas's country club circle. She deserved to live out his retirement in peace.

She glared at her phone and the upsetting email still on its screen, then slid it across the counter for her husband to see. "Why is our daughter bringing her family to this birthday lūʻau? They barely know my aunt. Why should they care if Kaʻahumanu turns eighty-five?"

Douglas adjusted his reading glasses and peered at the email's small print. "Cynthia says they have something they want to share."

"What, like a present? Couldn't they have sent it in the mail? And why are they bringing Alexa? I'm sure she has graduate-college work to do."

Douglas peered over his glasses. "Maybe they want a vacation."

"On Kaua'i?"

"Why not? It's the most beautiful island."

"If you like a jungle."

Douglas reached across the counter and patted the Tiffany engagement ring and wedding band on Kay's hand. "Maybe their tastes aren't as discriminating as yours."

"Nonsense. Cynthia takes after me. Her husband is a tech giant. Why would either of them want to fly all this way for a homestead lū'au?"

Douglas checked the email. "They're staying at the Grand Hyatt on Po'ipū Beach. I'm sure they'll have all the five-star amenities they could want. Perhaps Alexa wants to connect to her Hawaiian roots."

Kay groaned. "Our granddaughter's roots are with us in Honolulu, not on a seedy homestead in Anahola."

"You grew up on a homestead."

"Not that one. I lived with my father's family in Wailua, crammed into his childhood room. Good thing my mother couldn't have any more children after me or we wouldn't have fit." Kay shivered with disgust. "Can you imagine ten Kealohas stuffed into four bedrooms and no indoor plumbing? Is that what you want Cynthia and Alexa to see? Because I'm sure my aunty's Anahola homestead will be just as bad. Chickens running inside and out. Muddy feet traipsing through a shack. They probably slaughter their own pigs."

Douglas took off his glasses and crinkled the corners of his pale-blue eyes. "Think they'll cook one in an imu?"

Kay sighed. "And probably pound their own poi."

He chuckled. "Sounds delicious to me."

"Only because you never had to eat it to survive. My mother made bad choices all her life—ran around with men, married my father, alienated her family to move in with his. Couldn't she see we would never escape?"

Bitterness churned in Kay's gut. If only her privileged haole husband could truly understand.

"My father's family begged neighbors for food. Mom's family had it a little better, but she wouldn't go to any of the Pahukulas for help. My mother was as thankful to get away from them as I was to get away from her."

Kay swallowed the acid that came up in her throat. She wanted nothing to do with the good-for-nothing Kealohas or the Pahukula brood.

"My grandmother birthed ten children. *Ten.* Can you believe it? Popped them out like kittens. All gone now except for her precious Ka'ahumanu." Kay rubbed her sore belly. "Who has a tenth child so late in life? My mother, God rest her soul, should have been the last. She was the favorite child until Ka'ahumanu came along."

Douglas must have been tired of hearing this again, but he came around the counter and brushed the worry from her face. "You'll aggravate your ulcer if you keep complaining like this. I know you don't want to go to the lū'au, but Ka'ahumanu is your only living aunt."

"She's only two years older than me."

"Exactly. And you're younger, richer, and more beautiful. Can't you celebrate that?"

Kay swatted his hand. After all these years, he still made her smile. "Can we stay at the Hyatt?"

"I already booked a suite. Think of it as a family resort vacation for us with a historic detour into old Hawaiian times."

She kissed him on the cheek. "My life would have been very different if I hadn't met you."

He winked. "Maybe so. But you still would have done well."

Douglas was right. Kay had come to the big city with a fire in her belly to elevate her life, and that started with a name change: she dropped the name her mother gave her, Kēhau, opting for the simpler *Kay*. If she hadn't snagged him, she would have attracted another rich suitor with her island beauty and strategically polished ways. Not only had she surrounded herself with mainlander friends to erase the local lilt from her voice and the Pidgin English from her speech, but she had also

21

joined the debate team at UH, read widely, and kept abreast of world events. She spent her meager earnings buying the cheapest drinks at exclusive hotel lounges and bars so she could mingle with an influential crowd. When a new friend invited her to a Wai'alae Country Club event, she spotted young Douglas Ornelas making a big impression on the real estate elite. By the end of the evening, she had made her own impression on him.

"Why are you frowning, Kay? You have nothing to be ashamed of. Cynthia and Alexa will feel even more proud of you when they see how far you have come."

"I suppose you're right. I can handle a brief and private embarrassment. No photographs. At the first sign of organizing a family portrait, we make our excuses and leave. I don't want it showing up in the local papers, linking us to them."

"No one we know would see it."

"Not in a Kaua'i paper. But if they mention our names, rest assured the Honolulu news will report it as well."

"Would that be so bad?"

"I have a hundred relatives who might attend this lū'au. What kind of lives do you think they lead? A whiff of scandal and everyone in Honolulu will be talking about us."

CHAPTER FIVE

Makalani grabbed a pack of dried cuttlefish and went to her bedroom to store her gear. The airy room faced the front lānai with a pocket door that opened onto the side deck opposite Aunty Maile's family wing. This bedroom had been Aunty Maile's before she married Sanji Muramoto.

Makalani opened the window and door to let the cool breeze circulate through the room. After the surprise snow in Oregon, Kaua'i's supposedly cool January weather had her sweating through her shirt.

"You all settled in?" Pāpā asked from behind.

She turned and smiled. "Where's the fish?"

"Dropped um in da kitchen when I came through da back. What you doing in here? Māmā and Tūtū kick you out already?"

"You know it." She nodded at the open door across the deck. "Is Linda in there?"

"Nah. She drove back to town." Pāpā frowned as she chuckled. "Eh, no laugh."

"Sorry. But after living in Portland, it's hard to think of tiny Kapa'a as a town."

"What you call it, den?"

"A neighborhood?"

"Huh. You need rewire your head." He swept his hand around the room to encompass the traditional quilts and pillows Makalani had stitched, the sailing outrigger model she had constructed, and the photographs of her hiking, kayaking, and building affordable houses all around Kaua'i. "Good t'ing you come home. Stay time fo' remembah who you are."

He picked up a childhood photograph of Makalani helping her baby sister to walk. It was taken in this same room, before Pāpā had moved Pua into Aunty Kaulana's old bedroom and built a private wing for the Chings. Now that Pua lived in Honolulu, this side of the house was usually empty.

"You talk to your sistah much?"

"Not enough."

He set down the picture frame. "She stay come on Saturday. You get four days of quiet all fo' yourself."

Makalani laughed. Pua worked as a restaurant manager in Waikīkī. While the lifestyle suited her gregarious sister, Makalani preferred talking to the mountains and the ocean.

"Wanna paddle downstream with me?" she asked.

"T'anks, but no. I get more chores to do."

"Want help?"

"Nah. Go enjoy da water. Dis your vacation, not mine."

She watched him leave and then unpacked her gear—quick work, since an island stay didn't require much. She kept old jackets and sweaters in the closet if the weather turned bad. The only bulky item she had brought were the boots she had worn on the plane.

Once changed into a triangle top and board shorts, she piled her hair under a paddler's hat and walked onto the side deck. The open pocket door to the Muramoto wing invited her inside. The door to Aunty Maile's suite on the right was shut tight. The door to James and Linda's old room in the center was locked. When Makalani tried the door beyond the bathroom on the left, she paused.

Would Solomon mind if she entered his space without permission?

Too bad, she thought, and opened the door.

The corner bedroom Becky and her younger sister shared as kids had its own access to the front lānai and windows on two sides. It should have been the brightest room in the house. Why had Solomon drawn all the shades?

She closed the door and switched on the ceiling light and fan. The stuffy air stank of soiled clothes, shoes, and beer. Stale kakimochi added seaweed and soy sauce to the scent. She poked the hardened dried mango beside the rice crackers in a bowl.

Would he have left out his snacks if he intended to leave overnight?

She swished the open can of beer.

Would he have left it unfinished?

Solomon wasn't the neatest guy in town, but he wasn't a slob. And if tales of his drinking problem were true, he would have gulped down the rest. What she saw in his bedroom did not fit the cousin she knew.

Clothes were piled high beneath the far window. Only one dented pillow rested on the unmade bed. If Solomon had a girlfriend, she hadn't slept here.

Surf posters and unframed photographs curled from the coral-pink walls over the ghostly impressions where Becky's corkboard and mirror had hung. None of the photos showed Solomon playing football, nor were any of his trophies or framed newspaper features in sight.

No girlfriend. No past. What matters to you now?

She checked the closet and found his memorabilia stuffed on one side, under a sheet. Solomon had been more than a big fish in a tiny pond. With his talent and drive, he could have followed Kaua'i boys Nate Herbig and Jordon Dizon into the NFL. Dizon had blown out his knee after two seasons with the Detroit Lions. Poor Solomon had lasted only a few NCAA Division I games. If only he could feel proud of that accomplishment instead of shattered by heartbreak, he might find a new passion in his life and pull himself from despair.

She slumped against the wall as a grimmer possibility entered her mind.

What if his depression got so bad that he . . .

She slammed the door to his closet before she could finish the thought.

Hands trembling, she said a quick prayer. She had to believe her cousin was okay. Depressed and in trouble, perhaps. Missing, for sure. But ultimately, fine. She loved him like a brother. Once she found him, she would make sure he felt her empathy, love, and support.

She coughed out a laugh.

Then I'll kick your butt for all the trouble you've caused.

Feeling calmer and more in control, Makalani examined the photographs on his wall for places or people Solomon might visit, which included a recent shot of him and his high school buddies drinking beer at Anahola Beach Park. Back in the day, Da Braddahs had ruled Kapaʻa High, with Solomon as the star and the other two providing solid support on the team. Although his friends had always been huge, their bulky muscles had sagged into fat. Beside them, Solomon's extra weight and slovenly appearance looked fine.

Another photo showed his big feet in front of Uluwehi Falls. Had he kayaked up the Wailua River from the ocean or put in at the state park? Either way led to an uphill, slippery hike. Good to know he got off his ʻōkole once in a while.

A third photo showed their whole family, posed on the rear lānai, three summers back. Solomon had moved into this room by then and was still recovering from reconstructive ACL and MCL surgery. Makalani sat in front of him while fourteen-year-old Becky hung on his arm. Their vivacious cousin had always loved him best.

The last photo showed Solomon and Becky, more recently, sitting on the sand. Someone had shot them from behind and caught a humpback whale in midbreach. Becky rested her head on Solomon's shoulder while he leaned back on his hands. If Becky *was* crushing on him, as Aunty Kaulana had said, Solomon didn't seem to object.

Makalani stepped back with apprehension. They weren't first cousins, and yet . . .

Did Solomon display this photo on the wall to remind himself of the whale . . . or Becky?

CHAPTER SIX

Finished with her snooping, Makalani headed toward the river down the rear lānai steps, where egg-laying hens pecked bugs and centipedes out of the grass. Other hens ate duckweed and water spinach growing in a plastic trough. Since the birds had no natural predators on the island and the neighborhood dogs and cats stayed close to their homes, the Pahukula chickens roamed freely throughout the property, sometimes up the steps and into the house. The only threats to their health were diseases wild chickens might pass to the flock, which is why Pāpā shot them on sight. Not one to waste, Tūtū simmered them into a flavorful broth. The local joke was to boil them with a hunk of lava, throw out the chicken, and then eat the rock. Tūtū claimed the meat wasn't that tough . . . with a good set of teeth.

Even thinking of junglefowl made Makalani's stomach growl. With all the commotion, she had forgotten to eat. Now that she was alone, her hunger had returned. She stopped at a small grove of papaya and banana trees to check for ripe fruit. When she didn't find any, she picked a cucumber off the trellised vines.

Her mother rotated the vegetables in their garden to vary their diet and replenish the soil. Only the kalo—or taro—paddies remained constant, except for the year when the river had flooded the loʻi and swept half of the crop into the bay. Their family had to buy poi for a year to supplement the corms they had lost. Fresh vegetables, like the cucumber Makalani now crunched, had sustained them through many difficult times.

She found the fishing kayak drying in the sun on the grass. Another kayak sat farther from the water under the shade of a tree. Her grandparents used to have an outrigger, given to them as a wedding gift, that Makalani would paddle while sitting in Pāpā's lap. Although he had done all the work at first, she had learned at a young age how to work as a team. She loved that canoe. But when University of Colorado Boulder sent an acceptance letter, Tūtū sold it to help pay the expense. Her grandmother's generosity had overwhelmed her then as it did now. Makalani felt the weight of responsibility.

How will I ever repay such a gift?

She gazed back at the house. If Tūtū hadn't shooed her out of the kitchen, she would have marched back inside to work. Instead, she finished her snack and dragged the kayak down to the grassy ramp.

Anahola Stream began high in the Keālia Forest Reserve. It widened as it passed underneath the highway and grew deep at the Pahukulas' bank. Many locals called it Anahola River instead. The lower course of the waterway meandered between properties hidden by dense vegetation. Every fifty yards or so, a neighbor's stilt house, pastures, or groves could be seen. Only the new fancy estates groomed their river frontage all the way to the bank.

As she approached the ocean, the river bulged and grew shallow. During high tide, the fresh water and seawater mingled across the beach. At low-tide hours like this, the river funneled through a slender channel. Makalani dragged the kayak across the sand and paddled into the gentle surf of Anahola Bay.

Twelve years ago, when she was only sixteen, Makalani had paddled through heavier surf with Solomon on a high-tide winter day. He was ten at the time, full of energy he hadn't figured out how to release. A neighbor had given the Pahukula kids an old canoe to play with after its outrigger had broken off in a storm. Although the slim hull maneuvered well on a calm river, it capsized easily in the surf—which had made it more fun.

"Solomon!" she had yelled. "Steer into the wave."

Makalani drove him hard as they crested the wave and paddled through incoming swells. Only when they reached calmer water did she ease the pace.

Solomon whipped his head around to grin and nearly toppled the boat. "Dat was so rad. Can we do it again?"

She nodded toward the sheltered beach of the bay where their 'ohana had gathered for a picnic. "After we eat. For now, let's paddle and swim."

Anahola Bay formed a hook at the northeastern lobe of Kaua'i with a stretch of beach running up the coast from the river mouth to Kuaehu Point. When the waves were pumping in the winter, the point break offered a long and exciting ride.

Makalani steered the canoe toward the shallow bay on the right where the reef calmed the water and attracted the turtles. "If we're lucky, a honu will come say hello."

"Or maybe a shark."

"In December? I doubt it. The wiliwili are no longer in bloom."
When the flowers of the wiliwili tree blossom, the shark god bites.

It was part of a longer Hawaiian proverb that compared the blossoms to beautiful women and the sharks to young men. The 'ōlelo no'eau described how the law must step in to break up the rivalry between men that sometimes arose when they fought for a wahine's attention. Although Solomon was too young to care about such things, he laughed with glee when she spoke the line and emphasized *bites*.

When they reached a sandy gap in the water, she stopped paddling. "You want to swim?"

He touched the water and pretended to shiver. "I'm good."

She laughed and rolled over the edge. Although brisk in December, the shallow bay always felt warm to her. Tūtū believed the snow goddess,

Poli'ahu, had touched Makalani at birth, because she never got cold like everyone else. Even at the top of Mauna Kea, Makalani felt warm.

She sank beneath the clear aqua water and opened her eyes, blinking as she grew accustomed to the brine. Unless a storm brought bacteria down the river, she didn't worry about infection. Her family had been swimming and spearfishing in this bay for generations. She wanted a moment of quiet and a peaceful underwater view.

She breaststroked through the water, like the sea turtles she hoped to find, until Solomon yelled and rocked the canoe. She surfaced to find him waving frantically at her.

"Shark, Makalani! Shark."

"Where?"

"Ovah dea."

"Quiet. Or you'll draw it to me."

"Too late. It already turned around." He rose out of his seat and pointed as a fin wove across the surface at a languid pace. "You think it's Punahele?"

"Let's hope. It's too close for me to risk swimming to you." The best thing she could do was to remain calm and stay still.

As was frequently the case with protective Hawaiian ancestors, Great-Grandmother Punahele had transformed into an 'aumakua after her death, which meant she could manifest as certain animals or objects of nature. Although sharks were not a common vessel for a Kaua'i family's 'aumakua, Tūtū swore her mother had chosen this animal because of a close encounter Punahele had experienced as a child. It felt natural to Tūtū when her mother appeared in manō form a week after her death.

Pāpā had also seen the tiger shark with marks around its head like Punahele's wavy silver hair. She scared away the fish, but she had never bothered him. If this shark was Manō Nui Punahele, she might not recognize Makalani. Better to take precautions than to hope the predator wouldn't eat her.

Makalani took a huge breath and sank below the surface to watch so the shark would think of her as a fellow predator and treat her with respect.

It glided through the water about twenty yards away, shifting side to side at a leisurely pace. It must have come in through the channel, because it was too big for the reef. From its twelve-foot length and faded patterns along its body, she guessed it to be a female of considerable age. As it swam closer, she saw the wavy silver streaks on its head.

She stared into its shiny blue eye and greeted the shark god with her thoughts.

Aloha mai, Manō Nui Punahele. I am the granddaughter of Ka'ahumanu Pahukula. I mean you no harm.

It swept its tail and regarded her with interest, sending tingles of dread and excitement through her limbs. Could this ancient female be her great-grandmother transformed?

It angled its nose in a straight line toward her before sinking below her belly and grazing its fin along her thigh. Makalani gasped in a mouthful of water as the last feet of the god passed within reach of her hands. It was so beautiful she couldn't resist. With the utmost care and respect, she held out her palms and brushed Manō Nui Punahele's light-green skin.

Makalani broke the surface and filled her lungs with air.

Solomon tracked the shark's progress with his finger and waved. "Ba-bye, manō. Go eat someone else."

Makalani hoisted herself out of the water and intentionally rocked the boat. "Show some respect. That wasn't any shark."

"Fo' real?"

She nodded. "It had Punahele's hair."

Makalani smiled at the distant memory. It was so vivid she scanned the water's surface for the side-to-side wave of her great-grandmother's fin.

When she reached the spot in the bay with the sandy bottom, she laid the kayak paddle across her lap.

"Aloha mai, Manō Nui Punahele. It is me, Makalani Pahukula, daughter of Kawika, granddaughter of your youngest daughter, Ka'ahumanu. I hope you are well and have many 'ono fish and monk seals to eat. If you have the time in your busy life, please send blessings to your human 'ohana. Some of us have lost our way and need your wisdom to guide us home."

She breathed in the salty tang of the bay as the sun set behind the Kalalea Mountain Range and painted the sky around Hōkū'alele Peak and Manō Mountain with streaks of lavender and peach. Tourists saw a likeness to King Kong's head in the mountain on the right. Makalani always saw the shark's fin for which the promontory was named.

On the shore, a family packed up to leave. It reminded Makalani of the picnic she and young Solomon had joined after seeing the shark. The moment they had dragged the old canoe onto the shore, five-year-old Becky had broken away from the family and run down the beach. Solomon had scooped her up before she crashed against the hull.

"Put me down, put me down. I wanna go in the canoe."

Solomon mussed little Becky's straight hair. "We stay pau already. We like grind some lunch."

"No, no, no." She reached for the paddle and fell out of his arms.

Makalani caught her before she hit the sand and plopped her into the canoe. "Be good, okay? We'll give you a ride."

"Gimme da paddle," Becky begged.

"Alright," Makalani said. "But you gotta sit down."

She handed Becky a paddle and glared at Solomon. "You goin' help, or what?"

He laughed and grabbed his side of the bow. Together, they pulled a triumphant Becky up the beach toward the food.

All that afternoon, five-year-old Becky pretended she was on an exciting voyage. When her parents coaxed her to play with her little sister, she crawled under the benches and refused to come out. Only

Solomon joined in her fun. He pulled the boat in the shade so she wouldn't get burned, rocked the hull as if she had paddled into a storm, and brought her cans of Pass-O-Guava juice and plastic-wrapped musubi for her provisions. He even circled her boat with his hand like a shark's fin on the back of his head. From that moment on, Solomon was Becky's favorite person on earth.

Makalani turned her kayak and looked out to sea.

Could seventeen-year-old Becky have convinced Solomon to take her on an *actual* voyage? What had happened to that old, broken canoe?

CHAPTER SEVEN

Ikaika ʻŌpūnui trudged up the trail and scowled at the tracks. They didn't belong to pigs or goats. An ATV's tires had torn up the ground. The mainland farmers had arrived a couple of years ago and set up stakes on his mountain, without a single offering to the gods. No prayer. No request. They unloaded their shovels and dug into the ʻāina as if it were their own.

Ikaika knelt between the ruts in the red earth, made deeper from the repeated treads of the ATV's tires. The previous night's rain had puddled and spilled down the route. The incoming storm would carve gullies into these treads if those haoles didn't vary how they drove down this trail.

Enough was enough.

Ikaika had given them time to settle in and adapt to the island way of life. The mainlanders hadn't even tried. They dug irrigation channels wherever they wanted instead of following the natural lay of the land. They sprayed their crops with pesticides that soaked into the ʻāina and traveled downstream. They hid beneath camouflage nets that disturbed the flight and nesting of birds. The time had come to teach these interlopers how to show some respect.

He hefted his rifle under his arm and marched through the trees on what had been a pig path for years. When he crested the ridge, he spotted the compound below. Like him, they squatted on government land. Unlike him, they gave nothing in return.

Ikaika had lived off the grid ever since he lost his landscaping job and his landlord had kicked him out of his apartment and tripled the rents. With no income or shelter, he sold his truck for provisions and hiked into the wilderness to live. Every week, he picked up camp and trekked higher and deeper into the forest reserve until he found a valley where he could farm in the old ways and call home. He built a shack near a stream and survived on what he could grow, gather, and hunt. He gave thanks for the bounty and never disturbed the natural watershed of the mountain or the topography of the land.

Ikaika cared for the ʻāina. The ʻāina cared for him.

He picked up a crumpled cigarette pack and stuffed it in the litter pouch dangling from his belt. The mainlanders showed no mālama for anything but themselves. He hoped the evidence in his pouch would help them appreciate their disregard.

"Drop your gun," a man said, emerging from the rocks along the ridge. His red beard matched the dirt stains on his shirt. He pointed a semiautomatic rifle at Ikaika's chest. It had a scope and an external magazine.

Ikaika lowered his own bolt-action rifle but did not put it on the ground. Rain had softened the earth into red, sticky mud. This rifle was the only weapon he possessed. Without it, he couldn't hunt for game.

"No need to threaten me," he said, using his clearest, most polite English to calm the man down. "I only came by to say hello and to return the litter you mistakenly dropped."

"You're the one who's made the mistake. Who are you? Why are you here?"

"My name is Ikaika ʻŌpūnui. I live in this forest. I want to teach you how to live in harmony with the land."

"Go back where you came from and consider me taught."

Ikaika shook his head. "What you do in your compound damages the watershed and affects every plant and creature in this forest, including me."

The man's pale eyes squinted as he laughed. "Hey, buddy. No one's forcing you to buy what we grow."

"It's not the product. It's the practice. Please, accept my kōkua. Let me help you live and farm *with* the land."

"Or what?"

Ikaika sighed. "Or I will bring up people you cannot ignore."

"Wrong answer."

The man raised his rifle and shot.

Ikaika dodged behind a tree, blood running down his arm. His shoulder felt numb. He had only hunted wild fowl and game. This man intended to kill *him*.

"Okay," he yelled. "I'll go home and leave you alone."

"Sorry, buddy. It's too late for that."

The man's next shot chipped bark into his face.

The narrow trunk wouldn't protect Ikaika for long. With his left arm too weak to aim the rifle, he ran toward the ravine. If he found a natural water chute, he might be able to slide down the mountain without breaking his neck. If he survived, maybe someone would find him and help. The odds were against him. If he stayed on the ridge, the haole grower would kill him for sure.

Ikaika jumped behind a rock cluster as the man fired again. He lay on the ground and slipped the rifle's barrel through a crack. When the bushes moved, he shot.

The man yelped in pain.

As Ikaika ran for the ravine, a root tripped his foot. Not a root. A hand. He kicked the bearded man's face. He kicked again and knocked the assault rifle into the shrubs. No matter how hard he kicked, the man wouldn't let go. Slick with blood from the bullet wound in Ikaika's shoulder and the other man's arm, they howled as they wrestled on the slippery red slope, creeping ever closer toward the edge of the cliff.

This wasn't supposed to happen.

Ikaika had come on this mission to protect the ʻāina.

Why wouldn't the land protect him in return?

CHAPTER EIGHT

By the time Makalani had stored the kayak under the shelter and changed out of her bathing suit top and shorts, the scent of baking pāpio permeated the house. In addition to onions, peppers, and garlic, she also detected frying oil, ginger, and soy. Whatever the method or recipe, her belly approved.

Māmā peeked through the bedroom door, her long hair swinging into the room. Although full like Makalani's, the strands were fine and the color of dark rum. Māmā's half-Irish genes also sharpened the bridge of her Hawaiian nose and lightened the natural base of her skin, always tan from working in the sun. Her near half-Chinese blood, slightly less than Makalani's father and aunties, showed in the high angles of her cheekbones and the low double-lids of her eyes. To Makalani, Julia Manu Pahukula was the most beautiful woman in the world.

Māmā picked Makalani's travel clothes off the floor. "Dinner's almost ready."

"I can smell it. What did you make?"

"Not me. Your aunties channeled their anger into competing recipes for fish."

"What about Pāpā?"

"He's acting like Switzerland with sashimi on a plate."

Makalani laughed. "Not taking sides, huh?"

"Not a chance. Which reminds me, try not to rile them up."

Makalani accepted the cargo pants and folded them dutifully on the bed. "Why would I do that?"

Māmā handed her the shirt. "You have a big heart, my love. But not everyone wants your help."

Makalani gave her a look.

"I know. Calling the kettle black. You know what I mean. Remember when you repaired Aunty Maile's rocking chair when she really wanted Sanji to see how bad it was and buy her the new model from the store? Or the way you fixed Uncle Eric's fishing net when he didn't really want to fish? Or the way—"

"I get it. I'll keep my thoughts to myself."

"Not all your thoughts." She winked. "Only the ones likely to start a fight." She considered a moment and laughed. "Or maybe don't talk at all."

Makalani dropped her jaw in pretend surprise.

"Kidding," Māmā said, tickling her ribs.

Makalani tickled back. Her longer reach made her mother squeal in surrender and plop giggling on the bed.

"You're too big for me now," Māmā said.

"I've been bigger than you since the seventh grade."

Māmā sighed. "You were so cute before then."

Makalani play-slapped her mother's arm. Coming from anyone else, she would have second-guessed the joke. Even so, Makalani knew she had been cuter before she grew into her size. Baby mice were cute. Oxen were not.

"Bet I could still carry you up from the river."

Māmā fake-glared. "Bet you don't want to try."

It felt good to joke with her mother and cuddle in comfy sweats on the bed. Back in Oregon, Makalani didn't even have a cat.

She stroked the back of her mother's graceful hand. "You still hula?"

"Sometimes. When I don't have work to do."

"Which is?"

"Never."

Makalani laughed. "Guess I know where I get it then."

"No way. You are *far* more driven than me. I just do what I can to help the farm." She tried to cover Makalani's hand with her own. "This used to fit in my palm."

"Are you sad I'm not a little kid anymore?"

She shrugged. "You were awfully cute."

"I'm still plenty cute."

"And so modest."

Makalani stuck out her tongue. She missed joking with her mother most of all. "Remember the days when everyone could make fun and no one would take offense?"

"You mean like Linda?"

"Yeah. Aunty Maile and Aunty Kaulana, too. What's going on with everyone?" Despite Makalani's challenges with friends, she had always felt comfortable with them.

Māmā started to joke, then grew serious. "Things changed after the new bill passed. Before then, everyone felt equal because only your father and his sisters could inherit Tūtū's land. When the Department of Hawaiian Home Lands lowered the successor quantum to twenty-five percent, you, Pua, and Solomon became eligible, but it excluded James and his kids. What was supposed to benefit all kānaka maoli caused a rift for us."

"I didn't notice."

"You were living in Boulder and training to become a national park ranger. It didn't matter that you qualified to inherit because you didn't want to come home and farm."

"*You* came back after college."

"Only because I met your dad. I was a Honolulu girl until he introduced me to homesteading. Now I can't imagine a better way to live."

Makalani frowned. "Do you think I take it for granted because it's all I've ever known?"

"Nah. Your adventures are too big for this little farm."

Makalani studied her mother for signs of reproach, but all she saw was acceptance and love. If Māmā wrestled with the doubts that kept Makalani up at night, they didn't show on her face. Her heart was big enough to want her daughter home and still support her decision to leave.

"I love you, Māmā."

"And I love you, my voyager."

My voyager.

Although the nickname had empowered Makalani to follow her dreams, the only adventure that mattered at the moment was finding her cousins and bringing them safely home. "Do you remember that picnic at the beach when Becky was five?"

"The one where she wouldn't get out of the boat?"

Makalani nodded. "And she screamed whenever James tried to pull her out?"

Māmā laughed. "That girl had a mind of her own and a will to match."

Makalani's heart skipped with worry. "Had?"

"Oh, no," Māmā said. "That's not what I meant. I'm sure she's fine." She paused to consider. "But she's still pretty willful."

Makalani laughed with nervousness and relief. "Relentless, more like."

"Look who's talking." Māmā pulled her off the bed. "Come and eat before they pick the fish to the bones."

They walked arm in arm to the dining area, bumping hips and giggling like kids, and arrived as Aunty Maile set a foil-covered tray on the table between a platter of Cantonese sweet-and-sour fried fish and a plank of translucent sashimi. A leafy cucumber salad and a large bowl of white rice completed the meal.

Uncle Eric hovered over his wife's sweet-and-sour with a fork. He picked off a crunchy cube of fish drenched in sticky pineapple sauce and stabbed something crispy from the side.

"What's that?" Makalani asked.

"Pork rind."

"Seriously?"

"Don't knock it till you try. So 'ono. Gon' broke your mouth."

She watched skeptically as he ate it and grinned. Then he cleansed his palate with a gulp of cheap beer.

"How do you stay so lean eating and drinking like that?"

Aunty Kaulana came up from behind and planted her meaty hands on his bony shoulders. "He gives his calories to me." She was as tall as Makalani but twice the size. She was also an impeccable cook. If she added pork rinds to her famous sweet-and-sour fish, it had to be epic.

Aunty Maile stopped Makalani before she scooped a second helping onto her plate, uncovered the foil lid of her own masterpiece, and released a mouthwatering steam. She had stuffed the belly of the fish and surrounded it with sliced yellow peppers, tomatoes, and green onions with a layer of buttery garlic, ginger, and pepper on top. She grabbed a set of chopsticks off the table and selected a delicate morsel of pāpio with each ingredient of her stuffing.

Makalani smiled. Of all Tūtū's children, Aunty Maile most resembled their Chinese father, Hing Fat, who passed away when Makalani was ten. Grandpa Hing had a slim build and a quiet nature. Although Aunty Maile resembled him physically, she acquired her domineering presence on her own.

Aunty Maile blew on the fish and held it up for Makalani to taste.

Makalani groaned as it melted in her mouth. "Like buttery heaven."

"Right?"

Makalani nodded. "So good."

Aunty Maile smirked at Aunty Kaulana as she carried the foil into the kitchen.

Pāpā gestured to his simple sashimi and shrugged. "You like try?"

Makalani pinched a slice with her chopsticks and dipped it into the bowl of vinegar and soy. Nothing more was needed with freshly caught fish.

Tūtū carried in a plate of 'ulu lemon bars and waved everyone to sit down. "This isn't a competition. 'Ai ā mā'ona." *Eat all you want.*

Pāpā scooped a double helping of rice and passed the bowl to Makalani. "You have a nice paddle?"

"I did. The sunset was gorgeous." She took one scoop and passed it along. "Has anyone seen Manō Nui recently?"

Tūtū perked up. "Did Punahele visit you?"

"Not today. But I was remembering the time she grazed my foot with her fin."

Tūtū nodded sagely and smoothed her own wild silver hair. "She recognized you."

"I felt her blessing." Makalani chuckled. "And also relief that she didn't eat me or capsize the boat. Whatever happened to that old canoe?"

Māmā flashed Makalani a warning glance.

Pāpā didn't notice. "Da one wit' da broken outrigger? We gave it to James fo' da keiki, long time back."

"Do Becky and Emma still use it?"

"They took it to Kapaʻa. So, maybe around dea."

"At the beach?" Makalani asked.

He shrugged. "Or Wailua River."

"Who wants sashimi?" Māmā said, louder than necessary.

Aunty Maile narrowed her eyes at Makalani. "Why do you ask?"

"I was remembering that picnic we all had on the beach after Solomon and I spotted Manō Nui Punahele. Becky played in that canoe all day, pretending she was on a voyage."

Aunty Maile sighed. "She was so excited when *Moana* came out a few years later. She saw it three times."

"With Solomon, right?"

Māmā shook her head in warning, but Makalani forged on. "Do you think Becky might have convinced him to take her on an actual voyage?"

Aunty Maile sneered. "My granddaughter is missing, and you're blaming her?"

Aunty Kaulana muttered, "Who else?"

"Not blaming," Makalani said. "Wondering where else we might search."

Aunty Maile snapped her chopsticks in two. "Sanji is with our son right now, trying to keep his wife and younger daughter calm." She shoved back her chair and popped her head toward Eric and Kaulana. "You want to play detective? Interrogate *them*."

The family froze as Aunty Maile stormed onto the rear lānai and vanished around the bend. A moment later, the door to her compound slammed shut.

Māmā shook her head at Makalani and sighed.

CHAPTER NINE

The next morning, Makalani ducked out of the house with only a passing goodbye to her mother and grandmother. Although the toasted Portuguese sweet bread smelled delicious, she craved a hearty Kalalea Juice Hale bowl. Had the local joint been her only destination, she would have enjoyed the walk. Since she had another errand in mind, she packed up her rental car with assorted outdoor gear and drove.

A couple of local guys hung out at a picnic table under the coconut trees, talking story over mounds of granola topped with honey-drizzled fruit. They nodded in greeting, offered a quick "howzit," and then shoveled another bite of lilikoʻi into their mouths.

Makalani used to know all her neighbors. She would greet them by name, ask about their husbands or wives, their aging kūpuna, or how their keiki were doing in school. After so many years living away from home, the community had changed. Families that had lived in Anahola for generations had been forced out by the escalating real estate prices. It was happening all over Kauaʻi. Locals who weren't already invested in property couldn't afford to buy a home. The apartment rentals had become equally steep. The hotels and fancy restaurants offered a decent wage up in Princeville and down in Poʻipū, but the only way to get there was to drive around the east side. The inland mountains and the sheer spires of the Nā Pali Coast—made famous in movies like *Jurassic Park* and *King Kong*—made it impossible to cut across the island or drive from the north to the west. Some locals traveled an hour each way to work. Aside from homes passed down through generations, subsidized by the government, or leased through the Department of Hawaiian Home Lands soon, there wouldn't be anywhere on Kaua'i where the average kanaka could afford to live.

"Why you look so sad?" a teenager asked through the order window from inside the orange shack. She looked old enough to have graduated high school and was probably a friend or cousin of the owners.

Makalani didn't recognize her, either.

The teenager shook her head when Makalani didn't answer and went back to scooping out papaya seeds. She dropped the spoonful of the black slime into a bucket and shrugged. "Go hang at da beach. It's a beautiful day."

It irked Makalani to be treated like a mainlander who had to be taught how to unwind. She felt even worse when she realized it was true. This was her first morning back home, and she had loaded her schedule with work. Even during her most ambitious time growing up, she had never forgotten how to chill.

Have I really changed that much?

Her hair was still long and wavy. She wore the same board shorts and tee that she kept in her bedroom closet. Was it the trekking sandals instead of slippers that marked her as other? Why did she feel so out of place?

She thought about dinner the previous night and the way she had upset Aunty Maile. Māmā had tried to stop her from asking about the canoe, and Makalani had forged ahead like a bull.

Bull-headed more like.

Clearly, her issues ran deeper than clothes. She had felt out of step with the island from the moment she arrived.

Feeling too conspicuous to hang out and eat, she ordered a Zen Masta smoothie and headed for the car.

She surfed the radio stations as she drove down the highway through abandoned sugarcane fields. Aside from guinea grass, only the toughest trees and shrubs grew in the depleted plantation soil. Every so often, banks of red dirt would rise along the highway with colorful sprays of hardy bougainvillea before flattening back into the plains. The monotony focused Makalani's mind. Until she found Becky and Solomon, she wouldn't be able to kick back and relax.

She stopped the radio scan on the soothing island reggae coming from KKCR. The nonprofit station showcased volunteer DJs and talk show hosts with a wide variety of local music from classical 'ukulele and slack key guitar to contemporary Hawaiian reggae and pop. Although she would have welcomed one of the Talk Story segments, tuning in to the volunteer station made her feel more connected to home.

As the song faded, a cheerful kāne and wahine disc jockey team, who called themselves L & L, complimented the artist and switched to the news.

"Ho, Leilani. Did you read dis one report?"

"I did, Liko. So sad, yeah? The body of a man was found by pig-hunting dogs early this morning in the Keālia Forest Reserve."

The man hummed in sad agreement. "The hunters notified officials before dawn. They didn't want to disturb the body, so one of them stayed and the other two hiked back to their car."

"Yeah," Leilani said. "There's no cell reception up there. What else could they do?"

"Right? KPD is still trying to identify the body. So if any of our listeners are missing a kāne friend or family member, you better let them know."

"Did they give a description?" Leilani asked.

"Nah. Sounds like the body was out there overnight."

Leilani made a grimacing noise. "Think the pua'a got to him?"

"Could be. You know how those pigs are."

"Ew . . . I need to wash away this image. Tell me about today's surf."

Makalani tuned out Liko's voice as he listed the wave heights, swell periods, wind directions, and tides of all the surfing beaches on Kaua'i. None of it washed away the image of Solomon's pig-ravaged body crumpled in the brush.

She called the homestead. "Eh, Tūtū. It's Makalani. Have you guys listened to the news this morning? A man's body was found by hunters in the Keālia Forest Reserve."

Tūtū gasped. "You t'ink it Solomon?"

"God, I hope not. The police haven't released the name. Either they're still trying to identify the body or they're contacting the family first."

"No one come to da house or call hea except fo' you."

"That's good." Makalani didn't mention the possibility of disfigurement by pigs. She didn't want her grandmother plagued by the gruesome images that played in her mind. "What about Uncle Eric and Aunty Kaulana? Has anyone called them on their cell?"

"Dey sleep late. If da police had woken dem wit' such horrible news, dey would have come running to us."

Makalani's mother asked questions in the background. A moment later, she took over the phone. "What's this about a body?"

Makalani filled her in. "It's probably unrelated, but Aunty Kaulana needs to report Solomon missing."

"Your Aunty Maile won't like it."

"He isn't her son."

"I know," Māmā said. "But the Muramotos are convinced Solomon is with Becky. If we report him missing, it could force them to do the same. You've only been home one night. Are you sure you want these bad feelings directed at you?"

Makalani ignored the implication and stuck to the issue at hand. "What if I called the police and gave them a description of Solomon. I could tell them I flew in from the mainland, heard the report on the news, and got worried."

"Why would you be worried?" Māmā said.

"Because he was supposed to hunt pig for Tūtū's lūʻau."

"You know that's not true."

"It would have been if he hadn't disappeared."

"Good point."

"So . . . ?" Makalani asked, raising her tone.

"I don't know," Māmā said. "That poor man probably died in a hunting accident. If you put Solomon in the same area, the police might think he did something bad."

"He would never."

Her mother paused for an uncomfortable long time. "Maybe not on purpose."

What did that mean?

"So what then?"

Her mother heaved a sigh. "I think we should sit tight and wait."

CHAPTER TEN

Makalani needed to speak with her cousin James. After she straightened him out, she would talk to her father about encouraging Aunty Kaulana and Uncle Eric to report Solomon missing. Although she appreciated her mother's concerns, the Investigative Services Bureau had resources a patrol officer like Kimo would not. That said, she no longer believed the poor man found in the forest could be Solomon. From all accounts, her cousin had become too lazy to go hunting on his own.

As the ocean view opened up at Keālia Beach, she worried again about the broken canoe. Even people who grew up in Hawai'i could get caught in the currents and pulled out to sea. Had anyone checked with the fire department or lifeguards? Her aunties and Linda were so intent upon pointing fingers at each other Makalani feared no one had considered the natural hazards of island life. The man found this morning had probably slipped off a ridge or been gored by a pig.

When she crossed the border into Kapa'a, her worries shifted to more urban concerns. Becky and her family lived in Kaua'i's most populated town through which everyone traveling from one end of the island to the other would pass. Although only a narrow strip from mountain to sea, the ahupua'a subdivision of Kapa'a had the richest resources of all. The ancient Hawaiians' method of dividing land gave each community timber from the mountains, dry and wet agricultural land, plus ocean access to fish. In this way, kānaka maoli could live in balance with nature and ensure good stewardship for generations to come. Each ahupua'a varied in size according to the richness of the land and were marked with an ahu of stones and a carved wooden image of a pig. In the old days, many of the commoners would lay an actual pua'a on top of the altar as a tax to the chief.

Why not fish?

How odd that so much of her island's culture centered around pigs.

Colored flags fluttered happily in the breeze as she drove past grassy lots with freestanding huts, food carts, and outdoor craft displays. Small homes with open yards sat between low multishop buildings with long porches and wooden balconies reminiscent of America's Old West and Hawai'i's paniolo days. The local commerce, schools, and dwellings extended into the hills. But even the tourist ideal of a sleepy Hawaiian town didn't shield it from crime. Kapa'a scored below the national safety average for US cities of its size, with high incidence of vandalism, burglary, and theft. Makalani couldn't remember anyone being kidnapped or murdered, but with all the people who drove through its coastal border, it wouldn't be hard to abduct a wayward teen.

She shook off the thought. Becky's side of the family seemed convinced she had run off with Solomon. Her cousins were probably too self-absorbed to realize the worry they had caused. Makalani looked from the vast ocean to the forested hills. Either that, or they had run into trouble like that man.

A man. Not Solomon.

She thought about her mother's long pause. What if her cousin had been in the forest for another purpose than to hunt?

"Nonsense," she said, calming her nerves by speaking out loud. "What other reason could he have?"

As she crossed the next stream, the touristy shops crowded together and blocked her view of the coast. The congestion made Kapa'a feel more like a typical town, with traffic lights and cars parked along the curbs. When Kūhiō Highway branched off into State Highway 581, she followed the new road up a block to the general store and the second-floor apartment where Becky's family now lived.

At nine thirty in the morning, she expected to find James's pickup truck and customer cars parked behind the building. All she found was dry grassy dirt and a lonely picnic table in the yard under a tree. Muramoto Market provided dry goods and basic groceries to neighbors who didn't want to drive the extra few minutes to a supermarket, health food store, or hardware store. James had moved out of Tūtū's homestead and into the second-floor apartment. How could he afford to pay the rent if no one came to shop?

She parked at the foot of the outdoor staircase where she imagined Linda normally parked.

A CLOSED sign hung on the market's rear door.

She headed up the apartment stairs, and paused. James was nine years older. They had never been close. He and his younger sister, who was only two years older than Makalani, had preferred to play with their Japanese father's nieces and nephews. While the siblings played with Pokémon, Nintendo, and the glass ohajiki discs, Makalani built banana stalk forts in the forest. She hung out with neighborhood kids and babysat Solomon until he grew old enough to paddle, surf, and hike. By the time James attended Kaua'i Community College, they hardly ever spoke. When Makalani moved to Colorado to attend UCB, the silence between them increased. Now he owned a market in Kapa'a, and his sister had married a man in Illinois. What could Makalani possibly say that would ease her worried cousin's heart?

She knocked and braced herself for an unfriendly welcome. When no one answered, she hurried down the stairs. Like many homes built near the ocean or rivers, this building stood a few feet aboveground. If James still had the old canoe, he would keep it there.

All Makalani found were drag marks in the dirt.

CHAPTER ELEVEN

The Kapaʻa Fire Station sat on the mauka side of the highway, past Safeway and before the big coconut grove. The trees had been planted by a German immigrant in the late 1800s and became the site of the old Coco Palms Resort. Before that, the Wailua River basin portion of the Wailua ahupuaʻa had been the home and birthing site of kings. Whenever Makalani came home, she reserved one morning to greet the rising sun at the rock wall remnants of the Hikinaakalā Heiau.

She bypassed the place of worship and pulled into the fire station's lot, where a heavy-duty pickup truck was backing toward the open garage. A gleaming brushfire truck and a rescue whaler sat inside.

A stocky hapa-Hawaiian lieutenant came over to her car as she parked on the grass. "Can I help you?"

"I'm looking for information about my missing cousins."

"Call 911."

"It's a quick question. Have there been any water rescues in the last couple of days?"

He frowned as if she had asked for state secrets. "We don't give out that kind of information. Call the dispatch nonemergency number."

"Sure, but . . ."

He walked away.

A woman yelled her name from the garage. When Makalani looked, her childhood friend, now a firefighter, emerged.

"Eh, Sandy."

"Eh, Miss Pahukula. What are you doing here? Aren't you supposed to be freezing your butt off in Oregon?"

"Home for Tūtū's birthday. You going out on a call?"

"Getting ready to. Wassup?"

Makalani checked to make sure the lieutenant had gone inside before walking toward her friend.

Sandy Hall had moved to Kapa'a in the ninth grade after her Montana-born parents got sick of the snow. They sold their ranch and bought a rustic house on acres of leased land in the hills off Olohena Road, also known as State Highway 581. Olohena Road made a big loop through open land between the Wailua Homesteads and the Nounou Forest Reserve, before following Kuamo'o Road back down to the shore. Very country. Very local. The blue-eyed mainlander had struggled to fit in. Until the day she rode her horse to school. When the kids saw Sandy Hall riding as well as any paniolo, they showed her respect. When she volunteered to build houses for Habitat for Humanity, she and Makalani became good friends.

Sandy stood beside the boat trailer, bringing her hands together as the driver backed closer to the hitch. "You met our new lieutenant?"

"The guy with the sweet disposition?"

"Yep. Hank 'Iao. He transferred from Honolulu last year. Very by-the-book kind of guy."

She clapped her hands together, telling the driver to stop.

"Why'd he want to come here?" Makalani asked.

"He wasn't given a choice." She cranked the boat trailer's coupler onto the truck's ball hitch and glanced to make sure the lieutenant wasn't around. "I heard he pissed off the higher-ups. They didn't want him around."

"I don't think Kapa'a has made him any friendlier. When I asked about recent rescues, he shut me down."

She secured the hitch and fastened the chain. "Why do you want to know about that?"

"My seventeen-year-old cousin is missing. I'm afraid she might have paddled into rough water."

Makalani didn't mention Solomon. A missing teenager elicited sympathy. A missing twenty-two-year-old unemployed college dropout with a bad rep in town? Not so much.

"How long has she been gone?"

"Monday night."

"It's only Wednesday morning. Are you sure she didn't skip out with friends?"

"That's what her parents think," Makalani said. "I'm not so sure. Where are you taking the whaler?"

"Upriver. A hiker slipped on the trail to Secret Falls. The tour guide said he hurt himself pretty bad. Didn't want to hurt the guy worse by trying to bring him back without help."

Secret Falls was another name for Uluwehi Falls, where Solomon had taken the picture of his big lū'au feet—big and flat from running around barefoot or in slippers all his life—and hung it on his bedroom wall next to the photo of him and Becky watching the whale.

"Mind if I tag along?"

"I can ask."

Hank 'Iao approached the whaler. "Ask about what?"

"This is my good friend Makalani Pahukula. She's looking for her teenage cousin and thinks she might be in trouble. Makalani is a national park ranger in Oregon. If I bring her with me, she could lend a hand, especially if the hiker needs carrying."

The lieutenant eyed Makalani, no doubt taking in her size and probable strength. "Fine. As a civilian. Nothing official. I don't want anyone thinking we can't handle our own."

"Copy that."

The lieutenant went back inside.

Sandy smiled. "We better go before he changes his mind."

Makalani nodded toward her car. "I'll meet you at the driveway. I need to grab something from my trunk."

"Let me guess. A hiking pack, rations, and emergency gear."

"You know me well."

"Only because you never change."

Makalani thought about Sandy's comment as she grabbed her pack and dropped her water bottles into the sleeves. Was Sandy right? If so, why was Makalani having such a hard time slipping back into her life?

They drove down the highway to the marina on the south side of Wailua River where the Smith's Fern Grotto Tour barges were docked and other outboard motorboats could launch. Kayaks and canoes usually launched from the state park ramp on the north side of the river between the private estates and the thrift shop, visitor center, and paddle craft rentals. The last time Makalani had paddled up Wailua, it was in an outrigger with Pāpā's canoe club.

Did he still paddle with them?

Makalani didn't know. Yet another example of her disconnect.

They motored out of the marina and swung up the river past kayaks, paddleboards, and canoes. The morning water-skiers, if there had been any, were gone. Wakeboards, tubes, and foils would come out soon. They chopped up the water and ruined the peace. Since Wailua was the only river in all of Hawai'i wide and deep enough for motorboats, the opportunity for tourism and commerce was too good to resist. Only the Smith's Fern Grotto boats that toured up the southern bank were quiet and slow.

Makalani stared at the grimy green water as the rescue whaler picked up speed. "Brown water alert today?"

Sandy yelled over the noise, "January storms. A ton of rain dumped over the weekend. The river is loaded with bacteria and debris from Wai'ale'ale on down."

Makalani nodded. Leptospirosis was no joke. The bacteria came from the urine of infected animals. Since Wai'ale'ale was one of the rainiest spots on earth, it often flooded the rivers and streams, pulling contaminated soil from the banks. Bacteria could enter the human body through the nose, mouth, eyes, or broken skin. Ninety percent of the cases were mild. If left untreated, severe cases could kill.

"Have you rescued any paddlers in an old two-person canoe?"

"No calls for us. But sometimes the tour guides or rangers give them a tow."

"I didn't know the rangers patrolled over here."

"They don't. But they join up with the volunteer groups and the tour and rental companies when the trails wash out. The heavy rainfall on the mountain causes the river to rise dangerously at the crossings and muddies the trails to Uluwehi Falls. If someone gets into trouble, they call 911, and dispatch connects the caller to KFD, KPD, or AMR, depending what kind of assistance is required." She laughed into the wind. "Our park rangers aren't like yours. And they definitely don't carry guns."

Makalani slapped the sides of her board shorts. "Not packing today."

Her duties as a law enforcement ranger at Crater Lake National Park included emergency medical assistance, search and rescue, firefighting, and visitor safety. She enforced the federal laws and regulations of the park as well as any Oregon criminal statutes and vehicle codes. Her duties were more similar to the armed Kaua'i officers from the Department of Conservation and Resources Enforcement, who policed the hunting areas in the parks, wilderness, and forest reserves. The DOCARE officers, who worked for the DLNR—Department of Land and Natural Resources—also conducted search and rescue operations, like she did.

They zipped up the center of the river while kayakers paddled along the north bank. When one of them became tangled in the mangrove, the tour guide called for the other kayakers to stop. If Becky and Solomon had run into trouble here, someone would have helped.

Later, where the river narrowed and wound through the jungle, Makalani wasn't as sure. No paddlers. No tour barge. Only the trees, the river, and the mountain ahead. What if no one else had been around?

She chanted the opening lines of the admittance song for Wailua River. It was originally sung by the goddess Hiʻiaka and later adopted by hula practitioners, like her mother, as a metaphor to request admittance into their school. The mele described the steep slope of Mount Waiʻaleʻale, standing in calm, lifting to the heavens above Wailua. The meaning of the final line felt most appropriate for the day.

Do not withhold the voice. Speak the call to come in.

CHAPTER TWELVE

Kay tossed the newspaper on her husband's empty breakfast plate. "Did you see this? They found a body in the Keālia Forest Reserve."

Douglas set aside his book and searched the newsprint for what she meant. "Who is they?"

"Pig hunters. Ugh. You see what I left behind? Do you see why I don't want Cynthia and her family to come?"

He read the small paragraph. "Actually, no. What does this man's misfortune have to do with us?"

"Nothing. *Everything.* You don't understand."

He rocked back in the wicker chair, annoyingly relaxed in his bird-of-paradise aloha shirt and his silvery-blond hair shining in the morning light.

His hand drifted to his novel, eager to return to his fantasyland while their actual life burned. Couldn't he see how the hillbilly taint of her origins could reflect poorly on them? Pig-hunting poverty was not the image she had worked so hard to project.

Kay took a breath as her old Kēhau temper rose. "Read your book, Douglas. I'm going to call Cynthia and convince them not to come."

She stormed off the lānai as loudly as her padded house slippers would allow. Their gentle slap on the tiles infuriated her more. She picked up the new phone Cynthia and her husband had encouraged her to buy, then gave up on its supposedly intuitive technology and marched into the kitchen to place the call. Her daughter's exasperated response made her want to scream.

"Why didn't you FaceTime me from the new phone?" Cynthia asked.

"Good morning to you, too."

"Sorry. It's just . . . no one uses landlines anymore."

"No one young. Is that what you mean?"

Cynthia heaved an audible sigh. "Never mind. I'll see your beautiful face soon enough."

"That's why I called. I don't think you should come."

"We've been over this, Mom. Alexa wants to meet her great-grandaunt, and I haven't seen Aunty Ka'ahumanu since I graduated from Punahou School. She's turning eighty-five. This is a big deal, not only for her but for us."

"I don't see why."

"Because she's family."

"You never cared about family before."

"Because you kept me away."

"I did no such thing. Besides, you're a big girl. You can go where you please."

"I know. But it would have felt uncomfortable barging into their lives on my own. This way, we can meet everyone with you."

"Ha. I haven't been to Kaua'i since the last of my other aunties and uncles died, ten years already. I never knew their children. No one will remember me any more than I remember them."

"Well, they should," Cynthia said. "After Aunty Ka'ahumanu, you're the eldest kupuna in the Pahukula line."

"Kupuna? Listen to you, sounding all Hawaiian li'dat." Kay grimaced at the slang. If she didn't hold it in check, the old speech patterns would return. If even discussing her family reverted her to the old ways, how would she sound after an entire day with the Pahukula clan?

"I know about kūpuna, Mom. Even when I lived in Honolulu, I spoke more 'ōlelo Hawai'i than you. Now that Alexa is studying our language, she has refreshed my memory and taught me new words."

"Why does Alexa even care? She lives in California. Shouldn't she be studying Spanish?"

"She did, in high school. Then Mandarin in college. Now that she's in graduate school and researching global cultures, she wanted to learn a language closer to her own roots."

"I'm surprised UC Berkeley even offers Hawaiian."

"They don't. She's taking it online from a kumu on Moloka'i. Cynthia plans to learn Cantonese at some point as well."

"Why Cantonese?"

"The Wongs emigrated from Canton."

"Who?"

"Your great-grandfather and his brothers? How could you not know?"

"Of course I know. But there are billions of Wongs in the world."

"We were discussing *our* roots," Cynthia said.

"No, darling. *You* were discussing our roots. I'm trying to understand why Alexa would waste her valuable education studying an obscure language like Hawaiian. I mean, why bother? It's only useful if you live out here in the sticks."

"Seriously, Mom? How can you live in Honolulu and not be aware of Hawai'i's cultural renaissance?"

Kay laughed. "Renaissance? This isn't Europe, dear. We are rocks in an ocean. If it weren't for tourism, no one would care."

Cynthia growled in frustration. "That's exactly the point. Hawai'i had a globally recognized sovereignty before it was illegally annexed by the US."

"Oh, dear lord. You sound like those protesters up on Mauna Kea. If we hadn't joined America, we would have been eaten by some other country. Have you ever thought of that?"

"What are you even saying?"

"I'm saying you should be thankful for the life you have led." Kay took a breath then added more calmly, "And that there's no reason for you and your family to attend this lū'au on Kaua'i."

"So that's what this is about."

Kay bit her lips. She hated the silence, but what else could she say? Her daughter had inherited the Pahukula stubborn streak. If she met her 'ohana, she might actually fit in. Which, as Cynthia had said, was exactly the point.

"Why do you hate your family?" Cynthia asked.

"I don't."

"Seems like you do."

Kay shook her head. *Hate* felt like too strong of a word. *Embarrassment* and *resentment* were closer to the mark. If she dug into her past, Cynthia would never let her stop.

After a pause, her daughter forged ahead. "Did you know I was the only local girl at Punahou who grew up with no relatives? You never even taught me to hula. I'm more than a quarter Hawaiian, and you treated me as if I were white."

"You say that like it's a bad thing."

"It was!"

"Don't yell at me."

"I'm not yelling. I'm upset. Do you have any idea how screwed up I felt? Too brown to be white. Too disconnected to be local. I've struggled with my identity all my life. Thad and his family were the first people to make me feel valued as a person of color."

"Person of color? I don't understand. You're not Black. Neither are they."

"Oh my god, Mom. There are more skin colors in the world than black and white. Every shade of brown counts. Every person *of color* has a heritage and life experience that differs from the white-majority. You should have taught me to honor our Hawaiian heritage. Instead, you treated it like something we should hide or ignore."

"I never—"

"But here's the thing, Mom. People on the mainland see my brown skin and group me with whatever minority they expect to find— Mexican or Native American in California; Puerto Rican, Middle

Eastern, or Black in New York; Cuban in Florida. But you know what they've never seen me as? White."

"But—"

"And you know what else, Mom? The same goes for you. Despite your bleached-out skin and highlighted hair, the women in Kahala see your broad nose and know exactly who you are. The irony is—if you owned it, you could wear it with pride."

Kay coughed out her bitterness. "You think you know how it is, but you don't."

"Because you have never shared anything about your life. I don't know you. I only know what you want everyone to see."

Kay took a breath. She didn't want to go down this path. But if digging up the pain would convince her daughter to drop this nonsense about color and pride, she probably should.

"When I was a kid, my skin was so dark from working my father's land that my mother called me Black Sand Girl. When I grew breasts, the local boys came around, trying to lure me into the bushes or the backs of their father's trucks. I never went. I saw what happened to my mother's life, and she had been even more beautiful than me. I don't say that to brag. It was simply the truth.

"When I came to Honolulu, I got lots of attention but very little respect. The haole men only wanted me for sex. They saw me as an exotic fling. When it came to actual relationships, they always chose white. Meanwhile, the local men didn't think I was local enough. They belittled my aspirations and made fun when I spoke proper English instead of Pidgin like them. The local women snubbed me and called me names behind my back. So you see, my darling, you can save your lectures about not fitting in. I know exactly how it feels to be too white for brown and too brown for white."

Cynthia remained silent, probably hoping her mother would say more, but Kay had shared all the personal insights she had the stomach to share.

"What about Dad?" Cynthia asked.

"Your father was the one exception. Which was why I married him."

Kay let the lie sit. Then she decided her daughter needed more of the truth—enough to make Cynthia appreciate the reality of Honolulu society life.

"By the time I met your father, I had lightened my skin and polished my ways. I had a degree in literature and an influential circle of mainlander friends. Although your father knew I was local, I acted haole like him."

"Was that really necessary?" Cynthia asked. "I mean, he fell in love with you, right?"

"Yes. With the woman I had transformed myself to become. He wouldn't have looked twice at the girl I had been. If I had stayed connected to my family or invited them to our wedding, their appearance and behavior would have affected how he and his family perceived me. It's the same with our country club. Although I could have helped your father land the rich Asian clients if I had befriended the local Chinese wives, it would have marked me as one of their clique. Even then, I wouldn't have been at the top. I'm mostly Hawaiian, after all. Honolulu's high society are primarily Chinese or Japanese. I gained wider acceptance in the country club society by playing golf and tennis with the haole wives."

"That's horrible."

"Is it? Look at how you were raised and the benefits you gained. You don't value them because you don't know how your life could have been."

"You don't, either."

"Yes, I do. If you go to Anahola, you will see what I mean. But you'll see it from your privileged perspective that my decisions allow you to have. Being Hawaiian, even in Hawai'i, is not as romantic as you and Alexa believe. Hawaiians have the highest percentage of homelessness and poverty. We fight to resurrect a language no one else speaks and wield power about things no one else values. Aside from exotic novelty or fulfilling an employer's diversification requirements, promoting your kanaka maoli blood will not help you at all."

"I'm not looking for a handout. I want to connect. I want to meet our family and learn more about our culture. I want Alexa to feel as though she belongs. This lū'au is important for her identity and for her work."

"What work?"

"She'll explain when we see you."

Kay emitted a long sigh of defeat. "And if I don't go?"

"We're coming to the lū'au, Mom, with or without you."

CHAPTER THIRTEEN

Makalani eyed the dead branches jutting from the water. "Are you sure this part of the river is deep enough for us?"

Sandy had slowed the rescue boat so the wake wouldn't overturn the kayakers paddling in front of Kamokila Village. She paid closer attention now because the river had narrowed and grown shallower on the way to the fork.

"The channel depth drops to three feet near the middle bank," Sandy said. "It's about six feet where we are now. The whaler can cruise in less than a foot of water if I raise the motor." She nodded toward the tour boat across the river taking the South Fork to the Fern Grotto cave. "They come up here even during the dry season. We'll be fine as long as we don't snag on a log or get too close to the trees."

Mangrove branches invaded from the shore and narrowed the river by several feet. A couple in a kayak caught their paddle in the tangle and paused to record the moment on their phone.

Sandy waved to the paddlers. "You guys okay?"

When they gave the thumbs-up, she slowed to a no-wake speed and headed up the North Fork toward the trailhead to the falls. Although both forks of Wailua River ran for miles into the mountains, the north fork waterway became impassable soon after the trailhead beach. At eleven in the morning, kayaks were already parked on the sand—which was why most locals only came up here on weekends when the tour companies weren't permitted to rent out their crafts.

Sandy cut off the engine and glided the rescue whaler onto the shore.

As soon as they landed, a frantic young woman approached. "I'm so glad you're here. My boyfriend paddled up the river. I told him not to go under the rope, but he wouldn't listen."

"He went past the trail crossing?" Sandy asked.

The woman nodded. "I followed him as far as I could go, but it was too hard to paddle against the current. He said he'd meet me at the falls."

"How long ago was that?"

"Couple hours. We came up early to beat the crowds."

"Are you here with a guide?"

The woman frowned. "He said they're too touristy. He wanted a real adventure. I waited for him at the falls, but he never showed up."

"Did you call 911?"

"I was about to when I saw you."

Sandy turned to Makalani. "The call for the injured hiker came in first."

"You go. I'll check on the adventurous boyfriend."

"You sure?"

"Hey. It's what I do." Makalani turned to the woman. "What's your boyfriend's name?"

"Keith."

"And you?"

"Patty."

"May I borrow your kayak, Patty?"

"Of course."

Sandy frowned. "You don't have to do this."

Makalani strapped on her backpack and jumped off the bow. "I wanted to check up there anyway in case my cousins were dumb enough to—" She glanced at the woman. "In case they also wanted a *real* adventure. If I make it back before you do, I'll meet you at the falls."

Sandy nodded. "Watch yourself. I don't want to rescue you, too."

By the time Makalani had borrowed Patty's kayak and paddled toward the river crossing, Sandy had jogged up the trail and waded into the water with her work pants and boots. The heavy rains had raised the river level to her thighs, almost to the height where hikers were cautioned to wait it out on the banks. She grabbed the guide rope for balance on the slippery rocks.

"You okay?" Makalani yelled.

Sandy waved from the bank and disappeared up the trail.

Makalani paddled against the current and ducked under the rope, glad she wouldn't need to drag the kayak through the rocky crossing as she normally would. Was this why Keith had ventured up the North Fork? Because the opportunity was too good to resist? If the conditions were similar two days ago, maybe Becky and Solomon had done the same.

Makalani saw hikers moving through the trees, then the trail veered uphill, and they left her alone. The water babbled gently as the obstacles decreased, making it easier to paddle until she wound around the bend. As the river narrowed into more of a stream, the vegetation grew so thick she couldn't see beyond the banks.

She yelled for Keith. Birds chirped in response.

The mangrove grew taller and the hau trees pressed in from the sides, closing her into a lush and isolating channel of green. When she called for Keith again, the jungle swallowed her voice. Ignoring the claustrophobic dread, she yelled again with more conviction. Wings fluttered out of the trees. Insects buzzed past her face. The only human sound she could hear was her own.

Makalani had solo hiked and paddled throughout Colorado and the Pacific Northwest. It invigorated her spirit and challenged her skill. Here on Kauaʻi, she felt something more. Without the noise and industry of people, she could almost hear Papahānaumoku's beating heart.

She lay back and hugged the oar to her chest as the hau branches knitted overhead. Aligning the paddles with the bow and the stern, she coasted through the living tunnel as if flowing through the Earth

Mother's veins. Sunlight dappled her face with Sky Father's kisses while Papahānaumoku rocked her in a tender embrace. Makalani breathed in the love and enjoyed the moment of peace. No worries. No doubt. No conflict. Only the tropical fragrance of home.

She pulled herself through the tunnel until the constriction of branches eased enough to sit. The filtered sunlight grew brighter up ahead. Keith must have noticed. Why else would he have continued past this point?

She detached the center lock of her oar to create a single paddle and forged ahead with short, shallow strokes. One thing was certain: Solomon and Becky couldn't have passed through here on a two-person canoe.

When she rounded a bend, the river widened and a slice of blue sky appeared. Mount Waiʻaleʻale peeked over the trees. She paddled harder, then slowed as branches snagged her from below. What if Keith had ditched his girlfriend and headed downriver on his own?

She checked the sky again—this time, looking for dark clouds. The tangle of hau branches blocked her from the bank. She couldn't even climb up a tree. If a storm broke, the flood would drown her for sure.

She paddled forward to a wider spot. She'd give Keith one more chance before she turned her kayak around.

She raised the pitch of her voice and yelled like she was calling to a friend down the beach. "Hūi! Keith. Are you there?"

She had almost given up when she heard a weak response.

"Hello?"

"Keith?"

"Yes. I'm here. I need help."

"Hold on. I'm coming."

She found him in a yellow kayak, wedged sideways in a thicket where he must have foolishly tried to turn. He dangled a bleeding leg over the side. The gash on his calf looked deep.

"Eh, Keith. I'm Makalani. I'm a ranger up in Oregon. Patty sent me to find you. How'd you hurt your leg?"

He breathed through the pain. "I got caught in the branches. Went in the water to turn the kayak and slid onto something sharp."

Makalani looked where he indicated, but the water was clouded with bacteria-rich soil.

"Do you have any water?"

"Drank it."

"Did you pour any of it on that wound?"

He shook his head and moaned. "Too thirsty."

Makalani sighed. The guy didn't know the danger he was in.

"Put your legs back in the kayak so you're stable." She connected her oar and stretched a paddle toward him. "Hold it as close to the bow as you can."

By the time she turned his kayak and hauled him out of the thicket, her face was dripping with sweat. He followed her into the wider spot, where she turned her own vessel and clipped her deck alongside his. She brought out one of her water bottles and flipped up the top.

"I need to clean that wound. Rest your foot on my bow and let your calf hang over the gap."

When he did as she asked, she held on to his ankle and squirted the water in a forceful stream down his gash. He cried out and tried to break free, but she had anticipated this and held him in place.

He panted with relief when she stopped. "Anyone teach you to be gentle?"

Anyone teach you to be smart?

Keeping the thought to herself, she tossed him the water bottle so he could drink what was left and pulled the antiseptic solution from her pack. "This might sting, but it's nothing compared to the pain of infection. The soil that comes down after a storm is contaminated by leptospirosis bacteria, which are so happy right now because they've found a new home in your calf."

"That's gross."

"And dangerous. Didn't the rental people tell you about the brown water alert?"

She covered the long gash with three pads of gauze and pressed until the bleeding slowed. "You could die from this. We need to get you to the hospital so the doctors can stitch it up and give you antibiotics."

She wrapped the pads with gauze and handed him another water bottle. "You're probably dehydrated from the exertion and adrenaline, not to mention the time you spent in the river."

She brought out a Mars bar. "Are you diabetic?"

"No."

She tore open the wrapper. "Sugar, protein, fat, caffeine—perfect energy boost on the go."

He accepted the candy and glanced at her pack. "You got anything in there for pain?"

"Acetaminophen. I'll give you two extra-strength, but we have to tell the paramedics. A lot of prescription painkillers are mixed with acetaminophen. Too much can kill you."

"Anything out here that can't kill me?"

She wanted to say, *intelligence*, but let that one pass, too.

She unclipped the bungees and brought out a bundle of reflective pink paracord. It was wound on a tactical tool with a cutting edge and lived in her backpack along with the first aid kit and emergency supplies. Although she could have cut it to fit, she tied a series of knots to anchor the bundle to the back of her kayak and tied the end onto the static cord at his bow. She preferred to keep full length of the paracord intact.

"Are you strong enough to paddle, or do you need a tow?"

He mustered his pride and sat up tall. "Stronger than you."

She laughed. "Yeah? We'll see about that."

CHAPTER FOURTEEN

Makalani and Keith paddled back to the whaler in half the time it had taken either of them to struggle up the North Fork. Knowing what hazards to expect helped almost as much as the current gently pushing them down the mountain. When the banks separated, the vegetation thinned enough to see hikers descending from Uluwehi Falls. Others crossed the river ahead. Makalani called for them to clear as she steered between the rocks. To his credit, Keith managed to keep up without damaging his kayak, a hiker, or himself. When they reached the beach, his girlfriend rushed over to help.

Makalani yelled to Keith, "Stay in the kayak until we get you on the sand."

Once he was safely moored, Patty descended on him with a tight embrace. "What were you thinking? I was so worried. You could have been hurt."

"He was." Makalani nodded to his bandaged calf, where blood had seeped through the pads and into the gauze. "He needs to go to the hospital." She held up her hand. "Before you start asking questions, did my firefighter friend return?"

"No."

Makalani checked her watch. An hour had passed since they parted. What could be taking Sandy so long?

"Okay, you guys. Stay here. Stay dry. He's too wiped out to paddle back against the wind. If you can help him into the shade, that's fine. Anything more might cause the wound to bleed."

She dug into her backpack and tossed them a bag of trail mix. Then she climbed into the whaler for water, tossed two bottles to Patty, and kept a third for herself.

"Rest up. I'll be back as soon as I can."

She drank a few swallows and headed up the trail. Once she crossed the river, she made good time. The mud sucked at her soles, but her trekking sandals held fast to her feet. When she reached the boardwalk planks that ran above the river, she jogged until the corner where the trail veered up the hill. A tour group slipped down the trail.

"Did you see a firefighter up at the falls?"

The tour guide nodded. "A guy broke his ankle. She and some others are trying to carry him out."

Makalani climbed up the rocks and roots to the next muddy trail where she spotted Sandy and another guy about to carry the injured man across a stream. Although her friend was strong, the man she was trying to carry was too big. Sandy could break her own ankle if she slipped.

"Hold up," Makalani yelled, and hurried to help.

Sandy settled the injured man on a stump while the guy who had helped her sat beside him on a rock to rest. Behind them, a haole couple and three kids examined plants along the trail.

"Eh, Makalani. Did you find the missing boyfriend?"

"Yeah. He gashed his leg in the contaminated water. He's going to need stitches and antibiotics."

"Where is he now?"

"Waiting on the beach."

Sandy nodded at the injured man. "Broken ankle. The guide's been helpful, but he's not accustomed to coordinating with someone else. I'm afraid he'll slip in the stream and bring us all down."

"How about you?"

"I can manage. With your help."

Makalani smiled. "Let's do it then."

They walked the injured man to the shore, put their shoulders under his armpits, and raised him up by the thighs. With him suspended in a seated position, they picked their way carefully across the stream. After that, Makalani—who was stronger than Sandy and closer to the man's height—continued to brace him as he hobbled down the trail. By the time they hoisted him and Keith into the whaler, Makalani was spent.

Sandy tossed her a water. "This could have gone bad if you hadn't come along."

"You would have gotten the job done."

"Maybe. But I'm glad I didn't have to try."

"What about the kayaks?" Makalani asked.

"The rental company can pick them up. They'll slow us down if we carry or tow."

As they shoved into the water and eased out of the North Fork, Makalani called to the injured man's tour guide as he led his remaining kayakers down the north side of the bank. "Eh, were you working on Monday?"

"Yeah. Why?"

"Did you see a hapa teenage girl paddling an old wooden canoe? She might have been with a big Hawaiian guy a few years older than her."

"Not on Monday. But a few rowdy girls cracked the hull of their junky canoe last Friday. They were paddling on the wrong side of the river and ran into a Fern Grotto tour boat."

"Were they okay?"

"Yeah. The pilot gave them a ride back to the marina, but they started singing and dancing along with the performers and disrupted the show. I'm friends with one of the tour guides. He said they were drunk."

CHAPTER FIFTEEN

Makalani sat under the shade of a kiawe tree, gazing at the ocean and finishing her lunch of pork laulau, sesame ahi poke, i'a lomi salmon, and two scoops of rice. Although famished after her river adventures, she had unwrapped the laulau with care, savoring the juicy bites of steamed kalo leaves and the fatty chunks of pork. The kind with butterfish was harder to find since black cod was an expensive North Pacific fish. Of all the food in Hawai'i, she missed laulau with steamed kalo leaves the most. Even L&L Hawaiian Barbecue in Oregon didn't serve that. And like the plate lunches at Pono Market, L&L's didn't include poi.

What self-respecting kanaka ate laulau and i'a lomi salmon without dipping it into day-old, two-finger poi?

She bagged her trash and lay on the sandy grass, intending to watch the breeze push clouds across the sky. All she could think of was Becky and her friends. Had they been the rowdy girls who capsized their canoe last Friday? If so, why was her cousin drunk on a river when she should have been at school?

According to Pāpā, Becky's parents had grounded her for staying out past curfew on Sunday night. If this was a pattern of poor behavior, it might explain why they didn't want to report her to the police. Not only would their parenting skills come into question, Becky might push back even harder if KPD interfered. Then again, a ride in the back seat of a squad car might scare her onto the right path.

Unless this isn't the path she intended to be on.

Makalani hadn't spoken to Becky for over a year. Even then, their conversations at family reunions had been shallow and brief. No matter how hard Makalani had tried to engage, Becky had snubbed her like the cool kids from Makalani's past. To assuage the hurt, Makalani had dismissed her cousin as a typical teen and scoured the kitchen until it sparkled as an excuse not to engage.

She sat up with a start. What if Becky hid behind rude and rebellious behavior the way Makalani hid behind work? If so, her cousin might not be the person she presents.

Or maybe she has a deeper reason for pushing everyone away.

Although hard to fathom, Makalani vowed to keep an open mind. After all, she knew more than anyone how truth could differ from facade.

And what about Solomon? Is he doing as poorly as everyone thinks?

When her mind drifted to the body found in the forest, she reminded herself of all the reasons it couldn't be him—too lazy to hike, too smart to hunt alone, no dreaded call from the police to break the sad news. Seventy-five thousand people lived on the island. There was no reason to believe the unfortunate man was him. And yet, that didn't mean he was okay.

She brushed the sand from her arms. There would be no cloud watching today, or any day, until both of her cousins were safely at home. Only then could she relax into island life and feel as if she truly belonged. Or not. Maybe living on the mainland had changed her in fundamental ways.

Find your cousins. The rest will fall into place.

She dropped her trash in a can and ambled down the path to her car. She could have easily walked the few blocks to the Muramoto Market, above which James and his family lived, but she wanted to check the radio for news. After a bit of channel surfing, she heard an update about the unfortunate man.

"KPD has identified the body found in Keālia Forest Reserve as Ikaika 'Ōpūnui, a former landscaper for the Kaua'i Beach Resort and

Spa who has been living off the grid in the forest for years. Although shot in the shoulder and ravaged by animals, they believe he died from blunt force trauma to the head, either in a fight or when sliding off the cliff. Detectives from the Investigative Services Bureau division are looking at 'Ōpūnui's death as a possible homicide. Anyone with information should contact ISB."

Makalani switched off the radio and sat in the heat.

Not Solomon.

Despite her logical arguments for why it couldn't be him, she still sighed with relief to hear the man's name. Ikaika 'Ōpūnui didn't sound familiar at all. The odds that his death had anything to do with her missing cousins were next to nil. Even so, a homicide investigation on sleepy Kaua'i did not bode well. What if Becky or Solomon were victims of violent crime?

She drove up the sandy road to the single-lane highway that connected the north side of the island to the south. A couple of tourists paused in their shopping to watch a rooster peck in the grass. Kapa'a wasn't Portland. Despite its high incidence of tourist-related theft, Kapa'a's violent crimes had always been low. Whatever had happened to Ikaika 'Ōpūnui was probably a fluke.

She crossed Kūhiō to the mauka side of the road and drove the back way to Muramoto Market. This time, she found two vehicles parked in James's backyard lot—his green pickup and a white SUV with the blue stripe and emblem of the Kaua'i Police.

CHAPTER SIXTEEN

Empty beer bottles littered the picnic table under the shower tree along the fence. Annoyed that no one had thrown away the trash, Makalani picked up the bottles and dumped them into the garbage pail. Cigarette butts had been ground into the dirt. An empty pack of Elements rolling paper, popular with paka lōlō smokers, sat among the trash.

Did James and Linda know their customers toked in their yard? What about Becky? Medical marijuana was legal. Recreational use was not.

Makalani entered the store through the rear entrance and found a familiar bolo-head cop grilling James at the front counter. Officer Kimo Tagaloa was a massive human being, half Samoan, half Hawaiian-Portuguese. His shiny brown head glistened with sweat. He had shaved it in high school and had continued the tough-guy look and bullying attitude throughout the years. From the way he loomed over her cousin, nothing much had changed.

Kimo had held the line on the Kapa'a High football team with the same hardcore attitude he used for chasing haoles off locals-only turf—which to him, was anywhere he happened to be. His size and aggression earned him a varsity spot. Unlike Solomon, he never put in the work. While Kimo played at being the star, Solomon set school records for tackles, forced fumbles, and epic touchdowns from interceptions caught at his own goal. Once the sports community glimpsed his stardom, they stopped caring about Kimo's immovable wall.

Standing across from Kimo, James looked like a kid. Although part Chinese and Hawaiian like Makalani and Solomon, James had inherited his Japanese father's slender build and his paternal grandmother's mild disposition.

Kimo crossed his bulky arms as he loomed over James. "It been two days already, and Becky still no come home? Dis no good, brah. Da longer she stay runaway, da more bad it look fo' you."

James backed away from the cash register, as if wanting more distance than the counter could provide. "Why me? I didn't do anything wrong. I want to find my daughter without making a fuss."

The roll of neck fat scraped against Kimo's collar as he laughed. "It no work li'dat, brah. You know how it is. Da sins of the kid fall on da faddah."

James straightened his slim back. "I thought it was the other way around."

Kimo leaned in. "What you saying, brah? You got sin you like confess?"

"No, of course not. And Becky doesn't, either. She's acting out. You know how it is with teenagers. But after two nights—" James shook his head. "Her rebellion is getting out of hand."

Kimo raised the glass lid off a crack seed jar and stuck his meaty fingers inside for a wet preserved plum. When he popped it in his mouth, James closed the lid and covered it with the unused tongs.

Kimo spit the plum seed into his palm and slapped it on the counter. "Don't know what to tell you, James. I check all dakine hospitals and jails. I even checked da shelters fo' runaway kids. And when I call dat list of Becky's good friends? Guess what? They all stay at home where they should be. No one stay missing except fo' Solomon."

"Then go find him. We already told you how much time he spends with Becky. It's not right. She listens to him more than she listens to me."

"Oh-ho. You jealous, or what?"

"Don't be crazy. Solomon is twenty-two. Becky's only seventeen. She should hang with her friends and seek guidance from us."

Kimo leaned over the counter toward James, who backed up as far as the wall would allow. "You better think twice before you call me lōlō again. Because right now, my eyes are on you." He moved aside the tongs, licked his fingers, and took another sticky plum. "When you last see Becky?"

"I told you. In the morning. Before Linda drove her to school."

"How she get home?"

"One of her friends lives near here. They were supposed to give her a ride." James sealed the glass lid on the jar. "We told you all of this yesterday."

"Yeah, but maybe you left something out. Like, how you closed your store in da middle of da day."

"I didn't."

"No try lie to me, brah. I get friends who came by on Monday and say your store was all closed up. Dey had to go all da way to Safeway fo' chips. Why dat, brah?"

"I had an errand. I wasn't gone long."

"You sure 'bout dat? Because I get dis oddah friend who came by fo' nails. Guess what? You still not hea." Kimo looked around. "Dese shelves look plenny kine stocked. How you make a living if you nevah hea to sell?"

"My business is fine. Solomon's the one who doesn't work."

"You speaking to da choir, brah. Everybody knows he one big disappointment fo' da whole Pahukula 'ohana. All you guys so proud li'dat, t'inking he go pro or whatevah. All he tackles now are coolers of beer." Kimo shook his head sadly. "Befo' time, Solomon get all da wahine he want. Now da girls no care. Must be hard lose all dakine attention. Where you t'ink he get it now?"

Makalani slammed the door.

Kimo and James looked at her in surprise.

"Eh, cuz." She walked up the aisle and stopped in front of Officer Tagaloa. "Eh, Kimo. I didn't see you there."

He snorted. "Still think you funny, eh Makalani?"

She shrugged. "Somebody's gotta be. You find Becky yet?"

"Working on it." He focused his cop stare on her. "When did *you* get in?"

"You mean was I on Kaua'i when she went missing? No. I flew in yesterday. Wanna see my ticket stub?" She smiled warmly at James. "Eh, cuz. How you holding up? This must be nerve-racking on you and Linda."

He exhaled with relief. "Yes. We're all very worried. Emma, too."

Kimo moved between them. "'Bout that . . . I need talk to your younger daughter."

"She doesn't know anything."

"Maybe. Maybe not. Kids keep secrets. When she get home?"

James shrugged. "It depends. The bus leaves right after school ends. If she misses it, Linda picks her up or she catches a ride with a friend."

"What friend?"

"I don't know. A neighbor or maybe one of Becky's?"

"Huh. Sounds like your girls could be up to all kine trouble and you wouldn't know."

"Of course we'd know. Linda and I are good parents. We don't hover. We give our girls room to practice autonomy."

"Autonomy? Listen to you, all educated li'dat. If I didn't know bettah, I t'ink you grew up on da mainland like your haole wife. Maybe you guys need rethink your—what dey call it? Oh, wait, I know dis one—your *parenting philosophy.*" He grabbed chips off a shelf. "Dis kine good?" He nodded as if James had answered. "I go try, 'kay? I come back when Emma get home. We can sit down, get your stories straight." He jerked his head at Makalani. "You in town fo' da lū'au?"

"That's the plan."

"Huh. My invitation musta got lost."

"Family affair."

"I get it. But your tūtū be plenny kine sad if I no can find your cousins by den." He twitched up his brows in case she hadn't caught the threat. Then he took his pilfered chips and left.

Makalani grunted in disgust. "Well, that was unpleasant. You okay?"

James sagged with relief. "I'm fine. He's doing his job."

"It's not really his job to do. Did you file a police report?"

"Kimo will find her."

"Kimo's only good at finding his next meal. You need to file a police report and get Investigative Services involved."

"Who?"

"The division of KPD that handles general crime, missing persons, and vice."

"Vice? Like drug dealers and murderers. You said it yourself, this is a family affair."

"I was talking about Tūtū's birthday, not finding your missing daughter. Kimo's a patrol cop. This is out of his league. Becky could be in real trouble."

"You think I don't know that? A dead body was found in the Keālia Reserve this morning. My first thought was, *Please, God, don't let it be Becky.* When they said it was a man, I nearly cried with relief."

"You didn't worry about Solomon?" Makalani asked.

"Nah. He's with Becky. I guarantee it."

"Why are you so sure?"

"Because I live here, Makalani. You don't."

James shook his head and scooped out the top layer of preserved plums that Kimo had touched, dumped them in the trash, then wiped the rim with a paper towel.

"Kimo's a disgusting person," he said. "But he's still a police officer with resources and connections we don't have." He crumpled the paper towel and hurled it into the trash. "I have work to do. So, you know . . ."

Makalani glanced around the store while James straightened the perfectly aligned cigarette packs on the wall. She went to the refrigerator for water and noted the aisles of overstocked goods. Everything looked perfect without a customer in sight. What kind of work did James have to do?

She browsed through the local snacks, most of it flavored with li hing spice, ground from dried plum skins previously preserved in a blend of licorice, sugar, and salt. She loved the distinctive flavor and the memories it evoked. Grandpa Hing had told her that li hing mui meant *traveling plum* and that his father had eaten them on the boat from Guangdong. Now Hawaiians added li hing to everything from candy to margaritas. Aunty Kaulana even added it to her recipes for hulihuli chicken and mango jam.

Makalani set a bag of li hing apples, okoshi puffed rice, and a bottle of water on the counter. James never offered an 'ohana discount. She never asked.

"Store looks nice, cuz. Last time I was here, it was so crowded I could hardly move. Is this your quiet time, after lunch, before school lets out?"

He swiped her card, then snapped it on the counter. "Did you come to gloat? Look around. No customers. No daughter. You think my life is a mess? You think yours is so much better than mine? Sheesh. Nothing ever changes with you."

Makalani gaped. "I didn't say any of that. All I did was compliment your store and save you from Kimo's interrogation."

"He wasn't interrogating me."

"Oh, yeah? Asking about your whereabouts and questioning your feelings about your daughter didn't sound like a friendly conversation to me. Isn't that what you were trying to avoid by not filing a missing person's report?"

"She's not missing. She ran away with our degenerate cousin."

"Solomon is not a degenerate."

"Really? When was the last time you saw him? Oh, I forget. You don't live here anymore." He slid her snacks across the counter. "You left, Makalani. Don't pretend to care."

She winced as if James had slapped her in the face. Although indifferent to her, he had never been cruel. "You really think I don't care?"

"I don't have time to worry about what you do or do not think. Go back to the homestead. Let Tūtū and everybody else shower you with attention. This isn't your business."

"Of course it is. I love Becky. I want her home safe. But asking Kimo to find her is like . . ." She shook her head in frustration. "Look, I'm trying to help."

"How? You work in a park."

"I'm a law enforcement ranger."

"In *Oregon*."

Silence grew between them like a wall, mortared by resentments too strong for mere words to dissolve. Makalani collected her water and snacks with a nod. Words had no meaning. Only actions would make things right.

CHAPTER SEVENTEEN

Julia slid the macadamia nuts off the wire tray and onto the cloth. She had dehydrated three pounds overnight and roasted them after lunch. Once she pounded them into pieces, she would bake a dozen loaves of banana nut bread for Saturday's lūʻau.

She folded the cloth and rested her hand lovingly on the lumps. "Remember how Makalani used to swaddle the nuts like a baby?"

Kawika nodded as he stole an escapee and popped it into his mouth. "Always careful, dat girl."

Julia picked up a mallet. "Then she'd smash them into pulp."

He laughed. "Thorough, too."

Julia tapped the lumps in the corner and slowly worked her mallet through the bundle of nuts. "I added ground macadamia into everything for a month. Cookies, crust, smoothies. I even coated a pork roast."

Kawika smacked his lips. "I remembah dat one. You should do it again."

"Are you kidding? When we're done with this lūʻau, I'm going on vacation."

"To where?"

"Somewhere I don't have to cook."

She whacked the bundle harder than intended and shot out a renegade nut. Kawika caught it before it rolled off the counter and slipped it back into the fold.

"Nobody will know if you don't make dakine bread."

"It's not that."

"Den what?"

She set down the mallet. "Our daughter finally comes home and she's still not here."

"Her cousins went missing. You know how she is. If she thinks there's something she can do, she gon' do it. Wait and see. Once they come back, she stay glued to your side."

"You think?"

"I know. You two stay close, yeah? Like hale koa seeds in a pod."

She cracked a smile. "Cute."

"Always." He picked up the mallet, daintily tapped a few nuts, and then pounded them with his fist.

"Hey. I need pieces not paste."

She shoved away his arm and continued her methodical work. When she was done, she slid the uniform bits into a bowl, smoothed the empty cloth flat, and filled it with the next batch of nuts. This would have been fun to do with Makalani. Alone, it felt like a chore.

"Shame on me," she said. "Solomon and Becky are missing, and I'm sulking because our daughter cares more about finding them than spending time with me." She pounded the nuts, then stopped. "Do you think they're really in trouble?"

"Definitely."

"*Definitely?*"

"Come on. You know those two. Only question is what kine and how much."

"So, you don't think it's serious?"

Kawika growled. "It will be if they no come home and help us wit' all dakine work."

She laughed.

"I mean it. My sistahs barely help. Dea husbands no care. Da kids are all ovah da place. Da only ones who work dis farm are you, me, and Mom. Dis lūʻau is supposed to be in her honor. So why no one step up?"

Julia slid the broken nuts into the bowl. "I've been wondering the same thing."

"And?"

"They don't want to live the homesteading life."

His broad shoulders slumped beneath the weight of her words.

Her husband had worked every day on this farm since he was a kid, feeding chickens, picking fruit, and gathering nuts. For him, play and work had always been one and the same. He had wrestled with friends in the muddy kalo paddies while he tended the plants. He surfed the waves with his canoe when he paddled out to fish. He sang and laughed while he pounded the poi. He turned every chore into an opportunity for fun and had tried to pass that joy on to their daughters.

"Eh," she said. "Remember the tag games you and the girls played with the wild chickens? You could have caught them so easy."

He shrugged. "No fun in dat."

"Or the contests you made up for who could carry the most buckets of mangoes back to the house?"

"No can let um rot."

"Or the crazy hairdos you made with the coconut husks before you ripped them off the shells."

He grinned. "And da bowling games we played before I hammered da picks in da eye sockets fo' juice." He gave an evil laugh, then sighed. "I remembah all dakine stuff. Wass your point?"

"You did everything you could to engage the kids and keep the work fun. But the new generations want more."

"Like what? Fame? Money? Ambition? Look what alla dat did to Solomon. Dat boy had everyt'ing goin' fo' him. He was a big star on dis island. But he wanted more."

"It's natural, though."

"Is it? What about gratitude and contentment? What could be more natural dan living off da 'āina and feeling da grace of God in everyt'ing you do? And what about Pua, yeah? A single, young woman working in Waikīkī? Evah wonder what she doing ovah dea? Auwē. Da t'ought of it keeps me up at night."

Julia bit down her smile. "Waikīkī isn't the den of iniquity you imagine. I grew up in Honolulu. I didn't turn out so bad."

"Because you have values."

"So does Pua."

He grunted with doubt.

"What about Makalani? She traveled all the way to the mainland. You don't seem worried about her."

"Dass different."

"Why?"

"Because she's . . . Makalani."

Julia shook her head. "No. Because she's more like you."

He drummed his fingers in thought. "Maybe. Okay, yeah. Is dat such a bad t'ing?"

"Of course not. But Pua isn't the same. She's a city girl. She likes the bustle of Honolulu life."

Julia reached for his sun-blackened hands and ran her slender fingers over the cracked and calloused terrain. "You want coconut oil for this?"

"Nah. I get homesteading hands. Soak um up and dry out again." He raised one of hers to inspect. "Not like yours. Look how graceful. You should be teaching hula, not cracking nuts."

"I'm not good enough to be a kumu."

"Well, you too good fo' dis." He popped another macadamia piece into his mouth and watched as she slid the next tray of roasted nuts onto her cloth. "You evah like go back to O'ahu?"

She folded the bundle and gave it a whack. "And give up all of this?"

"You can pound nuts in da city."

"But I wouldn't. I'd buy them in the baking aisle of Foodland and make bread with bananas ripened on my counter instead of a tree.

The end result would please everyone else and leave me yearning for something more."

He nodded with understanding. "Da 'āina."

"Yes. The love of working it with my hands."

"Auwē. Guess you meant to be hea."

"I am. And Pua is meant to be there."

CHAPTER EIGHTEEN

It took seven minutes for Makalani to drive up the coast to Kapaʻa High School and another five to snag an empty space in the student parking lot across from the bus and pickup area. Although permit only, no one would check this late in the day. School let out in five minutes. From what Makalani remembered from her own middle school and high school days, the buses would leave soon after that. If she could find Emma in time, she could offer her a ride home.

She passed the pickup gazebo on the corner and headed along the driveway toward the most direct route for bus riders to board. Seconds after the school bell rang, kids poured out of the buildings and swarmed up the paths. Makalani searched the faces for her cousin, spotted her walking with a friend along the grass, and caught up with the girls as they planted themselves in the shade of a tree. Unlike her early-maturing sister, Emma still looked like a gangly kid.

"Howzit, cuz," Makalani said. "Long time no see."

Emma's jaw dropped in surprise. "OMG! What are you doing here?"

Makalani held out her arms as her tiny cousin came in for a hug. While Becky had her mother's height, coloring, and figure, Emma could pass for full Japanese.

"Look at you, all grown up. Those turquoise glasses are chic."

Emma squealed. "You think? Mom doesn't like the color, or the rhinestones, or the style. She wanted me to get plain clear glass."

"Are you kidding? They suit you perfectly."

Emma shone like a polished-up stone. The kid had second child syndrome for sure.

She pointed to her friend still sitting on the grass. "This is Kathy. Kathy, this my cousin Makalani. She's a ranger in Oregon. Isn't that cool?"

Kathy nodded, then scrolled through her phone.

Emma continued without missing a beat. "What are you doing here?"

"I saw your dad. He thought you might like a ride home."

Emma rolled her eyes.

"What?"

"I've been doing science club every Wednesday for months, and he still has no idea."

"Why aren't you in science club right now?"

"We have a competition next month. I told him club was canceled and that Kathy and I would be working on our project at her house after school. But does he listen? No. All he cares about is his store."

"I think he's also worried about your sister."

"Ha. Don't get me started about Becky. Right, Kath?"

"Yups."

"I'm sick of her. Even when she's gone, she gets all the attention. I'm the one with the good grades. Does anyone care about me, Kath?"

"Nope."

"Aren't you worried about her?" Makalani asked.

"What for? Becky cuts school all the time."

"Your sister has been gone for two nights."

"And when she comes back, she won't even get in trouble. Mom will let her skate like she does with Dad."

"What do you mean?"

"You haven't heard? Dad's losing his store. He wants us to move back to Tūtū Nui's homestead, into the same tiny room where Becky and I grew up."

"Solomon's living there."

"Not for long."

A car beeped twice from the road. Kathy's head popped up from her phone.

Emma grabbed her backpack off the grass. "I've got to go. You're coming to the lū'au, right? We can talk more later."

"Wait. What about Becky's friends? Where would I find them?"

"The Queen Bees?" Emma nodded toward three hapa-Hawaiian girls sitting on the steps. "Holding court over there. Stuck-up titas. Good luck with that."

Emma ran after her friend without a backward glance.

What was happening to James's family? One daughter went missing. The other felt invisible. Meanwhile, his wife piled up her resentments like lava rocks on a wall. And now James was losing his store? The Muramotos were suffering. So were the Chings. The only thriving branch of her family tree appeared to be her own.

Makalani sighed with frustration and looked toward Becky's friends.

The Queen Bees, as Emma had tagged them, sat on the top step between two rows of classroom buildings, blocking the exit for students who wanted to pass. Most turned and went the other way. A few squeezed through along the railing. No one objected or bumped into them as they passed. Although they didn't look tough in a beat-your-ass-if-you-mess-with-us kind of way, Makalani assumed their social venom must sting. They didn't wear expensive clothes like the private school elite on the mainland or even in Honolulu. This was Kapa'a. The Queen Bees' power resided in their attitude, beauty, and blood. Tanned legs crossed beneath the hems of their shorts. Slippers dangled from their feet. If they had accepted haole-looking Becky into their ranks, she must have grown even more gorgeous and popular in the last year.

Although Makalani had never met the Queen Bees before, she recalled the sting from similar girls. So she leaned in to her ranger authority and approached with a smile. "Howzit. I'm Makalani Pahukula. My cousin Emma Muramoto said you're Becky's friends. You guys know where she is?"

The girl in the center shrugged. The other girls did the same.

Makalani furrowed her brows. "She hasn't been home for two nights. We're all pretty worried. We want to make sure she's safe."

"You da cousin from da mainland?" the leader said.

"From Anahola. But, yeah. I live in Oregon now."

The girls nodded at each other as if that explained everything.

Makalani bit back the urge to ask why she no longer fit in. She didn't want to set herself up to be stung. "Were you guys paddling with Becky on Friday when she capsized the canoe?"

The girl on the left giggled.

The leader elbowed her in the ribs. "Stay good fun, dass all. Nobody get hurt." She chuckled. "Except dat junk boat."

Makalani rolled her eyes. At least one mystery was solved.

"When did you last see Becky?"

The leader shrugged. "Monday li'dat?"

"During school?"

The girl on the left chuckled. "Part-time, anyways."

"What time did she ditch?"

"Hey. I nevah say she ditched."

Makalani sighed. "What time did she leave campus?"

"Lunchtime. Maybe."

The leader interrupted. "We stay seniors already. So what if Becky ditched?"

"She hasn't come home."

The other girls chuckled.

Makalani felt her old insecurities return. "Why are you laughing? Is she with a guy?"

"If she's lucky." The third girl, more animated than the others, reached across the leader with an exploding fist bump to her friend.

The leader rolled her eyes. "No listen to Kimi. She in love wit' Solomon."

"Try wait, tho," Kimi said. "You wen see him lately? Boom kanani! Solomon is so hot."

Makalani grimaced. "He's my cousin."

Kimi snickered. "He's Becky's cousin, too."

Makalani shook her head and focused on the leader, who seemed the most levelheaded of the three. "Is that who you think she's with?"

The leader shrugged. "If Becky wore him down. She pretty li'dat, but Solomon treats her like one kid."

"How would she wear him down?"

"You know." The leader tossed her hair and pitched her voice in a high whine like Becky's. "Take me to da movies. Take me to da beach. Take me hiking up Pihea Trail."

The other girls laughed.

Kimi slapped her knee. "Shoots. You nailed it."

"What trail did you say?" Makalani asked the leader, eager to steer the conversation away from Kimi's antics to something she understood.

"Pihea. In Kōke'e State Park. You know da one, yeah? Starts at Pu'u o Kila Lookout and goes through da Alaka'i Swamp? Becky like hike up to Kilohana Lookout long time, but nobody like go."

Makalani wasn't surprised. It would take a couple of hours to drive around the island and up the mountain to the trailhead, plus another four hours for the eight-mile hike. With beautiful trails closer to home, no one would want to drive all that way, especially for a pampered girl who would probably break down and whine.

"When did you last see Becky with Solomon?"

"Not see, but she used my phone to call him on Monday."

"From school?"

"Yeah. Her parents took her phone away when she came home late Sunday night. She stay plenny mad, whined to Solomon all morning. Say she like cut out and do somet'ing fun." She leaned forward. "Maybe he finally agreed."

CHAPTER NINETEEN

With no time to drive around the island, Makalani returned home. Her second day on Kaua'i had felt more stressful than the first. She was tempted to pitch a chair beside Uncle Eric and kick back with a beer. When she drove down to the old banyan tree, his favorite spot among the roots lay bare.

Is he picking fruit for the lū'au?

She laughed. Any fruit Uncle Eric picked would go straight into his mouth.

With juicy sweetness on her mind, she drove through the orchard toward the gully and parked.

Back in the day, she and Pāpā would run down the rocky trail on tough bare feet. When they reached the mountain apple tree, he would lift her on his shoulders so she could climb onto the lowest branch. He never worried that she might fall. Makalani always knew her limits no matter how adventurous she became. While other moms and dads had panicked whenever she climbed a cliff or jumped off a tall rock, Makalani's parents watched and smiled. Their calm belief in her judgment and skills had empowered her to leave the island and explore.

Isn't that what the ancient Polynesians had done?

She skipped down the trail in her hiking sandals, feeling more comfortable in her skin. The native-born were not defined by their footwear or the toughness of their feet. A kama'āina was defined by the goodness of their actions and the generosity in their heart. If she wanted to feel more local, all she had to do was show kuleana for her family, her people, and the land.

She ran her hand up the trunk of the 'ōhi'a 'ai tree and plucked a ruby-ripe fruit. Unlike other apples that grew from the ends of branches, Hawaiian mountain apples could grow anywhere on the tree, even on the trunk—a saving grace since Makalani had grown too heavy for the slender branches to support.

She bit into the fruit and slurped the sweet juice. It flowed like water from a mountain stream, connecting her to a past long before Western explorers had arrived. Before they had brought diseases that would decimate the Hawaiian population. Before they replaced 'ōlelo Hawai'i with English. Before they stole the 'āina that King Kamehameha III had intended to safeguard for his people. Makalani thought about all of this as she drank the sweet juice. History flowed through every living being in Hawai'i. All she had to do was open herself up and feel.

She tossed the avocado-size seed into the gully and wiped her hands on her shorts, erasing the stickiness of her day along with the fruit.

Hungry for family, she checked every room and wing in the house. She wandered through the farm, barefoot this time so she could feel the grass between her toes. She couldn't find anyone. She petted the new piglets and scattered grain for the chickens. When she finally spotted Tūtū near the river pulling kalo plants from the lo'i, she cupped her hands and yelled, "Hūi."

Tūtū looked up and waved a stalk with giant elephant-ear leaves above her silver hair.

Makalani continued her greeting in 'ōlelo Hawai'i, declaring herself as Tūtū's granddaughter and the daughter of Kawika and Julia Pahukula, come to say hello.

Tūtū answered more fluently, blending her vowels across words wherever an 'okina didn't force a glottal stop between sounds. When the old-timers spoke 'ōlelo Hawai'i, it could be hard to understand. Even so, Tūtū's meaning was clear.

"This is Ka'ahumanu Pahukula, your grandmother and daughter of Punahele Kahananui and Mahi'ai Pahukula, welcoming you home."

Tūtū waded to the edge of the row, placed the plant carefully on the bank, and rose to her full majestic height. Standing thigh-deep in muddy water with her strong arms at her sides, she took a deep breath and began a welcoming chant. Her low voice vibrated with an 'i'i so slow it resonated inside Makalani's bones, calling for attention as Tūtū sent her aloha on the breeze.

"Onaona i ka hala me ka lehua. He hale lehua no ia na ka noe."

Makalani breathed in the music of her native language, infused with Tūtū's loving intent. Although not fluent, Makalani remembered the meaning behind the beautiful words.

Fragrant with the breath of hala and lehua, this is the sight I long to see.

Tears welled in Makalani's eyes as Tūtū continued until the final, "Aloha e."

Her grandmother climbed out of the lo'i and rolled her hand for Makalani to come. Without the distraction of yesterday's family bickering and dinner preparations, they held each other's faces, touched their foreheads, and shared the presence of their breath.

After a long moment, Tūtū pulled back and smiled. "My heart sings to have you home, mo'opuna. It's been too long since you worked in da lo'i wit' me."

"I know."

"How you doing?"

"I'm okay. Better now that I'm with you." Makalani nodded toward the lo'i. "May I help you pick?"

"Of course. Working da 'āina will help you, too."

Makalani stepped into the paddy. Mud squished between her toes. As with Tūtū, Pāpā, and Aunty Kaulana, the water only reached her thighs. When Grandpa Hing was still alive, it came all the way to his waist. Her elder aunt was tiny like him.

"Does Aunty Maile ever help?"

"In da mud?" Tūtū laughed. "Too fastidious, dat one. She won't even feed da chickens."

They waded past the younger plants to the section where Tūtū had pulled the huge, leafy kalo from the muddy berm. When they had collected as many as they could hold, they carried the stalks back to the bank and laid them on the grass. After several more trips, they climbed out of the lo'i and sat. Dangling their feet and calves in the water, arms and legs coated with mud, they washed and picked the roots from the corms.

"You wen find Becky and Solomon today?" Tūtū asked.

"I tried. Rescued a couple hikers up Wailua instead."

"Dass you. Always kōkua fo' everybody. Nobody kōkua fo' you."

"That's not true. Besides, what do I need help for? I have everything I want right here."

"Oh, yeah? Den why you live so far away?"

They rose from the mud and laid the washed plants on a low table fashioned from two stumps and a plank. With buckets for them to sit on and containers for stalks and trash, they began cutting the plants into edible parts. They stacked the big leaves for laulau and stews, cut the stalks for replanting, and trimmed the corms to be cooked in a variety of recipes or pounded into poi. Some of the corms had sprouted new bulbs, which they gently removed to replant with the stalks.

"I spoke with James today," Makalani said. "He thinks I left Hawai'i because I don't care about our 'ohana. Is that how you feel?"

"*Mmm.* Yes and no."

Makalani dropped the plant in surprise. "Really?"

"What you like hear? Dat we stop needing you because you don't need us? Dass not how it works. Whether good or bad, da family's behavior is judged as one. We bring each other up, or we pull each other down. You still Pahukula, no matter how far away you live."

Makalani picked up the kalo and sorted her feelings as she trimmed and sorted the plants. She wished she could separate herself like the leaves and corms, feed her Oregon life with her mind and effort, sustain her family with her heart. Why did she have to shrink her adventures into a homesteading way of life? And why was her eighty-five-year-old grandmother pulling kalo plants alone?

"The house was empty when I came home. Where did everybody go?"

"Your māmā wen hula, Kaulana and Eric wen visit wit' friends. Maile and Sanji just . . . went. And your pāpā stay meet wit' da Anahola Homestead Committee."

"Is there a problem?"

"Who knows? Always some kine problem wit' them. Kawika handles it. I'm too old fo' da stress."

"But not too old for hauling kalo?"

Tūtū glanced at the heavy containers they had filled. "You think I go carry dat? No way, mo'opuna. Dass fo' you."

As Tūtū carried the leaves, Makalani added water to the container of replanting stalks and hauled the plastic bucket of kalo corms up the hill to the house. Since the calcium oxalate in kalo made the mouth and skin itch, the corms and leaves had to be cooked before eating or pounding into poi.

She set the heavy container on the picnic table and stretched her back. After supporting the injured man's weight on the hike back to the rescue boat, the field work and carrying the heavy bucket up the rear lānai steps had taken its toll.

Tūtū patted her shoulder. "Rest, Makalani."

"I'm okay."

"I no talk about your body. I stay talk about your mind. You been up hea two seconds and already da lines in your forehead look like Waimea Canyon."

Makalani shook out her arms and head, looked at her grandmother, and smiled. "Better?"

Tūtū sighed. "Sit. Enjoy da view."

"I could clean the kalo."

"Auwē. You no can be still fo' one minute? Sit."

She picked up the bucket of corms. When Makalani started to object, Tūtū's stink eye shut her up quick.

"Stay hea, Makalani. Watch da river. Breathe. You need relax more dan I need your help."

CHAPTER TWENTY

Makalani sat on the lānai bench and watched the clouds travel across the peach-and-aqua sky. As the sun set on another day, she prayed Becky and Solomon were together and safe.

Footsteps thumped as Pāpā stepped onto the deck. "Nice view, yeah?" Makalani checked out his clean T-shirt and shorts. "How was the meeting?"

He shook his head. "Da water pump stay broke. We need conserve our water little bit mo' time. Da new homesteaders from da Kuleana Program have big trouble wit' dea lots."

"What's wrong with them?"

"Everything. In before time, dat land was fo' grow pineapple and sugarcane. Now everyt'ing stay covered in pili grass and albizia trees. No roads. No utilities. HHC expects da homesteaders to clear da land and put all o' dat in fo' themselves. But wit' what money? Da commission acts li'dis one great gift fo' our people, but it nevah should have been theirs to give."

He swept his hand angrily toward the mountains. "Tūtū's ancestors on both sides of our family were awarded allodial rights—absolute ownership—during da Great Māhele, but dey nevah know enough to file claims. Dey already lived and worked da 'āina fo' da konohiki chiefs wit' rights to gather, hunt, and fish. What more did dey need? Like most maka'āinana, dey nevah imagine dea children's children would get no place to live."

He planted his hands on the railing and exhaled the frustration from his lungs. "If our kūpuna had filed dose claims, our 'ohana would own over one hundred acres of land."

Makalani joined him at the railing and rested her head on his shoulder.

"Nevah mind me. I get tired of da fighting." He patted her back. "How you stay?"

She shrugged. "Worried."

"About Solomon and Becky?"

"Yeah. I spoke with Becky's friends at school. They think she may have convinced Solomon to take her to Kōke'e Park for a hike."

"Da Moloa'a trail ovah hea mo' bettah. Why go all da way ovah dea?"

"She wanted to hike the Pihea Trail up to Kilohana Lookout."

Pāpā laughed. "Wit' Solomon? No way. Dat boy too moloā to hike up one mountain."

There it was again—lazy. The Solomon she knew would have run to Hanalei for fun.

"I don't know," she said. "There's something going on. I spoke with Emma as well. She told me Uncle James is losing his store. She said he wants to move back here."

Pāpā snorted. "Bumbai everybody come back, but nobody want work. Your māmā and tūtū bust dea 'ōkole. My sistahs bickah all da time. Your uncle Eric drink mo' beer dan his son. Maile's husband wastes time talking story wit' friends. Everybody wants da land. Nobody shows it respect."

He heaved a sigh. "Listen to me squawk, like a myna bird in a tree. Dis up to your tūtū. Whatevah she wants, fine by me. But I don't see how Solomon goin' fit in his parents' side of da house. Kaulana and Eric filled his old bedroom wit' junk."

"So you think he's okay? You're not worried?"

"I don't know. Maybe he come back. Maybe da police catch him. What difference it make? He still lost."

"He's not a criminal, Pāpā."

"I hope not, but you nevah know. Your cousin change plenny since you left. Becky, too. You don't know how they are anymore. Becky all ovah da place. Wild, dat one. And Solomon? Sheesh. He get more like Eric every day."

"They could still be in trouble."

Pāpā frowned. "James get Kimo to help though, right? He'll look into it."

She shook her head. "I spoke to him and James at the store. Kimo will only see what he wants to find."

"So what den?"

"I'm going to hike Pihea Trail in the morning. Want to come?"

"Nah. I get too much work for Tūtū's lū'au. But be careful, yeah? After all dakine rain, dat trail goin' be hamajang."

CHAPTER TWENTY-ONE

Kaulana walked through her friend's dumpy new house, imagining what it might look like if throw rugs covered the warped vinyl planks. Water stains bled across the ceiling and down some of the walls. Her friend claimed the roof hadn't leaked in the last rain—which was quite a relief since Noa and Lani had bought the house "as is."

Lani opened the door to a tiny room crammed with everything that wouldn't fit in the other two bedrooms. "Can you believe it, tita? We finally get one house."

Kaulana nodded agreeably. "What kine mortgage you get?"

"Two hundred twenty-three."

"*Thousand?* Auwē. We could nevah afford dat."

"Dey get empty lots fo' cheaper, but dey make you build up to code. And you still have to qualify for da loan. It's not like you can build something simple and live off da land."

Kaulana knew this all too well, which was why she and Eric still lived in her mother's house.

Lani led her to the kitchen. "You know Ua, yeah? She took her mother's place on da list after she died. Been waiting twenty-five years. When houses come up, she has to let dem go. She no can make one offer because she can't qualify fo' a loan. How's da Department of Hawaiian Home Lands goin' make good fo' her or any of da poor Hawaiians dey say they like help?"

Lani poured chips into a monkeypod bowl and handed Kaulana a beer. "I know it's not fair to da people waiting longer dan us, but Noa and me are so grateful to have dis crap place."

Kaulana followed her outside. Eric and Noa sat in beach chairs on the dried-up grass beside two more chairs and a lauhala mat. No shade. No green. Laundry fluttered along the carport. Hale koa bushes invaded from the ravine. Only the mountains offered a beautiful view.

Eric patted the chair beside him. "Isn't dis great? They live on top of da mountain like kings."

Kaulana frowned. "Must be a lot of work, though, yeah?"

Noa shrugged. "Little bit here, little bit there. Now dat we're in, we can take our time. Bumbai, it all come togeddah jus' right."

Kaulana folded up the lawn chair, too flimsy for her weight, and sat on the mat wondering how long *bumbai* might actually take.

Eric grinned. "Noa says he get one side hustle to help pay da mortgage."

"Oh, yeah?"

Noa shook his head and grabbed some chips.

Kaulana noted the man's red eyes and wondered if his side hustle might have to do with drugs. If so, she definitely did not want her husband involved.

"Eh," Noa said. "Wass up wit' dat son of yours? Bet he could work if he stay off da beer."

Kaulana also did not want Noa corrupting her son. She counted six empty cans between Lani's husband and hers. What right did Noa have to judge? Solomon could have become an NFL star while the best Noa could hope for was better landscaping and a fresh coat of paint.

Still, the look of accomplishment she saw in his eyes made her question if she and Eric were doing right by their son. What if Noa's side hustle was legit? Maybe Kaulana's brother and mother were right about Solomon needing a push. Maybe working the homestead would help him out of his slump and prevent him from disappointing his future wife the way Eric had disappointed her.

She thought about Makalani and how confident she seemed, working her mainland job, flying home on her own dime. Kaulana would never admit it, but her niece made her feel small.

When they finished the chips, Lani jumped to her feet. "Who wants to help me fix dinner?"

Eric laughed. "Nah. I stay perfect right here."

"Me, too," Noa said, cracking open another beer.

"I'll help," Kaulana said, crawling to her feet.

Sitting on the ground had grown uncomfortable after she gained the last hundred pounds. Her lean husband could sit all day long.

"You coming?" Lani asked.

Kaulana nodded. Who was she to judge? All she ever did was cook, eat, and complain. She had no purpose in her life, no big dream she was trying to pursue. Her friend had a house and was willing to work hard to make it a home. Kaulana already lived in a beautiful home. Maybe she would feel better if she did her share of the work.

CHAPTER TWENTY-TWO

Makalani pulled the quilt over her face and willed herself back to sleep, as she had done at eleven, and one, and two. With so much churning in her mind, she couldn't shut down.

A wild rooster crowed, answered by the rooster in their coop, a soothing sound she associated with home. Even their song, which drove most visitors nuts, couldn't lull Makalani back to sleep.

She rolled over and checked her watch. Three in the morning wasn't too obnoxious if she pretended to still be on Portland time.

Creeping through the house, she gathered provisions for a full day—with extra rations in case she found Becky and Solomon in dire straits. She checked the first aid kit she kept in her closet and added it to her backpack with her standard emergency gear. This time she dressed for a serious hike: wicking base-layer shirt, convertible cargo pants with the calf portions zipped off, a breathable waterproof jacket, and a brimmed airflow hat under which she could stuff her hair when it got hot. After rolling and packing the bottom legs of her pants and a long sleeve shirt, she exited her side door and walked quietly around the deck to the bench where she had stored her boots.

Crickets chirped in the darkness lit only by moonlight filtered through the trees. Although the evening's rain had unlocked the sweet fragrance of wild ginger and pua kenikeni, it hadn't rained hard enough to muddy the gravel path to her car. She opened and closed the door quietly and drove up the slope.

The journey to Kōkeʻe State Park took Makalani down the east coast to Līhuʻe and across the Kaumualiʻi Highway that skirted the mountain range blocking the southern tip of Poʻipū. Although she could feel the elevation changes as she drove, the forest hid behind an impenetrable night. When the land leveled, the tiny lights of Kalāheo appeared. Knowing she was within reach of the largest coffee farm in Hawaiʻi and all the US made her crave a hot cup of the rich Kauaʻi brew.

Later. When I've found them.

She couldn't afford to drink coffee before an eight-mile hike. Instead, she guzzled the last twenty-two ounces of the water she had brought for the ride. Hydration before a hike cut down the emergency water she would need to carry.

Town lights dwindled into the moonlit expanse of coastal and inland plains, then appeared again with scattered home lights from the early risers in Waimea. With no daylight saving time in Hawaiʻi, the first hint of dawn was still an hour away.

She rolled her window all the way down and enjoyed the last breath of ocean as she left Kekaha Beach and wound up the narrowing mountain road. As she climbed higher in elevation, the temperature cooled. The air grew thick with moisture and the pungent scent of rain-soaked earth. Pāpā wasn't kidding about hamajang trails. The hike would be a slippery mess.

Her tires skidded.

Apparently, so was the road.

Forty minutes later, she reached Puʻu o Kila Lookout and pulled behind a lonely SUV. Although camping sites collected fees from visitors, lookout and trailhead parking remained free and unmonitored for residents and tourists alike. Unless someone reported an accident or a washed-out trail, Makalani doubted anyone from park services would patrol way up here.

Keeping her headlamps on, she got out of the car and checked the rear of the beat-up Explorer. The window and bumper were decorated with the UH football team's green-and-white decals and a faded sticker from Kapa'a High. It had to be Solomon's. She peered into the hatch. A pink hibiscus backpack sat in the cluttered trunk.

Becky's?

But if they were camping, why park up here? Why camp at all?

Makalani pushed away her doubt. No matter how low Solomon had sunk or how desperate for attention and affirmation he had become, he would never cross that line. Becky was their cousin. Their *underage* cousin.

How much did she really know about Solomon as an adult? She had left the islands when he was twelve. As the years had passed, he had made less and less time to visit when she came home. In the two years since he dropped out of UH, she had hardly seen him at all.

She hadn't seen Becky, either, but that was a relief.

The older her young cousin became, the more she reminded Makalani of her own tormentors from school. Like her cousin, those girls had been pretty, popular, and mean. They had dispelled competition with brutal social assaults and manipulated anyone who could further their goals or desires. Boys, grades, homecoming court—anyone who stood in their path or could help them was fair game.

Oh, Becky. Have you become one of them?

As much as her cousin's attitude and behavior triggered bad memories, Makalani loved the girl fiercely and wanted her to be safe. Given time and empathy, Becky would grow out of her teenage angst and become the beautiful, caring woman she was destined to be. But for now, Aunty Kaulana had not been entirely wrong when she called Becky stuck-up and said she clung to Solomon like sweat. Even during her infrequent visits, Makalani had noticed the same. None of this explained why Solomon—even if he had taken Becky hiking without permission—had parked so far from a campsite if they had planned to stay overnight.

She moved her car beside the Explorer and prepared for the trek. Although it was cold at four thousand feet, she kept her pants converted into shorts. The high elevation kept mosquitos away. Jacket zipped, hat and shoulder straps in place, she headed up the road to the promontory where the slender ridge of Puʻu o Kila Lookout plunged into the Kalalau Valley and the Nā Pali Coast. The east side of the lookout faced Mount Waiʻaleʻale, backlit by the rising glow of dawn. The vast quantities of rain that drained down its western slopes had formed the Alakaʻi Swamp, the highest alpine bog in the world, currently hidden by fog.

Rain drizzled as she headed down the smooth, hard-packed earth and rock formations to the broad rim of the Kalalau Valley. This part of Pihea Trail had been graded for a road intended to connect Kōkeʻe to Hanalei before the muddy terrain ended the overly ambitious dream. Between the jagged cliffs and the near-constant rain, it became impossible for road builders to close the gap in the north.

The sloping trail grew slick as the drizzle increased to showers. Thankful for high-traction boots, she descended carefully, but quickened her pace as the trail rose. When she reached the offshoot to Pihea Vista, she passed it by—certain that neither of her cousins would want to work that hard for another view of Kalalau Valley—and descended along the hog fence into the forest.

Makalani had hiked this route many times during drier months when the red dirt was hard, not when the January rains had turned it to mud and eroded deep grooves between the roots. Grabbing one branch and then the next, she made her way through the most treacherous sections and picked up her pace where the terrain seemed to ease. A foolish mistake. Her boots shot out from under her. She slid down the chute, careening out of control, until she jammed her feet against the rocks at the turn. Between her legs, she saw a canopy of green.

Was this how Ikaika ʻŌpūnui had met his demise, slipping off that cliff in the Keālia Forest Reserve? Or had he been pushed after someone clubbed him in the head?

Trembling from near disaster, she climbed to her feet. Pāpā and Tūtū were right: Makalani had been away from home too long. Like an arrogant malihini, she had underestimated the local terrain. From here on in, she'd monitor her speed and check every turn in the trail for signs of a slide. She had skills her cousins did not. What had happened to her could easily have happened to them.

CHAPTER TWENTY-THREE

Makalani picked up her pace as the morning grew brighter and descended the double-plank boardwalk into the ʻOlokele Plateau. Although unstable in places, the boardwalk was safer than mud and reduced the environmental impact of hikers wandering off the trail. Pāpā had told her about the damage trekkers had done before the boardwalk construction began in 1991, and how their destructive wanderings had widened the trail in certain places to as much as thirty feet. Now the fertile ecosystem had taken back the land.

Fronds of ʻamaʻu and hāpuʻu ferns brushed against her legs. She paused for water and enjoyed the company of the honeycreepers defending their territory from the trees. The bright-yellow males would trill from dawn to dusk now that breeding season had begun. Other birds chirped in chorus, greeting the morning, saying hello.

As she trod along the planks, she breathed in the sweet fragrance of kāhili ginger growing in tall columns amid the ferns, shrubs, and trees. The delicate blossoms sprouted around a central stem like the royal standards for which they were named. In ancient times, the actual kāhili were made from bones of vanquished enemies and the feathers of predatory birds, symbols of power, protection, and divinity. Kāhili bearers would herald their monarch's arrival and wave the feathers over their monarch's body to call on ancestors after they had died.

After a mile, she reached the juncture for the Alakaʻi Swamp Trail, a crossroad of newly installed composite-board planks. A hard left would lead her into the ʻōhiʻa lehua forest and the alpine bog before rising up to Kilohana Lookout, where Becky's friends said she had wanted to go. If Makalani continued on Pihea Trail, she would reach Kawaikōī and Sugi Grove campgrounds where Solomon and Becky might have pitched a tent.

Would her cousins have circumvented the reservation process, counting on the recent rains to make the unpaved access road impossible for rangers to patrol?

Makalani had experienced that rough ride as a kid while camping with middle school friends. Not *her* friends. The girls were friendly with each other. Makalani had been invited by the parents as a favor to her mom.

Why did some girls bond and other girls drift?

That's what she had been wondering in the back seat, squished against the door while Ona, Roselani, and Ann chatted merrily among themselves. Makalani didn't have her mother's grace with people. She didn't know how to be fun like her dad. She wasn't even bossy like Aunty Maile. She was just . . . *her* . . . a too-serious giant who would rather be alone.

When they arrived at the small campground, she helped Ona's parents unload the truck. While the girls raced to the stream, Makalani carried containers of food to the camp. Ona's tiny mom had been amazed.

"You're as strong as a man." Her tone made Makalani feel like a freak. "Go play with the girls. We'll be fine on our own."

Makalani nodded but continued to work. Without purpose and exertion, she didn't know how to be.

Ona's tiny mother had viewed Makalani's strength with what would become an all-too-familiar mixture of awe and distaste. Even so, Makalani preferred function over grace. If other kids had valued this as well, she might have had more fun growing up and spent less time alone or fixated on work. As it was, she never fit in.

Ona and her friends spent all night telling ghost stories in the tent and giggling about the hottest boys in their class. Makalani shared a real-life story about her father's fight with a wild boar.

Ona crinkled her nose. "Ew, too much blood. We want scary not gross."

The girls shifted away, formed their own island, and left Makalani at sea.

That night, her stomach hurt so bad she could barely sleep. Māmā called them stress aches. But they never came when she studied for tests, spoke to grown-ups, or gave presentations in class. The pains only happened when she hung out with kids.

After everyone ate breakfast the next morning, Makalani wandered up Pihea Trail. When she reached the crossroad of composite planks, where she now stood, she took the boardwalk trail to the Alaka'i Swamp. Maybe her younger self was giving her a sign.

She followed the boardwalk into a familiar tunnel of trees where the newer planks reverted to rotted wood. Abandoned telephone poles, planted in World War II for advance warning of another Japanese attack, stood sentry, wires lost over the years. Their steadfast solitude drew Makalani along the boardwalk as they had when she was a child.

The farther she went from people, the closer she felt to herself.

She descended chicken-wired steps, amid giant tī plants and ferns, then crossed the flooded stream, and hiked along another fence built to keep out the destructive wild pigs. The moisture trapped by Mount Wai'ale'ale combined with the elevation made this ecosystem wetter and cooler than any place on the island. It could also disorient a hiker in the fog.

"Becky," she yelled. "Solomon?"

When no one answered, she continued to the swampy plateau. Fog shrouded the trees, stunted to shoulder height by the waterlogged earth.

Rotted planks sagged below the surface while stronger beams formed an unstable bridge. In places, newer composite planks ran alongside. Makalani alternated between them through the storm-flooded swamp.

In drier months, hikers could wander off the planks and get lost on islands of spongy land as her mother had done when she was a child before the boardwalks had been built. Back then, a curious visitor could wander the bog in search of endangered birds, Venus flytraps, and rare botanical discoveries not visible anywhere else in the world. Even on clear, sunny days, a misstep could swallow a child up to their waist. Which was why Ona's parents had been so angry when Makalani had finally returned to their camp.

"You've been gone for hours. Where have you been?" Ona's mom said.

"I followed the trail to Alaka'i Swamp."

"You're a kid," said Ona's dad. "You shouldn't have done that alone."

Makalani didn't tell them how often she solo-hiked in the Anahola hills or how her father had taught her to care for herself. Instead, she apologized and spent the rest of the weekend shadowing the girls, even though they clearly did not want her around.

Makalani exhaled the tension the memory had brought. She was almost as old as Ona's parents had been then. There was no reason to carry that memory forward when she could bury it in the bog.

She jumped across a break in the boardwalk, hurried up a sagging plank, and teetered across two-by-fours to the bank. Could a hazard like this have knocked her cousins off the trail? Or had Becky wandered through a bed of ferns and low flowering shrubs in search of Venus flytraps to bring home? The little girl Makalani had known would have shown them off at school. But what would captivate her jaded cousin at seventeen?

Makalani cupped her hands and yelled, "Becky? Solomon."

Silence answered, followed by a scurry of hooves and a flutter of wings.

A crimson 'apapane settled between the sprays of red lehua blossoms on the branch of a stunted 'ōhi'a tree. The little bird clicked and trilled an energetic song.

"Have you seen my cousins?" Makalani asked.

The tiny honeycreeper squeaked in answer, then vanished into the mist.

CHAPTER TWENTY-FOUR

Julia squeezed lime on to Kawika's breakfast papaya but neglected her own. Although they had a big day in front of them, she didn't want to eat.

"I'm worried about her."

"Who?" Kawika said, scooping out a giant bite of the sweet orange flesh.

"Makalani. She's so focused on Solomon and Becky, I'm afraid she'll make herself sick."

"She hasn't done that long time, not since she became one ranger. I think helping others gives her one outlet fo' all da bad feelings she get."

Julia sighed. "How would we know? She only tells us what we want to hear."

He scooped the last bit of fruit from the skin. "She one strong wahine. She can handle whatevah people say 'bout her."

"Even us?"

"Especially us."

Julia wasn't so sure. Their eldest daughter had manifested physiological reactions to emotional stress since she was a kid. The stomach pains increased most notably when she was having trouble with other children or when she felt she had let down an adult she admired. Although the doctors couldn't confirm this connection, they had no other plausible explanation for Makalani's pains. She handled life-or-death emergency with calm and steady efficiency. Throw her into emotional strife, and her body shut down.

Kawika covered Julia's graceful hands with his own. "Dat emotional stuff happened when she was young. She grown up now. She can handle pissed-off relatives."

"Not if she thinks she caused their suffering."

"What suffering could she have caused in two days? Nah. Makalani get in trouble because she care too much, not about what people t'ink but about what dey *do*. She no can stay home and do not'ing any more dan she could not breathe. Da only time she get sick is when people no let her help."

"By driving to the other side of the island at three in the morning? You heard her car leave. Isn't that a little obsessive even for her?"

Kawika chuckled. "Remembah da haad time she gave Kaulana when she started smoking da cigarettes? Or when James wen to community college instead of applying to UH?"

Julia smirked. "Or when you paddled to Ni'ihau after the boar gored your leg?"

"It was mostly healed. Besides, I paddle wit' my arms and back."

"But you brace with your legs, so Makalani was right."

"Which is exactly my point. If she t'inks she need drive and hike all dat way to find her cousins, maybe it's a good t'ing dat she does."

"I guess." Julia passed her untouched papaya to him. "She still thinks of her cousins the way they used to be. She doesn't know how they are now. I mean, let's face it, neither Solomon nor Becky would win best kid of the year."

"Not like Makalani?"

Julia shrugged. "I might be partial."

"You t'ink?" He took a bite and passed the papaya back to her.

She flashed him a stink eye and returned it to him. "Do I play favorites with our daughters?"

"Little bit. But Pua always had da easier time. Girlfriends, boyfriends, decent grades, happy kid. No reason to lose sleep ovah her. Not like Makalani. Everyt'ing haad wit' dat one."

"You think that's why she's so critical of others?"

132

"Critical? Nah. More like high expectation. She like everyone do dea best, including her."

Julia frowned. "No one is ever one hundred percent at their best."

"You come pretty close."

"Flatterer."

"No lie. You like Mary Poppins, yeah? Practically perfect in every way."

Only his sweet smile kept her from smacking his hand. *Mary Poppins.* If that were true, wouldn't her daughters enjoy her company more? Pua lived in Honolulu, where she managed a hotel restaurant in Waikīkī. Makalani lived in Oregon, keeping the peace in a national park. Both of her daughters had moved away from home the first chance they could.

"I'm going to bake banana nut bread."

"Now?" he asked. "Da lū'au is still two days away."

"I know. But Friday will be crazy. Saturday worse. We still have fifty laulau to prepare for your imu, not to mention the decorations and the other food we have to prepare. If I bake this morning, the bread will be fresh enough."

She peeled bananas into a bowl and tried to mash her worries along with the fruit.

Although Julia adored their younger daughter, she didn't think about her as much. Nor did Pua appear to think about them. Makalani, on the other hand, called twice a week to check on the family and the farm. When asked about her own life, she gave the briefest answers and turned the conversation around. Although she seemed happy in Oregon and established in her career, Julia was concerned. Did her daughter have friends? Did she miss home? Was her job as a law enforcement ranger more dangerous than she claimed? These questions kept Julia awake at night.

Kawika finished the papaya and fetched a ziplock bag of macadamia nut pieces she had prepared the previous day. "You two always had one special bond. Now dat Makalani's home, you want her all for yourself."

"You make me sound so selfish."

"Nah. You've been waiting fo' her to come home long time to talk story and bake banana bread wit' you. Dis business wit' Solomon and Becky is stealing your togeddah time."

"You don't think they're in trouble?"

"Probably. But not dakine everybody t'ink. Dose kids are close, but not in a bad way. Dey come home soon. Probably skipped off da island fo' fun."

"Should we call Pua?"

"Already did," he said. "If dey wen to O'ahu, dey didn't call her."

"Solomon and Becky have friends on other islands," Julia said. "He's broke, but she could have had money for tickets. Did you mention your theory to James and Linda?"

"Nah. You heard how defensive dey get wit' Makalani. Better to let t'ings play out and see."

CHAPTER TWENTY-FIVE

The rain returned as Makalani climbed the steep boardwalk steps out of 'Olokele Plateau. Between the downpour, the fog, and the press of the forest, her world had shrunk to the few yards in front of her feet.

The downpour ended as she crossed over a small pond and climbed up the final leg of the hike where Kilohana Lookout welcomed her with warmth and the resounding chorus of fully woken birds. She took off her hat and raised her face to the sun. Although gentle trade winds opened the gray sky, puffy white clouds hugged the jagged cliffs running from Mount Wai'ale'ale to the shore. On a clear day, she could have zoomed in with her phone to see waterfalls plunging thousands of feet down the ridge. As it was, she could barely see the lush Wainiha and Lumiha'i valleys or the northern coast and Hanalei Bay.

After water and a snack, she left her backpack on the bench and stepped off the warped deck and back into the mud. Trees and ferns encroached from all sides, even climbing up the cliff with a thousand-foot drop. No railings. No barriers. Just a hard-packed edge, slippery from the rain. Although muddy, the promontory was relatively smooth with only a few old impressions where a heavy hiker had gouged a deep boot print that had hardened in the sun. Aside from these, no other prints remained. She searched the thick foliage on the left, then inched her way carefully along the sheer drop. The hillside ferns and trees obscured any signs of a possible slide.

"Solomon! Becky!"

She checked her phone for bars. Kaua'i had notoriously bad cell reception, especially in the forests. But on clear days, at this particular lookout, lucky hikers could sometimes connect. Zero bars. This was not one of those days.

She pocketed the phone and squatted to stretch the kinks from her back. Two hours driving in the dark plus three more trudging through mud, swamp, and rain. For what? To trap herself on a lonely lookout?

She thumped her head and muttered, "Damn it, Solomon. Where have you gone?"

Frustration brewed like a storm, drawing from every mistake she had made, not only from this morning but since she had butted her nose into her family's business. James and Linda would find their wayward daughter. Solomon would wander home whenever he pleased. Only arrogance made her think she knew better than her cousins, aunts, uncles, and the police. Like a typical mainlander, she had barged in as if she knew best.

She guided a millipede out of a puddle, glad to have rescued something on this trek, and tilted her head to make sense of what she saw—an indentation as if caused by the front of a pivoting boot. She traced the ridges of the tread then touched the smaller, deeper indentation of a heel. It was deep, as if dug into the ground by the full weight of a man.

Makalani bolted from up from her squat. Her legs and back seized. Rather than give herself time to adjust, she hobbled toward the cliff. The rains had smoothed away other possible clues, but she might find something if she looked over the edge. She stopped herself midstep and backed away toward the bench. Her impulsive heart had led long enough. From now on, she needed to listen to her head.

She detached the yellow rescue sack she had hooked to her backpack and pulled out a coil of bright-orange climbing rope with carabiners attached to the loops and the ends. Since the metal posts of the bench were sharp and not cemented into the ground, she found a healthy tree behind it to use as an anchor. She wrapped several arm lengths of rope around the trunk. Although the friction would anchor it in place, she clipped the carabiner to the load strand for insurance, and threaded the coil under the bench so the rope wouldn't rub against the wood. She tied the remainder around her upper chest and tied it off with a rewoven figure eight. Satisfied with her safety measures, she wrapped the load line around her forearm, grabbed hold of the rope, and leaned out over the cliff.

Wind buffeted her jacket and face, more strongly now without the shelter of the trees. If she hadn't tied on, it would have knocked her over the edge.

She spat out her hair and searched the vegetation below for broken branches or shrubs ripped from the soil. A small landslide on the slope beneath her might have been caused by a person sliding over the edge or, just as likely, from rain destabilizing the earth. She loosened the coils around her arm and leaned a few more inches out into space, stretching the rope as far as it could go.

"Solomon? Becky."

Tiny brown birds fluttered from the treetops as she yelled, scolding her with their tweets. They might have been rare 'elepaio, but she didn't care enough to look. The only thing that mattered to her in this moment was finding her cousins and bringing them home.

She called again. When no one answered, she pulled herself back to standing and sighed with defeat. She had uncoiled the rope from her arm when she heard a faint call in the wind.

"Hello?" she said. "Is anyone there?"

"Hey." The voice sounded distant, weak, and male.

"Solomon? Is that you?" She strained to listen but heard only the wind. "It's Makalani. Can you hear me?"

If he slipped down the cliff on Monday afternoon, he would have been without water for almost three full days. He wouldn't be thinking clearly. His throat would be parched. She needed to ask clear questions with yes-or-no answers.

"Are you injured?"

"Nah."

"Is your position secure?" When he didn't answer, she yelled, "Are you stuck in a tree?"

"Yeah."

"A long way down?"

"Plenny far."

Although hoarse, he sounded surprisingly coherent. The low temperatures, tree shade, and immobility must have slowed dehydration. Even so, he would need water. And soon.

She relooped the rope around her arm and leaned out again, searching the vegetation for any color other than green.

"Say something."

"Like what?"

She spotted downturned branches in the shrubs on the right. If he had slipped through there, he might have fallen twenty or thirty yards.

"You got water?" he asked.

"I do."

"Good," he said. "Drink some fo' me."

She barked out a laugh, surprised and relieved at the humor. "I'd be happy to share if I knew where you were."

"Slipped off on da right."

She pulled herself back, glanced at the tree trunk to make sure her loops hadn't budged, and then switched hands so she would face in the correct direction when she hung out again. This time, she spotted the slide, through the downturned branches and into the tree tops below.

"Can you wave a hand?"

"I am."

"I can't see you."

"Try listen den."

Crackle, crackle, crunch.

Crackle, crackle, crunch.

She followed the sound to a flash of red she had previously mistaken for lehua blossoms.

"I see you."

He coughed, and the crackling stopped.

"What was that sound?"

"Plastic bottle."

"You had water?"

"Did. All pau."

That explained why Solomon sounded coherent and was able to talk.

"When did you run out?"

"Yesterday."

"Are you wearing a backpack?"

"Yeah. Becky wanted me to carry da lunch."

Becky.

In the excitement of finding Solomon, Makalani had forgotten all about her. Now that she remembered, she was terrified to ask.

"Eh, Mak?"

"Yeah?"

"Is Becky wit' you?"

CHAPTER TWENTY-SIX

Kay laid her long floral dress beside her suitcase with the rest of her clothes. She had it custom made for a Waiʻalae Country Club lūʻau the previous year. While many of the women had come in shapeless muʻumuʻu, she had chosen a vibrant blue rayon gown with a more elegant cut. The shallow scoop neck and tapered three-quarter sleeves hid the age spots on her chest and arms while the semifitted sheath showed off her still-graceful figure. Compared to her peers, Kay Ornelas had looked pretty darn good.

She picked up the dress, listened for sounds of her husband nearby, then slipped it on to make sure of the fit. The plumeria dress was the most Hawaiian-style garment she owned. Whenever she wore it, it made her want to hula.

She curled her short white hair around her ear and imagined it flowing over her shoulders to her waist as it had in her youth. Back then, she would have slipped a Tahitian gardenia behind her ear—right for available, left if she was dating a boy. When Douglas bought her this house, she planted a bush in their backyard for the scent. She didn't wear any of the flowers in her newly bobbed hair. If Douglas missed her tresses, he never said a word.

With eyes on the mirror, Kay sank into her knees and swayed forward with two tentative steps. As her hips moved, her hands swept up and paused on the right like the slope of a cliff. With slow, rolling sways, she trickled her fingers like rain.

She froze, hands suspended, eyes lost in the mist of her memories: The cloudy peak of Mount Wai'ale'ale. The sound of birds chirping in the trees. The cool trade winds carrying the sweet scent of mountain ginger and rain. The salty crust of dried seawater in her hair.

Kay dropped her hands, surprised by the longing she felt. Although she had never admitted it to Douglas, she loved Kaua'i the most. Not even Maui could compare to the lush beauty of the rainiest island in the chain. It was more than gorgeous scenery. Despite her denial, Kay missed the feeling of home.

She smoothed her dress, confused by the word. Home was where she had built a happy life with Douglas, not the unwelcoming place she had worked hard to escape. A few graceful hand gestures couldn't wipe that away. She needed armor or, at the very least, a shield behind which she could hide.

She smiled at her reflection, then retrieved a box from under her bed.

Kay had last worn the piko'ole pāpale when crownless, woven hats had surged in popularity with the golf ladies at the club. Her full-brim pāpale had been woven, lauhala style, from slimmer straw. The open top kept her head cool on the golf course and her hair looking nice at the dining room—the "nineteenth hole"—afterward, for lunch. She received many compliments, but she never told anyone the skillful weaver was her aunt.

Years had passed before Kay truly appreciated the thoughtful wedding gift.

Thoughtful and valuable.

In addition to the fine weave of the hat, Ka'ahumanu had encircled the crown with a wide cowrie shell band. The lei pāpale alone would have sold for $500 in a Honolulu boutique. Her gift note said she hoped the local straw and shells would remind Kēhau of home.

How precious yet awkward this gift had been since Kēhau—or Kay, as she had begun calling herself—hadn't invited Ka'ahumanu or any of her relatives to the wedding. Even her parents did not attend, having been told there would be only a courthouse ceremony. In truth, a hundred of Douglas's friends, family, and business associates had witnessed their union at a sunset, beachside ceremony on the Wai'alae Country Club lawn, followed by a lavish reception inside. Kay had only invited her Honolulu friends.

She ran her fingers along the hatband.

She had stressed about Ka'ahumanu's gift for weeks before sending a brief card of thanks. Out of embarrassment, she kept it generic and didn't mention the extraordinary craftsmanship or the thoughtful meaning of the shells. Now it was too late. As the saying went, *The overripe hala fruit had already fallen to the ground.*

She placed the hat on her head and fluffed her white hair through the open crown, pleased with how the color complemented the shells and accented the white plumerias against the vibrant blue leaves and background on her dress. Although average in height, she felt almost as regal as Ka'ahumanu always looked.

Kay tipped her head and peeked at her reflection beneath the protective shield of the brim. If she wore the hat to the lū'au, would her aunty be flattered or annoyed by her slight?

The problem with having an aunt so close in age was the competition that naturally arose. Although Kay's mother had kept her away from the Pahukula side of the family, the girls had seen each other every day at school, where a two-year advantage was huge. Ka'ahumanu knew everyone and did everything first. She excelled in paddling, basketball, weaving pāpale, and braiding haku leis with flowers and shells. She danced beautiful hula that she learned from her mother and, because of her majestic height, represented the Big Island of Hawai'i in every May Day hula pageant court. During her senior year, the student body even voted her queen.

Not so with Kēhau.

Although beautiful and graceful, she had lacked the authentic training her aunt had received and was passed over every year. In every way that mattered on the east side of Kaua'i, Kēhau lived in the shadow of her slightly older aunt. Despite the poverty they both shared,

Ka'ahumanu had the emotional support and respected Kaua'i pedigree of the Pahukula clan. Kay's father's 'ohana, the Kealohas, had moved to the island from Lāna'i and never amounted to much.

All that changed when Kēhau moved to Honolulu and transformed herself into Kay.

She dressed in ways that accentuated the slenderness of her formerly "too scrawny" figure, excelled in business and marketing courses, joined the popular clubs with the rich haole girls, and attracted the notice of ambitious young men. She stopped swimming and paddling and took up golf and tennis, instead. And she never danced the hula again.

Kay adjusted the brim of her fortifying hat and caught the reflection of her Tiffany rings as they sparkled in the light. In every way that mattered to her now, Kēhau Kealoha Ornelas had won.

CHAPTER TWENTY-SEVEN

Makalani had a hard decision to make. Although the sky was clearing and the clouds had mostly blown away, the signal reception was still weak. If the weather continued to improve, she might have a clear shot to the cell towers in Hanalei. But could she really afford to wait?

An hour spent with Solomon was another hour tacked on to her trip back into town. Even if Kawaikōī Stream hadn't swelled into an impassable river and the mud on Pihea Trail had dried, it would take her at least two hours to hike back to the car and another forty-five minutes to drive down the mountain into Waimea where she'd have enough bars for a call. That was three hours *plus* another twenty minutes before KFD's Air 1 rescue helicopter could make it to Kilohana Lookout.

If she lucked out with cell reception, first responders could rescue Solomon within the hour.

She laid her emergency tarp on the muddy ground a couple of feet from the edge so she could rest her body within hearing distance of him. After explaining her plan—and despite pangs of guilt—she ate, drank, and studied the sky.

"How many bars?" Solomon asked, his voice raspier than before.

This time, she opened her Android settings and checked the SIM status for decibel levels. Since bars were subjective from phone to phone, this was the only way to accurately measure Kilohana's cell signal. Whereas her phone had shown one bar, her decibels had improved to -105. She was six decibels away from an average signal that would hopefully connect.

She placed another call. When it didn't work, she texted 911.

"Not enough," she yelled. "But the clouds are clearing."

Although some moisture in the air facilitated signal transmission, too much interfered and caused a delay. Thirty minutes had passed since Solomon had asked about Becky. Makalani had waited another fifteen to see which way the weather might go. She asked numerous questions during that time, but Solomon was only able to answer the most urgent one before a coughing fit had made him stop. He had saved Becky from falling before he slipped off the cliff.

"Eh, Mak?"

"I'm here."

"Tell me a story." His voice sounded weak and scared.

"Sure." She squeezed back the rising tears.

Her poor cousin had been trapped in those branches for almost seventy hours, not knowing when one of them might break or if anyone would find him before he died. Although he had experienced close encounters with death while surfing or hunting or that football concussion that had landed him in the hospital in tenth grade, the prolonged danger and uncertainty of this situation had to be much worse. If he hadn't crackled that water bottle, she would never have distinguished the glimpse of his red shirt from the lehua blossoms on the trees. And just like that, she knew which story to tell.

"Long ago, before the first malihini walked on our land, a beautiful warrior named ʻŌhiʻa lived on the island of Hawaiʻi. He stood as tall and straight as the cliffs, with legs as strong as the trunks of the trees. His brown skin gleamed like oiled koa as he worked, fought, or played. He excelled at every sport the Hawaiians loved best. Everyone who met him said he was the bravest, kindest, most noble man they had ever known. So when he met a woman as lovely and perfect as him, it surprised no one when they fell madly in love.

"Lehua had eyes as round as the moon. Her smile was as bright as the midday sun. She showed kindness to everyone and had a gentle nature the tiny red 'apapane birds adored. They fluttered around her flowing black hair and followed her wherever she went. When 'Ōhi'a would serenade Lehua on his bamboo nose flute, they added to his melody with their high trilling song. They married and lived happily in the forest.

"One day, while 'Ōhi'a played his 'ohe hano ihu, a beautiful stranger appeared. When she flirted with him, he politely refused. She appeared the next day, more beautiful and determined than before, but still, 'Ōhi'a politely refused. He was in love with Lehua and could not be swayed.

"'Do you know who I am?' the stranger said, her eyes burning with fire.

"'You're Madame Pele, the goddess of volcanos. I'm a mortal in love with my wife.'

"When Lehua arrived, he enveloped her in his strong arms and kissed her gently on the mouth. Inflamed by jealousy and fury, Madame Pele encircled the lovers with lava, but left a clear path to herself.

"'Choose me over her, and I'll let you both live. Stay with your wife, and you die.'

"As the burning lava crept closer, 'Ōhi'a raised Lehua over his head. He begged Madame Pele to spare his beloved, but the goddess refused. Lava climbed up his legs and transformed his body into a twisted, ugly tree.

"Lehua cried out in horror, 'Please, Tūtū Pele, do the same to me so I can always be with my dearest 'Ōhi'a.'

"Pele vanished, leaving Lehua weeping in the branches of her love.

"The little 'apapane flew to the gods to tell them what Madame Pele had done. When the gods saw Lehua's despair, they turned her into a fiery blossom, forever uniting the lovers as the 'ōhi'a lehua tree.

"Now, whenever the flowers are picked on the way into the forest without greeting the lovers and asking their permission, tears of rain fall from the sky. To this day, the loyal 'apapane flutter and kiss Lehua's lovely face."

Makalani gazed over the valley and waited for Solomon's response. Had the old legend lulled him into sleep? If so, she prayed for sweet and comforting dreams.

After a moment, he called up to her, voice raspy from talking so much. "What you t'ink? Try stay? Or go?"

She checked the SIM status again—still a poor signal but a little improved. She sent another text. It failed. But as the sun warmed the air, the humidity would decrease. Another half hour of waiting could possibly have Solomon rescued by noon.

"The signal is improving. Let's wait fifteen minutes and see how it goes."

"What about da gray?" he said.

"What gray?"

"Coming in ovah da ridge."

She stood and walked to the far side where she could see Mount Wai'ale'ale in the east. Sure enough, The Rainmaker was at it again.

CHAPTER TWENTY-EIGHT

Makalani packed up her gear and called over the edge. "Are you sure you'll be okay? I hate to leave you if another storm rolls in."

Solomon grunted a harsh sound between a laugh and a cough. "Go, already. Da trees keep me dry bettah dan you."

Makalani nodded at the obvious truth. With no clear path through the vegetation, she couldn't even lower a reflective emergency blanket or water. The only thing she could do was keep him company or find help. She tightened the straps on her backpack and stuffed her hair beneath her hat. The hike back would be quick, dirty, and hot.

She tried to call one more time. When it didn't go through, she texted the emergency situation and location to 911 and waited for the failure notice to appear.

"Oh my god, Solomon. The text went through."

"What dey say?"

She gripped the phone tight.

Please, please, please.

"Makalani?"

"Wait." Seconds ticked by without a response. "Nothing yet."

"Not'ing?"

Makalani checked the SIM status on her phone. The decibels had dropped. "I've lost the signal."

"Dey get your text?"

"I think so. But I can't be sure."

"So what den?"

She walked to the left side of the bluff and peered across the canyon toward the east. The gathering clouds had grown dense.

"I'm going to hike out and call for help in town. With luck, you'll already be rescued."

Solomon scoffed. "Do I seem lucky to you?"

Makalani muttered a curse. She couldn't risk waiting for a helicopter that might never come, but she didn't want to leave him in a precarious emotional state. If he thought things were hopeless, he might try to climb up the cliff on his own. What would happen if the tree limbs broke? What would happen if he decided he didn't care?

"You *are* lucky, Solomon. Lucky and smart. You're in a secure position. When the rescue helicopter comes, it won't have enough room for me. I'll have to hike out anyway. If I leave now, I'll make it to the hospital soon after you arrive."

When he didn't respond, she dug her fingernails into her palms. She should have contained her excitement about the text and left with him still feeling—or at least pretending to feel—brave. A moment ago, he had encouraged her to leave. Now she feared he was falling into despair.

"Go," he said.

"You sure?"

"Yeah."

She analyzed his tone for clues about his intentions or psychological state. A survival attitude depended on a positive outlook, a rational mind, and a fierce determination to live. She heard a hint of steel in his voice.

"Okay. Sit tight and rest. The less you exert your body and mind, the less energy you'll burn and the less water you'll need. You have a secure and protected position. I described your location and let them know you're wearing red. Helicopters are loud. You'll hear it for sure."

"Got it."

He sounded stronger than before. She didn't want to add anything that would plant a seedling of doubt or sound like a final farewell.

"I'll see you at the hospital," she shouted over the cliff.

She whispered quietly to herself, "I love you, cuz," and ran.

She kept a steady pace down the boardwalk, across the pond, and up to the bog, trying not to worry that she still hadn't passed a single person on one of the island's most popular hikes. Had the stream overflowed and turned them away? The ranger in her hoped visitors would stay off the trails. The cousin in her hoped she could send determined hikers to Solomon in her place. When she jumped to a rotted plank and nearly fell into the bog, she focused her attention on the dangers at her feet. Although the fog had lifted, the boardwalk was as unstable as before.

A man on the far bank of Kawaikōī Stream held out his hands as she hurried down the stairs. "You have to wait. The current's too strong."

The babbling stream she had crossed earlier had swelled and grown swift.

Makalani took off her backpack, uncoiled several yards of her rope, and tossed the remainder over the rushing stream to the man.

"My cousin fell off a cliff. I can't afford to wait. Wrap that around a tree a few times and hang on to the end."

She tied a loop around her chest for safety, put on her backpack, and waded into the rapids. Leaning against the current, she planted her boots as firmly as she could, grabbing on to the boulders for balance when she slipped. By the time she reached the other side, the water had soaked through her shirt and washed her muddy boots and shorts clean.

"Thanks for your help." She unwound her rope and stuffed it into her pack. "Another storm is coming. You should hike out before it hits."

The woman beside him looked up at the sun. "Are you sure? We drove all the way from Princeville to see the swamp."

Makalani glanced at the woman's formerly white running shoes, now stained and caked with iron-rich mud. "You'll have a hard enough time hiking back to your car. If you get stuck in a downpour, I'll have to send another rescue crew for you."

Having issued her warning, Makalani strapped on her backpack and resumed her trail-running pace. By the time she reached the parking lot, she was exhausted and covered from chest to boots in mud.

She stopped another family as they pulled backpacks and water from their car. "It's not safe today. Enjoy the lookout, then do something else."

They took in her mud-wrestling appearance and tossed their gear back on the seat.

When she reached her own car, she threw a towel over the front seat, and drove down the winding road as fast as safety would allow.

CHAPTER TWENTY-NINE

Makalani blasted into the ER reception area like a bull through a gate. "Solomon Ching. Have the first responders brought him in yet?"

The admittance nurse looked up from her magazine. "The hiker who fell off Kilohana Lookout?"

Makalani sighed with relief. "That's him."

She smiled reassuringly. "He arrived two hours ago. They moved him out of the ER. Family is with him now."

"I'm his cousin."

"Then he'll be happy to see you, mud and all. Go around the corridor to the main side and ask for him at the nurses' station."

Makalani followed the instructions, but when she reached the station, she found her family already spilling into the hall.

Māmā spotted her first and stopped short of an embrace. "Are you okay? Solomon said the conditions were bad when you hiked out, but look at you, you're covered in mud."

"I'm fine."

Māmā's lip quivered as she wiped Makalani's face. "The red dirt looks like blood."

"It's not. Really, I'm okay. How is Solomon?"

Pāpā answered instead. "He stay dehydrated but surprisingly okay. If you nevah went up dea to search—" He shook the thought from his mind and pulled her into a hug, staining his sweatshirt red. "I should have gone wit' you. I should have believed."

"There wasn't anything you could have done. It was actually better that I went alone." *And that I went so early,* she thought. An hour later, she wouldn't have crossed the stream.

Pāpā rubbed her trembling arms. "You cold?"

"Adrenaline drop. I left my jacket in the car."

"I get it fo' you."

"You sure?"

"Gimme da keys. Go see your cousin."

"I parked in front of the ER."

"Of course you did. You're smarter dan all of us combined."

"Go," said Māmā. "I'll wait out here or you won't fit in that room."

She wasn't kidding. James, Linda, and both of her aunts and uncles stood around Solomon as Officer Kimo Tagaloa—taking up space for two people—questioned him from the foot of the bed. Everyone turned when Makalani entered. She ignored the onslaught of questions and squeezed past Aunty Kaulana and Uncle Eric to Solomon's side.

He had changed considerably since she had seen him the previous year, when his muscle had turned to flab. Although he still had a gut, his skin hung slack on his chest. Mostly, he looked weak. Sunken eyes. Scruffy beard over chapped lips. Broken-out skin. How much of this could be blamed on three days and nights trapped on a cliff?

She ran her hand down his scratched-up arm and held his fingers below the needle in his vein. If she hadn't found him this morning, they might have lost him for good.

He sighed with relief. "You made it."

"Told you I would." She took in the saline drip and monitoring wires. "How you feeling?"

"Glad to be out of dat tree."

They laughed.

Linda cut them off. "What about Becky? Did you find any sign of her? Solomon claims he saved her from falling before he slipped off the cliff."

"Eh, now," Kimo said. "Leave da questions fo' da police."

"Then ask them. Our daughter is still missing. This one might know where she is."

This one? Makalani didn't care for Linda's tone.

"Try wait, 'kay?" Kimo said. "Let me do my job."

He looked at Makalani. "So? What else you find besides dis one in a tree?"

"Dis one?" Makalani had had enough. "Solomon and I have names. Try show us some respect." If Kimo wanted to keep up his Samoan moke attitude, she'd show him how tough a Hawaiian tita could be.

"Relax, Makalani. Tell me what you saw."

Aunty Kaulana nodded in agreement. "Please. We all want to hear."

Makalani took a breath and put her indignation aside. "Rain washed away most of the prints. I only noticed Solomon's because his boot had dug a hole in the mud next to the cliff."

"Fresh hole?" Kimo asked.

"No. Days old. None of the prints looked fresh."

"Any sign of Becky?"

"No."

"A struggle?"

"No. But Solomon's boot had been dug into the ground with a lot of weight. Like he pivoted to save Becky from falling."

"Any slides?"

"Only where he slipped off the edge."

Kimo rubbed a meaty hand across his bolo head. "You sure it was only Solomon?"

Makalani started to answer, then read the energy in the room. Aside from Aunty Kaulana, Uncle Eric, and Solomon, everyone else radiated worry and distrust. Uncle Sanji glared at her from across the bed. This was the first time she had seen him since she'd been home. His hair had grayed. His short, stocky body had thickened. He looked even angrier than Aunty Maile.

Makalani nodded to Kimo. "The slide was small, not wide enough for two."

"You one expert on geology now?"

"You asked. I answered." She turned to Uncle Sanji, hoping Becky's grandfather would have more sway. "Solomon said he saved her. I'm sure that he did. Has anyone reported Becky's absence to the Investigative Services Bureau? They're the ones at KPD who search for missing people."

"I'm handling it," Kimo said.

You're a patrol cop with a beef against my cousin, she wanted to say. Instead, she kept her voice neutral and addressed Uncle Sanji, Aunty Maile, Linda, and James.

"If you officially report Becky missing and tell them what Solomon said, they'll assign detectives to her case and reach out to DOCARE officers at the DLNR."

Kimo scoffed. "How da Department of Land and Natural Resources goin' find dea keiki?"

"Because Kōke'e State Park is a hunting ground. The Conservation and Resource Enforcement officers know the terrain."

Linda gasped. "Are you suggesting that my daughter could be shot, dying in the woods, mistaken for a pig?"

"Of course not. But if she's lost in the forest reserve, DOCARE officers and hunters need to be warned."

Kimo held out his hands. "Eh, nobody say nothing 'bout mistaking Becky fo' one pig."

Makalani leaned over the bed. "She could be lost in the forest."

Kimo glared back. "Or Solomon could have shoved her off da cliff."

The room erupted as everyone shouted at once. Solomon's parents defended his honor. Becky's parents and grandparents yelled accusations no one would ever forget. The chasm between Chings and Muramotos grew wider than Solomon's bed.

Kimo patted the air with his hands. This time, nobody calmed.

Makalani walked around the bed to confront Kimo. "How could you say something like that?"

"Back off, Makalani."

"Look what you did. Your incompetence and prejudice are tearing my family apart."

He grabbed his handcuffs and stuck a palm in front of her chest. "Back off or I'll arrest *you*."

"For what?"

"Enough," Pāpā yelled from the door.

His authority as the eldest Pahukula silenced the room. He helped Makalani into her jacket and whispered into her ear. "Wass goin' on?"

"Kimo accused Solomon of shoving Becky off a cliff."

"Auwē."

She grunted. *Auwē, indeed.*

Pāpā scolded each family member with his gaze, then settled on Kimo with a courteous smile. "We all happy to get Solomon back safe. I'm sure you feel da same. You and Solomon stay good friends from befo' time, right? We all lucky to have a braddah on da force helping us out."

Kimo puffed up and adjusted the belt around his belly.

Pāpā pulled Makalani to the front. "We also lucky to have one brave and determined wahine like Makalani in our 'ohana who nevah give up on her cousins, who risk herself to bring Solomon home, and who still doing all she can to find Becky. Dass what we all want, right? To find Becky and bring her home safe." He stared across the bed at James and Linda. "I know you like keep family business private, but there's no shame in asking for kōkua."

James shook his head. "They'll dig into things that have nothing to do with Becky."

"Like what?"

"Business, lives, what difference does it make? The point is, they don't know us."

"He's right." Kimo looked down his nose at James in the same way he had done at the store. "At least wit' me, all da questions come from love."

Makalani choked down the bile that rose in her throat. How dare this bully pretend to care.

"Maybe Kawika is right," Aunty Maile said, rubbing her hand along her son's back.

James shook it off. "Becky is my daughter. I say what's best."

"What about me?" Linda said. "She's my daughter, too. Don't I get a say?"

"Of course you do. But I'm the father."

Pāpā interrupted. "Both parents are important. So is Becky. Report her missing. Let's bring our girl home."

Uncle Sanji patted his son's back. "Your uncle Kawika is right, James. She's been gone too long." He faced Kimo and offered a slight bow. "We appreciate everything you've done, Officer Tagaloa, but it's time to get more help."

Kimo narrowed his eyes, but Uncle Sanji held firm. James, on the other hand, looked ready to be sick.

After a moment, Kimo chuckled. "I drove all da way out hea 'cause you asked fo' my kōkua. But, hey, whatevah you want to do is fine wit' me."

He grabbed the footrail of the bed and leered at Solomon. "Feel better, yeah? You need get strong to answer all da questions da detectives will ask."

He grinned cruelly at James. "Same goes fo' you."

CHAPTER THIRTY

Once Kimo and the Muramotos had gone, Pāpā and Uncle Eric went to fetch Solomon's Explorer while Makalani, Māmā, and Aunty Kaulana kept Solomon company. After watching him sleep for hours, they met Pāpā and Uncle Eric at Hoku's Food Truck. The doctors wanted to pump Solomon full of fluids and monitor his electrolytes before they decided whether or not to keep him overnight. Since it would take a while, Māmā insisted they eat. Makalani had devoured a double helping of kalbi ribs and half of her fried saimin before finally slowing down.

Aunty Kaulana slid her kimchi into Makalani's container. "'Ono, yeah? All dat hiking make you mo' hungry dan me."

Māmā rubbed Makalani's back. "Solomon's not the only one who needs care. The salt and fluids are good for her, too."

Aunty Kaulana nodded and set down her spoon. "You one good cousin, Makalani. Eric and me . . ." She sniffed back an onslaught of emotion.

Makalani reached across the picnic table for her hand. It was larger and more sunbaked than her own, soft from fat, yet calloused in places from homesteading life.

"He's going to be okay," Makalani said.

Aunty Kaulana shrugged. "Dat boy hasn't been okay since he came home from UH. All da time sleep or drink. Nevah do nothing to care fo' himself." She took back her hand and sighed. "Stay like he crossed da huaka'i pō and nevah show um respect. Now all da time bad luck."

The huaka'i pō was a sacred band of ghost warriors that roamed the night and enforced Hawaiian law. If someone was unlucky enough to encounter the ghosts on their march, they were supposed to prostrate themselves and avert their gaze.

"Solomon's injury was bad luck fo' sure," Pāpā said. "But da rest is on him. He needs meaningful work to feel like a man."

"Like what?" Aunty Kaulana said. "Dig and fish like you?"

"Why not? It's pono work."

"Because he shoulda been one star, dass why. He bettah dan dis. He bettah dan you."

Pāpā accepted her insult with a shrug. "Maybe. Or maybe working da 'aina would strengthen his mana. Dat boy need be of service to replace da life energy he lost."

Uncle Eric waved his quesadilla, as a Buddhist monk waves incense to purify the air. "Solomon find his way soon. Football hard kine work. It's okay to take one break."

They finished the meal without further comment and headed back to the hospital where they found Solomon, dressed and waiting, finishing his dessert of yogurt and fruit. Between the nurse's care and the intravenous fluids, he looked markedly better than before—plump skin, brushed hair, *slightly* less straggly mustache and beard.

"Eh, what take you so long? Dey say I can leave already."

Aunty Kaulana narrowed her eyes. "Fo' real?"

"Yeah." He nodded to the man beside him. "Ask da nurse. I'm jus' waiting on you." He gestured to his purple Kilohana Canoe Club T-shirt and pink pajama pants. "He even gave me church donation clothes to wear home."

The burly nurse handed Aunty Kaulana the discharge instructions. "Dr. Chin wrote down foods and drinks he should have and avoid. Make an appointment with his primary doctor for next week." He glanced at Solomon. "Alcohol dehydrates the body. He should lay off the beer."

Having issued his instructions, he helped Solomon into a wheelchair and rolled him out the door. Since Makalani had come on her own, she convinced everyone that Solomon would be more comfortable in her car where he could stretch out his legs and tilt back the seat.

"You feeling okay?" she asked, when they left the lights of Waimea and Hanapēpē behind.

"Yeah. Jus' tired. Dat was a real shit show wit' Kimo. I mean, sheesh. Guy used to be a braddah. Now he jus' one pig. And why everybody so pissed off? Calling me degenerate. Saying I took Becky. She da one who called me. You t'ink I like drive all da way out hea? Oh, shit. What about my truck?"

"Our dads brought it down before dinner. Your parents are driving it home."

"Good. I get any parking tickets?"

"Nope. But I saw Becky's pink backpack sitting in the trunk."

He snorted. "Dat girl so much trouble."

"She's seventeen."

"Ha. She older dan you think."

"What's that supposed to mean?"

He shook his head and muttered, "I'm done wit' her."

He shoved his seat all the way down.

"Solomon, we need to talk."

He crossed his arms and turned his face to the door.

CHAPTER THIRTY-ONE

Makalani yelped as a muscle cramp tore her from sleep. She beat the gripping calf with her fist. When it wouldn't release, she pulled at her toes and fell onto her side, curling like a fish. This wouldn't be happening if she had accepted the second dinner Tūtū had prepared and guzzled another liter of water. But when Solomon had refused to talk and went straight to bed, Makalani had done the same.

Tūtū eyed Makalani's stooped posture as she hobbled into the kitchen. "You walk like an old kupuna wahine."

Makalani poured a glass of water and drank it down. "I feel like one."

Tūtū handed her a banana. "Nothing remains in da corners wit' you."

"What do you mean?"

"You nevah heard dat 'ōlelo no'eau?" She repeated the proverb in Hawaiian. "'A'ohe mea koe ma kū'ono. It is said of someone who gives without reservation, like you."

Makalani peeled the potassium-rich fruit. "Sounds more like you than me."

Tūtū shrugged. "If so, it came from my makuahine. She had ten children. I evah tell you dat? Three died young. I was da youngest, so I nevah met dem. I surprised everyone. Came out sixteen years after she thought she was done. Nevah slow her down. She took good care of me. She look out fo' all of us now."

"As Manō Nui Punahele?"

"Dass right. Your great-grandmother's spirit was so big in life she transformed into an 'aumakua and became our most powerful ancestral god."

Tūtū opened the orange Hawaiian sweet bread bag, tore a small piece from the round loaf, gave it a kiss, and set it aside.

"Is that for Manō Nui?" Makalani asked.

Tūtū winked. "Even a shark god enjoys something sweet." She patted the loaf. "You want french toast?"

"King's recipe?"

"Bes' kine. I can scramble Podagee sausage and eggs, too."

"You're spoiling me."

"You saved two people since you been home. Least I can do is fill your 'ōpū."

Makalani sat at the counter and stretched her sore back side to side. "How's the lū'au prep coming along?"

"Everybody pitch in. Your mother bake ten loaves of her famous banana nut bread. Annabelle Pahukula is bringing i'a lomi salmon. My nephew Paul caught um fresh. Our neighbors been dropping off pork belly, chicken, and fish to make laulau. Your parents stay outside pounding kalo and ribbing tī leaves so dey soft enough to' wrap. And latah tonight, your pāpā goin' steam da pig Solomon's friends volunteered to hunt."

"Why them?"

"Dey get dogs."

She set a plate in front of Makalani with two thick slices of King's Bakery french toast, creamy eggs, and spicy Portuguese sausage. "You should go. Da Braddahs will be happy to have you. I know you like hunt."

"With Pāpā," she said. "Might be weird to hunt with them."

"What might be weird?" Solomon spoke fast as he came through the rear lānai door. He wore last night's church donation pajama pants and shirt. Although rumpled in appearance, his eyes looked wide awake.

"Hunting pig with your friends," Makalani said.

"Oh, yeah, I forget about dat, we stay go out tonight." He ran his words together in a single stream of thought.

"You're not going."

"Yeah I am. I haven't moved in three days." He was talking really fast.

"I thought you were supposed to be lazy."

"Huh, everybody talk, nobody understand." He nodded toward Makalani's breakfast. "Eh, Tūtū, can I get some of dat?"

She set down a big glass of water and a plate piled high with food. "Already made extra fo' you."

He stabbed the french toast, stuffed half of it into his mouth, and followed it with two scoops of eggs. His hand trembled despite his throttling grip on the fork.

Makalani peered around the curtain of his tangled hair. "Slow down, cuz. The eggs won't run away."

He nodded but kept shoveling in the food. "Can I get coffee?"

Makalani shook her head at Tūtū. "It's on the doctor's list to avoid. Besides, you're kinda hyper. You feeling okay?"

"I jus' want coffee. Dat too much to ask?"

"No, but—"

"But what?"

Tūtū poured a short coffee and filled the cup to the rim with milk. Then she set it in front of him with a smirk.

"Wass dis?" he asked.

"You act like one keiki, you get keiki coffee."

Makalani sniggered into her eggs as Solomon glared from the cup to their grandmother.

"No flash stink eye at me," she said. "I'm not your parents or your cousin. I'm your kupuna. You will show me respect."

Solomon nodded and inhaled a steadying breath. "E kala mai iaʻu."

Tūtū accepted his request for forgiveness. "Mahalo. Aloha wau iā ʻoe." *Thank you. I love you.*

With the air cleared between them, Solomon drank his keiki coffee and finished his french toast, this time, cutting it into more reasonable bites.

Native Hawaiians believed forgiveness was only truly achieved when everyone let go of their bad feelings. They didn't pretend to forgive, then grumble behind someone's back. Nor did they harbor a grudge to use as ammunition for a subsequent fight. Rather than toss out a flippant "I'm sorry," they said, "Please forgive me," from the heart.

Tūtū had taught her 'ohana to follow the old ways. Every transgression, no matter how heinous, must be forgiven on all sides to restore balance and make the heart right.

"You mean no one gets punished?" Makalani had asked as a child.

"Justice and forgiveness are not da same," Tūtū had explained. "Some transgressions must be punished for da safety and welfare of da people. We need consider past actions when we decide what to do and who we should trust. But we can't let bad feelings eat a hole in our belly and damage our heart."

"Like Mr. Pineda's ulcer?"

Tūtū had smiled. "Could be li'dat. But I stay talk about emotions. We need forgive and let go."

As Makalani watched Solomon, she saw the power of forgiveness at work. But had he asked forgiveness for his rudeness this morning, or for something worse he had yet to reveal?

CHAPTER THIRTY-TWO

James opened the front door to two uniformed detectives, a tall haole man and a short Hawaiian Chinese woman.

The man showed his credentials and nodded to his partner. "I'm Detective Shaw, and this is Detective Lee. We received the report about your missing daughter. May we come in and speak to you and your wife?"

James ignored the knot in his stomach and gestured for them to enter, embarrassed when there was no place to sit. Every surface spilled over with cast-off blouses, sweaters, yoga pants, books, magazines, school bags, brushes, and those cloth rings his daughters and wife used to tie back their hair. He had grown so accustomed to the daily explosion of femininity he hadn't noticed the mess. Is this what his parents saw every time they came over? Was that why his father seemed forever displeased?

"Linda," he called. "The detectives are here to speak with us." He cleared Emma's book bag and magazines from the chairs. "Please. Have a seat."

She hurried in from the kitchen, looking both relieved and frazzled.

Detective Shaw remained standing to greet her. "Mrs. Muramoto. I'm Detective Shaw, and this is Detective Lee."

"Would you like some coffee?"

"We're fine, thank you. Could we sit?"

"Of course."

James beckoned Linda to the couch beside him and gave her a reassuring smile. He had rehearsed what he would say to the police when they finally arrived. As long as she let him do the talking, they'd be fine.

Detective Shaw waited for them to settle, glanced at his partner, then took the lead. "The report said that your daughter went missing Monday after school."

"That's right," James said.

"This is Friday. Why did you wait until last night to report her missing?"

"Our daughter is seventeen. Do you have children of your own?" When neither detective responded, he patted Linda's hand. "Well, girls are a handful at that age. This isn't the first time Becky stayed out with friends without letting us know. We were angry, of course, but we didn't start to worry until last night when her other cousin was found."

"That would be Solomon Ching?"

"Yes. He and Becky went for a hike. He said he tried to save her from falling off Kilohana Lookout before he slipped off the cliff."

"And that's when your other cousin found him?"

"Yes. Makalani Pahukula. When she found Solomon but not Becky, we decided to call you."

Detective Shaw glanced at his partner, who kept her expression attentive yet bland. "Tell us about Becky. You said she stayed out all night before?"

Linda waved her hand, dismissively. "Only for a night or two. She's a good girl. But not always very considerate at this age."

James brought down her hand and gave it a squeeze.

"Has she gotten into any trouble at school?"

"What kind of trouble?" James asked.

Detective Shaw shrugged. "Detention, fights, weapons, drugs?"

"Of course not," Linda said. "I told you, she's a good girl."

"Even good girls can get roped into criminal activity. We've had an uptick of drug-related crimes on the island. We need to make sure your daughter isn't involved."

"Don't be ridiculous," James said.

"You mean like the dead man they found two days ago?" Linda asked. "The one in the forest? Eaten by pigs?"

Detective Shaw leaned in. "Does the name Ikaika 'Ōpūnui mean anything to you?"

"No." She glanced worriedly at James, who shook his head as well.

"He was a local man in his forties, medium height, stocky build, probably had a beard."

"Probably?" Linda asked.

"From what we could tell. Have you seen anyone like that hanging around your store or your daughter? A customer, perhaps?"

James shook his head.

Linda freaked out. "Did he kidnap our Becky? Oh my god, James. She could be trapped in a crazy man's survival bunker and never be found."

The lady detective held out her hand. "Please, Mrs. Muramoto. That's not what we meant. We want to know if this man might have come in contact with Becky. That's all. The more we know about your daughter, the easier she'll be to find."

James squeezed his wife's fingers, willing her to stop talking and calm down. These detectives were trying to connect their family to that man's murder and whatever crimes he might have committed. If they thought Becky knew the dead man in the forest, they might investigate James and chase even more customers from the store.

Detective Lee studied James, then rose to admire the photographs on the wall. "Becky is such a pretty girl. Does she have any boyfriends?"

James winced at the plural use of the word. "Our daughter wasn't dating anyone, let alone more than one boy."

Detective Lee cocked her head in doubt, then glanced at a particularly vivacious shot of Becky in a revealing sundress, tossing her auburn hair. "Well, I'm sure boys took an interest in her."

"How would we know? We don't follow her around at school."

"What about your store?" Detective Shaw asked. "I saw a picnic table and benches under a tree out back. Have you seen Becky hanging with anyone out there?"

James tensed. "You know how it is with teenagers. She doesn't spend any of her free time near us."

"It's also near the stairs to your apartment. Certainly your daughter would have walked past customers on her way to and from home. Have you seen any unsavory types hanging around back longer than they should? Tourists? Locals? Anyone suspicious at all?"

Was this detective leading James back to 'Ōpūnui's murder? Why wouldn't he leave that theory alone?

Linda looked at James. "What about the guys hanging at our picnic table? They looked pretty unsavory to me."

"What guys?" Detective Shaw asked.

"A rowdy gang."

James cringed. Linda's helpful intervention was making things worse.

"They're not a gang," he said. "Just ordinary young men."

Detective Lee turned on James. "Men?"

"Maybe some girls."

"Girls?"

"Women. I don't know. Young people. Whatever you want to call them."

Detective Lee addressed Linda. "Have you spoken to these men?"

James rested his hand on Linda's knee. "Why would she? The store is my business. My wife has activities of her own."

"Like caring for your daughters?"

"I do a lot more than that," Linda said. "School functions, yoga, the community bazaar."

Detective Lee focused her scrupulous dark eyes on James. "When do these young people normally visit your store?"

"No particular time."

Why won't she leave this alone?

He rose from the couch and pulled Linda to her feet. "You should get them a list of Becky's friends." He looked at the tall haole detective, feeling much more comfortable with him. "We've spoken with her friends and their parents, but they might have more to say to you."

Detective Lee cocked her head. "Why would you think that?"

"Um . . . I don't know." He glanced at Detective Shaw for help. "Don't people say more to detectives?"

The man studied James for an uncomfortably long time, then turned to his partner.

Detective Lee smiled coldly at James. "No, Mr. Muramoto. They don't."

When Linda returned with the list, James hurried them out the door then sighed with relief as they got in their car. Although late for opening his store at nine, the only cars parked behind the market belonged to the detectives, Linda, and him.

"What was that about?" she asked as he closed and locked the door.

"They needed a list."

"I'm not talking about Becky's friends. Why did you interrupt me when I mentioned those men?"

"We're losing the store. I can't have them harassing the few customers I have left."

Linda recoiled. "*We're* losing it? A moment ago, the store was all yours."

"Fine. *I'm* losing it. Is that what you want to hear? How much of a failure I am?"

"I didn't say that."

"You didn't need to. I see it in your eyes every day. Your failure of a husband who couldn't make it even with a helping hand."

"You opened Muramoto Market on your own."

171

"Only because my father lost his own lease. If the landlord hadn't priced him out of business, he wouldn't have retired and given his inventory to me."

"And his debt." Linda's eyes burned like blue fire. "Everything with your family comes with a price."

"What do you want me to do?" he asked. "Sell everything and move to Wisconsin? Live in your parents' house? Open a Japanese market on an all-white street?"

"I want you to be a man and stand up to those drug dealers in our own backyard. That detective was right. Our daughters walk past them every day. What if one of them did something to Becky? What if she's lying in a ditch strung out on heroin?"

"Don't be so dramatic. That gang doesn't sell heroin. They grow pot in the hills."

"And that's okay with you?"

"Of course not. But you need to calm down."

James sank onto the couch, exhausted by his wife, his daughter, and this whole unsavory mess. "The next time the gang comes around, I'll ask them about Becky. Me. Not you. It has to be done carefully, or they could cause us more trouble than they already have."

CHAPTER THIRTY-THREE

Pāpā walked into the kitchen carrying tī leaf bundles of newly pounded pa'i 'ai—the denser kalo paste that could be diluted quickly into poi.

"Is dat all you made?" Tūtū asked.

"Nah, dea plenny more. Julia's still working. I only stopped because of da cops."

"What cops?" Makalani asked.

"Detectives. Two o' dem, waiting out front. Da haole guy get muddy boots. I wasn't sure he'd take um off."

Makalani nudged her cousin. "Let's go see what they want."

"You go," Solomon said. "Tell um I'm asleep."

"But you're not."

"I could be."

Makalani looked from him to Pāpā. "What's wrong with you guys?"

Both of them shrugged.

Makalani lowered Solomon's coffee mug before it reached his mouth. "Look, I know James them gave you a hard time last night, but the detectives are here to help. The sooner you talk, the sooner they can find Becky."

Coffee sloshed over the rim as he set down the mug. "Why you gotta push all da time? You been hea—what—three days?"

"Our cousin is missing."

"So was I."

"And look how that turned out."

"What you like me say, Makalani? How grateful I am? How, once again, you saved me from my stupid mistakes? Because dat got tired years ago." He shoved back his stool. "You like me go talk to da cops? Fine. I'll talk. But don't t'ink for one minute dis goin' come out good fo' me."

Pāpā nodded. "He's right, you know. Dis conversation might not go how you plan."

Pāpā left the tī leaf bundles on the counter and led Makalani and Solomon across the main room to the detectives, waiting on the front lānai. The tall haole sat in an overstuffed chair, ankle crossed at his knee, displaying a sturdy boot with mud in the tread. The hapa-Hawaiian woman scrolled through her phone beside him. Both of them rose as Makalani and Solomon walked through the door.

"Good morning. I'm Detective Shaw, and this is Detective Lee. We'd like to ask you a few questions about your cousin Becky."

He motioned toward the other chairs as he and his partner sat. Pāpā leaned against the railing behind them, clearly not intending to leave.

Makalani ignored her father and focused on them. "Thanks for coming so quickly. Have you had a chance to contact DOCARE?"

"Not yet."

"Why wait? Didn't my cousin James tell dispatch that his daughter might be lost in Kōke'e Park?"

"He did. We need information from the two of you first."

Detective Lee straightened up on the edge of her seat and offered Makalani a winning smile. She took in Solomon's appearance, from his messed-up hair to his purple and pink clothes. "You've had quite an ordeal, Mr. Ching. Are you feeling better?"

Solomon nodded. "Glad to be home."

"When did you last see Becky?"

"Monday late afternoon. Maybe two, three o'clock."

"How were the weather conditions that day?"

"No rain. But da trails were pretty messed up."

"And you thought it would be a good idea to take your teenage cousin on a hike?"

"She really wanted to go."

Detective Lee cocked her head in doubt.

"Hey, you don't know Becky," Solomon said. "She can be super persuasive."

"In what way?"

"Texting, calling. She kept at it fo' months. All da time wanting to go on dat hike."

"Do you still have the text on your phone?"

"Beats me."

"May we see the phone?"

"Might have fell off da cliff."

"Might have or did?"

"I don't know. I jus' woke up. I haven't had time to check."

"Would you check now, please?"

Pāpā interrupted. "I'm sure you have oddah questions to ask."

Detective Lee nodded. "That's true, Mr. Pahukula. We have quite a few."

Detective Shaw took over. "Mr. Ching, why did you think it would be okay to help Becky cut out of school?"

"It wasn't li'dat."

Makalani held out a hand. "Solomon's right. You don't know our cousin. She can be a real handful."

Detective Shaw nodded. "So we've heard." He focused back on Solomon. "But she wouldn't have gone on the hike without you, her much older and, presumably, wiser cousin."

Papa snorted. "Not sure 'bout wiser. But Solomon and Makalani are right 'bout Becky. Dat girl no listen to nobody but herself."

The detectives exchanged looks.

"Did Becky have her own car?" Detective Lee asked.

Pāpā shook his head.

"But you do," she said, focusing on Solomon. "And you drove her."

"Yeah. I mean . . . kinda."

"Which is it, Mr. Ching?"

"I have a car. She drove."

"Seriously?" Makalani said.

He held out his hands. "She has her license."

"How about you?" Detective Lee asked, then shook her head. "You know what? We'll circle back to that. Tell me what happened at Kilohana Lookout."

Solomon shifted in his seat. "It's a tough hike. Becky slipped couple times and messed up her clothes."

"What was she wearing?" Detective Shaw asked, lounging comfortably in his chair.

"Blue top, hoodie, shorts, Vans."

"What kind of top?"

"I don't know. Tight. Long sleeve."

"Sounds kind of sexy for school."

"Maybe. I don't know. Dass jus' what she wears."

Detective Lee leaned forward. "What happened at the lookout?"

He shrugged. "She was whining, hanging on me like she was tired. 'Solomon, hold me up. Solomon, carry me.' Goofing around, wrestling li'dat."

"Wrestling?"

"Playing."

"Playing?"

"You know, like kids do?"

Detective Lee interrupted. "Your cousin is seventeen, Mr. Ching. She's hardly a kid."

Solomon ignored the woman and looked back at the man. "She nevah realize how close she was to da edge. I grabbed her arm and yanked her back."

"And that's when you fell off the cliff?"

"Yeah. Got scratched up from da bushes and landed in a tree."

"We heard you were wearing your backpack."

"Lucky, right? I coulda died out dea wi' no food and water."

Detective Shaw studied him. "That's a whole lot of luck."

Makalani bristled at his tone. "I've seen luckier hikers in Oregon."

Detective Shaw checked the notes on his phone. "As a law enforcement ranger at Crater Lake National Park?"

"That's correct."

"Then Solomon is even luckier to have a devoted cousin like you."

Makalani gritted her teeth. "I'm saying that I've seen hikers get caught in the trees or saved by foliage when they fall."

"And when did you fly in?"

"Tuesday afternoon."

"Did you come straight to the homestead?"

"Yes."

"When did you learn your cousins were missing?"

"As soon as I got home."

Pāpā was right. This is definitely not going as planned.

"What did you think happened?"

"I thought they might have gotten lost or pulled out with the tide."

"That's an interesting theory."

Makalani shrugged. "Becky had this old canoe. I had been remembering how she used to beg Solomon to take her on a voyage. It was on my mind, so I wanted to check."

"And how did you do that?"

Makalani explained about the missing canoe, her firefighter friend, the two rescues up Wailua River, and how four rowdy girls had been rescued from a sinking canoe the previous week.

"You think that was Becky?"

"The description fit."

"And the behavior?"

Makalani sighed. "I don't think you guys appreciate my cousin's personality."

"We appreciate the personality profile all of you seem determined to give."

"What's that supposed to mean?"

Detective Lee cut in. "How did you learn about the hike?"

Makalani kept glaring at Detective Shaw, unwilling to let his implication that they were somehow colluding to give false testimony go without challenge.

"Miss Pahukula?" Detective Lee prodded.

Makalani sighed. Nothing good would come from setting the man straight. "Becky's friends mentioned it when I spoke with them at school."

"You always work this hard on vacation?"

Makalani laughed. *The question of the week.*

"Did I say something funny?"

Makalani pulled herself together. "No. As to your question, I've never had a family member go missing before."

Detective Lee nodded then turned back to Solomon. "Do you have a girlfriend?"

"No."

"Are you dating anyone?"

"No."

"How often do you drink alcohol?"

"What difference dat make?"

"Answer the question, please."

"I don't know. Maybe a beer now and den. Enough to have a good time."

"Is that important to you, Mr. Ching? Having a good time?"

Makalani held out her hand to keep him from answering. "What's this about?"

Detective Lee shrugged. "We're getting a feel for Mr. Ching's lifestyle." She looked back at him. "You've had a hard time since your knee injury took you out of football. I can't imagine the pain."

Solomon nodded. "Worse I evah felt."

"Did your doctors prescribe something to help?"

"Yeah, but it ran out pretty quick."

"What did you do?"

"'Bout what?"

"The pain."

"Not'ing. It jus' hurt."

"Did you try Tylenol or Advil?"

Solomon scoffed. "Dey nevah work."

"How about marijuana or a prescription from one of your friends?"

Pāpā cleared his throat at the railing. "Where you goin' wit' dis, Detective?"

The woman kept her eyes on Solomon. "Trying to establish if your nephew takes illegal drugs for his pain."

"What? No," Solomon said. "Dis not 'bout me. You're supposed to stay find my cousin."

Detective Lee nodded. "It would help us to know if you or she did any drugs."

Detective Shaw's voice dropped to a menacing pitch. "We know you don't have a job. We've heard you're a heavy drinker. You say you don't have a girlfriend. Yet you hang out with your rowdy teenage cousin. You see where I'm going with this?"

"No. I don't."

Detective Shaw leaned back in his chair, relaxed, as if talking story with good friends. "We're trying to figure out why a twenty-two-year-old man with no job who drinks too much and has no girlfriend would take his teenage cousin out of school to a remote location for an obviously dangerous hike."

Makalani gaped at the detective while, behind him, Pāpā sagged against the lānai's wooden support. He and Solomon were right. She shouldn't have convinced Uncle Sanji to report Becky missing. She should have returned to Kōke'e Park and searched for Becky herself.

"Where do you live, Mr. Ching?" Detective Lee asked.

"Huh?"

"You dropped out of UH two years ago. Where have you been living?"

"Wit' my parents."

"And now?"

He nodded over his shoulder at the Muramoto wing. "Ova dea. Becky's family move out last year. I took her room."

Detective Shaw narrowed his eyes. "You live in your cousin's bedroom?"

"Hers and Emma's. So what?"

"Did she leave any of her belongings?"

"Beats me."

"Mind if we have a look?"

"In my room?"

"You don't mind, do you?"

Pāpā stepped forward. "I cleaned it out before he moved in. Da girls nevah leave not'ing behind."

Detective Lee smiled. "It might help us to look around."

"No need. Ask your questions, den go find my niece."

Detective Lee nodded and spoke as sweetly as before. "Have you ever been arrested, Mr. Ching?"

"What?"

"It's a simple question."

Solomon shifted uncomfortably. "Um, yeah. But dey let me go."

She checked her notes. "You assaulted a man in a bar."

"He was talking crap 'bout Becky. What was I supposed to do? I punched da braddah in da mouth. Check it out fo' yourself if you nevah believe me. I'm telling da truth."

"And the DUI?"

Makalani flashed Solomon a look but kept her mouth shut.

"I was driving home from Kapa'a, practically my own neighborhood. I did my community service, rehabilitation program, alla dat."

"And your license?"

"I took da tests, paid da money, waiting fo' it to come in da mail."

Detective Shaw interrupted. "So, you picked up Becky without a license."

"*She* drove to Kōkeʻe."

"And I drove him home from the hospital," Makalani said.

Detective Lee frowned. "But Mr. Ching drove without a license to Becky's school."

Detective Shaw sighed. "Could be a month in jail. Hefty fine."

"And no more license," Detective Lee added.

"Wass goin' on here?" Pāpā asked. "Is my nephew a suspect?"

Detective Shaw kept his focus on Solomon. "One more question, Mr. Ching. Did you know Ikaika ʻŌpūnui?"

"Who?"

"The man found dead three days ago in Keālia Forest Reserve."

"Why would I know him?"

"His murder might have something to do with drugs."

"Pau," Pāpā said. He marched around the lānai chairs and pointed toward the steps. "Time fo' you to go."

The tall detective stood and looked Pāpā in the eyes. "We're officers of the law, Mr. Pahukula."

"Oh, yeah? Well dis is my land."

CHAPTER THIRTY-FOUR

Solomon and Pāpā waited for the detectives to drive up the dirt road and disappear behind the breadfruit trees before they broke off in two directions and left Makalani alone on the front lānai.

"Hey," she said. "Where are you guys going?"

Pāpā paused on the steps, his broad back and shoulders tense with anger. "To help your māmā pound poi."

Solomon marched toward his room.

"What about you?" she asked. "We have a few things to talk about, don't you think?"

"Like what, Makalani? How you turned me ovah to da police? How you always butt into everybody's business? I'm done talking wit' you."

"What about the cell phone? Could we at least check your room to see if it's still there?"

He opened his door, then shut it in her face.

Makalani slumped. None of this had gone as she expected. Once again, she had driven people away. But with Becky still missing, she couldn't let it slide.

She took a step toward the corner room and paused. Why hadn't Solomon stayed on the Ching side of the house? Where would he go if the Muramotos moved back in?

Worries about Becky and Solomon ate at her stomach. She hated to leave bad feelings and uncomfortable questions unresolved, but with Solomon refusing to speak with her, what could she do? As worried as she was about Becky, these problems would have to wait. The tension between her and Pāpā could not.

She found him in the grassy area beside the shed, sitting, knees open, at a heavy wooden pounding board propped on two wooden blocks. Māmā sat on a bucket on the opposite side of the papa kuʻi poi. Each of them worked the kalo at different stages in the pounding process.

"Have you come to help?" Māmā asked, scraping her fingers under the edge of the dense gray mass and flipping it onto itself.

"I will if you need it."

She chuckled. "Asking first? What have you done with my daughter?"

Pāpā snorted and smashed the kalo corms with the rounded base of his heavy stone pounder, scattering purple meat halfway across the board. Too much force. Too little care. No respect shown to the eldest brother of her people. This was not the way Makalani had been taught.

According to the Kumulipo creation chant, the first kalo plant grew from the buried stillborn son of Sky Father Wākea and Hoʻohōkūkalani, his daughter by Earth Mother Papahānaumoku. When their second son lived, they named him Hāloa, which means long or everlasting breath. Since this happened during creation and there was nothing to eat, the kalo plant that sprouted from Hāloa's elder brother's body provided sustenance not only for him but for the kānaka maoli to come and reminds the Hawaiian people of the kuleana the elder sibling has for the younger. Even the word ʻohana comes from the ʻohā starchy corm of the kalo plant her father had smashed with so little respect.

Pāpā glanced at Makalani, embarrassed. He gathered the scattered ʻohā meat with his hand, showing the mālama he should have demonstrated before.

"He aliʻi ka ʻāina; he kauwā ke kanaka," he said softly. "The land is a chief; the person is a servant."

This time he mashed more gently with the pōhaku kuʻi pounder, carved and smoothed from tight-pore lava in the traditional design.

Later in the process, he would pound its weight with force, breaking down the starch and turning the crumbly steamed corm into a dense, rubbery paste.

Māmā nodded as she slapped water against the stone and kneaded the pa'i 'ai away from her in firm but gentle strokes. She had also been taught to work the kalo with love and respect.

Unlike Pāpā, Makalani's mother worked with a rare ring-shaped pounder, used only on Kaua'i, where women had traditionally participated in this grueling work along with the men. Her pounder had an elongated bottom with a gap carved into the handle, wide enough for two-handed use. Tūtū owned two pōhaku ku'i 'ai puka that had been handed down in her family for generations. She had given one of them to Māmā as a wedding gift. She gave the other to Aunty Kaulana. The gifts didn't cause any bad feelings with Aunty Maile because she claimed she was too dainty for the work.

Māmā nodded toward the tī leaves. "Pull up a seat and wrap."

Makalani fetched a plastic bucket from the shed and set it, upside down, near the center of the pounding board beside the basket of long, shiny leaves. She sat and ran her hands along the smooth lip of the wood into the shallow well of the board that kept the water from sloshing over the edge.

"I remember when you made this," Makalani said.

Pāpā had carved and sanded the papa ku'i from a thick slab of monkeypod, then cured it in the ocean to kill the bacteria and swell the wood.

"You help some," he said as he placed another corm on top of his mash and crushed it gently with the edge of his pounder.

"Never as much as I think."

"But maybe mo' dan I like admit."

Having cleared the air a little, the three of them fell into amiable work. Pāpā mashed his 'ohā into paste. Makalani spread a stack of leaves on the board. Māmā cut her purple mass into sections with a plastic wedge. Makalani wet her hands and placed a hunk of pa'i 'ai on the top leaf. She folded up the ends, gave it a quarter turn, and repeated the process three more times. With the pa'i 'ai wrapped, she secured the bundle with a knot.

"Are these to dilute for poi or to eat?" she asked, pinching a small portion from the next hunk and popping it into her mouth.

"Both, yeah?" Māmā said. "And for your Aunty Kaulana's kūlolo."

Makalani salivated at the thought of the rich coconut cream and kalo dessert.

"Less talk. More wrap," Pāpā said.

He scraped his fingers under the paste, folded it over, and smashed the pōhaku ku'i onto the dough. Now that he was calmer, his hand and stone worked in seamless unity. He divided the mass into clumps and scraped them toward Makalani to wrap.

"When will you mix the poi?" she asked.

"Tomorrow morning," he said. "Befo' everybody stay come. Easier to store dis way in da kitchen or out hea."

Makalani nodded. Although poi could be kept without refrigeration for days, undiluted pa'i 'ai could be kept at room temperature for months. Pounding the starch molecules initiated the fermentation process. The longer it sat, the more sour and flavorful it became.

"You didn't want to make it earlier so the poi would turn sour?"

Pāpā placed new kalo corms on the board. "Wit' your cousins gone, all da lū'au prep got delayed."

"What happened with the police?" Māmā asked as she started a new batch.

Pāpā shrugged. "What everybody t'ought."

Makalani frowned. "Everybody but me."

He shook his head. "You been away."

"What difference does that make?"

"Shouldn't make any," he said. "But it does."

Makalani paused midknot. More and more, she was finding this to be true. Ten years on the mainland for college, ranger training, and work had disconnected her from island life in ways she had not foreseen, as if the veins connecting her to home had been cut. She felt the aloha, but her heart beat out of sync.

She tied off the bundle and started the next. She stacked a new set of tī leaves on the board like an alternating cross. She scraped up the next portion of pa'i 'ai, placed it in the center, then covered it with her hand. Eyes closed, she searched for the pulse of the island in the pounded kalo mound.

"You okay?" Pāpā asked.

Makalani smiled at him and lied. "Worried about Becky. Do you think she was in the bar with Solomon when he got into that fight?"

Māmā gasped. "Becky was in a bar?"

"Yeah. When some guy insulted her, Solomon punched him in the face."

Māmā rolled her eyes and slapped water on the stone.

Pāpā nodded in agreement, as if Māmā had spoken her thoughts. "Dat boy's reaction comes off more like one angry boyfriend dan one pissed-off cousin."

Makalani tied off her bundle and started anew. "The DUI didn't help. I wonder if it happened the same night. Solomon said he was driving home from Kapa'a. Do you think Becky was in the car?"

Pāpā shrugged. "Solomon get plenny kine friends in Kapa'a. He coulda visited one of dem. Either way, it didn't look good."

Makalani agreed. The detectives had treated Solomon like a suspect for good reason. "Do you think he still has his phone?"

"I don't know. Wit' him acting all sketchy, I bet dey come back wit' a warrant and check."

"What if we checked first?"

Māmā scraped the pa'i 'ai off the board and placed it squarely on the leaf. "I think we have enough bad feeling in our 'ohana without invading anyone's privacy." She wrapped the bundle and tied up the stems. "Take the pa'i 'ai to Tūtū. Your father and I can do the rest."

"You sure you don't want help?"

Māmā laughed. "Oh, is that what you think you're doing?"

Makalani knew she was making light of the situation, but the comment struck too close to the truth. She put the bundles in a basket and left her parents to do their work.

When she reached the front lānai, she knocked quietly on her cousin's door. "Solomon? I want to apologize. Can we talk?"

When he didn't answer, she turned the door's handle. This time, it was locked.

She walked up the side deck to the rear lānai and found Tūtū trimming banana leaves at the picnic table.

"You look sad, moʻopuna. Did da talk not go well?"

Makalani plopped onto the bench. "Everyone's angry with me."

"Maybe you need clear da air."

"Solomon won't answer my knock. He locked himself in his room."

Tūtū's eyes widened. No one in their family ever locked their door. "Give him time. Go talk to your cousin James instead."

"I'll only make it worse."

"You still need try, right?"

Makalani fought back an unexpected rush of tears. "What if something really bad is about to happen to Becky, and I . . . and I can't find her in time?"

Tūtū sat on the bench and clasped Makalani's hands as she cried. "You only one person, moʻopuna. You no can do everyt'ing all at once. I know it hurts to not help Becky right now, but you *can* bring comfort to James. ʻIke aku, ʻike mai. Kōkua aku, kōkua mai. Pēlā iho lā ka noho ʻana ʻohana. You remembah dis ʻōlelo noʻeau?"

Makalani nodded. "Recognize others, be recognized. Help others, be helped. This is how the family lives."

"Dass right. If you like help and feel bettah, make someone else feel bettah. See him. Help him. You and James mo' alike dan you know."

CHAPTER THIRTY-FIVE

Despite her reservations, Makalani took her grandmother's advice and went to make peace with James. She even stopped at Passion Bakery for a box of deep-fried malasadas stuffed with an assortment of ube, lilikoʻi, mango, coconut, and chocolate cream—special occasion treats he wouldn't buy for himself. All her good feelings fled when she saw the gang hanging at the picnic table in his back lot.

Two local men in their twenties—a scraggly blond and a Chinese guy with buzz-cut hair—sat on the table with their slippered feet on the bench. A kanaka maoli man in his thirties, wearing a Hawaiian Sovereignty long-sleeve T-shirt, reclined on the bench beside their dirty legs. Sitting at the end, a muscular hapa-Filipino man handed a roach clip to the woman standing next to him. She had the same hard features and matted black hair. From their rugged, unwashed appearance and the mud-splattered Jeep parked under the tree, Makalani guessed the gang had returned from a camping trip or lived in the wild. Although not legal to do so, some native-born kamaʻāina had chosen to survive off the land.

Like Ikaika ʻŌpūnui?

Makalani left her window down as she turned off her engine so she could hear them talking behind her in the yard.

The scowling woman passed the clip to a sunburned tourist wearing a Pi Kappa Alpha tee. He took a long toke, nodding with approval as he held in the smoke. He offered the roach to his friend, a Black guy in cutoff shorts only a mainlander would wear.

"This is smooth shit, man. You gotta try it."

The friend sucked in what was left, then coughed out a laugh.

The scowling woman took back the clip. "You want it?"

Frat Boy nodded and brought out his wallet to pay.

When Makalani had come here before and found the empty Elements packs in the trash, she had given James the benefit of the doubt. But how could he *not* know this gang was dealing in his yard? How could he allow illegal activity on his property so close to his kids?

She gripped the malasada box in her lap. If she marched into James's store all high and mighty, she'd drive the wedge between them even deeper than before. She needed to calm down and begin their conversation with an open heart.

'Ike aku, 'ike mai. Kōkua aku, kōkua mai.

If she saw others, she would be seen in return. If she helped others, she would be helped. *'Ike* meant more than *see*. She needed to recognize James as a person and perceive who he really was. Only in this way could she truly understand and offer meaningful help.

She put the gang out of her mind, walked into the store with pono intentions, and found James standing at the front window, staring at the street.

"Eh, cuz."

He turned in surprise. "What are you doing here?"

She held up the box. "I brought fancy kine malasadas. Thought you guys deserved a treat."

"For what? Driving our daughter away?" Sadness softened the sting of his words.

She set the box on the counter. "Teenagers are rough, especially ones as confident as Becky."

"You never ran away."

"I wasn't confident."

"What are you talking about? You're the most confident person I know."

"Not when I was a kid. I hung out with bratty Solomon because I didn't have friends."

"That's not how I remember it," James said. "You were always at the center of things, building, organizing, leading. Everyone respected you."

"Respected isn't the same as liked. I stuck close to the homestead because I didn't feel like I belonged anywhere else."

James furrowed his brows. "I stuck to my father's relatives because I didn't feel at home with all of you." He opened the take-out container and smiled. A dozen stuffed malasadas had been squished inside to fit, each topped with a colorful dollop that matched the cream inside. "You really did get the fancy kine."

Makalani winked. "Only the best for my 'ohana."

He picked up the fried dough stuffed with purple ube cream. "You want?"

"All for you. I ate a liliko'i one after lunch on the way."

He bit into the treat as the college tourists barged through the rear entrance.

"You smell that?" Cutoff Jeans said.

Frat Boy grinned. "Oh, yeah."

"I told you they'd have snacks."

James closed the lid and stashed the malasadas behind the counter. He glanced at Makalani with alarm.

"I know," she said. "I saw them buying out back."

He nodded with resignation, then watched as the men browsed through the aisles, picking out items and replacing them carelessly on his shelves.

"You got anything fresh?" Frat Boy asked, pulling bags of cookies off display clips.

"Only what's in the refrigerator today."

Cutoff Jeans looked around. "You sure? I could have sworn I smelled doughnuts."

"Me, too, man. That would taste so freaking good right now."

An elderly Japanese woman entered through the front door as Cutoff Jeans gave a colorful f-bomb response. She gasped in shock at the tourists. She glared at James as if the profanity had come from him.

A sixty-ish woman entered behind her, carrying two empty tote bags. "Everything okay, Mom?"

The elderly woman replied in hushed Japanese while the men argued the merits of fruit-flavored beers.

James bowed in greeting. "Konnichiwa, Obāsan. How may I help you today?"

The elderly woman whispered another comment and walked out the door.

The younger woman glanced at the men, laughing in front of the open refrigerator, and shrugged apologetically to James. "My mother isn't comfortable shopping here."

"I understand. I hope she will feel more comfortable another day."

The daughter left, tote bags unfilled.

The stoned men marched to the counter with two tall boy beers and a giant bag of chips.

"Is this all you want?" James asked, eyeing his disrupted shelves.

"Unless you got doughnuts," Frat Boy said.

James took out the box of malasadas, released the mouthwatering scent, and bit into the sweet ube cream. "Check down the street. No doughnuts here."

Frat Boy moaned. "That's cruel, man."

James ignored him and pushed the box toward Makalani to choose.

When the disgruntled men left, she closed the lid and returned it to James. "Is this why you're losing business?"

"You saw them selling paka lōlō outside. They and their customers are scaring away my regulars. Mrs. Uchimura has shopped here twice a week for years. Now she's gone for good because these one-time stoner customers bought two beers and a bag of chips."

"Have you tried asking the gang to leave?"

"I've seen guns in their Jeep. They live off the grid. They could shoot one of us and be gone without a trace. Even Kimo ignores them when he's seen them here before."

"This isn't pono, James. Medical marijuana is legal. Recreational weed is not."

"I know. But we only have one dispensary on Kaua'i. With all the taxes and restrictions the government places on them, the prices are high. And that's only for the patients who are certified to buy. Potheads and people suffering who can't get their medical certifications get their paka lōlō from growers like the gang selling in my backyard."

Makalani understood the conundrum. Although Oregon had legalized recreational marijuana use in 2015, their illegal production had recently grown out of control. While residents were allowed to grow four plants for personal use, the licensed commercial production became so oversaturated that the Oregon Liquor and Cannabis Commission put a temporary freeze on applications. When the booming hemp market collapsed, many of those growers switched to psychoactive cannabis and hid the unlicensed plants in their fields.

She had heard horror stories from her counterparts in Oregon's Bureau of Land Management at the quarterly meetings. The situation worsened when cartels from Mexico, Eastern Europe, and China moved in. They trafficked labor or basically enslaved migrant workers who had lost their jobs after wildfires destroyed many of the agricultural farms. They dug unapproved wells or stole water from their neighbors' lands. They dumped waste and chemicals onto the ground. They terrorized their workers and committed violent crimes. Although communities suffered, many residents remained quiet or complained anonymously out of fear.

That's in Oregon. How bad could it be here?

Makalani wanted to ask if Becky smoked or hung around the paka lōlō gang, but she didn't want to break the fragile bond that had formed between her and James. It was a sticky situation. If there was any chance the gang outside had taken or harmed Becky, Vice needed to be called.

Although, from the questions Detective Shaw had asked Solomon, Vice might already know.

Makalani coughed out a laugh.

"What's so funny?" James asked.

"I was thinking what a pain in the ass detectives could be."

"They came to the homestead?"

"Yup. They come here, too?"

"Sure did. Made me feel like a criminal in my own home."

"Same here." She didn't mention how they treated Solomon like a suspect. "Mind if I look into that gang?"

"You're asking my permission to help?"

Makalani grinned. "I'm trying not to push where help isn't welcome. My parents appreciated it. I thought you might as well."

He puzzled over this as if it were a strange and wonderful occurrence.

"Hey. Don't act so surprised."

"This is kinda big, though. Maybe I should call the *Garden Island*."

She smacked his arm. "Shut up."

"Or Civil Beat."

"Keep it up and I'll eat every malasada in the box."

He laughed. "No more ube for you. Seriously, though, I can't afford worse trouble from those guys than I already have."

Makalani understood. With so much at stake, illegal growers often resorted to violence. The cartels in Oregon protected their billion-dollar industry with vigor from robbers and law enforcement alike. In Klamath County, south of Crater Lake, Bureau of Land Management agents had discovered plants worth $100 million. Neighbors said the growers threatened to burn down their houses or harm their families if they complained. Makalani didn't want to put James and his family at risk.

"If I don't tell them we're related, I doubt they will guess."

Makalani was five inches taller, twenty pounds heavier, and—despite her wimpy Oregon tan—looked every bit the quarter Hawaiian she was. Her slim older cousin looked decidedly Japanese.

James shook his head. "If they even *think* this is coming from me—"

"They won't."

He blew out his tension in a cheek-puffing gust. "Try, don't try. At this point, I don't really care. We can move back to the homestead if I lose the store. I'll find something to do. Right now, Becky is my only concern."

A horn blared outside, followed by loud voices and a woman's screech. James cursed and bolted for the rear door. Makalani followed close on his heels.

CHAPTER THIRTY-SIX

James stopped Makalani at the door. "Stay inside. I don't want anyone seeing you with me." He ran out and slammed the screen door shut.

Linda had abandoned her Prius in the middle of the lot, engine running, door open wide. "Where's my daughter? I told you guys to get off our property. Now she's gone."

The scowling woman at the picnic table puffed out her chest. "Back off, lady. We don't care 'bout your stupid daughter. We got every right to be hea. We paying customers. From dat empty lot, I say your husband need us more dan he need you."

James ran up to Linda and yanked her by the arm. "What are you doing? I told you to stay away from these people. Park your car, and get in the house."

"Are you taking their side?"

"I'm not taking sides. I don't want an argument in our lot if customers arrive."

"What customers? We haven't done good business in months."

The guy with the scraggly blond hair and his buzz-cut friend hopped off the picnic table and sauntered toward the Jeep. Although an older model, they had tricked it out with camouflage paint, roof racks, and a floodlight bar across the top. Buzz Cut swung open the tailgate to reveal a hunting rifle mounted in the trunk.

Makalani reached for her duty sidearm. Her hand grazed her hip and stomach where the gun should have been. The SIG Sauer P320 pistol was stored in a gun locker in her duplex at Crater Lake National Park. The matching SIG she had registered in Hawai'i was locked in Pāpā's gun cabinet at home.

James, having seen the rifle as well, turned Linda forcibly toward her car. After a heated exchange, she moved her Prius behind his truck and stormed up the stairs.

The gang piled inside the Jeep, turned on the engine, and blared Hawaiian rap music into the lot. Having reversed within inches of hitting James, they slammed into drive and left him in a cloud of dirt.

Rather than check on James as he hurried after Linda, Makalani bolted to her Hyundai and followed the Jeep. The booming bass notes led her away from the main strip, where she expected them to go. She caught up in time to see them veer off Olohena and take Ka'apuni Road into the hills.

The area had a classic East Kaua'i feel—humble homes, expansive land, wild grass, red dirt. Banana and coconut fronds swayed in the breeze. Farther up the road, the lots condensed into a rural suburban feel with a soccer field and school bus stops for the kids. Several of the residents ran fruit stands or other small businesses out of their yards. The higher she went, the flatter and more peaceful it became, disturbed only by the blaring Hawaiian rap. After a lovely stretch of well-maintained properties, the Jeep turned onto an offshoot road that ran along the edge of the forest reserve. As the road narrowed, the pristine horse properties with classic white fences devolved into rough pastures overgrown with pili grass and surrounded by wire. Rusted trucks and junk littered the few houses on the forest side of the road.

Makalani held back as the Jeep slowed and turned.

A ramshackle house on the right had a cattle gate a few yards onto the property, off to the side. From the street, it appeared to lead straight into trees. She wouldn't be able to follow in a rental car even if the gate hadn't been locked. She would need a mode of transportation that could handle the terrain.

Sandy answered on the second ring. "Wassup, woman?"

"You working today?"

"Nope. Doing chores on the ranch."

"You think we could ride?"

"When?"

"Now."

Sandy laughed. "Still on mainland time, huh? Okay. Why not? It beats mucking out the stalls. You remember where I live?"

"Actually, there's a trail I'd like to take off Kanepo'onui Road."

"I'm not aware of any trails over there. You sure you don't mean Makaleha or Moalepe?"

"No. It's a back-road access onto public land, maybe the Wailua Game Management Area or the Keālia Forest Reserve."

"You want to hunt on horseback?" she asked, incredulity in her tone.

"Not hunt. Search."

"Ah, for your cousins."

"One of them, yeah. I'll explain more along the way."

"Okay. I'll load a couple horses and bring the trailer to you."

"You're a good friend, Sandy."

"Ha. I'm just the only Kaua'i person you know who moves as fast as you."

CHAPTER THIRTY-SEVEN

Makalani waved to Sandy as she drove her horse trailer up the narrow country road. "Thanks for coming."

"No prob. Where should I park?"

"The gate is padlocked. Is there another route into the reserve?"

"We can try the end of this road. Hop in and we'll check."

They left Makalani's rental parked across from the gate and continued through the corridor of trees. The view opened briefly to neatly kept properties, then closed in again with thickets and dilapidated homes. Rusted trucks and junk cluttered the road's edge as the pavement deteriorated into packed red dirt.

Sandy pulled onto the grass at the end of the road and maneuvered her horse trailer until she had finally turned it around. The dead end butted up against untamed land. An entrance had been cut through the fence.

Sandy introduced Makalani to a blood bay quarter horse with a mischievous eye. "This is Kukui. I gave you a trail saddle so you'd feel more comfortable."

Makalani stroked the horse's neck. "Hello, Kukui. Want to go hunting paka lōlō growers with me?"

"Paka lōlō growers? I thought we were looking for your cousin?"

"We are. I found Solomon yesterday stranded on the cliff below Kilohana Lookout. He saved Becky from falling before he slipped. No one has found her. When the detectives questioned us at the homestead this morning, they were more interested in Solomon's bad behavior than finding Becky. They grilled him about drugs and asked if he knew the murdered man found in the forest the other day. When I visited my cousin James at his market, I saw a gang of paka lōlō growers hanging in his back lot. They had rifles racked in the trunk of their Jeep and yelled at his wife. Since the family lives above the market, Becky would have seen them often. I followed them here."

Sandy held the bridle so Makalani could mount. "It's like that line from *Silence of the Lambs*, 'We covet what we see.' Most victims are targeted by people they know." She patted Makalani's thigh. "Let your legs dangle a sec. They're longer than my dad's." She lengthened the stirrup straps. "You remember how to ride?"

"Are you kidding? After all the lessons you and your dad gave me growing up, I think I can manage."

Sandy hopped onto a bareback saddle with stirrups and lay over her palomino's neck for a hug. "This is Puka Shell. She loves to run. I'll keep her in check."

She led the way through the fence opening, into the trees, and emerged onto a soaked pasture. The recent rains had swollen the pond and turned the red dirt on the banks into a pasty goo.

"Stay behind me. Don't let Kukui find her own way. I don't want my horse getting stuck in the mud or trapped between rocks and breaking her leg."

She hugged the tree line to drier land, where tire marks splayed in numerous directions from hidden properties into the forest reserve. "I had no idea it was this busy over here. Want to pick a tread and see where it goes?"

Makalani counted too many options. She didn't want to waste time on the wrong trail. "Let's follow the treads back toward the homes and see if it leads to the padlocked gate."

After four tries, they found the correct path and returned to the fork where it veered in two directions into the forest.

"Which route do you want to take?" Sandy asked.

Makalani nodded to the well-worn path on the left. "We can make better time if we check that one first."

They loped through the forest until the ruts and roots slowed their pace.

Sandy sat back in her saddle and stroked the rump of her horse. "You think this gang we're hunting lives off the grid?"

"I think it's a strong possibility. Dirty clothes, unwashed bodies, fully loaded Jeep splattered with mud. When they split at James's store, they drove straight up here. They've been dealing on his property, scaring away the customers and intimidating Becky's parents. I'm afraid she might have been taken as leverage against them."

"Has anyone reported this gang to the police?"

"Not exactly. My cousins aren't telling me everything, but there's something sketchy going on. From what I'm hearing, Becky's turned into a wild child, out of control."

"Think she ran away?"

"Could be. If so, I don't want her anywhere near them."

The rutted road ended higher up the hill in a clearing large enough for a truck to turn. Hiking trails led into the trees.

Makalani circled Kukui around the boot and paw prints on the ground. "These trails are for hunting. Let's go back and check the other route."

They hurried back to the grassy plain and followed the less-traveled route, wide enough for a Jeep. They picked their way carefully over gnarled roots, treacherous ruts, and the aggressive tread of mud-terrain tires. Pāpā's truck wouldn't have made it up here. A mile up the steep grade, the haole koa shrubs closed in tight.

Sandy reined in her horse. "Those sons of bitches."

"What's wrong?"

"Cattle guard on the road."

A trench had been dug into the ground and covered by an iron grate six feet across. All-terrain tires could pass over the horizontal pipes.

A horse or other hoofed animals would step or slip through the gaps. The dense shrubs made it impossible to go around.

Sandy dismounted and dropped her reins, signaling her well-trained horse to wait. She pulled at the iron to see if it would lift.

"We had these in Montana to keep cattle on the ranch. The humane guards have small spaces between the pipes that make it unsettling for animals to cross. These gaps are big enough for a horse's leg to slide through." She shook the locked grate in frustration. "Broken limbs. Starvation. The animals die horribly if they aren't rescued."

Makalani noted the hooves and leg bones in the trench. "Or slaughtered for food."

Sandy mounted Puka Shell and turned her down the trail. "Either way, we're done for the day. If you want to follow your growers, you'll need to hike in on foot or find a vehicle that can handle this road."

CHAPTER THIRTY-EIGHT

Kay puckered her lips and set the Magma Margarita on the table.

"You don't like it?" Cynthia asked.

Kay shrugged. "The jalapeño is a bit much."

Her daughter laughed and clinked her glass against Thad's. "That's what makes it so good."

Her son-in-law leaned back as he sipped and took in the view, looking as comfortable and casual as if he owned the whole beach. When his tech company eventually went public, he probably could. Was that why Kay was trying so hard to impress? She should have joined Douglas in a clean sauvignon blanc.

Alexa held out her coconut rum concoction. "Want to try mine, Grandma?"

"No thank you, dear. But I would like to hear about this present you brought for my aunt. What is so important you couldn't send it in the mail?"

Alexa hovered over her straw, effectively hiding her eyes. "You'll find out at the lūʻau."

Kay noted Cynthia's and Thad's concerned expressions. "You both know what this is." She turned to her granddaughter. "Why do they get to know and not me?"

Cynthia dipped a wonton chip into the poke. "This is how Alexa wants it done. It's not that big of a deal, Mom. You'll find out soon enough."

But it did feel like a big deal. Being excluded from these plans reminded Kay that she wasn't as important as she thought.

She looked from her hapa-haole daughter to her honey-haired granddaughter with the light-hazel eyes, each generation whiter than the one before. Yet Alexa apparently wanted to reclaim her Polynesian roots. Was she exploiting her ability to claim a minority while passing as white? Or had the Hawaiian culture captured her heart?

"I hear you're learning the Hawaiian language. Do you plan to move here?"

Alexa nibbled her sashimi. "Not permanently. But I'd like to visit my teacher on Moloka'i at some point."

"Your ancestors on my father's side came from Moloka'i and Lāna'i."

"So I've learned."

"As part of your research project?"

"Mm-hmm."

Kay was baffled. "What are you trying to become? A Hawaiian historian? A genealogist?"

"My field of study is social-cultural anthropology. Creating my own family tree is just a stepping stone toward my master's degree."

"So, the depth of your interest in Hawai'i is shallow?"

"Not shallow, Grandma, *focused* on what's necessary for this task." She laughed. "Anthropology as a field of study is actually quite practical and in high demand."

"For whom?"

"International corporations, nonprofits, education. You'd be surprised by the career opportunities. These days, companies need specialists who understand the interaction between culturally diverse societies and their environment and how that impacts the company's goals. Someone like me could link local to global, past to present, by researching migration, nationalism, ethnicity, rituals, celebrations, cultural values, identity. All sorts of things."

Cynthia winked at her husband. "If only she had passion."

Thad chuckled. "Our daughter has never lacked that."

Alexa raised her creamy cocktail in a toast. "Blame yourselves." She took a sip, then raised her glass to Douglas. "You, too, Grandpa. I remember how passionate you were about your career before you retired. Maybe I inherited it from you."

But not me? Kay thought.

Douglas covered her hand and brought it to his lips for a kiss. "All the passion in my life has come from my beautiful bride."

Although sweet, it didn't ease the hurt.

"Of course, Grandma," Alexa added quickly. "You're the most passionate of all."

Everyone nodded in agreement, but no one drank.

CHAPTER THIRTY-NINE

Makalani returned to the homestead, discouraged and hungry. With the cattle guard blocking the trail, she and Sandy had given up their pursuit. Between the padlocked gate, the flooded stream blocking the route from the dead-end road, and the rough terrain of the paka lōlō growers' secret trail, the only way she'd be able to follow was by foot.

She found her father cleaning a fresh catch of squid.

"Is that for Aunty Kaulana's squid lū'au?"

"You know it."

Makalani salivated in anticipation. Most mainlanders couldn't get past the brownish-green mess of cooked kalo leaves. Those that could abandoned the dish when they spotted tentacles peeking out of the soupy green murk. Chicken lū'au was an easier sell. Makalani preferred the squid.

Pāpā cut off the feelers, grabbed the base of the head, and pulled the innards and ink sac out of the small body in one fluid move. After removing the spear-like cartilage, he peeled off the skin, cut the flaps, then squished out the remaining innards from the tube. He turned the body inside out on his finger and wiggled it in the air.

"You like help?"

She laughed. "You got this. Where's Māmā?"

"Wit' da hula hālau making haku leis." He swished the squid in water, rolled it off his finger, and sliced it into rings. "Dey need plenny kine fo' all da performers, fo' Tūtū's hat, and to decorate da mats."

"That's a lot of work."

"And a lot of flowers. Some of da guys found maile in da mountains yesterday. Getting haad to find. Dass why so expensive, yeah?"

"But special."

"Yeah," he said. "Very special. Hey, I'm glad you came back when you did. I get something to ask."

"Wassup?" she asked.

"Solomon's been acting suppah strange today. Hyper and irritable dis morning, mellow in da afternoon. Too mellow, you know? I t'ink he may be on somet'ing."

Makalani had wondered the same, but with everyone angry with her, she hadn't wanted to stir the pot. "What do you want me to do?"

"Da Braddahs stay come ovah to hunt pig. Go wit' dem. Look out fo' your cousin. Keep him out o' trouble."

Makalani understood his concern. Back in the day, her cousin was the voice of reason, keeping Da Braddahs on track for the high school games. Without football, they had no reason to restrain.

"Why would any of them listen to me?"

"Eh, don't sell yourself short. All dem guys look up to you, always have. Especially wit' da ranger work you do in Oregon."

Makalani rolled her eyes. They liked that she carried a gun on the job. "When are they coming?"

"Soon. Da pigs like forage in da late afternoon."

"Why didn't they hunt yesterday or this morning?"

"Dey planned to, yeah? But when your cousins wen' missing, da plans got hamajang. Now everybody scramble like crazy to make t'ings work. Relatives fly in from da mainland and oddah islands. We meant greet um at da airport. But, you know . . . no can."

"They're family. They'll understand."

"Some will. Some won't. Honestly, I expected mo' kōkua dan we get."

Makalani nodded. "'A'ohe hana nui ke alu 'ia."

"Dass right. No task too big when we all work togeddah." He raised his brows. "You'll go on da hunt?"

"Of course."

Da Braddahs arrived after she had hydrated and changed clothes, with the happy groove of Nesian N.I.N.E.'s "Show Me" booming from their truck. The difference in vibe between the Natives Inna New Era and the militant rap she had heard coming from the paka lōlō gang's Jeep gave her hope that Da Braddahs were still the good, fun guys she remembered.

Malosi stepped out of the passenger side first. He looked as strong as his Samoan name suggested, even though his belly had gone soft. He had held the line after Kimo Tagaloa had graduated from Kapa'a High School. When he spotted Makalani, he gave her a devilish grin, the kind that had made the Kapa'a girls swoon and their fathers want to bust him in the face. Although she doubted he would attract much attention from young women today, he had that capable energy that more mature women liked.

"Eh, Makalani. I heard you was back."

"Three days already."

Pupule jumped out next, landed hard on the dirt, and wiggled his saggy breasts to make her laugh.

"Oh my god," she said. "Do you ever change?"

"No way, tita. I still got all da papayas fo' you."

She covered her eyes against the hilarious sight. Pupule got his nickname back in junior high when he danced the "Princess Pupule" song for a talent show. *Pupule* meant crazy, and the touristy song by Alfred Apaka played on the double meaning of the papaya seller's ample breasts. Even in seventh grade, Solomon's friend had an unfortunately fleshy chest. He was also the class clown and played it to the hilt.

The driver came out last and waved a shaka sign in hello. "Howzit."

"Eh, Boy. How you doing?"

Boy had inherited his father's long Hawaiian name. Rather than call him *Junior*, as mainlanders might, the family called him *Boy*. It was pretty common. Shout *Boy* at a surfing or canoe paddling event, and at least two guys would turn and look.

This Boy was better known than most because his family had deep roots on Kaua'i that traced back to the late 1700s during the reign of Queen Kamakahelei. Although commoners, Boy's ancestors had distinguished themselves during the annual Makahiki games, the ancient Hawaiian version of today's Olympics where warriors could stay active and the maka'āinana could practice in case they were ever called upon to fight. Boy's ancestors had excelled in games of strength like hākā moa, where two players arm wrestled while standing on one leg and holding their foot; and moa pāhe'e, where competitors slid heavy torpedo-shaped darts fifty feet between stakes. In recent generations, his family excelled in football, wrestling, and baseball. One of his uncles coached for Līhu'e High School. The other coached for Kapa'a. Although Boy could have followed suit, he seemed content to hunt for local butchers and friends.

His football muscles had also softened to fat. His deep, resonant voice remained. "Good to have you back, Makalani."

"Couldn't miss Tūtū's eighty-fifth."

Pāpā patted Boy on the back. "You should take Makalani wit' you tonight."

"You like hunt pig?" Pupule asked.

"It's been a long time, but yeah." She nodded toward the mixed-breed hounds pacing in the cargo bed of the truck. "Never hunted with dogs."

"How you find um, den?" Pupule asked.

Pāpā winked. "Guess we track bettah dan you."

"Oh, ho. Game on, uncle. We goin' see what your girl can do."

Makalani patted the air to calm Pupule's excitement. "Don't expect too much, okay?"

"You still get a gun?" Malosi asked.

Although she had it holstered inside her waistband, she didn't like the glint in his eyes. "I thought you guys hunted with knives."

"We do. But it nevah hurts to have insurance. I got busted wit'out a license last month. Game warden took um away."

Pupule laughed. "Nevah stop us before. Why should it stop us now?"

Solomon came out of his room and onto the deck looking more ready for a nap than a hunt. "Stop you from what?"

Boy scoffed. "Look at you, brah. You jus' wake up, or what?"

"Why you guys here so early?"

"Early? Stay four thirty already. Da pua'a forage earlier dis time of year."

"Dass right, braddah," Pupule said. "We like hit da trail before dark. Hurry up. We goin' hunt fo' one big suckah pig."

"Why's Makalani here?"

Pupule draped his arm around her shoulders. "Fo' decoration. Nah, just kidding. Why you think?"

Makalani smiled sweetly. "You don't mind, do you, cuz?"

Solomon grunted his displeasure and got in the back seat.

She peeled off Pupule's arm, mindful of the infatuation he had felt for her since he was a kid.

He laughed it off. "No be mad at me, ranger. I share what I got."

"Eh, Uncle Kawika," Boy said. "How many people da pua'a gotta feed?"

"Hundred say dey come. Hundred fifty could show up. You know how it is. Bettah have leftovahs den run out o' food."

Boy nodded and opened the driver's-side door. Malosi took the passenger seat in the front. Pupule held the rear door for Makalani to climb in the middle next to Solomon, who leaned against the window so they wouldn't have to touch. They hadn't even left, and it was already an uncomfortable trip.

CHAPTER FORTY

Hōkū'alele Peak and Manō Mountain waited in the distance as Boy drove through lush neighborhoods toward the forest reserve. Before the road turned, he pulled into a small grassy lot with shade trees and a firepit, not recently used.

"Is this your land, Boy?"

"Nah. Belongs to a friend. Been in his family fo' decades. Dey no can afford build. Live on da Big Island now. Dey camp hea whenevah dey come back."

He drove toward the line of trees and turned onto a hidden trail. The dogs barked and paced in the cargo bed, eager to be released.

Makalani had only hunted with guns, never the local way with dogs and knives. Sometimes pua'a would wander onto their property, digging up the fields. With no natural predators and a prolific fertility rate, the feral-pig population grew exponentially every year. To keep it under control, 70 percent of the population needed to be killed.

Makalani leaned forward in her seat as the truck bounced over a big root. "You got a good set of tires on this thing?"

Boy glanced over his shoulder and grinned. "It can handle."

Makalani thought about the paw prints she had seen from atop Sandy's horse. "You ever hunt off Kanepo'onui Road?"

"Sometimes."

"Ever run into any paka lōlō farms?"

Pupule bumped her arm. "Why you ask? You like bust, or what?"

She laughed it off. "Nothing like that. I was horseback riding with a friend, and we ran into a cattle guard blocking the trail."

Malosi turned in the passenger seat, his dark eyes narrowed in warning. "Dakine wit' pipes fo' catch da hooves?"

"Yeah."

"Stay away from dea, Makalani."

"Does it lead to a farm?"

"Could be Kalei dem," Pupule said.

"Who's that?" she asked.

"Tough tita. She and her braddah run a farm in da mountains. They sell good shit. I can hook you up if you like."

Solomon scoffed. "As if."

"What?" Pupule said. "Even rangers like party some time. Right, Makalani?"

She flashed a stink eye at Solomon. "They grow everything themselves?" she asked Pupule.

"Nah. Dey get one compound fo' da whole gang. I nevah been, but it sounds like a sweet way to live—no rent, no neighbors, no hassle. Little bit work. All da time high. Shoots. Sounds maika'i to me."

"You ever been to their farm?"

"No way. Dey secretive li'dat. Fo' good reason, tho. Dey get primo paka lōlō."

Boy gassed the truck over a particularly big root and bounced Pupule in his seat. "Enough weed talk. We hea to hunt pig."

The road widened in a dead end with enough room for Boy to turn the truck and park. As he shifted forward and back, Makalani considered what she had learned.

Pupule's description of Kalei and her brother fit the scowling Filipina woman and the man who resembled her that Makalani had seen selling weed. Although three other men had been lounging at that picnic table—one Hawaiian, one haole, and a young Chinese guy with buzz-cut hair—the woman had handled all the negotiations. When

Linda drove up later and shouted at them to leave, it was the woman, not the men, who told her to back off.

They had to be the same growers. But did they have anything to do with Ikaika 'Ōpūnui's death? She glanced at Solomon sulking beside her in the truck. If Pupule and the others bought weed from this gang, it seemed likely that he and Becky did, too.

Malosi opened the tailgate and released the pack, who happily marked their territory against the nearby trees. The six dogs were each a mix of two or three breeds—pit bull and bulldog for power; Lab, pointer, and bloodhound to track; and Airedale, whose furry coat helped protect the dogs in the brush. Together, the hunting mutts made a fierce, effective team.

Solomon reached into the bed for the cooler. "You got beer in hea?"

"Fo' latahz," Pupule said.

Solomon grabbed a can and guzzled half of it before Pupule or Makalani could object.

"Hunting is dangerous, cuz. Don't you want a clear head?"

Solomon sneered at Makalani. "I don't know, *cuz*. Don't you want to mind your own business?"

Boy strapped on his backpack and closed the tailgate. "You coming, or what?" He whistled, and the dogs raced to respond, wagging and pacing at his feet. "Good boys. Go on, now. Find us one big, fat pig."

The dogs trotted up the trail, followed by Malosi, Boy, and Pupule. Two of the tracker dogs broke ahead of the rest and separated into the trees.

Makalani waited until Solomon gulped the last drop of beer and tossed the can in the back. "You good?"

"Do what you want, Makalani, but no nursemaid me." He jogged up to Pupule and left Makalani to bring up the rear.

They followed a trail into the forest amid saplings and loosely spaced trees. Fallen leaves covered the ground. When the path faded, they followed the dogs between the trees. With few ferns and minimal shrubs, the terrain wasn't too hard, until a tracker dog barked from somewhere down the ridge.

Boy changed his whistle. The other dogs ran toward the bark. Malosi bolted through the forest, beating a path through the obstacles as he had with football opponents on a field. Boy and Pupule followed with Solomon close behind. Makalani divided her attention between the tangle of roots, the branches near her face, and her cousin jogging ahead. So far, he was holding up okay.

When they reached a ridge, the hunters slid down the slope, grabbing trunks and branches for balance and avoiding the rocks. At the bottom, the dogs jumped into a shallow stream and scrambled up the mud. Da Braddahs hurried after them, Malosi in the lead. When he, Boy, and Pupule crested the next ridge, Solomon had only begun, panting loudly as he climbed.

"You okay?" she asked. His ordeal had depleted his strength.

Snarls mixed with barks up ahead.

"Take your time, cuz," she said. "You've been through a lot." It would be safer if the danger was done before he arrived. She didn't want him gored by tusks trying to prove his toughness.

They made it up the hill in time to see the snarling dogs, fanned around their catch like the petals of a flower. They had pinned a pig between tree trunks and a rock and were biting at its face, ears, and neck.

Malosi circled behind the pig. He grabbed it by the ankles and raised the hind legs. The terrified animal pawed the ground as the wagging, snarling pack continued to bite.

Boy and Pupule yanked on their collars.

"Uoki," Boy shouted, commanding the dogs to stop.

Malosi dragged the pig into the open and steered its tusks away from the dogs. Makalani could see it wasn't that big. Fifty pounds at most. Old enough to kill, but not big enough to fulfill her father's request. Malosi set it free. The pua'a bolted into the brush.

The men sagged, hands on knees, sucking in air. Only midtwenties, and they were already past their prime.

Makalani handed a water pouch to Malosi and Pupule, neither of whom had brought their own. Boy praised his dogs. Solomon sat on a rock to hide his fatigue.

Hunting with dogs was a lot more frantic than the way Makalani and her father had tracked. During those few times in her teenage years, they had spent full days hiking through the wilderness, communing with the land, and searching for pig scat, plant decimation, erosion, and trodden soil. The peaceful hunts had led to deep conversations and important decisions.

Boy patted his hounds and repeated his initial command. "Go find us one big, fat pig."

The pointer- and hound-mix dogs ran down the slope, sniffed the area, then vanished into the brush. The lead dogs had the hottest passion and drive for the hunt. As before, they circled back occasionally to check in with Boy, then ventured out again. The pit, bulldog, and Labrador mutts stayed closer to the men.

When Solomon pushed forward to join Malosi and Boy, Makalani held back and gave him his space. It also gave her time to speak with Pupule alone.

"Eh," she said. "If I wanted to score some of that primo paka lōlō, where would I find Kalei?"

"I can hook you up."

"I know. But if I wanted to do it myself."

"Supah easy. Dey hang out behind Muramoto Market. Your cousin owns da place. You nevah know?"

"About the growers? Yeah. But I wasn't sure if they were the same. You said their weed is the best, right?"

"Top shelf."

"Will they sell to anyone?"

"Unless you one cop." He laughed. "So maybe don't act so rangerly all da time."

"Excuse me?"

He laughed. "Yeah. Li'dat."

"Like what?"

"Tense shoulders, back supah straight, your forehead wrinkled up like one pissed-off teacher befo' she kick you outta class. Hey, I jus' keeping it real. You dress like one kama'aina, but you give off da mainlander-cop vibe."

Was that why she felt so out of place? Because she exuded what Pupule called her *rangerly* attitude? She sighed. It would have been easier to just change her clothes.

"Okay. Say I mellowed my *vibe*. Where would I find these growers if they don't show up at my cousin's store?"

"What, you mean like go to dey compound?"

"Why not? Boy said his truck could handle the roads."

Pupule rolled his eyes. "You been away too long, tita. Crash a secret farm, you get your ass shot. Tell you what, drop by my place tonight." He circled his hips. "I share everyt'ing I got."

She shielded her eyes from the ridiculous sight. "Keep it in your pants, keiki. I'm too old for you."

Before he could argue, the aces yipped and barked.

Pupule grinned as the other dogs bolted through the trees. "Hustle up, Makalani. Time shake dose old-lady legs."

CHAPTER FORTY-ONE

James stared at the tread marks Linda's tires had made when she tore out of the back lot to bring Emma home from school. Would she stay with him after Becky returned? Or would she finally take the girls to Wisconsin for the life she could have led? It wasn't only the Pahukula clan and the paka lōlō growers that irritated Linda. It was him.

She loved me once, he thought. But he didn't quite believe it.

They had met, poolside, at the Hanalei Bay Resort, a three-star vacation complex with condos and private units to rent. She was vacationing with her parents. He delivered their towels. When her parents left to play tennis, she stayed and flirted with him.

He could still remember her lounging on the sandy slope of the free-form pool, creamy shoulders beginning to burn, bikini-clad bottom flexing beneath the water as she swished her long legs.

"You're part Hawaiian?" she said. "That's so cool. I wish I had grown up on Kauai." She blended the last two syllables of *Kaua'i* so it sounded like *Cow-why.* "I'm so bored with my parents. Would you show me around?"

After taking her to see the actual Hanalei Bay, he had taken her down the northeast coast to Anahola Beach. Back then, only a few people lived out of their cars under the trees. Now, homeless families crowded the beachfront land. It had never occurred to either one of them that their future family might share such a fate.

Linda saw paradise. All James saw was her.

A month after her vacation ended, she dropped out of college and returned to Kauaʻi. Two months after that, they married, with Becky in her womb.

At first, Linda had enjoyed Hawaiian homesteading life, but after Becky was born, his childhood bedroom felt cramped. Even after they moved her into his younger sister's room—where Solomon now lived—it only gave James and Linda a month of breathing space before their youngest daughter was born. Linda begged James to move out on their own, but he couldn't find work that paid above minimum wage. Nor could she find work to cover the free childcare they would lose.

"How about Wisconsin?" she had said. "It's cheaper to live, and my family could help."

"Are there any Asians?"

"What difference does that make?"

"Our kids are mixed race."

"Are you saying it's okay for people to discriminate against me, but it's not okay if it happens to you and the kids? I survived. So will they."

"Survived what? No one discriminates against you."

"Oh, really? We live on a Hawaiian homestead in Anahola where ninety percent of the population looks like you. There are more brown people in Wisconsin than there are white people here."

"I thought you loved living in Hawaiʻi."

"I did."

When James's sister moved away to college, they moved Emma in with Becky, and stayed.

When his father lost his lease for the market in Līhuʻe, James jumped at the chance to open his own store. He used his father's inventory and appliances as collateral for a loan and rented the tiny commercial property in Kapaʻa. Once Muramoto Market began turning a profit, he stopped renting the second-floor apartment and moved himself and his family out of Tūtū's homestead for good.

Or so he had thought.

Linda blamed James for ruining paradise. James blamed Linda for revealing her true self. Who could they blame for Becky running away?

Once again, the Muramoto family's future teetered on the edge.

CHAPTER FORTY-TWO

Makalani chased Pupule through a tunnel of interlacing trees and vines. Solomon had vanished into the thicket. She needed to catch him, but she couldn't squeeze past.

The yips and occasional barks of the aces intensified as the lead dogs found their quarry and cut off its escape. The other dogs barked in answer as they closed in to attack.

"You hear dat?" Pupule yelled, beating his way through the vines. "Geev'um good, braddahs."

A boar roared in anger as the dogs snarled and barked. One yelped. Another cried out in pain. The men shouted at the dogs, each other, and the pig.

Makalani hurdled a shrub. "Do you see them yet?" Pupule's broad back blocked her view.

"In da gully by da stream." Splashing sounds confirmed his guess. The snarling, barking, and yelping increased.

Makalani shoved past Pupule and darted through the trees.

Malosi yelled, "No."

Solomon yelled, "I got it."

A man shrieked.

Makalani sprinted as fast as she could, grabbing at branches as she tripped over roots. She had come on this hunting trip for one purpose: to keep her cousin safe. How could she have let him out of her sight?

She broke out of the bushes into a clearing where foraging pigs had stripped the vegetation and eroded the soil. A huge boar thrashed in the stream below her, trying to shake the dogs from its neck and face. When one lost its grip, the boar gored it with its tusks. The bulldog mutt fell backward into the water with a horrible screech.

Boy dodged between his other dogs and lunged at the boar with his knife.

Solomon and Malosi floundered in the blood-tinted water behind.

Whose blood—dog, pig, or man?

Makalani unholstered her pistol.

Pupule checked her wrist. "Don't shoot. You'll hit one of the dogs."

He charged into the water and circled the animals as they thrashed.

Malosi and Solomon helped each other stand.

Makalani couldn't tell if either man had been hurt.

The injured dog leaped into the fray and clamped on to the boar's ear. As all six dogs pinned the animal's head, Boy stabbed his knife into the armpit and dug the blade deep. Blood ran into the water. Pupule grabbed the hind legs and helped secure the beast as Boy sawed through sinew and muscle to reach the heart.

Makalani holstered the SIG and hurried to help Solomon and Malosi out of the stream. Red splatters marked both of their shirts.

"Who's hurt?" she asked.

"Malosi," Solomon said, easing him onto a rock.

She could see a nasty wound through his ripped shirt where the boar had gored into his side. Bone showed through the blood. She unstrapped her backpack and laid it on the bank.

"Lift up his shirt."

She opened her emergency first aid kit and squeezed a stream of antiseptic solution into the gash.

Malosi pulled away.

"Hold still."

She packed the wound with gauze and pressed a trauma pad on top to soak up the blood. Beside the stream, Boy and Pupule hung up the boar and let it bleed out.

"How you doing, Malosi?" she asked.

He panted through the pain. "Okay. Howzit look?"

"Good."

She motioned for Solomon to press on the wound and gave him a warning look when he gaped at the blood. Malosi didn't need the whole ugly truth. Animal wounds were prone to infection. God only knew what bacteria had plunged into Malosi on the feral pig's tusk.

She tore open alcohol wipes, cleaned the area around the wound, and taped the trauma pad to his skin. She shooed Solomon out of the way and wrapped Malosi's torso with an elastic bandage to hold it in place. She cracked open an ice pack and pressed it against his side.

Malosi exhaled with relief.

She placed two extra-strength acetaminophen in his mouth and gave him a bottle of water to drink. "You good?"

"Yeah. Go deal wit' your boy."

She turned toward the tree where Boy had hung the boar and saw him and Pupule lowering the bled-out harvest onto the grass. "He looks okay."

"Not that boy," Malosi said. "Your cousin."

Solomon sat on a stump with his head between his knees.

"Is he hurt, too?"

"Only in da head. Dumb shit charged wit'out a knife, like he go wrestle da suckah barehanded li'dat. When I pull him away, da buggah pua'a gored me in da ribs."

"Solomon," Boy yelled. "You go help, or what?"

Boy was kneeling beside the harvest, gloves on, knife poised to cut. A few yards away, Solomon stared at the dirt. He didn't even flinch as the yipping dogs jumped against his legs.

Belligerent, reckless, and now despondent?

227

Every new behavior baffled Makalani more than the last.

Boy scowled with annoyance as he made the first cut. When he sliced open the belly, the dogs whined impatiently for their treats. Pupule held them back and scolded them whenever they tried to advance. They barked with excitement when Boy rolled the entrails onto the ground. He carved off the choice organs and gave the command to eat as he threw them to the dogs.

By the time Solomon finally showed up to help, Boy had rinsed the cavity with bottled water, wiped off most of the blood, and bagged the cloth and gloves.

"Want me carry da bag?" Solomon asked.

Boy tied the fore and hind legs together like the straps of a pack. "Nope. You goin' wear da pua'a back to da truck."

Makalani thought about the miles of rough terrain they had covered. How would her weakened cousin carry the animal on his own? Even gutted and bled, it had to weigh almost as much as her. When she started to object, Boy and Pupule silenced her with their glares. This was punishment for Malosi. No one would help.

Solomon slid his arms through the tied legs as the men hefted the pig's hairy body high against his back. He hugged a foreleg with one hand to keep it in place and grabbed a curled seven-inch tusk with the other. Since the jaw had been wired semishut, the beast appeared to glare over Solomon's ear as if on a piggyback ride.

Solomon staggered under the weight.

Makalani raced forward to help.

"No," Boy said. "He can handle on his own."

Pupule helped Malosi to his feet. "You can walk?"

"Yeah. I'm good." Malosi tossed the ice pack to Makalani. "Solomon will be fine. We all done dis before."

"Without taking turns?"

He shrugged.

"What about his knee?"

"What about Malosi?" Pupule said. "He wouldn't be hurt if Solomon had acted smart."

Solomon staggered up the slope.

"Accidents happen," she said. "Especially when hunting. You know that. You shouldn't have brought him along. Not after what he's been through."

Solomon slipped and fell against a tree, the hairy beast clinging to his back.

"Tita's right," Malosi said. "Go help Solomon, Makalani can help me."

Pupule scoffed. "Boy won't like it."

"Tell him I said."

Makalani slid her shoulder under Malosi's arm while Pupule hurried up the hill and supported the pig's weight from behind.

"Mahalo," she said.

Malosi grimaced. "I nevah do it fo' him."

He was right. If a fever set in, they'd have to carry a 250-pound man instead of a 160-pound pig.

CHAPTER FORTY-THREE

The dogs led the way, lighted by the headlamps Makalani had distributed to the men. They took turns supporting Malosi, whose strength had fled with the sun. When Solomon's knee gave out, they took turns carrying the dead pig. The final stretch of the pig relay belonged to Makalani. Although she had trained to rescue people with a fireman's carry, she had never worn a rank animal like a backpack before. Although the stream had rinsed the animal's hair, she could still smell the lingering stench of feces-coated mud and the urine male boars frequently sprayed on each other in greeting. The stench of the hair bothered her more than the blood.

"You want I take um?" Boy asked.

She shook her head and hitched the smelly beast higher on her back. "We're almost there."

"You one strong wahine, Makalani. I don't know any oddah woman who could carry li'dat."

She knew a few. Although she wouldn't wish this particular ordeal on any of them.

When they reached the truck, Boy untied the pig's ankles and covered it with a sheet, like a keiki ready for a nap. With the pig secured, Pupule climbed in to monitor the dogs.

"Where to first?" Makalani asked Boy. "Homestead or ER?"

"After all dat? No way we let dis meat spoil. Besides, your Tūtū's place is on da way."

Pāpā greeted them in the parking area, illuminated by the spotlights anchored in the trees. "Everything okay? I get worried when you guys stay out so late. How you hike in da dark?"

Pupule opened the tailgate as Boy and Makalani got out of the truck. "Your daughter brought headlamps."

Pāpā hugged her around the shoulders. "Of course she did. My akamai daughter is always prepared."

Boy grunted in agreement. "She also brought first aid."

Solomon limped out of the back seat.

"You okay?" Pāpā asked.

Solomon ignored him and headed for the steps.

"Eh. I asked you a question," Pāpā yelled. Then he saw Malosi wrapped in a foil blanket, reclined in the front seat. "What happened to him?"

Boy yanked the sheet off the pig. "Take um already. I need get to da hospital, not talk story wit' you."

Pāpā accepted Boy's anger and lifted the pig.

"Go," Makalani said. "Take care of Malosi. We'll see you guys at the lū'au tomorrow, yeah?"

Boy shut the tailgate with a nod.

Pāpā watched the truck leave. "What happened?"

She grabbed the pig's hindquarters to help him with the weight. "Solomon was drinking and acting stupid. He charged into a stream with the dogs and no weapon. When Malosi stopped him, the pig gored him in the side."

They glanced at the house and saw Aunty Kaulana follow Solomon into his room.

Pāpā marched down the hill, pulling Makalani along with the animal they carried. "Where were you?"

The accusation stung.

"Trapped behind Pupule while coming down the ravine."

They set the harvest on a bed of banana leaves. She had failed in her mission. There was nothing more to say.

Pāpā knelt beside the harvest. The firelight from the nearby imu illuminated the frustration on his face. After an uncomfortable silence, he breathed deeply and sighed. "It's a good-size pig."

"Yeah."

"Goin' feed plenny kine people."

She cracked a smile. "All of Anahola."

"Guess you and me bettah finish da imu. You like eat somet'ing before we work?"

"I'm already gross. Let's get it done and put this day to bed."

Truth be told, she could hardly stand on her feet. Nor could she stomach the thought of eating food with swine hair, blood, and stench coating her body like a glove. Once she showered away the grime, her body would collapse.

She checked the imu, still flickering around the bed of football-size rocks. Mounds of dirt rested on the sides of the pit beside more lava rocks, uprooted banana trees, and stacks of giant tī and banana leaves.

"You did all this work by yourself?"

"Nah. Da neighbors came by to help dig and split kiawe. Tūtū's nephew dropped off banana trees since dey had more dan dey need. Your māmā brought leftovah tī leaves from lei-making at da hālau. We store dem in da shed. Everything else, I did on my own."

"Where did you get the puka rocks?"

"We had extra from befo', collected up da mountain out of Anahola Stream. Pōhaku from fresh water get more holes in da lava to make good steam." He smiled. "They also make da rocks less likely to explode."

Makalani remembered a friend's lū'au when rocks had done exactly that, sounding like fireworks and shooting sparks through the burlap, tarp, and dirt.

"What about Aunty Kaulana and Uncle Eric? Didn't they help?"

Pāpā shook his head. "Both your aunties stay cook all day wit' Tūtū. Uncle Eric pretend to kōkua, but you know how he is, more trouble dan he worth. I worked faster once I send him away."

Makalani nodded. Some people sucked energy from others the way roots sucked moisture from the earth.

"Do you still light your imu with a wrapping paper tube?"

"Works da bes', right?"

While stacking the lava rocks on top of the logs, Pāpā would leave a space in the center for a cardboard tube. Once everything was set, he would tear off the pages of a magazine and twist them into a spear. After pouring vodka down the tube, he would light the spear with a match, and drop it before the fire reached his hand.

He wiggled his fingers. "Singed um good dis time."

She could tell by his smile that he had timed it perfectly.

Some people burned the wood before adding the rocks. Pāpā stacked his grid of branches and rocks so air could circulate and allow the fire to catch underneath. Even so, there was always a moment before the flames could be seen through the rocks where Makalani wondered if—this once—he had made a mistake.

Pāpā tested the edge of the hot pit with his slippered foot. "Stay burn five hours already. Almost time to rake da rocks."

Makalani had forgotten how meticulous her father could be when preparing an imu for a feast. She had attended lū'au where the host wasn't careful and dug out the meat before it was done. Every kālua pig Pāpā had ever cooked fell off the bone.

"You must have started this imu right after we left. I'm sorry we took so long."

"Patience yeah? Good t'ings take time." He glanced at the gutted pig lying on the banana-leaf bed. "I'll prepare da harvest. You cut da stalks."

Of the two chores, skinning required the most skill. He had taught her how, but she hadn't done it in years. While Pāpā outlined the pig with his knife, Makalani hacked the fronds from the banana trees and split open the stumps. The honeydew-green flesh of the tree held moisture that would steam the food and infuse the meat, adding to the distinct flavor of kālua pig. Meanwhile, Pāpā peeled and carved the skin from the flesh. When he had completed the first half, he rolled the animal to skin the other side.

"So," he said. "Tell me more 'bout da hunt."

With the stumps split, Makalani hacked the leaves from the stalks. "Solomon drank a beer at the truck. I don't know how many he might have had before. He definitely did not want me around."

"Drinking alcohol is not allowed in hunting areas."

"We parked on a private lot. I tried to stop him. He guzzled it down fast."

Pāpā shrugged. "Short of tackling him, what could you do?" He cut under the skin to begin a new flap. "Keep going. Tell me da rest."

She leaned her machete against a rock and piled the leaves into a giant mound. "We found the first pig quick, but we let it go because it wasn't big enough to feed all the guests. Solomon was so annoyed with me by then, he took off with Malosi and left me and Pupule behind. An hour later, the dogs chased another pua'a into a ravine. I didn't know anything was wrong until I heard shouting and someone cry out in pain."

"How did Solomon act after Malosi was gored? Was he filled wit' remorse? Did he accept responsibility fo' his actions?"

Makalani frowned. "He brought Malosi to the bank and helped me treat and bandage the wound. After that, he sulked beside the stream."

Pāpā snorted with disgust as he cut off the ears. "He nevah say not'ing?"

"Nope. Not even when Boy tied up the legs and put the pig on his back. I tried to object because of Solomon's bum knee. Da Braddahs shut me down."

Pāpā yanked the skin off the head. "A man has to accept da consequences of his actions. A woman does, too."

"You think this was my fault?"

"Only you know da answer to dat. I stay hea digging dis pit. But wit' two men injured, dat makes more work fo' you and me."

He cut around the hooves and skinned the rest of the pig.

"I'll pick up the slack," she said.

He gave a sharp nod. "Maika'i. Dass what I like hear."

CHAPTER FORTY-FOUR

Kaulana rushed onto the lānai when the hunting party returned. Dogs barked. Truck headlights shone in her eyes. She heard her brother talking near the truck.

"Everything okay? I get worried when you guys stay out so late. How you hike in da dark?" Kawika said.

Pupule answered, "Your daughter brought headlamps."

"Of course she did. My akamai daughter is always prepared."

Another truck door slammed shut as her brother spoke with the men. Kaulana peered through the light as someone limped toward the house.

Kawika yelled at the man. "Are you okay? Eh. I asked you a question."

Kaulana stopped listening when she saw her son's blood.

"Don't," Solomon said to her as she rushed forward to help. "I'm not hurt, okay? Leave me alone."

She froze, hand to her mouth, wondering what she should do—respect his privacy, or make sure he wasn't lying to her, again.

Someone shouted by the truck. "Take um already. I need get to da hospital, not talk story wit' you."

Kaulana flashed another look at her son while Makalani called, "Take care of Malosi." The tailgate rattled and slammed shut.

Respect be damned. Kaulana needed to know what was going on.

She caught Solomon's door before it closed and paused in the doorway, blocking the outdoor lights. A moment later, Solomon switched on a lamp.

"I said I was fine, Mom."

"You say a lot of things. No make any of dem true."

He pulled off his filthy shirt and tossed it on the floor. Seconds later, he added his pants.

"Dat your blood?" she asked.

"No."

He grabbed a T-shirt and jersey shorts off a pile.

The state of his once glorious body broke her heart. His magnificent torso had sagged into flab. His once powerful arms that had blocked and tackled looked too flimsy for such a punishing task. Worst of all were his atrophied legs that had once propelled him down the field with record-setting speed. Her heart still jumped whenever she replayed those interception touchdowns in her mind. The stretch of his body. The catch. The way he had run and run and run.

"Mom."

"What?"

"You're staring."

"Sorry." She lowered her eyes to his feeble leg and the scar running down the face of his now-swollen knee. "You should ice dat soon."

"Yup."

"You like me wrap it fo' you?"

"Nope."

He covered the scratches on his arms with his hands, but nothing he did could hide the shame on his face.

"What happened out dea?"

He went to the corner and opened a small refrigerator.

"When you get dat?"

The tiny fridge was stuffed with beer. He opened a can and gulped the contents in one pull. He took out another and started to do the same.

"You no like food or juice? I can fix you something more nutritious dan beer."

He sat on the bed and pressed the cold can against his knee.

"You sure you no want ice?"

"Mom. Stop, okay? Just . . . stop."

She took a beer for herself and sat beside him on the bed. The corner of the mattress sank beneath her weight. Instead of opening the beer, she pressed the cold can against the other side of his knee. He accepted the gesture with a nod of thanks.

"Is Malosi okay?" she asked.

"I don't know. I acted stupid. Da pig gored him. Wouldn't have happened if I wasn't dea."

She stifled the urge to comfort or deny. It was probably the truth. This was also the first real moment of conversation they had had since he came home from the hospital, hopeless and depressed. She was terrified he might shut her out again if she said the wrong thing.

He downed his beer and opened up hers, drank half, and returned it to his knee. "Get me one mo'?"

She wanted to yell, "No," and swat the other beer from his hand. She wanted to march him to the shower and make him wash off the stink of dead animal and blood. She wanted to shake him out of his self-pity and motivate him to find a new passion in life. She wanted to do anything other than enable his drunken, slovenly descent.

She closed her eyes and whispered, "You get more potential dan any oddah Pahukula kid. No let it go to waste."

He snorted a laugh. "You t'ink I did all dis on purpose? Dat I like being one useless drunk li' Dad?"

"I nevah say dat. I only meant—"

"I know what you meant. But I do not exist on dis planet to validate you."

Kaulana froze.

His vehemence dug into her heart. Did her only child truly blame her? The cruelty of his words would replay forever in her mind.

Solomon shoved himself from the bed and stumbled to the fridge. He opened another beer and gestured toward the door. "I don't need your help."

She sat in silence, waiting for an apology or a gesture of love. When neither came, she left—eyes forward, lips clenched. The door behind her clicked shut.

The night was quiet. The truck had left. Only the moon and a few tree lights illuminated the grounds. She wandered across the clearing into the trees, embraced a trunk, and cried. Solomon was right. She had shifted all her hopes and dreams onto him, as if his achievements could make up for her own disappointing life. How could she blame him for not wanting her help?

As she pressed her forehead into the bark and thanked the tree for accepting her tears, quiet voices floated up from the imu where the dying fire produced hot, glowing rocks. Makalani worked beside her father as Kaulana wished her own son would work beside her.

"He nevah say not'ing?" Kawika said, cutting off the pig's ears.

Makalani tossed hacked banana leaves onto a pile beside the pit. "Nope. Not even when Boy tied up the legs and put the pig on his back. I tried to object because of Solomon's bum knee. Da Braddahs shut me down."

So that's why his knee was swollen. His friends made him pay.

Kawika yanked the skin off the head. "A man has to accept da consequences of his actions. A woman does, too."

"You think this was my fault?"

"Only you know da answer to dat. I stay hea digging dis pit. But wit' two men injured, dat makes more work fo' you and me."

"I'll pick up the slack," Makalani said.

Kaulana would have given all she had to hear Solomon say the same. Her brother was clearly a better parent than her.

Makalani wrapped the skin and hooves in the leaves and carried it to the compost pit across the property near the fence.

Kaulana hid in the darkness with her shame. These two shouldn't be working alone while her son and husband drank beer. Although Kaulana had been cooking all day, she returned to the kitchen. Soon after, she walked into the firelight, carrying foil pans of tī leaf bundles, as Kawika washed and dried the skinned pig.

"You want help wit' da chicken wire?"

He looked up and smiled. "Always easier wit' two." He nodded at the stack of foil pans, so heavy they made her arms flex. "How many laulau you guys make?"

"Fifty big ones. At least two portions each."

She set the foil pans on a stump. The top one had a rectangular package inside. She had spread the dense kalo pudding on a layer of tī leaves then wrapped and tucked the ends like a present in the pan.

"Is dat your kūlolo?" he asked.

"Imu steaming is best. You mind?"

"Not if I get to eat it."

She smiled. "Remember dat time when Tūtū Punahele made kūlolo? You ate da whole t'ing before any of us even knew it was done? Shoots. I thought Kupunakāne would beat you, fo' sure."

He grinned. "Da body lives when da stomach is full."

Kaulana grabbed her belly and laughed. "Den I stay way mo' alive dan you."

Together, they unrolled the chicken wire and draped it over a worktable used especially for preparing meat, poultry, and fish. After laying a thick bed of banana leaves, they picked up the harvest at both ends.

"How much dis kine weigh?" she asked.

"Hundred sixty maybe?" He laughed. "Pretty damn big."

The powerful siblings, eldest and youngest, hefted the pig's body with ease and laid the harvest on the leaf-covered wire. It felt good to work with someone close to her size. Their petite sister, Maile, made Kaulana feel fat. Working with Kawika always made her feel strong.

He respected her size and welcomed her help. Why had she held it in reserve?

Makalani returned. Instead of interrupting her elders, she grabbed a shovel and began raking the fiery lava rocks into a smooth and even bed. All three of them had inherited the majestic Pahukula height. Only Maile took after their father, Hing Fat.

"I'm sorry 'bout Solomon," Kaulana said. "He should be out hea helping you."

Kawika shrugged. "Haad time."

"Yeah, well . . . been li'dat fo' years."

"Some people take longer to heal."

"You talking 'bout his knee?"

"Nope."

"His heart?"

Kawika nodded. "And his mind. But you're right. Da boy need labor and meaningful work."

A few yards away, Makalani's dirty face sweated from effort and heat. Even by firelight, she radiated the health and vigor Kaulana's son lacked.

"Pāpā," she said. "You need rocks for the pig?"

Kawika stuffed the belly with tī leaves. "A good-size one will do."

As Makalani chose a hot rock, Kaulana added more leaves. "You t'ink my boy was trying to save Becky when he fell down da cliff?"

"Any reason to think he would lie?"

"Haad to say. He nevah like share much wit' me."

"Where you want it?" Makalani asked, holding the glowing rock in her shovel.

Kawika held open the pig's legs. "In da belly on top of da leaves."

Kaulana covered the rock with more tī leaves and helped her brother tie the pig's legs.

"How's the cooking going?" Makalani asked Kaulana.

"Good. I get leftovahs in da kitchen if you like grind."

"Mahalo."

"No, Makalani, mahalo to you. I nevah thank you properly fo' saving my son. I heard what you told your father about da hunt. Sounds like you saved Malosi, too."

Makalani shrugged off the praise, as she frequently did, and returned to the imu where she piled the freshly hacked banana stalks on the rocks.

Kawika covered the pig with more leaves, then folded the chicken wire for Kaulana to grab. "Nevah mind my daughter. She always takes da blame."

Kaulana sighed. "Only because too many of us don't."

He thought a moment and nodded. "Yeah, me included. I was plenny haad on her tonight." He shook his head. "She's so competent, you know? Guess I expect mo' from her dan anybody else."

They tied the basket securely with wire. When the meat was done, it would fall off the bone. The leaves and cage would hold the pig together as they pulled it out of the pit.

Kawika grabbed the basket near the head. "You ready?"

Kaulana grabbed the rump. Together, they laid the harvest on the steaming bed of banana stalks and leaves. After Kawika and Makalani added more layers of juicy plants and hot rocks, Kaulana filled the rest of the space with her foil pans of laulau and kūlolo. After one more layer of stalks and leaves, they piled on wet burlap sacks. They trapped the steam with sheets of plastic and covered the entire mound with a tarp.

Makalani picked up the shovel to seal the imu with dirt.

Kaulana took it from her and nodded toward the house. "I got dis."

"You sure?"

"Yeah. It's late."

Her filthy niece was exhausted from work Kaulana's son and husband should have done. Kaulana would not allow her to work a minute longer while Solomon and Eric slept soundly in their beds.

Kawika grabbed a second shovel. "My sistah and I will finish. Go clean up and eat."

"Okay. I'll wake up early to help with the prep."

"Might as well sleep in. You on airport duty. Pua's flight arrives at ten thirty."

"Could she have cut it any closer?"

He jammed his shovel into the dirt and tossed it on the steaming tarp. "You know your sistah. People stay come around noon. If dea had been a ten-forty flight, she would have taken dat."

CHAPTER FORTY-FIVE

Pua sauntered through the breezy baggage claim area in a navy halter dress. The hem stopped midthigh over shapely tan legs. Yellow hibiscus descended from one breast and up the opposite well-rounded hip that swayed with each step on platform slippers that would have made Makalani trip. She had straightened her hair into sheets of coffee-colored rain, which she tossed off her shoulder as she waved.

"Eh, big sistah."

"Hey, little sis."

Makalani eyed the navy leather tote on Pua's bare shoulder and the wide-brimmed hat in her hand. "No carry-on?"

"I checked."

"For a two-night stay?"

Pua shook the hair off her face and set the hat carefully on her head. The yellow hatband completed the look as if she had stepped off the pages of a travel magazine. Makalani, on the other hand, was dressed for work in a T-shirt and shorts.

Pua held up her tote. "Why should I lug around a suitcase when this is all I need?"

Makalani glanced at the empty baggage carousel. "So we wouldn't have to wait."

"The lū'au doesn't start until noon. We'll get there in time."

"Time to what, greet people and eat? If you had chosen an earlier flight, we could have at least helped set up the tables, chairs, and mats."

Pua flashed a sly smile. "You're welcome." When Makalani frowned, Pua slapped her on the arm. "Kidding, okay? Lighten up. You're supposed to be on vacation. I had a late night at work. And before you ask, Friday nights are too busy to miss."

Since Pua managed a hotel restaurant, it was probably the truth, as was her avoidance of manual labor and dirt.

Makalani headed for the conveyor belt when the first piece of luggage slid down the chute. She caught Pua sizing up her appearance. "What?"

"Nothing. It's just, now that you live on the mainland, I thought you'd dress with more style."

"We're hosting the lūʻau. I have to help Pāpā dig out the pig."

Pua eyed Makalani's shirt. "Okay, but it's also a party, right?"

The shirt in question had a scooping neckline and a feminine drape with *Mālama i ka ʻĀina* arched over a blooming tree of life and *Respect and Care for the Land* completing the circle below.

"Tūtū loves this shirt."

"She's eighty-five years old."

"So?"

"Unless you like dating octogenarians, you need to seriously up your game. Maybe you could change into something more festive after you dig up the pig."

"It's a lūʻau on our homestead, Pua, not a Waikīkī bar. Our guests will be relatives and family friends."

"Who could introduce you to someone you might want to date."

Pua retrieved her rolling bag off the carousel and rested her matching tote on top.

Makalani had brought a backpack for a two-week stay.

When they reached the car, Makalani tossed Pua's suitcase in the trunk. "Did it ever occur to you that I might have a boyfriend back in Oregon?"

"Do you?"

"That's not the point. You act as if I'm undatable."

"Not undatable. Unfashionable." She struck a pose and floated a graceful hand down her curves. "You'd stop traffic if you wore a dress like mine."

"I'm fifty pounds heavier. I'd rip through the seams."

"You're also six inches taller and totally ripped. My god, Makalani. You have no idea how stunning you are."

"We don't have time for this nonsense. The lū'au starts in thirty minutes, and it takes twenty-five minutes to drive."

She hopped behind the wheel. Pua tossed her hat in the back and wiggled into her seat. How was a woman supposed to do any work or sit on the grass wearing such a ridiculous dress?

As they drove up the east coast—golf course on the right, pili grass and hills on the left—Pua's words replayed in her mind. Although she had sounded sincere, Makalani found the assertion hard to believe—unless by *stunning* Pua had meant imposing in size. If that was the case, Makalani would agree. She often drew attention simply by entering a room, especially on the mainland, where six-foot hapa-Hawaiian women were rare. After the initial surprise, men usually stayed clear.

"What are you snorting about?" Pua asked.

"I didn't snort."

"You most certainly did."

"I was picturing myself squeezed into your dress."

"You should let me take you shopping."

"In *Anahola*?"

"In Līhu'e. Wherever. I could change your whole self-image in one afternoon."

"I like who I am."

"Doesn't mean you can't make a few improvements. I think you'd be pleasantly surprised."

Makalani's last shopping excursion had been in Portland in search of rain gear and boots. She couldn't recall the last time she had shopped for—or even needed—a dress.

"I don't know, Pua. I'm more of a trek-through-the-mud kind of woman."

"Only because no one invites you to do anything else."

Makalani considered this theory as she drove toward a vast blue sky and white, puffy clouds. The only signs of civilization in this stretch of old sugarcane fields were the telephone poles and the wires lining the road.

"Come on," Pua said. "Sistahs' day out. I'll go nuts at the homestead if we don't do something fun."

That was the defining difference between the Pahukula girls: Pua worked to have fun. Makalani had fun doing work.

"You heard about Solomon and Becky?"

Pua rolled her eyes. "Typically dramatic."

"Them?"

"Eh, I'm dramatic in more advantageous ways. Becky's a drama queen. Solomon's a cliché."

"He's hurting."

"He's a high school football star who couldn't move on. He hangs out with Becky because she's a queen bee at Kapa'a High. He's trying to recapture his glory days through her."

"That's not fair."

"Oh, no? Why else would a twenty-two-year-old man hang out with a seventeen-year-old girl?" She cocked her head. "Because the alternative isn't nice."

"You can't believe that."

Pua shrugged. "Becky's been crushing on Solomon since she was a kid. He needs to be idolized. She fits the bill."

"That's cold."

"Maybe. But it's the way of weak men. Girls like Becky crave attention from older guys and work them like pros. I watch it happen every night at the bar."

"You let underage girls into your bar?"

"We serve food. As long as they don't order alcohol, I can't throw them out. Not even for their own good."

CHAPTER FORTY-SIX

At least fifty lūʻau guests had already arrived by the time Makalani turned onto the homestead road. Their cars and trucks filled the grassy lanes between the trees and lined the red-dirt slope all the way to the house. The only place to park was an orchard lane beneath a macadamia nut tree.

"Can't you park any closer?" Pua asked.

"If you wanted curbside service, you should have taken an earlier flight."

Makalani walked around to the trunk.

"Leave my bag for later," Pua said.

"You sure? I can carry."

She held up her tote. "I have everything I need."

Pua used the reflection in the window to adjust the angle of her hat and the silky drape of her hair. She would have looked perfect if not for her platform slippers teetering over the nuts.

"Barefoot is safer," Makalani said.

"In this outfit? Hele on, big sistah. You don't have to wait for me."

"Okay. But don't dawdle. We're already late."

"In Hawaiʻi? We could roll up an hour from now and still not be the last to arrive."

"We're not guests, Pua. We're the hosts. You haven't done a single thing to help."

"I'm here, aren't I?"

Makalani started to respond, then gave up. Even if she forced her sister to work, Pua's labor wouldn't come from the heart. Unlike T-shirt slogans that could remind kānaka to care for the land, kuleana for 'ohana was ingrained in people from birth.

How could they be so different?

What confounded Makalani the most was how happy everyone would be that Pua showed up. Was her sister that special, or were their expectations of her that low?

'Ukulele music beckoned from the clearing down the hill.

Pua swayed to the music, eyes closed, beautiful face upturned. No hurry. No cares. She lived in the moment in a way Makalani could not. People would feel this and want her around. Makalani did, too.

"I'm glad you're here, little sis. It means a lot that you came."

Pua blew her a kiss. "Go on. Do what you gotta do."

Makalani jogged out of the orchard and down the red-dirt slope, where she found the early arrivals in the flat grassy area beside the house. They mingled around flower-decorated tables and an assortment of mats laid on the ground while her family flitted between them and accepted their offerings for the growing buffet. By the time Makalani and Pāpā had dug out the pig, Tūtū would have an epic birthday feast.

An 'ukulele trio played in the stage area designated by kāhili ginger stalks. Four sets of pū'ili split-bamboo sticks and feathered 'uli'uli rattling gourds waited on the grass across the front. A polished double-gourd, called an ipu heke, sat on a quilted pounding mat to the side for a chanter to beat. While Makalani had picked up Pua, Māmā's hula hālau had been hard at work.

Tūtū waved at Makalani from a circle of elderly friends. The rounded ruffle collar of her red hibiscus mu'umu'u was already hidden by colorful leis—purple and green orchids, yellow plumeria, fiery cigar flowers, golden pua kenikeni, delicate ropes of orange 'ilima and white ginger on top. Twisted vines of maile hung down her dress with cascading strands of sweet pīkake draped in between. Her long silver hair was twisted into a bun and encircled by a leafy haku lei crown made of red ginger and white tuberose to match her dress. Within an hour, she would have leis piled up to her cheeks.

Makalani bypassed the gathering and headed straight for the house. Her aunties were in the kitchen, heating pots of squid lūʻau and chicken long rice.

Māmā handed Makalani a koa platter with tiny balls of paʻi ʻai. "Say hello to our guests, then help your father with the pig."

Makalani popped a purple-gray ball in her mouth. She loved the intensity of the pounded kalo before it had been diluted into poi.

"Hey," Māmā scolded. "Guests before hosts. Speaking of which, where's your sister?"

"Strolling in from the car. She's dressed for a party, so I wouldn't expect her to work."

Aunty Kaulana snorted. "Like everybody else."

Aunty Maile sneered. "You digging at my family again?"

"I nevah say dat. But I don't see Linda or Emma in dis kitchen, do you?"

"Dey bringing mochi from dea store."

"When? After da lūʻau stay pau?"

Makalani interrupted before the argument could grow. "They're worried about Becky. I'm sure they'll come soon."

"Exactly," Māmā said, covering the pots and turning off the burners. "We should be out there, as well. Grab a pūpū platter, sistahs. We have friends and family to greet."

As Makalani crossed the living area, a boy hurried in from the front lānai. He was followed by a middle-aged hapa-Hawaiian man, the son of Tūtū's eldest brother, ʻEleu.

"Long time no see, Makalani," Brian said. "Okay for dis one visit your lua?"

"Of course." Makalani pointed the squirming boy toward the bathroom, then smiled at her second cousin once removed. She had called him uncle while growing up because he was close to her parents in age. Once she became a ranger, he insisted she call him by name.

"How old is he now, Brian?"

"Vinnie? He's seven."

Makalani appreciated the refresher on the boy's name. Although Tūtū had provided a family tree and highlighted all her mother's descendants who planned to attend the lūʻau, Makalani still found it hard to get them all straight. When in doubt, she would call everyone aunty, uncle, sistah, braddah, or keiki.

"Is your sistah here yet?" she asked.

"Yeah. Kim flew in with her husband and daughter. She married a Dole, you know. Crazy right? I wonder if any of our ancestors worked on the pineapple plantations his family owned."

"Probably," Makalani said. "Great-Great-Grandpa was a contract laborer from Canton."

"Yups. And our great-grandfather was a farmer. He probably worked in the fields or the cannery when he was a young." Brian plucked a paʻi ʻai off her platter and popped it into his mouth. "Every family needs at least one farmer so they can live off the land."

"Do you have any?"

"Unfortunately, no. My family moved to Oʻahu. The closest my sister and I ever got to a farm growing up was driving through the Wahiawa plantations and a school excursion to visit Lani Moo."

Makalani laughed. "The Meadow Gold cow?"

"You know it. They gave us ice cream sandwiches. That field trip was a big deal. Now that we FBI, we see more ranches than farms, especially since my wife comes from old paniolo stock."

By *FBI*, her cousin meant *from the Big Island*, where the Hawaiian cowboy culture had begun.

Brian pointed to the lua. "Boy's taking kinda long. I better see what's up. Can I have one more of those? I only get paʻi ʻai when I visit here."

Makalani felt proud that her parents and grandmother lived off the land.

On the front lānai, Makalani found three elderly people resting in comfy chairs. The kūpuna were friends of Tūtū's and not related by blood.

"Aloha aunties, uncle. Would you like pa'i 'ai?"

The ladies accepted, but the man declined. "Gets stuck in da teeth."

Makalani smiled and continued down the steps, where a rainbow of kids scrambled away from the girl who was "it." Makalani hoped the older ones kept the younger kids away from the river as they raced down the hill. They had all learned to swim soon after they could walk, but they'd catch heck if they returned to their parents soaking wet.

She waded through the guests, overwhelmed by the friends and relatives she couldn't recall, especially those who greeted her by name.

"You've gotten so big, Makalani. Do you remember me? I danced with your mother back in the day."

"Eh, Makalani. I hear you one ranger up in Oregon. Way to represent."

"You're Kawika's eldest, right? You came hunting wit' me when you was a kid." The man patted his belly. "I had a big 'ōpū even back den."

Makalani responded with familiarity to all. "Of course, aunty. Mahalo, aunty. No way, uncle—you're as skinny as a kid."

After a dozen such responses, she spotted Sandy with relief.

"You made it." Makalani raised her voice to be heard over laughter, talking, and the hula hālau's show.

"Are you kidding? I felt honored to score an invite to the event of the year."

Cars and trucks filled the parking area, the orchard lanes, and both sides of the dirt driveway from Anahola Road. There must have been eighty people in the yard with more streaming down the hill. The 'ukulele players sang in lively falsetto while women wearing tī leaf skirts and double plumeria leis shook their feathered red-and-yellow 'ulī'ulī as they danced. All through the homestead, people of all ages—kūpuna to keiki—talked story, laughed, sang, and cheered. The buffet tables overflowed with offerings, most still covered, some left open to snack on before the feast.

"Your grandmother is well loved."

Sandy was right. All the locals in Anahola knew and respected Punahele's brood, especially her youngest child born so much later in life. Now that Punahele's other nine children had passed on, only Ka'ahumanu Pahukula remained. Since Tūtū had been born sixteen years after her youngest sibling, her surviving nephews and nieces were fairly close to her age.

"Thanks for inviting me," Sandy yelled as hula dancers smacked the feathered gourds on their thighs and rattled them loudly in the air.

Makalani leaned closer. "You're a good friend. It was the least I could do."

Sandy waved it off. "You carried your own weight upriver. Literally. That guy with the broken ankle weighed a ton." When the dance ended, she added more quietly, "As for the impromptu trail ride, I reported the cattle guard to DLNR. They said they'd check on it when they can. I think they have their hands full with the dead guy they found."

"Ikaika 'Ōpūnui."

"Yeah. They found his camp, a nice homestead with crops and old-style irrigation. It circulated from a nearby stream. He had even dug out a fishpond next to his kalo field and stocked it with 'o'opu. Pretty smart, right? Fresh fish. No refrigeration needed. Built a smokehouse, too."

"Did they find any paka lōlō?"

"Nope."

"Weapons?"

"Knives, machetes. No guns."

"What about the cliff where he slid? Did they find shell casings or signs of a fight at the top?"

"They found an old rifle, but it's been four days since he died. Any casings or footprints would have washed away in the rains."

Makalani thought of the downpours during her hike two days before. That was the west side of the island. The east side rained even more, especially in the forests away from the coast.

Sandy plucked a ball of pa'i 'ai off the platter. "They'll question hunters. But if someone shot him by mistake, they might not even know."

"What about the head trauma?"

"He might have bashed it against a rock on the way down. The case is still open, but the momentum has waned."

Sandy ate the morsel and smiled. "This is so good, and not just the pa'i 'ai. Look around you, Makalani. This lū'au is magical. Your tūtū looks like a queen. The homestead is overflowing with friends and family you probably haven't seen in years. Forget about all these troubles for a few hours and enjoy why you came home."

CHAPTER FORTY-SEVEN

Makalani followed Sandy's advice, set her worries aside, and enjoyed the party like everyone else. It was fun putting faces to names and tracing people's lineage back to Punahele's kids. After greeting the Doles and Hongs from Honolulu, Makalani ran into another Oʻahu relative no one in her family had seen in years.

"Aunty Kēhau," Makalani said. "I'm so glad you could come."

Only two years younger than Tūtū, the woman had a dramatically different style. She could have stepped out of a Tori Richard's catalog with her moisturized, sun-protected skin, subtle yet strategic makeup, and a bob of pretty white hair she had fluffed out the top of a crownless straw hat. A stunning band of white cowrie shells accented the white hibiscus on her elegant blue dress. Since Tūtū's eldest niece was several inches shorter than Makalani, the wide brim of her hat hid her eyes every time she looked away. It seemed intentional, but Makalani couldn't be sure.

"Thank you, dear. Please call me Aunty Kay. Are you one of Kaʻahumanu's grandchildren?"

"I am. My name is Makalani. I have a younger sister named Pua. Our father, Kawika, is Tūtū's son and eldest child. He and our mother, Julia, live and work on the homestead."

Aunty Kay forced a smile as if this were far more information than she had hoped to obtain. She beckoned to a slender hapa-haole woman, a haole man, and a woman in her early twenties—most likely their daughter—with honey-blond hair. Although Makalani could tell both women were part Hawaiian and Chinese, mainlanders might assume the mother was of Mexican, East Indian, or Native American descent. The daughter, with her hazel-green eyes, could almost pass as white.

Aunty Kay's diamond rings caught the light as she waved. "This is my daughter, Cynthia, her husband, Thad, and their daughter, Alexa. They flew in from San Francisco, where Alexa attends graduate school at UC Berkeley. My husband, Douglas, went for beverages. He'll be back soon."

Having made her introductions, Aunty Kay retreated behind her family. Since she had neglected to introduce Makalani—or had already forgotten her name—so Makalani introduced herself and offered everyone pa'i 'ai.

"Is that like poi?" Alexa asked, more eager to try it than anyone else.

Makalani smiled at her interest. "This is what poi looks like before we dilute it with water. My parents and I pounded the kalo yesterday. It's not as sour as I would like."

Cynthia took a piece. "Is kalo the same as taro?"

Alexa answered for Makalani. "'Ōlelo Hawai'i doesn't have t's." She pronounced *Hawai'i* with a hard *v* that bit her teeth into her lip, as though she had been studying the language and wanted to show off what she had learned.

"I know that, dear. When I grew up in Honolulu, we still called it taro."

"It's the same," Makalani said. "Captain Cook recognized the taro plant from his expeditions to New Zealand and Tahiti. The English language borrowed the word from them. A lot of my friends call it taro." Makalani smiled at Alexa. "So you know, we also call my grandmother Tūtū for short instead of kūkū wahine or kupuna wahine. It's a local thing. Although you're technically right about the t's."

Having, hopefully, appealed to them both, Makalani watched as they popped the balls of pa'i 'ai into their mouths. She hid her amusement when both mother and daughter winced at the taste.

She offered her platter to Thad. "Would you like to try?"

He glanced at the women and winked. "I think I'll pass."

She laughed at his honesty and decided she liked him most of all. "Were you born and raised in San Francisco?"

"In the neighboring areas. I'm in tech, so, Silicon Valley is a must. This is far more beautiful. When I retire, maybe we should move here."

Aunty Kay scoffed. "My son-in-law is far too modest. He grew up in Palo Alto and founded a Fortune 500 company. They have a gorgeous vacation home in Baja they can visit when they want to lounge on the beach."

Thad groaned. "You make me sound like a pretentious bum." He smiled at Makalani. "I'm addicted to fishing. Nothing beats yellowfin sashimi sliced on the boat."

"My dad would agree. Pāpā caught all of the ulua and squid for the poke and squid lū'au."

"I've tried poke before, but the *loo-ow* thing is something new. I thought it meant *feast*."

"It does. But lū'au is also the name for kalo leaves baked with coconut cream and chicken or squid. It looks kind of slimy, so visitors usually pass."

Thad chuckled. "Thanks for the heads-up. Which one of these strapping men is your father?"

"He's down by the imu, probably waiting for me to help him dig out the pig."

"That sounds like fun."

"You're welcome to help." She glanced at his cream-colored slacks. "Or watch."

Cynthia and Alexa turned toward the musicians as they began a new song. Dancers in long fitted dresses swayed onto the grassy stage.

Thad noted their excitement and shrugged. "Wish I could, but I think the hula dancers won the vote."

Makalani smiled. "Definitely the cleaner choice."

"Do you hula, Makalani?" Alexa asked.

"Not very well. My mother dances beautifully. This is her hula hālau."

"Your mother is Julia, right? Maiden name Manu, born in Honolulu, half-Irish, an eighth Hawaiian, and three-eighths Chinese."

"Whoa. How do you know all of that?"

Alexa smiled. "I'm pursuing a graduate degree in social-cultural anthropology. I researched Punahele's genealogy for my thesis paper on the *Social-Cultural Effect of Multiethnic Families in Hawai'i in the Past and Today.*"

"Sounds like a huge topic."

"It could be if I want to pursue it further, but I may choose something more globally relevant for my doctoral studies."

"I don't think anyone in our family has a PhD."

"They don't. I'd be the first."

Makalani laughed. "Well, congratulations in advance. Wish I had a copy of that genealogy right now."

Alexa beamed. "I'll share it with everyone in the family once I submit it to the Bishop Museum."

"The museum?"

"It's an extensive record. After I submit my report to my professor and receive his review, I'll make the necessary changes and send it to them." She leaned in to whisper. "I made something special for your grandmother's birthday. I hope it excites her as much as it did me."

Before Makalani could ask what it was, Alexa backed up and scooped her mother's arm. "Let's watch the show."

Thad shrugged at Makalani. "See what I mean?"

Makalani smiled and offered the final ball of pa'i 'ai to Aunty Kay. As she shook her head, the cowrie hatband caught Makalani's eye again.

"Your lei pāpale is stunning, Aunty Kay. The braiding in your hatband and the tight weave of your piko'ole pāpale are as fine as any I have seen."

Instead of beaming with delight, Aunty Kay's smile grew tense.

"Your grandmother made them for me as a wedding gift. This seemed like the right occasion to bring them out of the box."

She waved at a neatly dressed elderly man, approaching with drinks. "Come, Thad. I think Douglas has found you a beer."

When she turned, her wide-brimmed hat shut out Makalani like a wall.

CHAPTER FORTY-EIGHT

Makalani's mother intercepted her on the way back to the house and reached for the empty koa platter. "I'll take this. Your father needs help. How are you doing at remembering everyone's name?"

"Better than I thought, but not very good. We must have a hundred relatives."

"Only fifty are coming. The rest are friends."

"Oh, is that all?"

"Eh, you're lucky. You've been gone a long time. No one expects you to remember all their names. I, on the other hand, need to know everyone and how they relate."

"Alexa's genealogy should help."

"Alexa Worthington? That's Kēhau Ornelas's granddaughter, right? I didn't know she had a family tree."

"She researched it herself as part of her master's thesis. She even knows your maiden name and ethnicity."

Māmā rolled her eyes. "Oh, great. Now everyone will blame my temper on my Irish descent."

"What temper?"

"You'll find out quick if you don't help Pāpā unearth that pig." She pointed to a muscular hapa-Hawaiian man in his late thirties. "Ask Joseph Pahukula to help."

"Ahonui's grandson?" Makalani asked.

"Very good. He runs the old homestead now that his father works less."

"How old is his dad?"

"Late sixties. A lot younger than Tūtū. But you know how it is, she puts all her nieces and nephews to shame."

"How many of that generation are still with us?"

"Five," Māmā said. "Kēhau Ornelas is the eldest and lives on Oʻahu. She's the only child of Punahele's second-youngest daughter, Hoʻomana, who was born sixteen years before Tūtū. Although your grandmother is her aunty, Tūtū and Kēhau are only two years apart."

"I spoke with her a few minutes ago. She seemed shy and a little—"

"Stuck-up?"

Makalani laughed. "I was going to say reserved."

"You have a good heart, my daughter, but there's a reason you've only met her once before. Kēhau broke ties with the family when she moved to Honolulu. She didn't even invite her parents to her wedding. Tūtū made her a beautiful hat and lei pāpale out of shells. She received a belated, emotionless response. We were all quite surprised when she RSVP'd."

"She asked me to call her Aunty Kay."

Māmā nodded. "She signed her email with Kay Ornelas as well. I think her daughter and granddaughter pressured her to come, since they accepted our invitation a month before her. It's a shame, really. Kēhau and Tūtū went to school together. It would be nice if they mended whatever is between them while they're still young enough to connect."

Māmā smiled as a pregnant woman ambled up to Joseph. "You see the hāpai wahine standing beside Joseph? That's his youngest sister, Katherine Tavares. With all the Chinese, Japanese, haole, and Filipino mixed into this ʻohana, it's about time we had someone with Portuguese blood."

Makalani agreed. Kauaʻi had a rich immigration history to support its early sugarcane boom. Contract laborers and immigrants had come from China, Japan, the Philippines, Puerto Rico, and the Madeira and

266

Azores islands of Portugal off the African continent where sugarcane was grown. If not for the Portuguese, Hawai'i would have no malasadas, Hawaiian sweet bread, spicy Portuguese sausage, or even the 'ukulele accompaniment for the dancers of Māmā's hula hālau.

A slender man with thick, black hair and a matching mustache kissed Katherine's cheek.

Makalani smiled. "Their keiki goin' be loved."

"Right?" Māmā said.

She bumped Makalani with her hip. "Now, go say hello and ask Joseph to help you and Pāpā at the imu. Your aunties and I will bring out the rest of the food we made and uncover what everybody brought. I want all the kaukau set before Tūtū leads the blessing. As soon as that pig is out of the ground, our guests will storm the buffet tables, then bring their plates to you."

Makalani laughed. "Okay. I'll ready the troops."

As Māmā had predicted, Joseph Pahukula was happy to help.

"Anyone chipping in wit' da homestead?" he asked as they walked down the slope.

"Not really."

"Same here. My dad like fish. My mom still cooks. With two of my sistahs in San Diego and O'ahu, da rest is on my wife, Jackie, and me. My youngest sistah, Katherine, lives in Wailuku, Maui. She and her husband had a place in Lahaina fo' little bit time, but da big fire destroyed all dey had. Long time past already, but still plenny painful fo' dem."

"That must have been so hard. I wish I had been here to help."

"Nah, you were in Oregon. What could you do?"

The comment hit her hard. How many other opportunities to help had she missed while pursuing her career? If she moved back to the islands, she could be here for emergencies, celebrations, and the daily interactions that bonded a family. What did she have in Oregon besides work?

"Anyways, mahalo e ke Akua, all my sistahs stay happy and healthy. But, you know, dey all left da homestead as quick as dey could. Who knows what our keiki will do. Our kids are eight, eleven, and thirteen. When dey not in school, all dey care about are friends, sports, and girls."

"Girls?"

"Yeah. My oldest is a Romeo. God help us all." He nodded toward Solomon drinking beer under a tree. "Your cousin is strong even wit' dat bum knee. Why doesn't he help?"

Makalani shook her head. "I'm still trying to figure that out."

"Well, if he lived on our homestead, I'd put dat kāne to work."

She would have agreed if not for the trouble she had caused. She planned to give Solomon a wide berth.

When Pāpā saw them coming, he handed Makalani an extra shovel and tossed Joseph a large pair of gloves. "T'anks fo' da help."

Joseph grinned. "Your daughter nevah give me one choice."

"You volunteered," she said.

"Only to get first dibs at da pig." He winked at her father. "It smells 'ono, brah. How long it been in?"

"Since late last night. Da coals have cooled by now. Imu is keeping it warm."

The musicians stopped playing. Everyone clapped. A man spoke into the microphone and directed the guests to follow Tūtū down the slope. The flower leis were piled all the way to her radiant smile.

Makalani smiled. "She looks so happy."

"Yup," Pāpā said. "She yearned for dis reunion, long time." He frowned at Joseph. "I'm sorry da Aquinos and Cookes couldn't come."

Joseph shrugged. "It was too expensive for my eldest sistah to fly her family from San Diego, and my numbah two sistah had a Cooke family obligation on Oʻahu. I asked her to come alone, but she said she had to be dea."

"I understand. Similar thing wit' my niece, Kelly Oshima."

"Maile's daughter?"

"Yup. We offered little bit money, but da flights stay supah expensive from Illinois. Plus, Kelly no like bring her newborn on a flight. No can blame her. But wit' Becky still missing, James could have used his sistah's support."

Makalani could tell he had more thoughts to share. Instead, he patted his cousin on the back and looked beyond the imu as his mother approached. She held out her arms and clasped his face in her hands. They touched foreheads and exchanged the breath of aloha and a quiet greeting in 'ōlelo Hawai'i.

"Is da pua'a ready to be unearthed?"

"Yes, Māmā."

She looked at Makalani and Joseph. "Mākaukau 'oe no ke kōkua?" *Are you ready to help?*

"'Ae," they answered, and held up their shovel and gloves.

"Ho'omaika'i," she said, then turned to her guests.

Over one hundred family members and friends spread before her on the gentle slope and around the clearing where she now stood. People of all shades of brown and white, some from as far as Denver or as close as down the road, had assembled to celebrate the eighty-fifth birthday of Punahele Pahukula's only remaining child. Later during the lū'au, she would thank everyone for coming and give a heartfelt speech. This moment was to give thanks for the food they were about to receive.

Tūtū held out her strong arms in welcome. When everyone quieted, the eldest of the Pahukula 'ohana chanted the opening line of "Oli Mahalo," by Kēhau Camara, in the most evocatively deep voice Makalani had ever heard her use.

The crowd leaned forward. Many closed their eyes to better hear Tūtū's resonant tones. After letting the lowest note trail into silence, Ka'ahumanu Pahukula began the song again, an octave higher to carry through the homestead she and her late husband had built. Her face filled with joyful memories and love as she sang. She extended this aloha to every member of her 'ohana who had gathered and to those who were missed. Tūtū's aloha reflected back to her in the faces of her family and closest friends. She was more than her eighty-five years on this earth. She carried the history of the Pahukula lineage and their traditions in her blood. She kept them alive so they wouldn't be forgotten when others let them slip away.

When Tūtū chanted her gratitude to God and their ancestors, the divine power in her voice brought Punahele's spirit to life. Makalani felt her great-grandmother's presence so keenly she could see the icy-blue eyes of the shark god Punahele had become. Makalani's skin tingled where Manō Nui's fin had brushed her thigh.

As Tūtū repeated the final line of the oli, Makalani sang the words quietly to herself. "Mahalo me ke aloha lā."

Tears rolled down her face. Tears of gratitude with love.

CHAPTER FORTY-NINE

"Hold um tight," Pāpā said as Makalani shoveled dirt off the tarp.

Joseph pulled the plastic and stepped on the corner with his foot. When Makalani had cleared off the weight, the men grabbed the edges of the tarp and pulled it to the side. Next off came the layers of plastic and burlap sacks, followed by the withered banana leaves and stalks.

"Goin' be plenny hot," Pāpā warned.

While he and Joseph pulled the pans of laulau and kūlolo out of the pit, Makalani carried over a long, concave tray and set it on the ground. Then the men raised the pig cage out of the imu and lowered it onto the shiny stainless steel. Shriveled tī leaves stuck to the wire and poked through the holes. Joseph picked off an exposed piece of fatty meat and popped it into his mouth. The expression of ecstasy made Makalani laugh.

"Eh," Pāpā said. "More work, less taste."

Makalani nodded toward the slope as she moved the pans of laulau to the table. "Hungry people coming down. You guys better hurry up."

They grabbed the ends and lifted the pig on its steel gurney with a grunt.

Makalani slid her tin pans to the end of the table to make room. "Does Aunty Kaulana want us to serve the laulau or carry it up to the buffet?"

"Hea good," Pāpā said. "Unwrap da bundles and dump da lū'au leaves and meat back in da pans. People can take whatevah dey like."

True to Māmā's prediction, dozens of guests had already visited the buffet and were carrying down their plates.

Pāpā cut the bindings and peeled open the wire cage. The meat fell in succulent pieces off the bones. After removing the skeleton, he and Joseph wiggled the chicken wire out from under the pig and picked the renegade bones and tī leaves off the tray.

Makalani sneaked a piece of kālua pig and groaned with delight. Despite the laborious effort, meat cooked in the ground tasted the best.

"'Ono?" Pāpā asked.

"So good."

"Shred um up."

Starting at one end, they used hip bones and tongs to pull apart the meat and chop up the fat. They mixed everything together for the perfect balance of taste.

Pāpā handed Joseph a tin plate. "First dibs fo' da kōkua."

Joseph grinned. "Instant karma."

Makalani stole another bite, then waved in their relatives and friends. She laughed when she saw Pupule approach with two plates.

He held them to the sides as he shook his shoulders, jiggling his chest. When she laughed, he jiggled more.

She covered her eyes. "Oh my god, Pupule. Stop, okay? Please."

"Wassamatta, Makalani? No can handle my glorious physique?"

She shook her hand in front of her face, then continued mixing the meat.

He nodded at the tongs in her hand. "I want big kine helpings for Malosi."

"He came?"

"Oh, yeah. He stay wait up top under a shady tree."

"How's he feeling?"

"Sore befo', but pretty happy right now. The doctor gave him choke drugs. Primo kine. Greedy buggah won't even share. Come to think of it, put the choicest bits of kālua pig on my plate. Save da junk kine fo' his."

"Sorry, Pupule. No junk kine here."

He broke open a laulau still held together by the steamed lū'au leaves and revealed the pork belly, chicken, and fish steamed inside. "Dis butterfish?"

"Now who's da greedy buggah? Black cod is expensive. Our neighbors caught local fish."

"No worry beef curry. We grind it all da same."

Pāpā fake-glared at them as they laughed. "Move it, you two. You holding up da line." He gestured for Makalani's tongs. "Take da kūlolo to da kitchen so Aunty Kaulana can cut it up and serve how she like."

Pupule opened his mouth in exaggerated excitement as Makalani grabbed the pan. "I bettah come, make sure it get dea okay."

"You're a good friend, Pupule," she said with a smirk. Then she added more seriously, "Have you seen Solomon yet?"

"Up dea, waiting on Malosi like a nurse."

Makalani sighed with relief. "So, no hard feelings between them?"

"Little bit, maybe. Not'ing time and sucking up won't fix." He glanced at the kūlolo, wrapped in steamed tī leaves like a package in the pan. "Speaking of sucking up. Weren't you supposed to make sure your cousin nevah do not'ing stupid li'dat? I'm not saying it's your fault or anyt'ing." He stared at the kūlolo. "But if you wanted to make good . . ."

"What? Are you saying I owe you first dibs?"

He winked. "Or maybe somet'ing else."

"In your dreams." She held up the pan. "You can find this—and only this—on the dessert table with everybody else."

"Dea you go, acting all rangerly again. How you stay find one man if you no lighten up?"

"Who says I don't date. You know what? Never mind. My romantic affairs are none of your concern. Take care of Malosi. I'll come by later to say hello."

"Ooh. No can wait."

He held the plates to the sides, but she dashed up the hill before the jiggling began. Although he was mostly joking, his words stuck in her mind.

How you stay find one man if you no lighten up?

Was her serious nature keeping people at a distance? After four years in Oregon, she had only a handful of friends. The occasional blind dates and extra guys they invited to dinners never seemed to click. She had written it off to cultural differences and social discomfort. What if the problem was something more intrinsic with her? She didn't have Pua's ease with people or confidence in how she looked. She couldn't kick back and do nothing but talk. Working on a project with others made it easier for her to interact. Rather than using the opportunity to build friendships or flirt, she focused her attention entirely on the task.

She placed the pan on the kitchen counter, opening the leaves so the kūlolo would cool, and allowed the social tension she had locked in her shoulders to release. Even among old friends and family, Makalani rarely felt entirely relaxed. She never knew when something she said or did would elicit a negative response. Wariness made her awkward. Awkwardness made her tense. Tension caused the *rangerly* attitude Pupule had accused her of—twice.

Beneath it all, Makalani knew there was fear.

She fought against this emotion by helping others. Sometimes, the recipients appreciated her kōkua. Other times, they did not. Too frequently, her critical opinions about their actions seeped out. Although this attitude kept reckless Oregon park visitors and the Crater Lake community in line, her judgment was not appreciated by family and friends. The more she concealed her emotions, the more standoffish she appeared. The only solution she could think of was not to have opinions at all.

And Solomon?

How could she eradicate her judgment when so much of the trouble he encountered manifested from poor behavior and reckless mistakes?

James interrupted her thoughts with a bakery box of mochi. "Can I hide in here with you?"

She laughed. "Is that what I'm doing?"

"You tell me. There must be a hundred relatives and friends outside, yet you're hiding in the kitchen pretending to work."

She laughed it off, but her cousin was right. She could handle her family, one by one. The enormity of the group tied her stomach in a knot. So many opportunities to say or do the wrong thing. So many ways to overextend or be misunderstood. If her anxiety didn't pass, she wouldn't be able to eat.

"Did you come inside to give me a hard time?"

"Just lucky." He opened the box on the counter and revealed flour-dusted balls of multicolored mochi. "Linda thinks they'll be prettier on a plate. That said, I wouldn't mind hiding in here with you."

"Are people asking about Becky?"

"Asking or watching our every move. I swear all the talking stopped when the three of us walked down from the road."

Although Makalani was sure that didn't happen, she kept her mouth shut. James needed someone to listen, not to offer weak condolences or unwelcome advice.

"I can feel their judgment, looking at Linda and me, wondering what we did to make our daughter run away. Looking at Emma, wondering if she'll do the same. I've messed up my family so bad. I don't know how we'll recover from all of this."

Makalani brought out a plate. When he didn't keep talking, she asked if the detectives had any news.

"Nope. They say they'll be in touch when they have a definitive lead."

She placed the mochi in widening circles on a plate, taking her time so James wouldn't feel rushed.

"The detectives aren't treating her as a runaway. But honestly, Makalani. I'm afraid to consider anything else."

She positioned the final mochi.

James flattened the box. "We could stay in here. Eat all of these ourselves."

Makalani nodded. If they hid out a little longer, she might relax enough to eat—provided she didn't say anything judgmental that would aggravate James.

"Never mind," he said, letting her off the hook. "Linda would kill me if I left her out there alone. Even before all this unwanted attention, she always felt out of place."

"You two okay?"

He shrugged. "She wants to move home to her parents."

"With the kids?"

"Yeah."

"And with you?"

"Good question." He picked up the mochi and left.

CHAPTER FIFTY

Kay breathed in the sweet jasmine scent of pīkake, draped along the elegant neckline of her fitted blue-and-white hibiscus dress. When Kaʻahumanu had seen the white shell lei pāpale and hat she had made for Kay's wedding, she had insisted that Kay accept her five-strand lei of pīkake to match. Despite years of distancing, Kay's former classmate and aunt had greeted her with love. She had even seated Kay beside her at the family kūpuna table. Now that Kaʻahumanu's eldest niece and nephews had died, Kay—the daughter of Punahele's second youngest child—was senior cousin to all.

Kay tilted her head. The hat's brim had come in handy when she wanted to leave an uncomfortable conversation or hide when she felt insecure. It also allowed her to discreetly observe her cousins as they visited with one another and ate. She hadn't seen them since she had returned to Kauaʻi, without her family, for Grandma Punahele's celebration of life.

She scanned the clearing for their daughter and found Cynthia, Thad, and Alexa eating with relatives on a mat under a tree. They blended as a family more subtly than Douglas and Kay, producing a daughter with the gentle hapa-haole features Kay had always wanted for herself.

"Are you okay?" Douglas asked.

She nodded toward the tree. "Admiring Alexa."

He followed her glance and smiled. "She's having a great time. It's good that we came. Not only for her but for me."

"You?"

"Of course. This is the first time I've met your family. They're beautiful, welcoming people, like you."

Kay blinked in surprise, equally stunned by his assessment of her family as the incongruous comparison to her.

Welcoming?

Did he really find her so?

Douglas returned to his meal and took another bite of i'a lomi salmon, dipping it into the poi. He looked so happy and at ease. Had she made a mistake keeping him and her 'ohana apart?

Kawika arrived at the table in a dusty T-shirt and shorts. He carried a pan of kālua pig and laulau so the elders would not have to walk down the slope. He and his sisters, Maile and Kaulana, were the youngest cousins in Kay's generation. Although places had been left for them at the table, they had all been too busy to sit. When Kawika bent to serve his mother, she slipped a rope of tuberose around his thick neck. A sturdy lei for a sturdy, hardworking man.

"Eh, Kēhau," he said, offering the pan of food to her. "T'anks fo' coming. Haven't seen you long time. I hear your daughter's family flew in from California. Can't wait talk story wit' dem."

She smiled pleasantly. "Thank you, Kawika. This is my husband, Douglas."

"Howzit, Doug? You like try some kālua pig? Fresh out of da imu. My eldest daughter, Makalani, and my nephew, Solomon, went hunt wit' friends and brought down a good-size boar last night."

Kay took the cubes of chicken, fish, and steamed lū'au instead.

"Remembah da pork belly, Kēhau. Da fat make da laulau taste so sweet."

Although Kay wanted it, she declined. The only way she would survive the confusing onslaught of emotions was to limit her contact with the things she had loved in the past. The imu-steamed pork was at the top of her list. Even the Hawaiian food shops in Honolulu didn't cook their laulau or kālua pig in the ground. She found it less triggering to fill her plate with fruit, salads, poke, and chicken long rice from the potluck buffet. She avoided the roasted sweet potato and squid lū'au that reminded her too much of her homesteading life. And she absolutely did not take any poi.

"Where are your sisters?" she asked Kawika.

Based on the lū'au gossip Kay had already heard, it sounded as if his sisters were not getting along. Kaulana's son—the nephew Kawika had mentioned—had dropped out of UH, while Maile's teenage granddaughter sounded promiscuous and out of control. Becky was still missing. Makalani had, apparently, found Solomon dangling from a cliff. KPD detectives were investigating everyone for wrongdoing, including Becky's parents. One of Kay's relatives had even mentioned drugs.

Please, God, don't let this reach Honolulu and be connected to me.

Kawika smiled as if this soap opera scandal didn't exist. "Maile and Kaulana make sure everybody get fed. Dey come eat when dey pau."

"Will your wife be joining us at the table?" Douglas asked. "She's from O'ahu, isn't that right?"

"Julia? Yeah. But Mom wanted all her nieces and nephews at one table along wit' my sistahs and me. So, you know—" He grinned at his relatives and raised his voice to be heard. "Wit' alla you cousins and your spouses taking up space, *our* spouses no can fit."

Everyone laughed except for Kay. Her cousin's jovial slang had sent her back to the poverty and grime of her youth. Chicken manure and rotting wood. Unwashed bodies and too little food. All the while, her destitute family had laughed it off like a joke. Kēhau Kealoha had grown up in a sad little world. Kay Ornelas led a much better life.

As Kawika moved on to serve her cousins, each of them wearing one of Ka'ahumanu's leis, Kay felt a warm hand cover her own.

"I missed you, Kēhau." Ka'ahumanu's smile reached all the way to her eyes, conveying a genuine love for her niece that Kay did not feel in return. "Remember how close we was in school? Everybody t'ought we stay cousins instead of aunty and niece. Look at you now, so pretty and young. No one would evah make dat mistake. You look way younger dan me."

Close? Young?

Although the older woman clearly meant what she said, Kay knew it was a lie. They had never been friends. And despite hard labor and harmful UVA rays, homestead life had kept Ka'ahumanu youthful, happy, and strong. In the face of her radiance and assurance, Kay's armor of wealth and style disintegrated like tissue in the rain.

She hid beneath the brim of the hat this woman had made and struggled for something positive to say. When she came up short, her aunt filled the silence with a stream of Hawaiian Kay did not understand.

Ka'ahumanu switched to English. "Have you lost our language, Kēhau?"

"Lost?" Kay tensed. "Unlike you, I was never taught."

Sadness spread across Ka'ahumanu's face as if Kay had told her of a loved one's demise. "Ho'omana did you a disservice by keeping you from us. My sistah nevah cared much fo' da old ways. What about your makua kāne's 'ohana? Didn't any of dem have our language to share?"

Kay swallowed her bitterness. The Kealohas had added nothing of value to her life other than motivation to escape. Her aunt's suggestion that the Pahukula side of her family would have cared more made Kay want to choke.

Douglas squeezed her hand under the table, no doubt sensing her distress.

If only she had convinced their daughter not to come, Kay could have feigned an illness and stayed in Honolulu where she belonged. Whatever her granddaughter wanted to give Ka'ahumanu in person could not possibly be worth the anguish Kay felt.

CHAPTER FIFTY-ONE

Everyone had eaten their first round of food when Makalani's father took the stage. Rather than borrow a singer's microphone, he addressed the crowd in his booming bass voice.

"Mahalo no kou hele 'ana mai. T'ank you all fo' traveling hea from across da road, oddah islands, and all da way from California and Colorado. We miss da members of our 'ohana not able to join us—Mary Aquino's family in San Diego, Sara Cooke's family on O'ahu, and da family of Kelly Oshima, my sistah Maile's daughter, who jus' gave birth in Evanston, Illinois." He smiled through the applause. "Dey named him Lee." He held up his little finger. "Cute buggah already get his mākua wrapped around his manamana pili."

Everyone laughed.

"We give t'anks, as well, to our aunties, uncles, children, parents, and grandparents who have passed from dis earth. Although we no can see um wit' our eyes, we feel um in our hearts, looking out fo' us and blessing our lives."

He gestured toward the elderly friends and neighbors seated comfortably at a table while younger adults and keiki lounged on the mats and grass. "We feel gratitude fo' da kūpuna hea today who guide us wit' dey wisdom and knowledge. You stay good friends wit' my maddah and all of us who live hea in Anahola. Mahalo no kou hele 'ana mai."

He smiled at his first cousins, seated at Tūtū's table, and thumped his fist on his chest. "My heart leaps wit' joy to see my maddah surrounded by her nieces and nephews. Although me and my sistahs, Maile and Kaulana, are da same generation as dese cousins, we are babies compared to our kūpuna. I feel deep gratitude to Paul Pahukula, Ahonui's son who lives on Punahele's old homestead; Dana Fujita, ʻIolana's daughter, who traveled hea from Maui; Eva Loo, Lokelani's daughter, who flew all da way from Denver; Edward Ahuna, Lokelani's son, who lives on da south side of Kauaʻi; and our most senior kupuna, Kēhau Ornelas, Hoʻomana's daughter, who came in from Oʻahu. You carry our traditions and memories in your hearts. Mahalo iā ʻoe mai kākou a pau."

The kūpuna smiled broadly except for Aunty Kay, whose expression fluctuated between surprise, appreciation, and what appeared to be anger. Makalani could not imagine why. Pāpā had singled her out for senior respect. Had she expected something more? Something about the woman felt wrong.

Makalani forgot her concerns when she saw her father gazing at his mother with love. The bond between them went beyond parent and child. Kawika Pahukula carried the stewardship of his mother's land and descendants on his broad back. He spread his arms wider to include the family and friends watching from under the trees, beyond the tables, and on the shady front lānai. He smiled at his mother and gestured toward her.

"We gather today to share our mahalo and aloha to Punahele's only remaining child, Kaʻahumanu Pahukula. Although she married my faddah, Hing Fat, she retained da Pahukula name and keeps our kānaka maoli heritage alive."

He placed a hand on his chest and waited for the rush of emotion to pass. "Māmā, my heart cannot contain da love I feel fo' you."

The kūpuna and adults nodded their approval while the keiki squirmed on the mats. Pāpā noticed and smiled.

"Everybody get enough kaukau to eat?"

The kids and grown-ups cheered.

"You like da entertainment from da Sons of Anahola Trio and da Hula Hālau 'O Kalale'a?"

People clapped and yelled their approval.

Pāpā turned to the hula teacher, performers, and musicians. "Mahalo fo' making everyt'ing so beautiful and fo' sharing your talent and spirit wit' us."

"In little bit time, my sistah Maile goin' share her spectacular guava birt'day cake. But first, my wife, Julia, has a special hula she like dance. It's called 'Ka'ahumanu Ali'i.' Many of you know dis song by da Kahauanu Lake Trio and will understand, right away, why it so special to us. Fo' dose who may not know, I like share a bit of Pahukula history wit' you.

"My maddah was da baby of her family, Punahele's youngest child, born out of love so very late in life. After birt'ing ten children, three who died young, Punahele wanted her last child to have a powerful name. She named her Ka'ahumanu aftah one of da most powerful women in Hawaiian history, da first kuhina nui—coregent—in the Kingdom of Hawai'i, and also a grandaunt to Punahele herself.

"As most of you know, Queen Ka'ahumanu was da favorite wife of King Kamehameha I. He appointed her pu'uhonua, which means a place of sanctuary and peace. By her presence and authority, she could grant absolution and refuge fo' kānaka in need. All of you who have spent time wit' my maddah have felt da peace she radiates and da comfort she provides. As da saying goes: He 'ōpū hālau. Her heart—not her belly!—is as big as a long house." He quieted the laughter and smiled. "Like her great-grandaunt, Ka'ahumanu, my maddah, also has a deep faith in God."

His brows furrowed in thought. "Although our queen's acceptance and promotion of Christian missionaries had a devastating impact on our culture, her insistence dat all kānaka maoli be able to read da Bible made da Kingdom of Hawai'i da most literate nation in da world. She fought fo' women's rights before feminism was a t'ing. She helped abolish da ancient kapu laws dat prevented women from eating wit' men and consuming certain foods. As kuhina nui fo' her stepsons, Kings Kamehameha II and III, she led our ancestors wit' strength, compassion, and faith."

He held his palm out to Tūtū and lowered his gaze, giving everyone the time and privacy to make the connection between the two women on their own. He held his other hand out to Māmā and invited her to the grassy stage.

"Please welcome my wife, Julia Pahukula, as she dances to 'Ka'ahumanu Ali'i.'"

Makalani caught her breath as her mother, hair piled high on her head, glided across the grass in a fitted mu'umu'u the color of rich vanilla cream. A downy lei of goose feathers strung in the fluffy wili poepoe style draped around the collar of her dress. Brown nēnē geese took flight from the hem and vanished around her slim waist.

She extended her field-tanned arms to the 'ukulele player's vamp, undulating one hand at a time like a graceful wing while the other hand poised on her hip. When she reached the center of the stage, she swept her hands up to the side and began her story in the uplands of Mānoa where the beloved Queen Ka'ahumanu had lived in her final days.

While the singer's high falsetto voice told the tale in 'ōlelo Hawai'i, Māmā relayed the story with her hands, bringing to life the fragrant flowers and sounds of the birds. She transfixed her audience with arching rainbows, mountain mists, and Mānoa's famous Tuahine rain. She bowed with one foot forward to signify royalty and motioned in front of her heart for love. The gracefulness of every gesture and movement stole Makalani's breath.

It ended too soon with a declaration of love. "O Ka'ahumanu Ali'i, he aloha nō."

Māmā took her final vamp and ended with one hand extended to Tūtū in a shallow bow. The family went wild, hooting and calling out praise. The singer brought the standing microphone forward so Makalani's mother could speak.

"Mahalo, everyone. You're very kind. You're also family, so . . . you know . . . you're probably sucking up for Maile's guava cake."

Everyone laughed.

Joseph heckled. "Bring it out."

Māmā pointed fake-angry at him. "You get the last piece."

Everyone laughed again.

"Seriously, though, this song is special for all the reasons Kawika explained. What he didn't share is the meaning of the queen's and my mother-in-law's name. Ka'ahumanu is the mantle or cloak of feathers worn by Hawaiian royalty. In ancient times, vibrant feathers were gathered from Native Hawaiian birds, many of which are extinct or endangered today. As a result, most of the beautiful colors we see in modern feather work are dyed from geese."

Māmā extended her hand to an elderly woman at the kūpuna table. "When Aunty Lan agreed to teach me the basics of feather work, I asked for natural colors to reflect Mom's love for the 'āina and all creatures and plants in their natural state." She removed the fluffy lei of brown, gray, and white feathers and offered it to Tūtū. "Mom. I made this lei hulu manu for you."

Tūtū gasped and hurried toward the stage, tears rolling down her cheeks, watering her flower leis. When she reached Māmā, she clasped her face and exchanged the breath of love, forehead to forehead, careful not to crush the fragile creation Māmā held.

As Tūtū received her gift, Pāpā came forward with a quilted board. She examined and praised the craftsmanship, and then she laid the lei hulu manu carefully on the quilted board. Feathers were too delicate to wear on top of flowers. Tūtū would protect the fragile gift under glass until a special occasion arose.

Makalani's parents kissed Tūtū's cheeks and backed away so the family and friends could applaud.

Tūtū hummed quietly into the microphone to quiet them down.

"My heart is full of gratitude. I love you so much. I can't believe you all hea." She shook her head in wonder, then switched to 'ōlelo Hawai'i for the rest of her speech. Most of the kūpuna and some of the adults nodded with understanding. Everyone else divined her emotions from her expressions and tone. Even the small children stopped fidgeting as she spoke.

She switched back to English. "My hula is not as beautiful as Julia's. But since our 'ohana is gathered, I wish to pay tribute to my maddah, our matriarch, wit' dis beautiful song written by Keali'i Reichel. It speaks of his longing fo' his lover and future husband, declaring his love fo' his 'never-fading lei.' For me, 'Kawaipunahele' sings of my love fo' *our* Punahele because I know, when da time is right, we will be reunited once again."

Everyone sighed when the haunting melody began. Every heart swelled when Tūtū danced, knees deeply bent, fingers together and still in the old Hawaiian way. She infused her longing and adoration into every motion and expression until the trio's final notes and their heavenly falsettos floated into the sky. She touched her fingers to her lips and extended her aloha to them all.

CHAPTER FIFTY-TWO

Aunty Maile's guava cake was a hit. Good thing she made lots. People came back for seconds until every crumb was gone.

As Makalani cleared Tūtū's empty plate and set it with her own, friends and family came by to pay their respects and compliment Tūtū's beautiful hula. She thanked everyone and turned the conversation around to them. While she spoke with a neighbor, Alexa came to the table to check on Aunty Kay.

"Hi, Grandma. Did you enjoy the food?"

"Yes, dear. And you?"

"Are you kidding? It was the best." Alexa smiled at Makalani. "Did you and your dad really cook a whole pig in an imu?"

"Yeah. I can show you later if you want to see."

"That would be great." She glanced at Tūtū, as if unsure what to say.

When Aunty Kay didn't step in, Makalani made the introductions herself. "Tūtū, this is Aunty Kay's granddaughter, Alexa Worthington. She flew in from San Francisco."

Tūtū side-eyed her elderly niece. "You go by Kay now?"

The woman shrugged, eyes hidden by the brim of her hat.

Tūtū shook it off as nonsense and greeted the young woman with a welcoming smile. "Welina mai, Alexa. Are you having a good time?"

"I am. Happy birthday, Aunty Ka'ahumanu. Hau'oli lā hānau."

Tūtū's eyes widened. "You study 'ōlelo Hawai'i in San Francisco?"

"I'm studying online with Kumu Maile on Molokaʻi. It's part of my social anthropology studies at UC Berkeley."

Tūtū looked impressed and slightly confused. "Well . . . I guess any study dat connects you to Hawaiʻi is good."

Alexa beamed with delight. "I'm so glad you agree. I have a special birthday present for you and all our relatives. Would it be okay if I announced it from the stage?"

"Um . . ." Tūtū stumbled, clearly taken off guard by this strange request from a young relative she didn't know.

Aunty Kay seemed equally perturbed. "It's a big secret. Alexa and her parents wouldn't even tell me."

Tūtū smiled to hide her concern. "How exciting. Go ahead, Alexa. Ask da musicians fo' a microphone so everybody can hear."

As Alexa hurried to the stage, Tūtū leaned toward Makalani. "Any idea what dis wahine goin' say?"

"Nope."

"Auwē. I hope she no try sing in ʻōlelo Hawaiʻi. Her pronunciation is not very good." Tūtū giggled with Makalani, then turned her attention to the grassy stage.

Alexa looked sweet and nervous standing by herself behind the mic. She pulled her honey-blond hair in front of her shoulders and smoothed nonexistent wrinkles from her sunny-yellow dress.

"Aloha, everyone. I'm Alexa Worthington, daughter of Cynthia Ornelas Worthington, granddaughter of Kēhau Kealoha Ornelas, and great-granddaughter of Hoʻomana Pahukula Kealoha. I live in the San Francisco Bay area, where I attend graduate school at UC Berkeley. I'm up here because I have a very special birthday present for Aunty Kaʻahumanu and for all of you."

Makalani's parents joined her behind Tūtū.

"Wass all dis?" Pāpā said.

"Nobody knows," Makalani answered.

Māmā hushed them both with a look.

Alexa continued with more confidence. "For the last year and a half, I've been working on a genealogy project for my graduate studies in social anthropology. I'm excited to say that I am almost done."

Pāpā leaned over Tūtū. "I t'ought we already had one family tree."

"We do," she said. "But it's out o' date. Names and arrows all ovah da place."

Pāpā nodded, as if Alexa's project might improve what they had.

"My goal was to record a small section of our lineage in detail and deduce basic socio-anthropological affects as an example of multigenerational heterogeneous families from Hawai'i. I know that sounds lofty, but my professors and I are super excited about this project. I even contacted the Bishop Museum in Honolulu, and they *might* want to enter our lineage and my study into their archives."

Aunty Maile came over. "Wass all dis, Kawika?"

Pāpā shrugged. "Some cousin from da mainland made a family tree she like share."

"Why she doing it from da mic?"

"To get attention? I don't know. Maybe she makes a lot of speeches at school."

Makalani's family weren't the only people talking among themselves. Alexa's announcement had sparked equal amounts of curiosity and skepticism. One of Pāpā's friends from the Anahola Homestead Committee called her "a high maka maka wahine" as he passed the table on the way to the buffet for another helping of desserts.

The commotion didn't dampen Alexa's excitement in the least. "Our matriarch, Punahele, gave birth nine times."

"Ten," a man yelled. "You forgot da birthday girl."

Everybody laughed.

Alexa smiled. "I didn't forget."

Tūtū frowned. "What she mean by dat?"

This isn't good, Makalani thought, certain that whatever Alexa had meant should not be shared like this. "We should stop her."

"How?" Tūtū asked. "Yank her from da mic?"

"Sounds good to me," Pāpā said.

Māmā grabbed his arm. "It's too late. Look around. Everyone wants to know. If they don't hear it for themselves from her, they'll make up their own stories and hound Tūtū for the truth. Even then, they won't believe what she says if we shut down that girl."

"Punahele and the midwife were dear friends. So when Punahele begged a favor, the midwife listed her and Mahi'ai as the parents on Ka'ahumanu's Certificate of Hawaiian Birth."

The crowd muttered in confusion.

"But she recorded the names of Ka'ahumanu's *actual* parents in her journal."

"Dass enough," Pāpā yelled and raced to the stage, ripping the microphone out of Alexa's hand even as she started to speak. "Okay, okay, mahalo everybody. We get plenny mo' kaukau and desserts on da tables, please help yourself to whatevah you like."

"Let da wahine speak," a man yelled from the back.

"Yeah, Kawika," another man said from the lānai. "We like hear what she say."

A woman pointed her finger at him from a hala mat up front. "It's not our business."

"Dass right, Lani," Kawika said. "Our business is to celebrate my maddah and eat and drink way mo' dan we should."

He handed the mic back to the musicians and told them to play, and then he grabbed Alexa by the arm and escorted her off the stage with a big, fake smile on his face.

CHAPTER FIFTY-THREE

Tūtū stared at the elders in shock, her youthful effervescence wilted like the delicate ginger squashed beneath her mountain of leis. The woman of infinite strength in Makalani's life, the matriarch who shouldered the responsibility of all, the warrior always ready to stand up and fight for her community had withered into a frightened old woman who didn't know what to do.

"What did that girl mean?" Tūtū's nieces and nephews wanted to know.

"Are you still our aunty?"

"Who are your parents?"

"Why you keep dis secret from us?"

Aunty Kaulana and Aunty Maile tried to calm their elder cousins. Tūtū stared at Aunty Kay. "Did you know 'bout dis?"

Aunty Kay looked equally surprised. "They wouldn't tell me. This is as shocking to me as to you."

Makalani nudged her mother. "Escape with my aunties and meet me behind the house."

"Why?"

"That's where Pāpā took Alexa."

"He what?"

Before Māmā could ask any more questions, Makalani wrapped her arms around Tūtū and steered her away. "Excuse us a moment, Aunties,

Uncles, I promise we'll be right back." She whispered to Aunty Kay, "You should come with us."

Using her size to good advantage, Makalani shielded the elderly women from the prying crowd and guided her into the grove. From there, she cut through the parked cars to the mauka end of the yard and found Pāpā arguing with Alexa's father.

"What kine man you stay to allow your daughter pull one stunt li'dis?"

"Hold on, Kawika—"

"Mistah Pahukula to you."

"Come on, now," Makalani said, letting go of Tūtū and rushing to them. Compared to Pāpā's bulk, Alexa's tall, haole dad looked like a twig. "We're family, right?"

Pāpā scoffed. "I nevah met dem befo'. Have you?"

Aunty Kay came forward with her husband close behind. Although elderly, Douglas looked ready to take Pāpā on.

Aunty Kay glared at her granddaughter standing in her own daughter's embrace. "*This* was your surprise? You kept this from me because you knew I would have said no." She turned to her husband. "I told you we shouldn't have come." She turned on her daughter. "You should have respected my wishes and stayed home."

"Don't you want to know, Grandma?" Alexa said. "My discovery is also for you."

"For me? Oh, no, don't drag me into this Pahukula mess."

Tūtū came forward, still shellshocked but calmer now that Makalani had taken her away from the crowd. "Who are my parents, Alexa?"

Cynthia squeezed her daughter's shoulder. "Go ahead."

Aunty Kaulana and Aunty Maile arrived with Māmā, silent but ready to pounce.

"Answer my maddah," Pāpā said. "You tried tell da whole world our business, you bettah tell us."

Alexa flinched away from Pāpā and smiled at her grandmother and Tūtū instead. "I wanted you together when I shared this news."

"Why dis maddah?" Tūtū asked.

"Because you have the same mother."

"What?"

"That's why Punahele took Ho'omana to the other side of the island, not for comfort—as I'm sure you have always believed—but to hide her pregnancy until they figured out what to do. Ho'omana was only sixteen. Your father worked on a sugarcane plantation. Two months after you were born, he returned to Madeira, Portugal, with his parents."

"Dass not possible," Tūtū said, holding out her dark, sunbaked arms. "Look at me, Alexa. Do I look half Podagee to you?"

"The Madeira islands are off the North African coast. Your father's name is Felizardo Djoudi. Based on his surname, he probably had an ancestor from Algeria. You see why this is so exciting? By following the breadcrumbs, I was able to unearth a whole new lineage for your branch of the Pahukula tree."

"This is ridiculous," Aunty Kay said. "My mother didn't have any other children. Where did you find this so-called discovery of yours?"

"Research, Grandma. Creating a detailed genealogy is like being a detective and following the clues. Once I knew Ho'omana gave birth to Ka'ahumanu, I knew where to look. The midwife's daughter wasn't the only one with family journals and personal history. One of Ho'omana's girlfriends dated your father's friend. Both journals mentioned Felizardo Djoudi and said he was the child of a contract laborer from Portugal. I confirmed this with census, immigration, and emigration reports. This isn't a *so-called discovery*, Grandma, it's a fact."

Pāpā rubbed his hands over his face. "And you t'ought it would be okay to reveal dis *very personal information* at a lū'au, in front o' all our family and friends? Auwē. Your knowledge come at da expense o' your heart."

"Hold on, now," Thad said, coming to his daughter's defense. "Alexa may have been overly enthusiastic, but her research has opened up a whole new ancestral line for your family. When you've had a chance to sleep on it, I think you'll all be . . . grateful . . . for her hard work."

"Grateful? Today is my maddah's eighty-fifth birt'day. She is still da eldest living descendent of Punahele Pahukula's line. She share her wisdom and her aloha wit' everybody hea. And you get da nerve—"

Tūtū grabbed his arm. "E mālie, Kawika. Be calm." She turned to Aunty Kay. "I don't know what I am to you, Kēhau—aunty, half sistah—but my love feels da same. When love is given, love should be returned. Anger cannot sustain life. It hurts da person who feeds it as much, if not moa, dan everybody else." She opened her arms to everyone. "We get too much emotion hea today. Aloha mai nō, aloha aku; o ka hūhū ka mea e ola 'ole ai."

She reached for Aunty Kay's hand, but her sister recoiled as if Tūtū's touch had stung.

Police sirens wailed from the highway.

Aunty Kay grabbed her husband's hand. "I want to go home, Douglas. Right now."

Then the flashing red and blue lights stormed down the hill.

CHAPTER FIFTY-FOUR

Squad cars kicked up dirt as they descended and fanned to a stop at the edge of the hula hālau's grassy stage. Pāpā ran in front of his guests as uniformed officers poured from the cars. He yelled from his gut, "Wass goin' on?" so loud that every one of them stopped.

Detectives Shaw and Lee exited their gray sedan, the tall haole man taking the lead. "We have a warrant to search your property and your house."

"What? Dis one birthday party. Did someone complain?"

Detective Shaw handed him the warrant and addressed the confused and alarmed crowd. "Everyone who does not live on this homestead needs to vacate the property. Leave your names and contact information with the officers on your way out."

"Wait a minute," Pāpā said. "You no can give twenty minutes for a proper goodbye?"

"No, Mr. Pahukula. We can't."

Pāpā turned away in disgust and attempted to smile for the guests. "T'anks fo' coming, everyone. Take whatevah leftovers you like. If you want leave your contributions, we'll wash your plates and return dem to you." He shook his head, too overwhelmed to do anything but laugh. "What can I say? Mahalo fo' sharing dis, uh, *eventful* day wit' us."

The guests laughed and shouted in return.

"Mahalo, brah."

"Great party."

"We got your back."

"Call if you need us."

"I'm taking all da kālua pig!"

Pāpā pointed at his neighbor with fake ferocity, then thumped his chest in an acknowledgment of love.

All the while, Detective Shaw scanned the crowd. He signaled two officers and pointed at Solomon, standing beside his friends beneath a tree. They pressed forward, motioning lūʻau guests out of their way.

Da Braddahs stepped in front of Solomon, arms crossed, feet rooted to the ground, forming a defensive line as they had done in their youth.

The lead officer ordered Da Braddahs to step aside. When the men hesitated, he pulled out a baton.

"Solomon Ching," he said. "We need you to wait in a squad car while we execute the search. If you do not comply, we will arrest you and your friends."

Makalani rushed over. "Solomon, do as they say. If they don't find what they're looking for, they won't take you in." She turned to the officer. "Isn't that correct?"

"Yes, ma'am. Unless he resists."

"He won't." She glared at Boy, Pupule, and Malosi—who looked ready to fight despite the stitches in his side. "Back off, you guys. Let's not make anything worse."

Boy nodded and stepped to the side.

Solomon backed up. "I nevah do not'ing."

The lead officer advanced. "Are you refusing to comply?"

"I'm not refusing anyt'ing. I'm innocent. Leave me alone." He glanced at the river, as if ready to bolt.

"Don't be foolish, Mr. Ching. We're not arresting you—yet."

While the lead officer spoke, his partner circled around the men. He surprised Solomon and cuffed his hands behind his back.

"Is that really necessary?" Makalani said.

"Step aside, ma'am."

Solomon shot daggers at her while he passed.

"Be chill, cuz," she said. "This will be over soon."

Pāpā brought the search warrant as they moved Solomon to a car and invaded Tūtū's house. "Is dis legit, Makalani?"

Tūtū, Aunty Kaulana, and Uncle Eric came over while she read.

"Yes, Pāpā. I'm afraid so. They have the right to search Solomon's bedroom and devices for any images, correspondence, or possessions to, from, or belonging to Becky Muramoto or any underaged girls. They have the right to search the house, property, and his vehicle for firearms and illegal drugs, including but not limited to marijuana, flunitrazepam, gamma-hydroxybutyric acid, gamma-butyrolactone, and ketamine."

"Wass all dat?" Tūtū asked.

"Date rape drugs."

Aunty Kaulana gasped.

"What's going on?" James asked, trailed by his parents, wife, and daughter.

Aunty Kaulana shoved him back a step. "You tell us, James. What you say to da cops dat make them think Solomon could do such a thing?"

Aunty Maile stepped between them, a chihuahua protecting her pup. "Back off, tita."

"Whoa," Pāpā said, keeping them apart. "No give da cops a reason to arrest you."

As Māmā, Pua, and cousin Joseph encouraged all the lū'au guests to leave, the hula hālau and musicians packed up their equipment and the mats they had brought. Everyone looked shell-shocked and concerned. Several told Pāpā and Tūtū to call them if the family needed help.

Makalani watched the descendants of Punahele's kids pulled together into their separate lineage groups, dividing the Pahukula 'ohana into Hongs, Fujitas, Muramotos, Manlapits, Scotts, Tavareses, Ahunas, and Loos. Those who had elders seated at Tūtū's table brought them protectively into the fold. The Worthingtons banded together, Aunty Kay shielding her face with the brim of her hat. When the officer who was taking everyone's contact information reached her, the elderly woman refused.

"We have nothing to do with whatever this is. My husband is an important person in Honolulu. We don't want our names to be dragged into this mess."

Douglas quieted his wife and provided the information so he and his family could leave.

Aunty Kaulana hugged Uncle Eric so fiercely Makalani worried the smaller man might be crushed. "What dey goin' do to our son?"

Uncle Eric smoothed his hands over her back. "Nothing, Lana. Everyt'ing goin' be fine."

But as he guided Aunty Kaulana closer to their son, handcuffed in the squad car, Makalani wasn't so sure she agreed.

CHAPTER FIFTY-FIVE

Kay Ornelas whirled on her family when they finally reached their parked car. "How could you let Alexa humiliate me like that?"

"Grandma, I wasn't trying to humiliate you."

"No? You bared our dirty secrets in front of a crowd."

"They aren't dirty. I *shared* the news with your family and your half sister's friends."

Kay growled in fury. "That woman and I are not sisters. Do you understand me? I've spent my whole life trying to escape Ka'ahumanu and the whole Pahukula clan. You have ruined everything I worked so hard to create."

"I don't understand."

"Of course you don't. Because you are a self-centered, ignorant child."

"Mom," Cynthia yelled.

"What? You knew what she would say, and you did nothing to stop her. You kept it from me and acted as if her birthday present was a grand surprise. How could you do that to me, Cynthia? You are as complicit as her."

"Hold on," Thad said. "Alexa logged hundreds of hours on this project. It's an incredible body of work. You and your entire family should be grateful and impressed."

"Impressed? With what? My mother's shame? My grandmother's lies? Or your selfish daughter's plan to put it all on public record with Bishop Museum? Tell me, Thad, how grateful should I be when Honolulu society begins gossiping about us? Oh, I forgot. The Worthingtons will be in San Francisco where none of this touches you."

Kay glared at the three of them, daring someone to speak. Instead, they squeezed together in a protective hug as if Alexa—and not Kay—had been wronged.

Douglas broke the silence in his most reasonable voice. "I think we can all agree that Alexa should have consulted her grandmother in private before breaking such an important family discovery."

Alexa stiffened, but wisely did not speak.

"When things settle, you owe your grandmother and Ka'ahumanu a sincere apology for embarrassing them in public and ruining your aunty's birthday."

Alexa shook off her mother's embrace. "The police raid ruined the party, not me."

"Don't fool yourself," Douglas said. "Their arrival saved you from Kawika's wrath. You saw his face. Ka'ahumanu's son wanted to tear you apart." Douglas stopped Thad's objection with a look. "Your daughter owes an apology. See that it's done."

Douglas placed his arm around Kay. "What matters now is that Alexa moves forward in a way that respects the privacy of everyone involved. I suggest she distribute the lineage to members of the family, not to Bishop Museum."

Cynthia and Thad nodded.

Kay exhaled in relief. Although she'd rather erase everything Alexa had disclosed, at least the shameful truths would remain a private family affair.

"No," Alexa said.

She had stopped sniveling and stepped forward to face her grandfather like an adult.

"This genealogy and report will help me get into a PhD program, which will eventually launch my professional career. Not only will I give it to the museum, I will exploit my published works in every academic application and interview I have."

"Alexa," Cynthia whispered.

"No, Mom. This is too important to let go." She looked at Kay without an ounce of remorse. "I'm sorry the truth upsets you, Grandma, but our ancestry is a remarkable case study for the immigration influences of contract laborers on—"

"Yes, yes," Douglas said. "Post-territory, pre-statehood Hawai'i. You made a big show of that at the microphone."

"My study doesn't only reflect the past, Grandpa. It's relevant to modern Hawaiian society as well. This could be the foundation for future research, publication, and grants. It might even help me land a professorship at Berkeley or Stanford if I decide to go the academic route. So you see, this isn't limited to the family."

"Clearly not," Kay said. "Your so-called birthday present is all about you."

Alexa stiffened. "It was important for the entire family to hear."

"No. It was important that you be the star. You wanted the entire family focused on your grand announcement so they would see you as the Pahukula relative who returned to Hawai'i to elevate everyone back here. Your pretense about learning the Hawaiian language and researching our history comes from your ambition and your privileged ability to pass as white."

"Oh my god, Grandma. Are you accusing me of being a white savior?"

"I don't know what that means, but it sounds about right."

CHAPTER FIFTY-SIX

Detective Shaw beckoned Makalani from the top of the steps. "We found a gun cabinet in the house. We need it opened and permits for everything we find."

Makalani relayed the information to her parents and grandmother, huddled at a table in the shade. Aunty Kaulana and Uncle Eric sat closer to the squad car so they could keep an eye on their son. Aunty Maile and Uncle Sanji kept themselves busy by collecting the trash.

Pāpā shrugged. "All da guns are registered to me."

"Plus mine," Makalani said. "I have a permit in my room."

"Does Solomon have a gun?" Tūtū asked.

"Not in da cabinet," Pāpā said. "Maybe somewhere else."

"I should have checked his room more carefully," Makalani said.

"When?"

"My first day home, before I went paddling."

Pāpā shook his head. "Dis not on you."

As Makalani walked up the steps, she wasn't so sure.

Officers picked through Solomon's belongings, piled and stacked on the deck. A third officer worked inside the small space checking floorboards, closets, and walls. Two more carried Solomon's mattress onto the lānai and patted it down for hidden items. One of them returned to check the bed's headboard and frame.

If Solomon had hidden anything, it would be found.

Much to Makalani's relief, the communal areas of Tūtū's home had been treated with more respect.

Detective Shaw led them to the gun cabinet in her parents' bedroom and waited while Pāpā punched in the five-digit code. "Who else can open this safe?"

"My wife, my mother, and Makalani."

"Not your sisters or their husbands?"

"No."

"How about Solomon? Wouldn't he need a gun to hunt?"

"He and his friends hunt old school wit' dogs and knives. Da pistol belongs to Makalani. Da rifles and shotgun are mine."

As Detective Shaw checked Pāpā's permit, Detective Lee entered with a triumphant nod. After exchanging quiet words with her partner, she left and yelled for officers to stop their search.

"What is it?" Makalani said. "What did you find?"

Detective Shaw signaled an officer. "Pack the rifles. Leave the pistol." He turned to Pāpā. "We're done here, Mr. Pahukula. You can call the station Monday afternoon about your firearms. I cannot guarantee when or if they will be returned."

"I showed you my permits," Pāpā said.

"Routine check." The insincerity in the detective's eyes said something else.

Makalani locked her pistol in the safe and hurried out the door. Solomon's gutted mattress laid open on the deck while officers from inside his ravaged bedroom carried boxes of evidence out to a van.

Makalani rushed to Detective Shaw. "What about Solomon?"

"We're taking him in."

"On what charge?"

When he didn't answer, she rushed to the squad car and yelled at her cousin. "Ask for a lawyer and keep your mouth shut. They will assign a public defender to you. Do whatever they say."

The car backed in front of her as it turned. Solomon stared out the rear window, eyes widened with fright.

She ran beside his window. "Solomon. Did you hear what I said? Ask for a lawyer, and keep your mouth shut."

Aunty Kaulana bellowed like an angry bear. "Where you take my son?"

Detective Shaw stepped back, one hand forward, the other hovering at his hip. Although equally tall, he was outsized and ill equipped to handle her motherly rage.

Detective Lee spoke in a calming voice and used her diminutive size to deescalate the scene. "Mrs. Ching. We're taking your son to police headquarters in Līhuʻe."

"On what charges?" Makalani asked.

"Charges will be read at the arraignment."

"No way," Aunty Kaulana said. "You have to tell us now."

"No, Mrs. Ching. Regardless of what you see on television, we are not constitutionally bound to explain the details of this arrest beyond where we are taking your son."

"Dis is bull—"

Makalani stopped her aunt before she could finish. "How long before the arraignment?"

"Could be up to forty-eight hours."

"Not until Monday?" Aunty Kaulana asked.

"This is Saturday, Mrs. Ching. Monday is when the clock starts."

Unable to throttle the detective, Aunty Kaulana grabbed Makalani instead. "Is she saying dey can keep my son in jail, wit'out a trial, wit'out not'ing, until Wednesday?"

Makalani yelled as the detective walked away. "Solomon is an unemployed adult. He will need a public defender before he talks to you."

"That's up to Solomon, Miss Pahukula."

Detective Lee shut her car door. While officers prepared to leave, the detectives followed the squad car with Solomon up the hill.

"Is dis true?" Aunty Kaulana asked.

Makalani nodded. "Felony crimes are typically not charged right away. But if prosecutors don't think there's enough for a case, they won't charge at all. If that happens, Solomon won't have a criminal record."

"So, li'dis nevah happened?"

"Not exactly. This will be on his arrest record, along with the assault and DUI."

Aunty Kaulana sank to her knees.

Uncle Eric cradled her head against his side. "Can we see him at da station?"

"Maybe with an attorney. Not on your own."

"We should call da public defender's office," Pāpā said.

"It's Saturday."

Uncle Eric's eyes grew wide. "You mean dey can pressure Solomon all weekend wit'out any kine representation?"

"Not if he demands a lawyer."

"Two days in jail? No way. Dat boy goin' crack under pressure and talk."

Makalani didn't know what else to do. "Can we afford to hire an attorney?"

Tūtū shook her head. "And I'm not allowed to use da homestead as collateral fo' loans."

"But it's yours."

"It's a lease dat can be taken away."

CHAPTER FIFTY-SEVEN

Makalani dried the final serving bowl as the evening rain pattered gently on the river-view deck. After the frenzy of activity and emotions, she welcomed the peace.

Tempers had flared when Aunty Maile and Uncle Sanji saw Solomon's ransacked belongings blocking the deck to their wing. They calmed down when they realized their adjacent rooms had not been disturbed. With that settled, they left the search warrant mess for Aunty Kaulana and Uncle Eric to handle and helped Tūtū, Makalani, and her parents clean up the detritus of the abrupt departure of 150 guests.

Everyone had worked in silence, alone with their thoughts, until the homestead looked as neat as it had when Makalani first arrived home.

Four days since she landed.

Five hours since the raid.

One hundred eighty minutes since Solomon, handcuffed in the back of a squad car, had been driven off their land.

With so much to consider, no one wanted to talk. Not to mention the repercussions that might come from Alexa Worthington's shocking news. Tūtū was understandably upset. Her stoic silence set the tone for everyone else.

Makalani turned off the main kitchen light and listened to the rain. Although gentle evening showers were a frequent companion on Kaua'i, the weather forecasters predicted a big storm the following night. She prayed Becky was somewhere safe and dry.

According to Emma, her sister had stayed out overnight without permission before. Māmā said Becky had even gone on a weekend trip with a girlfriend's family and not let James or Linda know. No one had called her a runaway then. This time, she had been gone five days without a word. What if she didn't plan to return?

Didn't or couldn't?

Makalani ran through the list of horrors a missing teenager could face: sexual exploitation, drug abuse, abduction, crime. She could have been taken off the island and sent anywhere in the world.

Or she might never go anywhere again.

Makalani shook away the unthinkable and focused on what she could do that the detectives would not.

From the moment Makalani had convinced James to report his daughter missing, KPD and ISB had instigated all the protocols to find Becky and bring her home safely. They had resources Makalani did not have. Although aggravating, their investigation of Solomon and Becky's possible connection to drugs showed how seriously they were taking this case. As frightening as all this was, Makalani needed to focus and apply her particular skills on the cousin she could help.

She stared into the night and pictured Solomon's terrified eyes looking back.

What crime did the detectives suspect he had done? What had they found in his room? What had they discovered about him or Becky that Makalani didn't already know? She grabbed a pen and notepad from a drawer and sat at the dining table where she could see by the dim rear lānai lights.

She drew a line down the center and wrote *FACTS* on the left.

- Becky ran away from home on several occasions.
- Her parents didn't call the police then.
- If I hadn't insisted, they wouldn't have called them now.

Then she wrote *QUESTIONS* on the right:

- Did James or Linda need a perfect family image to attain an unknown goal?
- Did Becky have a reason to thwart their plans?
- Had she intentionally tried to hurt them before?
- If so, what could make her that angry—teenage angst, or had her parents wronged her in some legitimate way?

Three facts and four questions. Makalani's list already leaned toward the unknown.

She added another line to her *FACTS*:

- A gang of illegal paka lōlō growers sold their weed in Becky's backyard.

But more *QUESTIONS* appeared:

- Did Becky smoke pot?
- Did she hang out with this gang?
- Did they harass her in ways she was too embarrassed to admit to her parents or her friends?

If Makalani hadn't been so afraid of destroying her fragile relationship with James, she would have asked if Becky had ever stolen money from the family or the store. It didn't sound as if Becky had a job, yet she would need money if she bought weed from the gang. She would need even more for cocaine, oxy, or meth.

She added more *QUESTIONS*:

- Would Emma have tattled to her parents or told me if Becky took drugs?
- What would I have found if I had asked to search Becky's room?

The unknown column kept growing. Makalani needed more *FACTS.*

- Becky's friends confirmed her crush on Solomon.
- Becky instigated the road trip to Kōkeʻe Park and the dangerous hike.
- Solomon's level of dehydration matched his claim of being stranded for three days with only the food and water in his pack.

Makalani paused.

If Solomon had saved Becky as he claimed and let her drive to Kōkeʻe, why didn't she take his car and get help?

With all the evidence pointing to that hike, Kauaʻi Search and Rescue must have done a thorough check. Even so, Makalani knew how easily a person could be lost.

Pain stabbed into her gut.

She doubled over, squeezing her belly to contain the spreading fire. After all these years, the stress aches had finally returned—not from something she had said, but from things left undone.

She breathed through the pain. She knew from experience she had to expand her diaphragm and try to relax, but the ice picks kept stabbing into her gut. As counterintuitive as it felt, she stopped clutching her stomach and arched. Every gasping breath brought a little more relief.

When the stress aches had finally begun to subside, a new and disturbing possibility appeared. One that explained how Becky could vanish without taking Solomon's car and why Solomon stuck to a story about Becky slipping that no one seemed to believe.

Makalani poised her pen over the *FACTS* column and wrote.

- Detectives questioned Solomon about Ikaika ʻŌpūnui, found shot and dead in Keālia Forest Reserve.

- The gang keeps rifles inside their Jeep.
- Detectives confiscated Pāpā's rifles and left my pistol behind.

If her cousins had ripped off or double-crossed the gang in some way, Kalei and the men might have followed her cousins to the lookout and shoved them off that cliff. Although it seemed like a lot of trouble and exertion to settle a debt, it would have kept the murders far away from the gang's farm.

Makalani tore off her notes. Right column jammed with questions, left column skimpy with facts, her imagination spinning out of control. She needed to stay focused on things she could do to help.

She picked up the phone.

Only one course of action came to mind.

CHAPTER FIFTY-EIGHT

The morning sun cracked through the clouds as Boy drove the truck into the hills. He followed the same route Makalani had taken when following the paka lōlō gang's Jeep, through rural neighborhoods and plateaus of wild pili grass, rustic horse properties, and fields. They turned onto the offshoot road that ran alongside the forest reserve.

Makalani leaned forward between the bucket seats and pointed to the cattle gate in a lot beside the ramshackle house. "The gang drove through there." She pointed up the narrowing road. "It ends in a dirt cul-de-sac. My friend and I rode horses through a gap in the fence."

Boy shook his head. "My truck no can follow one horse. Da gate is locked. Goin' rain soon. You sure Kalei's gang took Becky to dea farm?"

"I'm not sure of anything. But this is the only lead I can pursue in the next few hours before this storm hits. When the detectives questioned Solomon and me, they asked him about drugs and if he knew Ikaika ʻŌpūnui."

"Da dead guy?"

"Yeah. I don't know what they discovered in Solomon's room, but if they found a stash of weed, all of this might connect to Kalei's gang. At the very least, the gang had access to Becky and had been harassing James's customers and his wife. Whether she ran away with her paka lōlō buddies or was kidnapped to use as leverage against James, my gut tells me she's with them."

Pupule studied the house. "Da people inside could be asleep. Maybe dis gate no belong to dem."

Boy shrugged. "Or it does, and dey come out shooting." He looked back at Makalani. "Your call. What you like do?"

Even from the distance, she could see the padlock on the chain. "I don't suppose they'd give us permission?"

Pupule snorted. "Not if dey buy weed from Kalei's gang."

If Makalani asked the guys to cut the chain, she—a federal officer— would be breaking the law.

She tugged nervously on her braid. "Do you know another way in?"

Boy shook his head. "We couldn't even see public land before dis."

Pupule held out his hands in a great show of surprise. "Ho. Den I guess dis must be da public hunting access."

"Not if it's padlocked," Makalani said.

He cocked his head. "You sure 'bout dat? You chat wit' Boy. I'll take a look."

Before she could argue, Pupule was out the door with a mini bolt cutter in his hand.

Boy ignored her frown and put the truck in gear. "If you like find Kalei's farm, dis *hunting access* is our way in."

He picked up Pupule and drove through the wide-open gate. Makalani breathed easier when no one stormed out of the house. If she found Becky held captive at the paka lōlō gang's farm, this petty bit of vandalism would be the least of the crimes she might have to commit. She was out of her jurisdiction. Forest reserves belonged to the state. Kaua'i didn't have any federal land.

Once across the pasture, Boy headed up the steep, muddy path, locking the differentials so all four wheels would pull over the rocks and through the deep ruts. "You weren't kidding 'bout rough conditions."

"It gets worse near the cattle guard."

"How far dat?"

"A mile? Maybe more."

"Good t'ing my truck midsize. You say da gang has a Jeep?"

"Yeah. Rugged tires. High off the ground."

He nodded. "And probably a sway bar disconnect system to handle severe tilt."

"Does your truck have that?"

"Yeah. But it still not a Jeep."

Makalani leaned against the door as the truck's left tires drove over a thick cluster of roots and then bounced back into place as they fell into a rut. "Good thing Malosi didn't come."

"He wanted to," Boy said. "Malosi still pissed at Solomon fo' acting stupid, but we all know your cousin could nevah do whatever da cops t'ink."

Makalani wasn't so sure. Although certain her cousin wouldn't have killed, kidnapped, or abused, she suspected he might have contributed to the delinquency of a minor. He had definitely taken Becky out of school. If the cops had found enough marijuana—or, God forbid, harder drugs—in his bedroom during their search, they could charge him with misdemeanor or felony crimes. The age difference between Solomon and Becky made everything worse.

She rolled up her window as a thicket of haole koa shrubs brushed her side of the truck. The foreign invaders wouldn't grow to the majestic heights of Hawaiian koa trees. But they could spread into dense walls up to thirty feet high.

"Ugly plants," Pupule said.

Makalani smiled. "I used to pick the pods and string the brown seeds into leis."

"Fo' real? I no can picture you sitting still fo' dat long."

"I did lots of arts and crafts. Still do."

"Like what?"

"Building models. I made a two-foot replica of the Hōkūle'a at home in Oregon."

Pupule laughed. "You need go on more dates. And by da way, dis *home in Oregon* stuff nevah goin' fly. You belong in Hawai'i wit' us."

Although she didn't respond, she had been wondering the same.

Makalani lived in a cozy community with other rangers and people who worked in Crater Lake National Park. The nearest town was an hour away. She rented a two-bedroom duplex on the park's property, socialized with other rangers and their families, and kept the peace in the park's community and wilderness year-round. Whether snow shoeing in the winter or hiking summer trails, she protected people, wildlife, and, especially, the land. He ali'i ka 'āina; he kauwā ke kanaka.

The land was the chief; people the servants. No matter where Makalani went, it was her mission to serve the land.

Oregon was a beautiful place to live. She loved the acceptance of others and forward-thinking views. She even loved the wet weather, although she did miss walking barefoot in warm Kaua'i rain. And she loved that forty thousand Oregonians self-reported as Native Hawaiian or Pacific Islander. Yet as much as she enjoyed where she lived and the EMT, search, and rescue work she did, Pupule was right, Oregon wasn't her home. If she moved back to Kaua'i, she could help her parents and Tūtū on the homestead. She could probably land a law enforcement or ranger position with the DLNR.

Pupule slammed his hands on the dashboard. "Watch out fo' da pig."

Boy drove to the edge of the cattle guard and stopped.

A terrified sow, funneled in by the shrubs, had attempted to cross and slipped between the pipes. Only her thrashing body remained above ground.

Boy shook his head in disgust. "Poor t'ing goin' die. I'd take it fo' meat if we were on our way home. Leaving it to suffah all day would be cruel."

"Plus it stay blockin' da road," Pupule said.

Makalani opened her door. "We have to get her out."

She approached slowly and cooed at the sow. When the animal stopped thrashing, Makalani stepped onto the grate. After petting the sow's neck gently, she slid her arms around the animal's chest. Pupule did the same at the flank. The sow twitched with alarm.

"Hold her tight," Makalani said. "She'll start thrashing as soon as we lift. We need to raise her up and toss her to the other side before she breaks one of her legs."

"I stay more worried about ours."

"Pupule's right," Boy said. "She could cut your calves wit' her hooves. Or you could break your ankle if your boot catch between da pipes."

"You want to kill her?" Makalani asked.

"I nevah say dat. But if you get hurt, we gotta go back."

She nodded, even more determined to find Kalei's gang.

"Ready, Pupule?"

"Yups."

In one coordinated move, they raised the struggling animal and tossed her onto the trail. The sow landed on her hooves and bounded up the hill. As she vanished into the forest, rain clouds passed overhead.

CHAPTER FIFTY-NINE

Kaulana charged into the house like a bull, slamming the screen door against the wall and rebounding it shut. Her heavy tread shook the floors like a magnitude eight quake. She hadn't seen or spoken to her son in seventeen hours. She wouldn't wait another second more.

Julia held out the kitchen phone.

Kaulana snatched it from her hand. "Solomon? Dat you?"

"Yeah, Mom."

She sniffed back the tears. Her big, beautiful son sounded frightened and weak. She needed to be strong and confident for him.

"We try see you last night. Da police station had a phone on da wall. We called. Dey no let us in. Told us go home, wait fo' your call." She sniffed again. "Your faddah and me wait all night. He fell asleep wit' da phone by his ear."

"I'm sorry, Mom. I didn't want to talk."

"Huh. And hea I t'ought da cell lines were down. I told him, 'No way our son be in jail and nevah call us.'" She shook off her frustration and sarcasm. "Why you call da house?"

"Dad didn't pick up."

She choked out a laugh. "Stupid buggah. Probably slept t'rough da ring."

"No worries. I got you now."

She took a steadying breath. "Dey feed you?"

"Yups. Dinner and breakfast."

She imagined a steel tray with a cup of water and a single slice of white bread.

Nah. Dis Hawai'i. More like scoops of macaroni salad and rice.

"You feeling okay?" she asked. "Want me ask fo' extra blankets?"

He grunted, then coughed. "It no work li'dat, Mom."

"Maybe mo' water."

"I'm good." His voice trembled.

Was he scared or going through withdrawals? He had sounded like this in the hospital after three days stuck on that cliff. Since then, he seemed drunk or high every minute of the day.

"Maybe time away from drinking is a good t'ing," she said. "Sober you up. Clean out your system."

"I no drink dat much."

"Really? Den why you get da shakes?"

He didn't answer.

"Nevah mind. How it go wit' da detectives? They give you one public defender?"

"Not until tomorrow."

"Dey question you? Because Makalani said—"

"I know what she said. All her talking landed me hea."

"Oh, baby. Dis not her fault."

"You t'ink it's mine?"

The hurt in his voice tore at her heart. Even so, she had to know. She pressed the phone hard against her face and braced herself for what she might hear.

"Tell me da truth, baby. Wass goin' on wit' you and Becky?"

"How you ask dat?"

"Jus' tell me. I promise I'll understand."

Would she, though? What if the rumors were true? How would she and the family handle a romance between these kids? Although not illegal since the age of consent in Hawai'i was sixteen, a relationship like that would cause embarrassment. Locals would talk stink about Solomon more than they already did.

"Not'ing to understand," he said. "Becky my cousin. She also da only person on dis whole island who still looks up to me and doesn't t'ink I'm a loser."

Hurt quickly replaced Kaulana's relief. "I don't t'ink dat."

"Of course you do. Everyone does. Everybody except Becky. Is it so wrong to want a little encouragement? To have someone believe I'm mo' dan I am? Becky looks up to me. I look out fo' her. Daas it."

Kaulana felt one knot of tension release. So many others remained.

"You know where she stay now?"

"You no t'ink I would have told someone already? I saved her from falling, jus' like I said. She could be anywhere—lost, hurt, scared. I stay worried sick. Cops should be tearing apart Kōke'e Park searching fo' her instead of locking me up."

"I know, baby. But right now, we stay worried 'bout you. Did you say anyt'ing to dakine detectives dat could get you in more trouble dan you are?"

He sucked in a cry. "I don't know. I'm so messed up, Mom."

"It's okay. I got you."

"I wish you were hea."

"Me, too, baby. Me, too."

She hugged the phone and muttered soothing words as he cried.

CHAPTER SIXTY

"We gotta stop," Boy said. "Or we nevah get out."

He drove between a gap in the trees and turned the truck in seven painstaking moves.

Makalani hopped out of the cab. The haole koa had given way to ferns, vines, and waxy-leaf shrubs. No dogs this time. Even if they had been given Becky's scent, they would have taken off after the first animal they spotted. The storm was coming. Makalani couldn't afford another reckless chase through slippery terrain.

She examined the tire tracks scraped across roots and carved into ruts.

Pupule strapped on his water pack and grabbed his rifle with a grin. "Time fo' hunt."

"Hold up," she said. "I need my gear."

In addition to the day's worth of food and water, Makalani had packed a thermal shirt, fleece-lined leggings, socks, a Mylar blanket, paracord, iodine tablets, first aid supplies, an accordion sleep mat, whistles, and extra rations in case she found Becky in bad shape. Although the extra water pouch added weight to her backpack, she never embarked on a rescue mission unprepared.

She checked the knife clipped inside her pocket and the pistol holstered at her appendix inside the waistband of her pants. She zipped up her jacket and secured the hat tie under her chin. Although the weather reports had predicted the storm to hit this area in the late afternoon, pillows of white and gray cumulus clouds already blocked out the sun.

Makalani took the lead, her long strides setting the pace up the rocky trail she hoped would lead to the paka lōlō gang's farm. If the thunderstorms dropped as much rain as she feared, the muddy trails wouldn't dry for a week. By then, who knew what charges Solomon might face?

"Slow down, tita," Pupule yelled. "My short legs no can keep up."

Even Boy lagged behind. Their hunting forays must not have conditioned them for vertical sprints.

She handed them each a whistle. "Go at your own pace, but keep an eye on the sky. If you need to turn back, blow two short bursts. If I need more time, I'll whistle back once. Otherwise, I'll answer with two bursts and meet you at the truck."

"Okay," Boy said. "But not too long. Kūlanihākoʻi will overflow soon."

He wasn't kidding. The clouds had already begun to swell into cauliflower tops. When the mythical lake flooded in the sky, rain would pour onto the earth. She hitched up her backpack and ran.

A hundred yards up, the trail forked: a goat path dropped into a valley on the left and a dry creek bed ran through a tunnel of trees on the right. Offroad tires had traveled in both directions. Only the tracks on the right had driven through fresh mud.

Makalani drew an arrow at the fork for the guys and ran up the pebbled path. She needed to find the gang's camp before the storm hit. Once the dry bed flooded, the trail would be lost. Even in dry weather, the tunnel of trees would hide this route from prying airborne eyes. Makalani needed photographic evidence to convince the detectives of what she hoped to find. Better yet, Becky in tow.

Doubt chipped at her confidence with every crunch of her boots.

What if the gang hadn't taken Becky?

What if some unknown entity was to blame?

What if Solomon said something incriminating and the detectives pinned everything on him?

Two blasts of a whistle stopped her runaway mind. The sky had darkened with the impending storm. Although Boy and Pupule had signaled, she couldn't give up yet.

She blew a single tweet in return, set the timer on her watch, and sprinted up the dry bed as fast as her tired lungs would allow. If she didn't spot signs of the gang's farm or camp in the next fifteen minutes, she'd abandon her quest and race down the mountain before the storm stranded Boy's truck.

Ten minutes later, she smelled frying meat.

She shut off her watch timer and proceeded with care. When she finally reached a gap in the trees, the threatening ho'oweliweli clouds had blocked out the sky.

"Chip," a man yelled in a high-pitched voice. "Come fetch da Spam."

"Chill, Russell. I'm putting on pants."

A moment later, the scraggly blond man Makalani had seen behind James's store appeared in the tarp-covered opening between two multiperson tents. Without a shirt, he looked more athletic than Makalani had originally assumed. He slipped his feet into rubber thongs and hurried to the firepit where Russell, the Chinese guy with the buzz-cut hair, handed him a plate.

Chip frowned at the Spam. "No rice?"

"Still cooking. Get me a tarp or something. It's starting to rain."

As Chip hurried back to the tents, the hapa-Filipino woman, Kalei, and her brother came around the bend.

"Did Inoa come back?" Kalei asked.

"No," Russell said. "He's checking da drainage trenches to make sure dey stay clear."

"You guys dug um deep, though, right?"

"Ask Gabe, he and Inoa finished da job."

She slapped her brother's arm. "Well?"

"Yeah," Gabe said languidly, as if he were stoned. "We dug till we hit rock."

She shook her head at the clouds. "It won't be enough."

As they debated the future of their fields, Makalani spotted a pair of dirty Vans drying on sticks.

CHAPTER SIXTY-ONE

Kay watched the storm clouds gather above the resort and beyond Shipwreck Beach. If only the imminent downpour could wash away the events and revelations of the previous day, she could return to her carefully manufactured life. Instead, childhood memories rolled in with the waves.

Once upon a time, Kay had loved visiting Grandma Punahele's homestead, nestled against the mountain, forest in the back, room in the front to run with the dogs and the goats. Grandma had a cow for milking and dozens of chickens for eating and laying eggs. Her orchard had the sweetest papayas, the biggest bananas, and the most plentiful crop of mangos—much tastier than the scrawny trees on the homestead where Kay had grown up. Grandpa Mahiʻai had even dug a pond for the ducks. To five-year-old Kēhau, Grandma Punahele's homestead was everything the Kealoha homestead was not—a plentiful wonderland tended with love.

Uncle ʻEleu and Aunty ʻIolana had moved to different parts of Kauaʻi by then, but Uncle Ahonui still lived on the homestead with his wife. They doted on Kēhau whenever she visited because God had not seen fit to give them a child. They would wait another twelve years before they were surprised with Paul, who would eventually marry and sire four children, including Joseph who now ran the farm.

Grandma Punahele had given birth to so many children Kēhau could hardly keep them straight, especially if she counted the one stillbirth and the two who died young. She often wondered if her grandparents' next four daughters, including Kēhau's mom, made up for the children they had lost.

Kēhau's elder aunties, Lokelani and Mālie, had been too involved with college and boyfriends to spend time with her, but her youngest aunty had always been happy to play. At seven years old to Kēhau's five, Ka'ahumanu had felt like a sister in those early days—before her parents had taken her away and uprooted her life. If Alexa's research was to be believed, she and Ka'ahumanu were sisters in truth.

The more Kēhau remembered of those childhood visits, the more it made sense. The longing in her mother's eyes whenever Ka'ahumanu called Grandma Punahele *Māmā* and ran to her for hugs. The sadness when Ka'ahumanu spoke a phrase in 'ōlelo Hawai'i that Kēhau hadn't been taught. The pride when Ka'ahumanu cheerfully cared for the animals and crops the way Kēhau never did. Kēhau's mother had been grieving for the special daughter she gave away—a daughter who was nothing like Kēhau.

When her mother stopped taking her to Grandma's homestead, she and Ka'ahumanu had drifted apart. The two years between them made a huge difference at school. Although Ka'ahumanu never snubbed her, she was always busy with activities and friends. The more the older girl succeeded, the smaller Kēhau felt. This, combined with the cultural and financial poverty she felt at home, made Kēhau hate everything Ka'ahumanu enjoyed. Her only protection was to deny. If she didn't want something, the lack of it couldn't hurt.

Kay wiped a tear from her cheek. She knew better now. Anger and denial had not protected her. Kay would always be Kēhau. The child inside her hadn't recovered from the hurt.

"Kay? Darling?" Douglas said. "Why are you sitting on the balcony when we have a whole resort to explore?"

"It's going to rain," she said, brushing the tears off her cheeks.

He sat in the matching chair. "We could join our family at the saltwater pool for a prestorm swim."

Kay choked out a laugh. "I have more family than I want."

He lowered her hand and gave it a kiss. "You don't mean that."

Tears streamed down her face. "In this moment, I really do."

Douglas—God bless him—shared her space without comment as she cried.

"I've been surprised with an elder sister I have envied all my life, humiliated in front of relatives I have snubbed, and betrayed by our granddaughter and the daughter we raised. Family is not as comforting as I once believed."

"For what it's worth, I'm still glad we came. I've always regretted not inviting your parents and relatives to our wedding. Now that I've met them, I'd like to keep them in our lives."

"That's a horrifying thought."

"Why? Because of Honolulu? Our friends are not as judgmental or snobbish as you believe. Even if they were, why should we care? I fell in love with you—Kay or Kēhau, short hair or long, only child or not. The determined, intelligent, fierce warrior woman I married remains. Your 'ohana adds to your history and depth."

"Even with a scandal?"

He laughed. "Scandals add spice. But I wouldn't call what your mother and grandmother did a scandal. They chose to keep your mother's firstborn child in the family however they could."

"My life would have been so different."

"Actually," he said. "You might not have been born. Caring for an infant would have derailed your mother's life. She might not have graduated high school or met your father. Ka'ahumanu might not have become the woman you envy or the sister you now have the opportunity to embrace."

He cradled Kay's hands in his own. "Put your anger aside, my love. It's time to make peace."

CHAPTER SIXTY-TWO

Makalani stared at the pink-and-white-checked shoes, too small for the men, too ridiculous for Kalei. The Vans had to be Becky's, as Solomon had described. Makalani crept to the left for a better look into the tents. Her cousin must be safe if the gang cared enough to dry her shoes. That, or they needed her able to walk on command. What if they kidnapped Becky to use as a camp slave, or worse?

Makalani was so tied up in worry, she didn't notice the trip wire strung low between the trees.

Cans clattered.

Russell overturned the rice pot as he leaped to his feet.

Chip swung his plate in her direction and toppled his Spam.

Kalei slapped her brother's arm and gestured toward the tent. "Get da guns and check it out. It might be one pig. If it stay something biggah, shoot it."

Makalani touched the handle of her SIG, but left it holstered in place. She had invaded the gang's territory. Although they had no legal rights to homestead on this land, the courts might uphold their castle rights to defend. Without spotting Becky or having any real cause to believe she was imprisoned in one of their tents, Makalani might be legally viewed as a trespassing threat.

Heavy footfalls came from behind as a big Hawaiian man with a machete and a shovel ran toward the camp, probably Inoa back from the fields.

Makalani bolted into the forest. Giant hāpuʻu fronds whipped against her face. Behind her, the men bickered loudly in pursuit.

"What set off da cans?" a deep voice asked.

Gabe responded in his lilting, sluggish tone. "We nevah see. Maybe one pig?"

"Nah. I saw boot prints," the deep voice answered. "Definitely a man."

"Maybe da haoles come sabotage our fields," Russell yelled in his higher-pitched voice.

"Right before a storm?" the deep voice asked. "No way. Gabe, you and me would have seen um fo' sure."

"No mattah, Inoa. My sistah wants um dead."

Makalani leaped over roots and slick mud as she ran, puzzling through what she had heard. The haole men her pursuers believed they were chasing must have seriously encroached on the gang. Competitors? Mainland survivalists living off the grid? Whoever they were, Makalani did not want to be mistaken for them. She was nearly six feet tall. It was not a good time to be the size of most men.

"Ovah dea," Gabe yelled.

A shotgun pumped with an unmistakable *ka-chunk*.

Makalani dived into the red-spotted ʻamaʻu ferns seconds before pellets shredded leaves.

Lightning flashed over the distant peaks.

Russell cheered with an even higher-pitched squeal. "Geev'um, brah. Da wild pigs goin' eat good tonight."

Thunder clapped in response as Kūlanihākoʻi drizzled its overflow waters on her face.

"You get um?" Inoa yelled.

Makalani rolled to her feet and ran toward a dense cluster of ʻōhiʻa and koa trees. If the land continued its ascent, she might find a defendable position on higher ground. With the gang on the hunt, castle rights no longer applied.

She barged through the shrubs as thunder rumbled again. If she couldn't hear her pursuers, they couldn't hear her. If only the forest floor would clear enough to see the slope of the land. With ferns reaching up to her waist, she couldn't predict where her next step would fall.

The men argued behind her as they hacked through the fronds.

"Dis way."

"Ovah hea."

"Rain get mo' bad. We gotta go back."

Inoa's voice yelled the loudest. "No way. We need shoot um, or Kalei goin' be pissed."

Makalani's boot sank into a hole, and she pitched forward into the trunk of a tree. She froze, hands on bark, a hairbreadth from having broken her shin. If she didn't find sparser terrain, they'd catch her for sure.

She dislodged her boot and bolted through an opening in the shrubs. Rather than ascend to higher ground, she careened down the slope, grabbing the thin trunks of strawberry guava trees for support. Now that the canopy had thinned, rain pounded against her bare head. Somewhere in her flight, branches had torn off her hat.

Earth slicked into mud, accelerating her speed. If she continued like this, she would smash onto the rocks in the gully below. Clawing at the mud, she straightened her slide and punched, feet first, through the wood rot of a log. Although it had saved her from breaking her feet on the rocks, it had also wedged her in place.

Muffled voices carried down the hill. She twisted her head and blinked against the falling rain. No sign of the men, only the muddy path she had swiped through the trees.

Makalani patted the pistol holstered against her belly, checked the knife in her pocket, and straightened the straps on her pack. Her wild hair was still in a braid. Other than her missing hat, everything was secure. It could have been so much worse. Even so, she had no idea where she was or how to find her way back to Boy's truck.

Rain pelted her head.

Are they even there? Or did they leave while they could?

She pried her legs out of the log and slid onto the rocky bank of the stream. The water was rising. She needed to hike out of this gully before the stream flooded and the already slick hillside turned into waterfalls of mud.

Makalani opened her arms to the sky. "Aloha mai, Lono. I know this is the last month of the Makahiki and the farmers are praying to you for rain, but would you *please* ease your blessings for a few hours until I get out of this mess?"

Lono roared from the mountain and shook the rock beneath her feet. She had neglected to honor him for too long and beseeched his aid too late. In moments, the overabundance of his blessings would rush down the canyon and wash her away. It wouldn't matter that she had found the gang's camp and spotted Becky's shoes. If she didn't survive this storm, those secrets would die with her.

CHAPTER SIXTY-THREE

"Do you think the river will flood?" Julia asked as sheets of rain pounded onto the rear deck.

Kawika handed her a cup of coffee. "It might. I'll pull da boats and kalo buckets up da bank."

"Ask Makalani to help you."

"Where is she?"

"Still asleep, I think."

Kawika widened his eyes in surprise. "At eleven thirty? Pua, maybe. Makalani, no way. She might be hiding out in her room, but she's definitely awake."

"I'm not hiding," Ka'ahumanu said. "I woke up hours befo' you."

Kawika set down his own coffee and greeted her with a hug. "How are you, Mom? I'm so sorry your birthday lū'au ended li'dat."

Ka'ahumanu shrugged, but her face showed the strain.

Julia couldn't imagine how it felt to have your history and identity rewritten so suddenly and in such a public way. "Is there anything we can do to help?"

Ka'ahumanu sank onto the bench. "How? Punahele and Ho'omana are dead. No one knows da truth except, maybe, Alexa. But if Ho'omana was my mother, why she no take an interest in my life? Why Alexa no come to me in private to share dis devastating news?" She shook her fists in frustration. "And how can I possibly be half Podagee?"

Julia gaped at her mother-in-law, who had always welcomed everyone with aloha. Not once, in all these years, had she said anything against the Portuguese people. How could such a loving woman harbor prejudice in her heart?

Kawika looked equally confused.

Ka'ahumanu squeezed back her tears. "You no understan'. If my father was full Podagee, dat means I no get da fifty-percent blood quantum fo' my lease. If DHHL find out, they will kick us off dis land."

With all the disruption from the lū'au, Julia had not done the math. Not only did Kawika and his sisters not have the quarter Hawaiian blood needed to inherit the homestead, Ka'ahumanu lacked the blood quantum to hold on to the one-dollar, ninety-nine-year lease. After a lifetime of work and raising two generations of Pahukulas on this land, Ka'ahumanu and all of them could lose their family home.

Kawika straightened his spine with conviction. "We gotta stop Alexa from making dis public."

His mother scoffed. "She told ovah a hundred people dat I not da birt' child of Punahele and Mahi'ai. You no t'ink everybody in Anahola talk story 'bout us?"

Thunder clapped as even more rain pounded on the roof.

"I t'ink they get bigger concerns," Kawika said. "Wit' luck, we could contain da damage and tell everyone it was a big mistake."

Ka'ahumanu turned to Julia. "Where Kay dem stay?"

"The Grand Hyatt."

Kawika frowned. "Dass a long way to drive in dis storm. Maybe try call?"

"Not good enough," his mother said. "I need speak wit' Alexa in person to explain how much trouble her genealogy will cause. And I need talk wit' my sistah, Kēhau. You saw her face. Her granddaughter dropped dis bomb on her, too."

Kawika took her hand. "You believe her, Mom?"

Ka'ahumanu nodded. "Alexa is callous and ambitious, but she seem plenny kine smart. Punahele was already fifty years old when I was

336

born. It make more sense dat she was protecting her daughter instead of having a baby so late in life. Although in hindsight, I no t'ink it helped very much. Ho'omana nevah smile when she visit. Either it pained her to see me, or her life was very sad."

"Her daughter, too," Kawika said.

"Kēhau? Yeah. Always angry dat one. No mattah what I do, she push me away. She get so many blessings, but it nevah enough."

Lightning flashed, followed a second later by a thunderous boom.

"Rain's coming down hard," Julia said.

"Yeah," Kawika said. "It's too dangerous to drive. We need secure da homestead in case of a flood."

"Mom," Pua yelled from the other side of the house.

She ran across the room in her cozy pajama pants and top. "I knocked on Makalani's door and found this on her bed."

She handed a note to Julia.

"What it say?" Kawika asked.

Julia read. "She went into the forest with Boy and Pupule to find an illegal paka lōlō farm."

"What?" Kawika yelled. "Why she do dat?"

"She says they've been selling weed on James's property and chasing off his customers. She thinks Becky might be with them either by choice or by force. She wanted to find them before the storm hits and before Solomon said anything stupid that could get him into more trouble than he's already in."

Kawika pointed to the downpour outside. "Da storm already hit."

"Calm down," his mother said, then turned to Julia. "Which trail dey take?"

"It doesn't say."

Ka'ahumanu turned to Pua. "Did your sistah say anyt'ing 'bout her plans?"

"No, Tūtū. This is all news to me."

Kawika shook with frustration. "How could she be so foolish? If she still out dea . . ." His voice cracked with fear.

Julia reached for Pua and squeezed the only daughter she could.

Ka'ahumanu remained calm. "We should call James. He might have heard from Makalani or know where dese growers live."

Pua held out her phone. "No bars."

Kawika picked up the landline and slammed it in the cradle. "Dead."

Julia took a breath and did what a mother does, hold on to the rudder and steer her family through the waves. "Makalani knows how to handle herself. She's with Boy and Pupule, so at least she's not alone. We can't contact James or the authorities. Even if we could and we knew exactly where she was, no one would search for her in the middle of a storm."

"Den what?" Kawika asked.

"We protect who and what we can."

Ka'ahumanu nodded. "We need focus on da crisis befo' us and do what we are each able to do."

"I'll pull up da boats," Kawika said. "And add gravel to our drive."

"I'll help," Pua said.

"Secure da animal shelters," Ka'ahumanu said. "Get Kaulana, Maile dem to help. Julia and me will fill da ice chests wit' food and heat leftovers while we have power. We no can tell how long Lono will bless us wit' rain. But we have to believe our Makalani will be okay."

CHAPTER SIXTY-FOUR

Makalani scrambled up the hillside shrubs before the wall of churning rapids ripped the rotted stump from the bank. The roots held long enough to dig in her boots and claw to the base of a strawberry guava tree. The invasive species anchored deeply into the ground. She clung to the trembling trunk as mud slid from above and the rapids devoured everything below.

I should have turned back at the whistle and returned after the storm.

"Stop it, Makalani."

The roar of the rising river swallowed her shout.

Should haves were an indulgence she couldn't afford. She needed to climb out of this death trap before a major landslide uprooted everything on the slope.

She sprang to another guava trunk six feet to the right, grabbed hold of a shrub, and climbed to another before it gave way. She scrambled at a diagonal against an onslaught of sliding mud.

Lightning flashed, illuminating a rocky ledge below and ten feet farther to the right. The rapids were rising. The ledge might be high enough to avoid getting hit.

Might.

It was too far to leap, but she didn't have a choice. Before her current perch could uproot, Makalani dived horizontally and swam against the sliding mud and brush. A rock slammed into her back. She rolled over the side and dangled off the ledge under a waterfall of earth. She kicked her legs and swung into a shallow cave. She scrambled backward until rocks dug into her spine. Only then, did she wipe the mud from her eyes and breathe.

Terror and adrenaline pounded through her heart. Mud and debris cascaded off the ledge. Although trapped and isolated, at least she was safe.

She peeled off her backpack, relieved to see it hadn't torn. She removed her jacket and waistband holster next, followed by her folding knife and every article of clothing, including her soaked underwear and bra. When it came to survival, staying warm was more important than food.

With no visible gashes she needed to treat, she used a foot of her gauze to clean the mud from her hands and her face. She squeezed the water from her braid and tied it in a knot. Having cleaned and dried herself as well as she could, she donned the fleece-lined leggings, thermal shirt, and extra socks she had packed. She unfolded the foam mat and wrapped herself in Mylar. Huddled in her silver cocoon, she stretched out her body to rest.

An hour later, she drank her fill of water and ate. Although she didn't know how long she might be stranded in the wilderness, it was essential that she remained mentally sharp and strong. If the rain stopped by morning, she planned to climb or slide out of this cave. If the storm lasted longer, she'd ration her supplies. When she finally escaped, she would use her iodine tablets to purify any water source she found until she made it off this mountain and found people who could help.

That was the plan.

As long as the wind didn't shift and start blowing the rain into her shelter or a landslide didn't rip the rocky cave from the slope, she would remain relatively warm and safe through the night.

"I am a wind-resisting 'a'ali'i," she whispered. "No gale can push me over."

Resolve strengthened, she settled on a smooth rock and stared at the rain. She prayed Boy and Pupule had made it to their truck and had driven down the mountain before the road became too slick. If they had waited for her, they could be stuck in a ditch or rolled off a ledge. She wouldn't forgive herself if her mission to save family had injured her friends.

What about Becky?

Makalani shook her head to dispel the negative thoughts. Becky would be fine. This was January. The gang must have endured rainy seasons before. If Inoa and Gabe had dug drainage ditches around their fields, they had probably done the same for their camp. Whatever hardship her young cousin faced during the storm was unlikely to be as dangerous as her own.

Unless she was a hostage they couldn't afford to keep.

Oh my god, what if they kill her because of me?

Lightning flashed, followed too closely by thunder so loud it vibrated the earth.

Makalani peered over the ledge. More trees had uprooted and slid down the slope. The rapids were rising. How long before the angry river reached her?

CHAPTER SIXTY-FIVE

James counted the seconds before the thunder clapped overhead. Somewhere in the storm, his eldest daughter wandered, hid, or cowered, away from his protection, possibly in danger, definitely scared. Was she crying for him now as she had as a child?

"Where are you, Becky?" he said into the storm. "Please, please be safe."

He hung on to the belief she had run away from home because the alternative ate at his soul.

Linda, on the other hand, channeled her fear at the easiest target within reach. She laid every possible theory for their daughter's absence squarely at his feet. His degenerate cousin. His horrible island. His failure as a father and husband that put their daughter at risk. If Becky *had* run away, she blamed his stubborn insistence to stay in flaky Kapa'a instead of moving to Wisconsin where they would have had her "responsible" family's support. When the police raided the lū'au, she had convicted Solomon in her mind before the squad car drove him to jail.

As angry at Solomon as James had been, he couldn't believe his cousin would actually do the horrid things Linda believed. Not only did she think Solomon had abducted Becky, she thought he had molested her in the past. When James demanded reasons for this belief, she said he was too blind and self-absorbed to see. But if this were the case, why hadn't Linda intervened? Surely a mother had the same duty as a father to protect their child?

The rear door slammed open before he answered this thought.

"James," a man yelled. "You hea?"

Solomon's high school football buddies hurried up the aisle. Boy and Pupule were muddy and soaked.

"What's going on?" James asked.

"Me and Pupule drove Makalani into da forest to find your daughter," Boy said. "Makalani nevah come back."

"What? Why? You're not making sense."

"Den listen mo' careful. We wen search for da paka lōlō gang's farm. Makalani t'inks Becky might be wit' dem."

"Why would she think that?"

"Because no way Solomon could hurt Becky," Pupule yelled.

"Chill, brah," Boy said, and turned back to James. "Da detectives questioned Solomon 'bout drugs and dat dead guy dey found in da forest. Kalei's gang practically lives behind your store. Makalani t'inks everyt'ing connects to dem. She wanted to find dea camp befo' da rains washed out da trails."

James panicked as he imagined his daughter in a grimy camp with those punks. "Did she?"

"We don't know. We split at a fork. When I blew da whistle, she nevah return."

"So you left?"

Boy looked upset. "Da storm hit hard. I promise you, we did not have a choice."

James turned from them to the rain pounding outside his store. "We have to do something."

Pupule threw out his hands. "Why you t'ink we stop hea?"

"Cell reception is down," Boy said. "Use your landline. Call her parents, da fire station, 911."

"What landline?" James said. "Becky convinced us they were obsolete. We use our cell phones for the store and our home."

He trembled with frustration. When Makalani had asked if she could help, he never dreamed she would do something so foolhardy—or brave. His cousin was risking her life to find Becky while he waited in his store.

He locked the front door and flipped the sign from OPEN to CLOSED.

Linda was right to hold him in such disdain. He should have been searching every inch of this island until he found their daughter and brought her safely home.

"Let's go," he said, grabbing his rain jacket at the back door. "The police substation is around the corner, across the park. Once they call Search and Rescue, we can drive up to Anahola and let Kawika and Julia know."

They took Boy's rugged truck and left James's pickup, with its wimpy tires, behind—another fitting reminder of how useless he had become. When this was done and Becky and his cousins—Solomon included—were safely at home, James would step up and take control of his life. No potheads in his yard. No wife picking him apart. No unrooted daughters wandering astray. He'd make Muramoto Market work or move his family back to the homestead and help Tūtū farm and professionally distribute her crops. If this crisis had taught him anything, it was the importance of 'ohana and how much stronger he and his children were with them than alone. If Linda wanted to move to Wisconsin, she'd have to leave the girls on Kaua'i with him. James wanted his daughters to learn the Hawaiian values that had made Makalani so strong.

When they reached the tiny substation, no one was there.

"Dey must be out on emergency calls," Boy said as they huddled in the alcove. "Let's try da fire station down da road."

"It's not much bigger," James warned. "If we had a landline, we could call. My cell still has no bars."

"Same hea," Pupule said. "And dis rain is coming down hard."

When they reached Boy's truck, only thirty steps away, the rain had soaked through James's pants.

Sure enough, the firefighters had left their station as well.

Boy looked at James. "I goin' be straight wit' you, brah. If we drive into da homestead, we might not get out. Does your wife and other daughter know where you at?"

"No. I ran out with you."

Boy was right. He couldn't leave Linda and Emma alone. As much as he wanted the strength of his 'ohana and his parents around him, he needed to protect his wife and daughter, their home, and his store. If the police miraculously found Becky, they would expect to find him there.

CHAPTER SIXTY-SIX

Makalani woke to silence. The rain had stopped. A glow of light heralded the approaching dawn. Her body ached from the rock beneath her mat and the battering it had endured the previous day. At least she was warm and dry in her Mylar cocoon.

After easing herself off the foam mat and stretching the kinks from her back, she relieved herself near the edge of the cave. Fully awake, she could hear the river rushing below.

Rushing.

Although too dark to see how high it had risen or the destruction it had caused, the river wasn't roaring as loudly as before.

By the time she consumed her 400-calorie survival bar and a half liter of water, the morning sun brightened the partially clouded sky. She bagged her dirty clothes and trash, folded the accordion mat, and wedged her warm-socked feet into damp hiking boots. She clipped her holster and gun inside her waistband and cinched her jacket below her hips. With the slippery terrain she would encounter, she wanted her firearm protected and secured.

As ready as possible, Makalani peeked over the edge.

Although the river had lowered six feet from the banks, it could still sweep her away if she slipped into its grip—which seemed likely since the landslide had swiped a muddy red streak below her cave. If she made it across the loose earth to the clinging plants, vines, and trees, would the roots hold against her weight?

A man cried weakly from above. "Gabe. Inoa. Russell. Can anyone hear me?"

Makalani held on to the side of the rock shelter and looked up the slope. The landslide had partially buried a man. Since he had called for the other three men, this must be Chip. If she could free him, he might know the way back to the camp. Either way, she couldn't leave him to die.

Back in Oregon, she had rescued a hiker on the opposite side of a landslide by tossing him a rope and having him tie it around a tree. Without that line, she would have slid down the mountain's face. Even if Chip had two free arms, the paracord she carried didn't weigh enough to throw up a hill. She might, however, be able to hook it on a tree.

She wrapped her hands in gauze like a boxer before a fight. She unpacked the cord and tied her backpack on the end. She tied the other end of the cord in a loose loop around the sleeve of her left wrist. This could be the cleverest or foolhardiest idea she had ever tried.

Pāpā's voice spoke in her mind.

If you no can do not'ing else, chance um big or go home.

Gripping the side of the rock shelter, she tossed the backpack across the landslide and over the tipping trunk of a strawberry guava tree. The thin cord slid through her gauze-protected hands as the pack slid downhill. She yanked it to a stop, then pulled and jiggled until she tangled the shoulder straps in the shrubs.

Assuming the land would give way, she launched herself from the ledge and scrambled as fast as she could, clawing the sliding mud as she crossed. The safety line yanked her wrist and swung her the last few feet over the landslide. Digging her boots into the hill, she climbed the paracord to the shrubs. When she reached her backpack, she gave thanks for the invasive tree's deep and stubborn roots.

"You made it," Chip yelled. "I can't believe it."

Neither could she.

"Can you get me out? I'm stuck."

That's the plan, she thought, but didn't waste the breath. Neither of them was out of danger yet.

Makalani slid the paracord loop off her wrist and untied the other end from her pack. As she wound it into a bundle, Chip whined from above.

"Can you move any faster? I really gotta pee."

"You've been up there all night. I'm sure you've figured out how to do that by now."

She slid her arms into the straps of her pack and clipped it at her waist. It would hug her jacket to her body and make it harder to unzip and draw her gun, but she cared more about losing the first aid and supplies than any danger Chip might present. The landslide would have buried any weapon he had carried. A night spent in damp earth would have depleted his strength. Besides, he didn't strike her as aggressive. From what she had seen and heard at the camp, he didn't seem particularly useful to the gang.

Testing the roots of every plant she grabbed, Makalani climbed up the hill. When she reached Chip, she took out a water pouch and enjoyed a long sip.

He opened his mouth expectantly, then frowned. "You goin' share?"

"Hmm. That depends."

"On what?"

"On whether you still plan to kill me."

"Eh, I nevah did. Dat was my friends. You trespassed. Dey defended what's ours." He smacked his dry mouth. "Come on. One sip."

She squirted an ounce of water into his mouth. He smacked his parched lips and opened them for more.

"Where's Becky Muramoto?" she said.

"What?"

"My cousin. I saw her Vans at your camp."

Chip looked confused. "You not a grower?"

"I'm an Oregon ranger."

"Oh, shit." He coughed. "Can I have mo' water?"

She looked up the hill and considered—for one tiny moment—leaving him behind.

"Please?" Mud clotted his hair. Red earth smeared his face. "Look, I'm sorry," he said. "We thought you came from da haole camp. No one would have shot if we knew what you were."

She gave him another sip. "Haole like you?"

"Eh, I'm local. Dey from da mainland. Big difference."

"And they grow?"

He struggled under the weight of mud and debris. "Little help?"

"Will you take me to Becky?"

"Sure, whatevah. Jus' dig me out, okay?"

Although his current position was anchored against roots, the situation could easily change.

Makalani returned the water pouch to her backpack and unclipped her knife. The Benchmade Freek was her favorite knife: light enough for everyday carry, heavy enough for surviving in the wild. Best of all, it was made by a company in Oregon where she lived.

She cut a branch off the heavy limb weighing on Chip's chest and used it to lever the rest out of the way, then dug until he was free. The guy was lucky. Layers of leaves and plants had stuck to his clothes and insulated him from the cold. It also absorbed the urine from the night. She grabbed his forearm and hauled him out of the earth.

He crawled to the side and clung to the shrubs.

She unwound the tattered gauze from her hands and waited for him to catch his breath. "Okay. Time to go."

Chip squinted up at the slope. "Right now?"

"You want to chance another slide?"

"No way."

She shoved him from behind as he climbed, turning her face away from the stench. When they reached the top, he sprawled on the ground. The T-shirt he must have pulled on before chasing her through the forest was stained with red mud. His drawstring pants had ripped down both sides. If he had switched his slippers for shoes, he had lost them during the slide.

She dug out yesterday's dirty socks and dropped them on his chest.

"What dis fo'?"

"Your feet."

"You get any shoes?"

She glanced at her boots. "Two of them, where they belong."

Chip made a face, then pulled on the socks.

She gave him a water pouch and an energy bar. "Not too fast or your stomach will cramp."

She cleaned her blade while he ate, then tucked it away. When he finished, she packed the trash and helped him to his feet. "Which way?"

He looked around him, scratching his face in thought. "Through here I t'ink."

"You *think*?"

"I wasn't paying attention. We were chasing you."

"*Hunting* me."

"I already told you why. Damn, girl, you sure hold a grudge."

Makalani gritted her teeth. "Don't call me *girl*. And don't make me sorry I dug you out of the mud."

"Whatevah," he said, and marched through the trees. "Jus' so you know, Becky called me, not da oddah way around."

She hurried alongside. "What do you mean?"

"She left one message, all upset. Begged me to drive all da way to Kōke'e and pick her up."

"When was this?"

"Monday."

"A week ago?"

"Yeah. She borrowed some lady's phone to make da call. Said she killed her cousin by mistake. Too freaked out to call her parents. Said dey would call da cops and throw her in jail."

"That's ridiculous. Did you tell her that wouldn't happen?"

"How I know dat? I've been living on da street since I was sixteen. My parents kick me out. Cops hassle me all da time. Maybe it's bettah if Becky take care of herself."

"Becky isn't like you. She has a family who cares about her. Besides, Solomon is fine."

"He is?" Chip seemed genuinely surprised. "She said she shoved him off a cliff."

"That's a bit dramatic even for Becky."

"Maybe. But she made it sound plenny bad. And she definitely did not want to go home."

He yelped as a stick stabbed through his sock. For someone who lived off the grid, he didn't have much wilderness sense. She spotted several smoother routes for his feet, but she didn't want to influence his direction or veer him off course.

"Why did she call you?"

He kept walking. "We talk sometimes."

"About what?"

"You know . . . school, parents, life."

"You guys are friends?"

"I guess. We hang out, alright? It's not a big deal."

"It is when you hide her in the wilderness."

"I didn't hide her. She refused to go home."

Makalani grabbed his arm. She dreaded to ask, but she needed to know. "Why? Is there something going on?"

He yanked back in surprise. "What, like abuse? She's your cousin. You tell me."

Makalani considered Becky's rebellious behavior over the years, Linda's anger, James's disregard. Did Becky cling to Solomon to get away from them? Or did she have other reasons to run away from home?

Chip plodded ahead.

Becky had family. Why would she have called *him*?

CHAPTER SIXTY-SEVEN

The last thing Julia wanted to do when Detectives Shaw and Lee knocked at the front door was to let them inside Tūtū's house.

She yelled for her family and met the detectives outside.

Kawika and Pua rushed out first, followed by Solomon's friends, Pupule and Boy. Kaulana and Eric came out of their wing on the left. Maile and Sanji walked onto the front lānai from the right. Tūtū approached from the yard, boots muddy, grimy work gloves on her hands.

The detectives backed up, surrounded on all sides by hostility and suspicion.

"What you want dis time?" Tūtū said from behind.

"Kawika and I called them as soon as the cell service came on," Julia said. "Isn't that why you're here? To give us news about our daughter?"

Detective Lee nodded.

Detective Shaw shrugged. "Kaua'i Search and Rescue won't search for a woman who may or may not be lost in the forest. They have their hands full with real emergencies after the storm."

Boy stepped forward. "*May or may not be lost?* We went wit' her. She nevah come back. What you call dat?"

Detective Shaw looked at Julia. "You didn't provide that information when you first called."

"I didn't know."

"We'll add it to the report," Detective Lee said.

"You mean you haven't already told them?" Julia said.

Detective Shaw intervened. "KSAR is conducting two other search and rescue missions. They have limited resources and one helicopter. Your daughter is a NPS ranger. She can handle an emergency better than most."

"Fine," Julia said. "If you won't send in a search party, we'll go on our own."

"Mrs. Pahukula—"

"No. Do your job, or we'll do it for you. Either way, my daughter is coming home—today."

Kawika and the braddahs stepped beside her, daring Detective Shaw to object. Behind them, the family stood united in support.

He eyed her linemen with a frown. "I understand your concern."

Julia cocked her head. "Which means what? You'll request a search and rescue?"

"We'll alert DLNR."

"Guess we'll wait by da cattle gate den," Boy said, eyeing the detective with distrust.

"That won't be necessary."

Julia stepped between them. "We will *all* be waiting, Detective. If no one shows up, we'll go in alone."

Detective Lee joined her partner. "Please, Mrs. Pahukula, don't make the situation any worse."

"Dass all you got?" Kawika said. "Our nephew is in jail, our grandniece is missing, our daughter was lost in da storm, in danger or possibly hurt. You guys do not'ing. How could we possibly make dis situation any worse?"

He opened the front door for Julia and Da Braddahs to go back in the house. "We wait one hour, den we go. Join us or don't."

CHAPTER SIXTY-EIGHT

If not for the storm, Makalani could have retraced her dash through the forest by the trail of broken branches and boot-crushed plants. Now every direction looked equally damaged and drenched clean.

Chip leaned against a koa tree, looking utterly spent. "I need mo' water."

"We've been wandering for hours," she said. "Are you sure this is the way?"

"Yeah. I mean, I think so. Can I get water, or what?"

Makalani took a swig and passed him the pouch. He gulped more than his share and returned it without thanks.

He lifted a foot and pointed to the rips in his mud-crusted sock. "Want me to go faster? Try give me your boots."

She ignored him and checked the forest for any indication of which way to go. With the foliage so dense, she couldn't see more than six feet.

Chip pointed to a channel in the ground between the ferns. "Dat might be da drainage ditch Inoa and Gabe dug near our field."

"Or the rain could have deepened a natural groove."

"You got a better idea?"

Makalani remembered running downhill through 'ama'u ferns. This could be the way.

"Fine," she said. "I'll follow you."

As exhausted as the guy seemed, Chip might attempt to run and alert the gang. Until she found Becky, she'd keep him in sight.

When they reached the rise, he yanked her to the ground. He pointed above them at a wooden sign nailed to a tree.

Keep out. Trespassers will be shot.

Chip muttered curses and tried to crawl back.

Makalani pinned him in place. "Whose sign is that?"

"Haole growers. We gotta go."

"Are they the ones who killed Ikaika 'Ōpūnui?"

"Who?"

"The homesteader who was murdered in the forest last week."

Chip shrugged. "Maybe. I mean, yeah. We're pretty sure it was dem."

She held him firmly as he tried to escape. "Hold still."

"For what, to get shot? No thanks."

She leaned her forearm on his chest. "Quiet. I need to think."

"About what?"

Rather than answer, she studied the terrain.

Flowering cannabis plants grew on the sunny hillside and plateau in uneven patterns, mixed in with wild local shrubs. From her vantage point, Makalani could spot several irrigation channels dug beneath the shelter of trees on the ridge, flowing into the fields beneath the cover of plants. Camouflage netting obscured the contours of a greenhouse and camp.

"How many plants do you think they have?"

Chip squirmed out of her grasp to look. "Couple hundred. Maybe more."

"So what? We're looking at two to three hundred grand?"

"For dis crop," Chip said. "Five times dat if dey grow five cycles a year."

Makalani hummed in thought. Illegal growers and cartels in Oregon had murdered for less.

Chip tugged at her sleeve. "Can we go now?"

"No." She took out her phone. "I need documentation for Vice."

He grabbed her wrist. "You can't bring dem hea. It's too close to our farm. If Vice busts dem, dey goin' bust us."

Makalani glared. "For growing or kidnapping?"

"I told you. Becky needed a place to stay. What was I supposed to do, leave her stranded at Kōke'e Park?"

Makalani peeled his fingers from her wrist. There were dozens of better choices Chip could have made, but this wasn't the time or place to explain.

She snapped pictures of the ridge, slope, plateau, and camp, including a shot with the direction of the morning sun. On her final photo, she noticed men in the field shaking rainwater from the plants. The one with the red beard had a black eye, a broken nose, and a bandage wrapped around his arm.

Makalani adjusted her position and zoomed in for a closer look.

The man looked up the ridge, straight at her.

He alerted the men, who ran back to the camp while he pulled a pistol from the back of his waist.

Chip sprang to his feet.

The bandaged man yelled back to the camp and pointed across the ridge—in the same direction Makalani's nervous guide had run. She called for Chip to stop and go another way, but he had already bolted through the trees.

Men could be following. Others might cut him off ahead. She unzipped her jacket for better access to her weapon and ran.

Chip tumbled and slid ahead of her down the mud. He slammed to a stop and sprawled onto a trail, face splashing into rain-drenched ruts.

Makalani jumped beside him and pulled him onto bare and bleeding feet. "Are you crazy? You could have been killed."

He brushed a branch off his pants. "Only because of you."

"Me? Oh, no. You and your gang brought all of this on yourself." She shoved him down the wide, muddy trail. "Sprint while you can. Once we gain distance, we'll lose them in the trees."

He stumble-jogged ahead, yelping whenever he hit something sharp. The last threads of her socks hugged his ankles like the fetlocks of a horse.

An engine rumbled from behind. The haole growers must use this trail as a road.

"Into the shrubs," she yelled.

"Not yet. I been hea before. Side trail coming up quick."

"They'll follow."

"No way. It's too narrow fo' a truck."

A gun fired.

Chip sprang ahead.

For the second time in twenty-four hours, Makalani ran for her life.

CHAPTER SIXTY-NINE

"Did you hear that?" Julia said, clutching the grab handle of Boy's truck and pointing up the trail.

"Sounded like a shot," Kawika said.

"Maybe," Boy said. "Or backfire from a truck."

Julia's gut clenched. "Can you drive any faster?"

"Not wit'out breaking an axle," Boy said.

"We'll buy you a new one. Hurry. Please."

Julia fell back as Boy jammed across roots and ruts eroded by the storms. The firearms were stored in the lockbox under her seat. When another shot fired up the mountain, she wished she had a rifle in her hands.

She squeezed Kawika's knee. "You think it's Makalani?"

"Or someone fighting her. Hunters wouldn't come out da morning aftah a storm. I hate to say it, but I wish dose detectives and oddah law enforcement had come. If Makalani took on drug dealers, we could be ovah our heads."

Julia fell against her husband as the truck jolted over high ground on the right.

Pupule clutched the window's edge and yelled. "Lean, you buggahs, before da truck tips."

Kawika shoved Julia toward the window while Boy accelerated over the high bank of the road. The truck teetered, then dropped onto four wheels.

Pupule whooped like a cowboy riding a bucking steer.

Kawika hugged Julia tightly through the jolts.

"Everyone okay?" Boy yelled.

Julia nodded.

Kawika yelled, "Good enough."

After several more yards, Boy stopped at a fork.

He turned in his seat and pointed to the right. "Makalani drew an arrow for us yesterday pointing into dat gully. Creek bed was dry. It won't be today."

"Wass on da left?" Kawika asked.

"We nevah check because it started to rain."

"The gunshots came from that direction," Julia said.

Boy cranked the steering wheel and charged up the hill. The truck canted on the rocks, thumped back to level, then ran up another rocky berm.

Julia hung on to the grab handle, certain they'd flip off the edge or into a ditch.

Boy slammed on the brakes and shifted into park. "Like I told your daughter, my truck can handle, but it still not a Jeep."

Julia grabbed his shoulder. "Boy, please. We can't give up."

Pupule grinned. "No worry beef curry, he nevah say dat." He opened his door and hopped to the ground. "Grab da rifles. It's time to go hunt."

CHAPTER SEVENTY

Makalani heaved Chip over a fallen tree and helped him to his feet. "They can't drive around this. We still have a chance."

He stumbled against her with the first step and cried out in pain. "I can't."

The vehicle rumbled closer.

A gun fired.

Bark chipped off the trunk.

Makalani swooped Chip into a fireman's carry and jogged around the bend. She chanted as she jogged, "Never. Say. Can't."

Skinny from rustic living and slim-frame genes, the young man barely weighed more than her mother, who Makalani had carried to Anahola River on a dare in her teens. If she could carry her mother back then, and support the muscular hiker out of Uluwehi Falls last week, she could certainly haul Chip's scrawny body today.

She hefted Chip higher on her shoulders and chanted an ʻōlelo noʻeau Tūtū had taught her to the beat of her feet. "E hume i ka malo, e hoʻokala i ka ihe." It was time to tighten her proverbial loincloth and sharpen her spear. Makalani Pahukula was going to war.

Vehicle doors slammed shut up the hill, followed by an assertive command and responses from at least two different men.

She lowered Chip to the ground and pushed him behind a rocky bank. "Climb up behind the trees. Be quiet, and don't move."

"What about you?"

She took cover and unholstered her gun. "I'll lead them down the trail and deal with them there."

He whispered in fear, "Wit'out me?"

"You'll be safer here."

Makalani tried to sound more confident than she felt. She understood what to do when Lono whipped the wind into a frenzy, flooded the rivers, and oversaturated the land. Until yesterday, no one had ever shot at her. How would she cope if she had to take someone's life?

She motioned for Chip to hide and peeked around the bend.

The man with the broken nose and bandaged arm led the way with a pistol. Two more men carried rifles. A fourth held a shotgun with a hunting knife holstered to his thigh. These weren't locals farming paka lōlō in the wilderness to survive. They were mainland invaders who would kill her and Chip as readily as they had probably killed Ikaika 'Ōpūnui and people who had threatened their operations in other states before. She couldn't afford to worry about how she might or might not cope. Violence had found her. Makalani needed to respond.

She sprinted down the trail and up the next rise, letting her boots fall heavily so the men would hear and follow her. When their voices grew louder, she dodged erratically to avoid being shot and took cover behind an outcropping against the hill.

A bullet shattered a nearby rock into dust.

Another splintered a branch from a tree.

Makalani peered around the boulder, aimed at the broken-nose man, and shot.

He cried out in pain.

She climbed to a higher vantage point as the other men fired where she had been. She lay on the iron-rich earth the color of dried blood as the third rule of gun safety replayed in her mind.

Don't aim your weapon at anything you are unwilling to kill or destroy.

Although she only intended to wound these men, once she pulled the trigger, the destruction she caused would be out of her control.

Better to kill and live than allow evil men to prevail.

The lead rifleman spotted her first. As he raised his gun to fire, she shot him center mass. She winged the second rifleman in the shoulder and hit the shotgun-carrying brute in the leg. She splayed flat against the hillside as bullets peppered the rocks beside her head.

Three men injured. One possibly dead.

She sprang to her feet and led the hunters farther away from Chip.

"Leave him," a man yelled.

The other two cursed and spewed vile acts of retribution they would inflict once they dragged her back to camp.

Makalani's only chance to retrieve Chip and rescue Becky was to scare the hunters off or incapacitate them all.

She darted into the pothos vines hanging from the trees. Although the giant leaves concealed her completely, she took cover behind a sturdy trunk—concealment versus cover, an important discrepancy to know.

Shotgun pellets and rifle bullets tore through the blanket of vines. Even injured, her opposition was three—possibly four—against one.

Makalani hadn't come prepared for a major gunfight. She had one magazine. Only nine rounds left. As she closed her eyes, she heard her mother's voice in her mind.

Makalani. Where are you?

Right here, Māmā, she wished she could say.

Julia Manu Pahukula was her mother, her role model, the sunrise of her dreams. Every aspiration Makalani had ever dared to pursue had begun with her mother's love and belief. Her tireless efforts and compassion, the way she created beauty in all aspects of life, the way she cared for others before she cared for herself. Makalani aspired to live up to her mother's ideal. To accomplish this, she first had to live.

"Makalani," her mother cried again, louder and more present than before.

Pāpā's shouted, "Julia. No."

Makalani shoved open the vines in time to see her father tackle her mother into the ferns a second before bullets fired into the trail where they had been. It all happened so fast.

Down the trail from her parents, Boy and Pupule ran up the hill.

Above Makalani's position, the mainland growers closed in on her parents.

Higher still, Chip hobbled down the rutted trail.

The clueless man was directly behind Makalani's line of fire. If she missed the growers, she might hit him. Even if all her bullets found their marks, they could still pass through body parts and strike Chip.

In the time it took to inhale, the four elements converged into place—her parents, her friends, her enemies, and Chip—spurning Makalani into the only action that made sense.

CHAPTER SEVENTY-ONE

Makalani ran onto the trail, pistol at the ready, yelling for Chip to get out of the way.

The battered man with the pistol swept his aim from her parents to her.

The rifleman aiming at Boy faltered at her shout.

The man with the shotgun followed her gaze and turned to see Chip rooted in place.

Makalani had given Chip a chance to move. There was nothing more she could do.

As she wrapped her finger around the trigger to shoot the man aiming at her, a bullet hit him in the chest. Blood stained the battered man's shirt. He dropped his pistol and crumpled to the ground.

Chip screamed and hit the dirt.

Boy slid the bolt of his rifle as the grower with the shotgun took aim.

With the area behind the grower cleared, Makalani shot him before he fired at Chip.

"Federal officer," she yelled at the last man standing. "Put down your weapon."

He swung his rifle from Pupule to her.

Makalani fired center mass while her father shot him in the head.

The man teetered a moment, as if not realizing all his options had passed. As if not understanding he was already dead. The grisly moment passed, and he fell to the ground.

Māmā ran to Makalani, hugged her tightly, then pushed her away. "Are you hurt? Oh my god, Makalani." She checked every inch for injuries. Having found nothing serious, she hugged her again.

"I'm fine, Māmā. A little battered, that's all."

Pāpā enveloped them both in his strong arms and squeezed, too overwhelmed by emotion to speak.

"You had us plenny worried," Boy said.

Makalani eased out of her parents' embrace. Boy held out his fist. She bypassed the offering and threw her arms around him instead.

"Eh, what about me?" Pupule said.

Makalani laughed and walked into his sweaty embrace.

"Mahalo for coming back," she said to both of them. "And for bringing my parents."

Boy nodded. "We try bring Search and Rescue, but dey nevah show. Da detectives who arrested Solomon said you could take care of yourself."

Pupule laughed. "Well, dey weren't wrong. Tita can handle."

"Um, you guys?" Chip said, hobbling down the trail, an enemy rifle cradled under his arm. "Dis one's moving."

The battered man with the bandaged arm was alive. Blood drenched his pant leg and shirt from gunshots courtesy of her and Boy.

She brushed the fallen pistol behind her with her boot. After checking to be sure the other two men were dead, she shrugged off the backpack she still wore, retrieved the Mylar blanket, and cut it into strips.

Pāpā unslung the hiking bag draped across his back. "I have gauze pads if you want."

"Thanks," she said. "I used mine to wrap my hands."

"How come?"

"Long story."

Makalani pressed the pads against the gunshot wounds and wrapped them with strips to hold them in place. The man woke with a moan, then passed out.

She nodded at the rifle Chip held. "What about the guy I shot up the road? Is he still alive?"

"Uh-huh. He cursed me out big time when I took his gun."

"That's a Browning semiautomatic," she said to her father. "Officers only took our rifles during the raid."

"I was t'inking da same t'ing," Pāpā said. "Maybe da cops nevah leave your pistol out of professional courtesy. Maybe dey left your pistol because it nevah fit dea ballistics report fo' da bullet found in Ikaika 'Ōpūnui."

Māmā gasped. "Is that what they think Solomon did?"

Makalani shrugged. "It would explain their aggressive attitude."

Chip dangled the rifle to the side like a poisonous snake. "Someone take it."

"We didn't say that was the gun," Makalani said. "Put it down before you shoot off your foot." She nodded to the bandaged man. "Besides, my money is on him."

Pāpā nudged the Smith & Wesson with his shoe. "He fired a pistol."

"Yeah, but if 'Ōpūnui shot him in the arm, firing a rifle would be hard. Maybe he switched weapons with somebody else."

In the momentary silence, the man up the road cried for help.

Boy's face tightened between a scowl and a grin. "Bet I could encourage him to share what he knows."

"No," Makalani said. "Bring him down with the others for law enforcement to find."

"What law enforcement?" Pupule said. "I only see us."

She looked to the sky as the rapid flap of helicopter blades grew loud. Detective Shaw stared down. With no room to land, he waved, and they left.

Pupule shook his fists and called them a string of colorful names.

"Relax," Makalani said. "He knows our location. KSAR will send their own helicopter that can airlift the injured to a hospital and the dead to a morgue." She turned to Chip. "We need to get Becky before they come back."

"Why you look at him?" Pāpā said.

"He's part of the paka lōlō gang that hangs behind James's store. Becky has been hiding from her parents and the cops at their camp. She thought she killed Solomon when he slipped off the cliff."

"She called dis guy instead of her *family*?"

"Apparently so."

"We friends, alright?" Chip said. "We not hurting anyone, jus' growing some weed." He pointed at Boy and Pupule. "You guys buy from us." He turned to Makalani. "Solomon does, too. It's no big deal. Please. You can't tell da cops or rangers 'bout us."

"You squatting on state land," Pāpā said.

"Our camp is da only home we got. Inoa's on da DHHL list, but he can't qualify fo' da homes or lots dat come up. Kalei and Gabe's landlord kicked dem out when he sold his crap building to a developer. Russell and me were camping on da beach befo' dis. You t'ink we like living in da sticks wit' no internet or TV? We got nowhere else to go."

Pāpā shook his head and looked at Makalani with concern. "I no like get you in trouble. But I feel kinda sorry fo' dese guys, especially now dat Tūtū might lose her land."

"What? Why?" Makalani asked.

"Tell you aftah we get Becky home."

Pāpā was right. Makalani had more pressing decisions to make. Although sworn to uphold the law, she hadn't actually witnessed Chip or the gang committing a crime. And with violent mainland growers in the forest, it made sense that they might have assumed she was with them.

She glared at Chip. "You fired on a federal officer."

"Not me."

"Doesn't matter. If you had shot me, you would have gone to prison with them."

"Would have?" he asked, eyes widened with hope.

Makalani sighed. "Take us to Becky. If she's okay—and if your gang doesn't do anything stupid—we'll take her home."

"And den?"

"You and your friends will stop hanging around my cousin's store. No selling on his property. No harassing his family or customers."

"Sure. Whatevah you say."

"And stay away from Becky and any other kids." When Chip hesitated, she added, "I don't care if you're friends."

Chip nodded, trembling beneath Makalani's glare. "Got it. Yes. Take your cousin and we done."

She leaned closer. "The deal is only good if Becky is unharmed. If my cousin is hurt or anyone fires on us—"

"Dey won't."

Pāpā gripped his rifle. "I'm coming wit' you."

"So am I," Boy said.

Pupule raised his rifle. "Me, too."

Makalani shook her head. "Pāpā and Boy will come with me. You stay here with my mother and guard the men. If you hear shots, all bets are off."

CHAPTER SEVENTY-TWO

Makalani shoved Chip forward toward the camp. "Make sure everyone stays calm, or my first bullet is for you."

Chip stumbled forward on cut and blistered feet, his torn clothes stained with red dirt, his straggly blond hair matted into muddy dreads. "Chill, okay? Everyt'ing goin' be fine. Jus' give me a chance to let um know wassup."

"You have thirty seconds," Pāpā said, bracing his rifle against his shoulder. Even with the barrel pointed toward the ground, his message was clear.

Chip ran into the camp, yelping with every painful step. "Eh, you guys. I'm back."

The gang stopped the poststorm repairs and watched their friend's approach with a mixture of surprise, shock, and relief.

Becky dropped a bucket and shrieked. She ran to Chip and threw her arms around him in a crushing embrace. "Oh my god, oh my god. You're alive." She kissed every inch of his filthy and embarrassed face.

Chip peeled her off him and shot a nervous glance toward the trees. "You guys, listen up. Becky's cousin pulled me out of a landslide. Her family is hea to take her home."

Becky jolted back in surprise while the gang ran for weapons or cover. Makalani didn't know which. One thing for certain, Chip did not have things under control.

Makalani stepped into the clearing, hands and pistol held up in peace. "This is not a bust. We're here for Becky. Everybody calm down."

Kalei turned with a shovel. Her brother held a tent stake. Russell gripped a cast iron pan. Inoa held a rifle across his waist, ready to raise and fire.

Chip yelled, "Everyone, chill out."

Kalei stepped forward. "I seen you befo'."

"Yes," Makalani said. "Three days ago behind Muramoto Market. You yelled at my cousin's wife."

Kalei grunted. "Dat lady's a bitch."

"That may be true, but you lied to her about not having Becky."

Pāpā and Boy emerged from the trees on either side of the camp. They held their rifles at the ready.

Kalei and the gang tensed.

"Uncle Kawika?" Becky's voice cracked with fear, like a mischievous child caught in the act. "What are you doing here?"

Pāpā glared. "Bringing you home."

Becky reached for Chip. When he backed away, she looked around her for support. She spotted Boy and started to cry.

"Solomon slipped," she said. "I didn't mean to kill him." She looked at Makalani and her uncle and sobbed. "I'm so sorry. It's all my fault."

"Come here," Pāpā said.

"But—"

"Now."

With a final pleading look at Chip, she bowed her head and obeyed.

Pāpā squeezed her shoulder in welcome and moved her behind him.

"You have what you came fo'," Kalei said.

"Not everything." Makalani looked at Chip. "Tell them."

Chip trembled as all eyes focused on him. He explained everything that had happened in one long and rambling burst. When he reached the deal he had struck, he stopped for a breath. "Dey promised not to call da cops."

"She's a ranger," Kalei said.

"Not with DLNR," Makalani said.

Kalei glared. "So what, if we stay away from your 'ohana, you no tell nobody 'bout us?"

Makalani nodded. "And no more selling to kids."

She groaned with frustration. "You get any idea how expensive it is to live on Kaua'i wit' hotel developers and rich haole buying up da land? Of course you don't. You live in Oregon. You not one of us."

"Eh," Boy said. "Makalani stay kanaka maoli jus' like me." He pointed at Pāpā, Inoa, and Russell. "Jus' like dem. I don't know what kine blood you and your braddah get in your veins, but don't—for one moment—pretend she not local enough to count."

Boy's words meant more to Makalani than he knew. They struck at the core of everything that had tugged at her heart since she had arrived. Although she wanted to thank him properly, all she could do at the moment was radiate her mahalo with her eyes.

She turned to Kalei. "Chip told me about your troubles. We won't tell anyone about your farm or your camp. That said, DLNR and KPD will come out in droves to investigate 'Ōpūnui's murder and what happened to us today. I can't promise they won't find this place on their own."

"And Becky?" Kalei asked.

"She needs to tell them the truth."

"That I killed Solomon?" Becky said, bursting into tears.

Makalani groaned in exasperation. "Oh my god, Becky, Solomon is alive. He tried to save you and slipped. Why didn't you call for help? Do you have any idea the trouble you've caused? Your family is worried sick, Solomon is in jail—"

"What?"

"Yes. The detectives think he abducted *you*." Makalani turned on Kalei and the gang. "They're investigating him for 'Ōpūnui's murder. Vice will comb this reserve for illegal cannabis farms. My advice to you is to get out while you can."

Kalei slapped Chip on the arm. "Dis all because of you and your stupid fling wit' dat girl."

"But I love him," Becky said.

Kalei grunted with disgust. "No you don't. You hang wit' Chip to piss off your parents because you are a spoiled, entitled little brat." She turned to Makalani. "Trust me. We are done wit' dis girl." She punched Chip in the arm. "Right?"

He nodded furiously and stared at the ground.

"Pack up," Kalei said. "We drive out da back way. If we get stuck, we hike into town." She narrowed her eyes at Becky. "Leave us out o' your drama. No weed, no kidnapping, no guns—none of dat stuff. You hid out wit' friends and got separated in da storm. You got no idea where we went, and you nevah expect to see us again."

Kalei jutted her chin at Makalani. "Dis work fo' you?"

Makalani exchanged concerned looks with Pāpā and Boy. "In theory, yes. But when the detectives question her, I don't want her to lie."

Chip stepped forward. "She won't lie if she tells dem 'bout me."

Makalani nodded. "That would work." She turned to Becky. "Tell them you called Chip from Kōke'e Park, like you did, and that you camped together because you were afraid you would be blamed for Solomon falling off the cliff. When you got separated in the storm, I found Chip, and we found you."

"Won't he get in trouble?" Becky asked.

"Chip is a witness. He's already involved."

Chip slumped, his momentary chivalry gone. "So, I gotta stay?"

Makalani nodded. "Yes. You need to come back with us."

Russell patted Chip's shoulder, then gave him a hug. "Catch you later, brah."

"No time fo' goodbyes," Kalei said. "We gotta run."

CHAPTER SEVENTY-THREE

Kay tuned out the back seat chatter as her son-in-law drove cautiously up the east coast. After her husband had convinced everyone to make this trip to Kaʻahumanu's homestead, they had pointedly ignored the genealogy issue and filled the silence with banal comments about the poststorm ocean, land, and sky.

Turquoise or azure? Brownish green or greenish brown? Cumulus or stratus?

Kay wanted to scream.

Thad paused at the top of the homestead's muddy drive. "We can slide down the hill, but we may have to wait for the mud to dry before we can leave."

Alexa leaned forward. "Dad, I have other interviews to conduct. I can't be stuck here all day."

Kay snapped. "You think it only rained here? Everyone on the island has to clean up. The last thing anyone wants is to heap your mess on top of theirs."

Cynthia pulled Alexa back and assured her everything would be fine.

How could that be when Cynthia's selfish daughter had upturned their world?

Kaʻahumanu emerged from the house as they parked, looking tired and disheveled from work. Her wrinkled high-water pants and cheap flower shirt made Kay feel self-conscious in the tailored pants and blouse she wore. The short hair she had styled felt contrived in contrast to the explosion of silver waves tied behind Ka'ahumanu's neck.

Her half sister beckoned them to the lānai. "E komo mai. Watch your step in da mud."

Douglas helped Kay up the stairs, then held back with the others so the half sisters could greet each other first. Although Kay appreciated the gesture, the contradicting emotions warring inside her had rendered her mute. She had always wanted an older sister to pave her way through childhood and guide her through hard times. The woman standing before her could have filled that empty spot—*had* filled it as a cousin before Kay's mother had kept them apart.

Our mother, she reminded herself. *Ka'ahumanu's and mine.*

Kay's elder sister had made the Pahukulas so proud. Had their mother regretted keeping Kay instead of her?

Ka'ahumanu placed her rough hands on Kay's cheeks, soaked in Kay's confusion with a nod, and then touched foreheads, bone to bone, where their ancestral DNA was contained. When their noses touched as well, Kay closed her eyes and breathed in the divine breath Ka'ahumanu shared—the same breath of God she also held in herself.

Decades of anger and resentment shed from her heart, making room for aloha so profound Kay started to cry. Her chest heaved with love and regret.

All these years, I could have felt this?

Ka'ahumanu soothed her as she cried with Hawaiian words she didn't understand. When the wave of emotion had passed, her elder sister separated slightly and gazed into Kay's eyes.

"I see you, Kēhau. You are my kaikaina, my younger sistah. I feel you in my bones."

Kay nodded and fell into Ka'ahumanu's embrace, resting her head against her taller sister's breast like a child. She breathed in the aloha and exhaled peace. She could have stayed like this forever.

Alexa whispered to her parents, "I told you this was a good thing."

Ka'ahumanu released Kay with a parting smile, then fixed Alexa with a scolding look. "Your news was poorly shared and brought trouble wit' da joy."

"I only wanted—"

Ka'ahumanu stopped her with a hand. "Pa'a ka waha. Be silent and listen. Wisdom cannot enter while foolish words exit your mouth." She gestured toward the house. "You are welcome in my hale. Leave your shoes and your foolishness at da door."

Ka'ahumanu's home was surprisingly spacious and neat. The style blended old and new Hawai'i with hand-stitched quilts, pillows, woven mats, and gourds amid bamboo furniture and contemporary local art. Although Kay had never been here before, she felt immediately at home.

Her sister's eldest daughter, Maile, and her granddaughter Pua served leftover lū'au food for lunch. Maile's husband, Sanji, brewed liliko'i iced tea. With a dining table and benches long enough for twelve, the nine of them had plenty of room. While they ate, drank, and enjoyed the view, Ka'ahumanu steered the conversation to pleasing topics everyone could enjoy.

"My husband grew kalo in Canton. He came ovah as a contract worker befo' he get one job at Kapa'a Cannery. When I get dis lease, we built da kalo paddy down by da river and planted vegetable and most of da fruit and nut trees up top." She looked around her with pride. "We built dis house and raised our keiki and dea keiki hea, too."

Thad nodded, clearly impressed. "So this is a completely self-sustaining farm?"

"It can be. We get chickens, pigs, easy access to da sea. My son is a good fisherman, so we get plenny to eat. We sell da excess and trade wit' our neighbors. It's a good life. What else could we need?"

After lunch, Ka'ahumanu took them outside on the rear deck, where they could see the river below. It was so beautiful, not the poverty-stricken dump Kay had imagined it would be. Her sister had created something truly special—a thriving farm and family commune even more magical than Kay's memory of Grandma Punahele's homestead. But when they retired to the living area, the peaceful mood fled.

Once everyone had found a comfortable place to sit, Ka'ahumanu brought up the elephant in the room. She explained what might happen to her homestead if Alexa proceeded as she planned. It was all so clear to Kay, yet her granddaughter refused to understand. Or perhaps, Alexa simply didn't care.

Kay gritted her teeth as her granddaughter defended her position—again—despite everything Ka'ahumanu had explained. This was about more than Alexa's ambition or Kay's embarrassment with her Honolulu society friends. Ka'ahumanu and her children might actually lose their home.

"You cannot send your genealogy to Bishop Museum," Kay said.

"I'm sorry, Grandma—"

"No, Alexa. No. Your pretend apology will not save this homestead. Weren't you listening? Once the Department of Hawaiian Home Lands learns that my sister is less than fifty percent Hawaiian, all of this—" She opened her arms to encompass the surprisingly lovely home Ka'ahumanu and her family had built. "All of this will be taken away."

Alexa nodded. "I understand what you're saying, Grandma. But this is the truth. It won't be my fault if your sister loses a property she never had a right to lease."

Pua leaped to her feet in front of her grandmother. "How dare you say that to my tūtū? You have no idea what she contributes to the local community. *Never had a right?* Are you even serious? Our ancestors owned land on this island. Not leased. Owned. And guess what? We still do."

"Then live there," Alexa said.

"We can't. Because the United States government won't give us back our land."

"Then you obviously don't own it now."

Pua and Alexa tilted their heads, like goats on a ridge, neither of them willing to budge.

Maile stepped between the cousins and told them to sit.

"My niece stay talk 'bout da Great Māhele and da Kuleana Act from 1850 dat allowed commoners, like our ancestors, to petition fo' title. But since my grandfaddah's parents already lived and farmed da 'āina, dey no understand dey had to apply. So da government deeded dea land to a local chief. Tūtū's maddah's family understood, but dey no get da money fo' all da required steps. If dey had, our 'ohana would own property all ovah Kaua'i."

Alexa smirked at Pua. "Like I said, you don't own it now."

"No," Maile said, rotating her hand to include Alexa, her parents, and Kay. "*We* don't own it now. Dat land is worth millions of dollars. All of us would have been entitled to a piece."

Ka'ahumanu sighed. "It's not 'bout da money. Dey called it da Kuleana Act because of our responsibility and sacred duty to care fo' da land. I lease dis homestead to show mālama and kuleana fo' dis place and all da 'āina we lost."

Maile and Pua knelt beside her chair and rested their heads against her arms. Kay wanted to join them, but her daughter's family looked unconvinced. As she debated what else she might say to sway their opinion, Kaulana—Ka'ahumanu's formidable youngest daughter— barged into the house with her skinny hapa-Pākē husband and their recently arrested son.

Kaulana cried out with joy, "Dey let Solomon go."

"Why?" Maile said, looking both alarmed and relieved.

Kaulana smiled at her sister. "Dey found Becky. Your granddaughter is safe."

Kay didn't know what had transpired between the sisters during this crisis, but in that moment, love washed away the tension in their eyes. Maile opened her slender arms. The giant woman hurried into her embrace. Once connected, Kaulana cradled her elder sister against her chest.

"I'm so sorry for talking stink 'bout Becky," Kaulana said.

Maile nodded. "And I nevah should have doubted your son."

Kaulana squeezed Maile tight. "I love you, tita."

Maile patted the sides of Kaulana's broad back. "Me, too, kaikaina. Me, too."

Calling the big woman *younger sibling* reminded Kay that nothing would ever change the order of birth—not size or sophistication or money. The elder would always have privileges the younger siblings would not. But they also had the responsibility to care for those who came next.

Maile squirmed out of her younger sister's embrace. "We good?"

Kaulana nodded. "Always."

Beyond them, Solomon Ching stood beside his father like a weary, invisible ghost—the object of discussion yet unimportant by himself.

Kay thought of the judgment she held in her heart and how she had dismissed him and the entire family as beneath her concern. How arrogant and wrong she had been. Although this young man had fallen from grace, it didn't mean he was unworthy or couldn't climb back on top.

Solomon glared at his mother and aunt, walked out of the house, and slammed the screen door shut.

Eric looked back from his departing son and found the whole family staring at him. He chuckled nervously and shrugged. "He jus' needs a couple beers and time by himself." He nodded at the floor as if struggling to believe his own words.

Kay doubted either of those things would help the troubled young man. From her half sister's expression, Kay thought Ka'ahumanu agreed.

A horn blared outside and voices yelled for Solomon to wait.

CHAPTER SEVENTY-FOUR

Makalani jumped out of Boy's truck and shouted for Solomon to wait.

James pulled up beside them. Becky dashed out of the pickup and ran up the steps. She jumped onto Solomon like a koala on a tree.

"You're alive," she cried. "I thought you were dead. I thought I killed you. I thought . . . oh my god, Solomon . . . you're alive."

He hugged her tight, tears rolling down his face.

Two cousins fused together by worry and relief.

Makalani waited with her parents and Boy at the bottom of the steps while James, Linda, and Emma approached from their truck. Tūtū and the rest of the family watched from behind the screen door. Although everyone had questions, no one wanted to infringe.

When Becky finally slid off Solomon, everyone rushed onto the lānai.

Aunty Maile and Uncle Sanji crushed Becky in a hug while Boy and Pupule hugged and patted their braddah on the back.

"What happened to you guys?" Solomon said. "You as dirty as pigs."

Pupule nodded toward Makalani. "It's your cousin's fault. She wen get lost in da storm last night looking fo' Becky, pissed off mainland drug dealers, and dragged us into a gunfight instead."

"She *what*?"

"No joke, braddah. Your cousin one badass tita. She shot um up and made Becky's boyfriend lead us back to dea camp."

He gaped at Becky. "What boyfriend?"

Pupule laughed. "Dat straggly guy, Chip. Ho, braddah. You shoulda seen Makalani face off wit' Kalei's gang, acting all rangerly li'dat."

Boy smacked Pupule's arm. "You weren't even there. You and Aunty Julia stayed behind wit' da bodies while Uncle Kawika and me went wit' Makalani to deal wit' da gang—who, by da way, none of us are supposed to mention, evah again."

Solomon shook his head in confusion. "What are you saying?"

"Makalani t'ought up a way to keep um away from da Muramotos wit'out turning um in to Vice. Your cousin's one stand-up tita. She saved you, Becky, and James's store pretty much all by herself."

"What bodies?" Tūtū asked Boy.

Makalani cringed. Her grandmother was angry. Her aunties and uncles looked confused. Aunty Kay and her family—*Why were they here?*—looked alarmed. Makalani couldn't stand any more of the hyperbole Solomon's buddies had spun.

"Don't listen to them," she said. "If my parents, Boy, and Pupule hadn't come when they did, Chip and I would have been killed."

The family gasped.

"No way," Pupule said. "Dose men would have killed *us* if you hadn't shot first."

"I didn't shoot first. And it wasn't just me."

Pāpā nodded. "We helped little bit. But I gotta say, Makalani, you da hero of dis story whether you like it or not."

"Kulikuli!" Tūtū yelled. "Enough squawking. I want to hear everyt'ing in order. No more nonsense. I want da truth. And I want to hear it from her."

Everyone turned to Makalani in agreement, waiting for her to speak.

She dropped her backpack at her mud-crusted boots and rubbed the tangled hair out of her face. Her sleeve and the rest of her clothes were stained with red dirt and blood. Now that her initial excitement at seeing Solomon had passed, her muscles trembled and threatened to give way.

She gripped the back of a chair. "Could I maybe clean up first? A shower and food would be great."

Solomon caught her as she swayed. "Talk can wait," he said to the family, slipped his shoulder under Makalani's arm, and walked her to the side lānai entrance of her room.

Each step made her more tired than before.

"You need to rest," he said.

"I'll be okay. If I drop my head on a pillow now, I'll sleep through the night."

"Dey can wait."

"And let Pupule control the narrative?" She laughed. "Not a chance."

"Yeah, well . . . whatevah you guys did out dea, I know it was ninety percent you. No try to deny it, Makalani. You always been dea fo' me, even when I was a kid. Even when I was one stuck-up football star. No mattah how drunk or depressed I get, I always listen. I nevah say not'ing. But I always hear what you say."

She hugged him tight. "When things calm down, we'll paddle out and have a good talk. But right now, I stink so bad I can't even think."

They laughed and crinkled their noses.

"Pilau," she said.

Solomon laughed harder. "You stink worse dan me."

When they finally calmed down, he held her steady while she shed her grimy boots on the deck.

"You need help inside?"

"Nah. I got it. I'll see you in a bit."

She made it inside before her body began to shake. Everything that had happened in the last twenty-eight hours hit her at once—finding Becky's shoes, running for her life, scrambling from the rapids, riding a landslide, huddling in a shallow cave.

She slid to the floor.

Saving Chip, confronting ʻŌpūnui's killers, firing her weapon—ending a life.

She had rescued Becky and cleared Solomon's name. In the process, she had risked her parents' and her friends' lives. How could she have lived with herself if things had ended another way?

It took half a bottle of conditioner to untangle her hair and all the hot water in the pipes before she felt clean.

All through the process, she cried.

Thirty minutes later, dressed in her pajamas and with her damp hair wound into a bun, she sat cross-legged in an armchair and explained the whole adventure, beginning with her hunt for Kalei's gang and ending with finding Becky and letting them off the hook.

"Wait," Solomon said. "You didn't turn dem in?"

Makalani shrugged. "They were struggling with housing issues, like a lot of locals here on Kauaʻi. Although I don't condone them squatting in the reserve, I can appreciate what led them to live off the grid. I also understand how frustrating our current cannabis laws are for recreational users like you. Even registered medicinal users can have a hard time acquiring the cannabis they need. Although the gang broke the law, they protected the natural watershed and didn't pollute the land. They also weren't violent like the growers who tried to kill us. In fact, they were afraid of them, too. I would have acted differently if I worked for KPD or DLNR." She turned to James and Linda. "But I made sure they won't bother your family or your customers again."

Linda squeezed Becky's hand. "You'll stay away from that Chip?"

Becky sulked. "I don't even know where he is."

"Keep it that way," James said. He nodded at Makalani. "Mahalo. For everything."

"Naʻu ka hauʻoli," she said. *The happiness belongs to me.*

Tūtū nodded with approval. "Dat's enough fo' now, moʻopuna. I am so grateful alla you are safe." She looked at everyone in the room. "Befo' we can call it quits, we need discuss somet'ing else."

When the family had settled, she turned to Aunty Kay.

"Too often in dis world, hardship accompanies da joy. So it is wit' dis news 'bout my parentage. Although my heart is full of aloha fo' you, Alexa's discovery means I am half Podagee."

Her eyes traveled around the room. "Which means I am only three-eighths Hawaiian."

She settled on Kaulana, who hadn't heard this before. "And you and your siblings are only three-sixteenths. You understan' what dis means, right?"

Aunty Kaulana sighed. "Dey goin' kick us off da land."

"Yeah," Tūtū said. "Dey probably will."

Pupule cut through the silence. "Not if dey don't know."

All eyes went to Alexa, sitting between her parents on a couch. The Worthingtons tensed for a fight.

Makalani thought she understood. "It's not as easy as that, Pupule. Alexa has researched our genealogy for a long time. This project will help her get a master's degree that could eventually launch her career, but only if she can publish and exploit her work. Isn't that right, Alexa?"

"Yes. Thank you for understanding."

Makalani smiled sadly. "Believe me, I do. I went to college in Colorado with big dreams of making an impact on a place bigger than here. I graduated with a bachelor's degree, went through ranger academy, law enforcement academy, and worked as a seasonal ranger before I landed a permanent position. Although I could have applied for one of the national parks in Hawai'i, I chose Oregon instead. I know how it feels to be disconnected from your family, part of the 'ohana, and yet, not quite."

Alexa nodded.

Makalani did, too.

"But this trip home has taught me something I didn't know. No matter where we live or how disconnected or alienated we feel, our blood and our ancestry connect us to each other with an unbreakable cord. All the success in the world cannot compare to the fulfillment family can provide."

She walked over to Alexa, hands extended, inviting her cousin to rise.

CHAPTER SEVENTY-FIVE

"Dis is pono," Tūtū said as Makalani and Alexa separated from their honi kiss. "But it is not complete. When I look at alla your faces, I see words and feelings left unsaid."

Makalani looked around her and understood. Her family had taken steps to mend their relationships, but no one had fully acknowledged or taken responsibility for what they had done. She returned to her cushion and, along with everyone—including the Worthingtons—listened to what the spiritual matriarch of their family had to say.

"Some of you know dis already, but it is important to repeat. Forgiveness is different in Hawai'i dan it is in da West. It's not enough to simply say *I am sorry* and go back to our lives. We must recognize da transgression we have committed and understand da injury dis transgression may have caused."

At the word *transgression*, the mainland members of Makalani's family flinched. Even Linda, who had lived on Kaua'i since she married James, tensed.

Tūtū chuckled. "You see? Forgiveness is not as easy as you t'ink."

Makalani's parents and aunties nodded in agreement. They had grown up with ho'oponopono, the Hawaiian practice of forgiveness and conflict resolution. So had Makalani and Pua. Although Solomon had grown up on Tūtū's homestead—and, for a limited time, James and his daughters as well—Aunties Kaulana and Maile had not perpetuated this tradition with any of them.

Tūtū smiled at her family. "*Transgression* is a potent word. It makes us t'ink of sin or crime. But you can also harm oddahs knowingly or unknowingly t'rough omission, forgetting to do somet'ing important, or by delaying a task. Dis kine transgression, called hala, may not sound important to you, but it can cause plenny kine pain."

Tūtū smiled at Makalani. "We can also do t'ings to excess, go overboard in our good intentions, or become so focused on what we believe is right dat we dominate conversations or take actions into our own hands. Dis kine transgression is called hewa." She looked at Solomon as she explained, "It includes unhealthy habits and addictions"—then turned to face Linda—"or when we allow anger and resentment to fester in our hearts." Finally, she returned her focus to Makalani. "Hewa also includes wallowing in guilt."

She let this sink in before taking a deep and cleansing breath.

"Den we get da big stuff. Dakine sin and crime everybody t'inks of first. But even da worst kine of 'ino transgression—dat should and must be punished—needs to be forgiven befo' da injured party can heal. Only den can we move forward and create da reality we want."

She paused as many of the family members wrestled with what she had said.

Linda shook her head. "I would never have forgiven anyone who had hurt my daughter."

Thad and Cynthia nodded and touched Alexa's hands.

"I understand," Tūtū said. "Heinous acts must be punished. But if we are to be pono, right wit' ourselves, we must let go of da hate and forgive."

Tūtū opened her arms to the family. "Fortunately, none of us have dis kine burden today."

"I do," Makalani said.

"Explain dis to me, mo'opuna. What 'ino do you t'ink you committed or need to forgive?"

"I shot four men. Two of them died."

"Pretty sure I killed one of dem," Pāpā said.

Māmā shook her head and looked at Pāpā, Boy, and Pupule for support. "They were trying to kill us. You all fired in self-defense."

"I hear what you're saying," Makalani said. "But those men wouldn't have come after us if Chip and I hadn't discovered their crops, which wouldn't have happened if I hadn't ignored Boy's whistle and gone to find Becky alone. I delayed because I thought I was right. I've trampled on everyone from the moment I stepped off the plane. I bullied Solomon, pressured James and Linda, and put Boy and Pupule at risk. I didn't tell you or Pāpā where I was going or what I intended to do. I even went to Emma's school to question her in front of her friend. I've acted all high maka maka to all of you as if I knew more than anyone here, as if living on the mainland had somehow made me smarter and more capable than everyone else. I have committed every one of these transgressions. I don't know if I've caused injury to Aunty Kay's family, but I know for a fact I have wronged each and every one of you."

She looked at each family member in turn. "E kala mai ia'u. Please forgive me."

Tūtū nodded. "Mahalo, Makalani. Aloha wau iā 'oe." She turned to Aunty Kay's family. "Dis means *thank you* and *I love you.* All of us who accepts Makalani's apology must say dis to her."

When everyone had thanked Makalani and told her they loved her in English or Hawaiian, Tūtū raised her brows expectantly back at her.

Makalani closed her eyes. Forgiveness was often hardest to ask and grant to one's self.

She whispered, "I'm sorry. Please forgive me. Thank you. I love you."

"Hana hou," Tūtū said.

Makalani took a breath and tried again. "I'm sorry. Please forgive me. Thank you. I love you."

"Louder."

Tears rolled down her face. "I'm sorry. Please forgive me. Thank you. I love you."

All eyes went to Tūtū as Makalani wept. When their matriarch finally nodded, everyone relaxed.

Solomon stood.

"I drink too much," he said. "I don't know if I'm an alcoholic, but I t'ink I should stop. I need to let go of da past and stop feeling so depressed. I don't know how. But I know my actions have worried Mom and Dad. Maybe if I pulled my weight around hea, it would help."

He looked at Makalani's father and Tūtū. "You guys do almost all da work and nevah say not'ing to make me feel bad." He sniffed. "I used to be stronger dan any of you, and I still nevah kōkua wit' anyt'ing or mālama dis family or da 'āina."

He turned to Becky. "If I really wanted to help, I should have told you to wise up and stay in school. Taking you to Kilohana Lookout was da biggest mistake I evah make in my life. I almost get both of us killed, not to mention Makalani, Uncle Kawika, Aunty Julia, Boy, Pupule, and poor Malosi, who would have been in dat gunfight if my stupid actions didn't get him gored by a pig."

He looked at all the Muramotos. "James, Linda, Emma, Uncle Sanji, Aunty Maile—I am so sorry I put Becky in danger and caused all of you pain. Please forgive me."

Uncle Eric rubbed Aunty Kaulana's shoulders as she sniffed back the tears. Their relief was mirrored by all the local family members in the room.

Tūtū nodded her approval. "Is dea anyt'ing anyone wants to add? Some way Solomon has harmed you? Somet'ing you need to unburden before you can let it go and restore balance in your heart?"

When everyone had shaken their heads no, Tūtū helped them and Solomon recite the words of forgiveness and love. As Solomon sat, she turned to Aunty Kay's husband and their daughter's family to explain.

"Ho'oponopono means to restore balance or make t'ings right. Our ancestors believed dey were responsible fo' everyt'ing dat happened in dea lives. So if someone in our 'ohana is suffering or causing harm, dis becomes all of our responsibility to heal."

She looked around the room. "Does anyone else have somet'ing to share?"

Aunties Maile and Kaulana spoke next, apologizing for their bad treatment of each other and the suspicions and judgment they held in their hearts. This led to a cleansing exchange between the other Muramotos and the Chings, which ended with everyone acknowledging the harm they had committed and asking forgiveness for the pain they had caused.

Only one Muramoto remained silent, digging her fingernails into her thighs.

"What 'bout you, Linda?" Tūtū asked. "What pain eats at your heart?"

Linda's eyes shifted toward James's knee, then back to her own. Whatever resentment she felt would not be shared today. From what James had told Makalani, she feared things between them would not be resolved.

"May I speak?" Becky asked Tūtū.

"Of course, dear one. Go ahead."

"Everything everyone did or said started with me. I've been really selfish and full of myself. My sister thinks my life is easy, and it probably is. But a lot of times, you know, it all feels hard. I shouldn't have cut out of school and put Solomon in that position. I shouldn't have hiked in those stupid, slippery shoes. I should have called for help when he fell. I should have gone home to my parents instead of running away. I'm so sorry, you guys. I really am. Thank you for finding me and bringing me home."

Emma hugged her sister as she cried.

"Mahalo, Becky. Aloha wau iā 'oe," Tūtū and everyone said, followed by Becky's hesitant mantra of forgiveness and love to herself.

All the locals in the room exhaled with relief.

Alexa and her parents looked more uncomfortable than before.

Tūtū leaned forward in her chair. "Hawaiians believe every t'ing and every person is our concern. We acknowledge our part in creating da mess and accept kuleana fo' making it right. But dis works both ways, yeah? Like when we show kuleana fo' da 'āina, da 'āina shows kuleana fo' us by providing food, shelter, and beauty. Same goes fo' our 'ohana. When someone suffahs, it stay our kuleana to help make things right. It is from dis place in my heart dat I goin' share my problem and my pain wit' all o' you."

Tūtū's children and grandchildren nodded in support.

"Alexa, I am grateful to you fo' uncovering da truth. I treasure having one sistah. But I am deeply afraid fo' my descendants. When me and my husband acquired dis lot, it nevah look li'dis. We cleared, planted, and built. We raised our keiki and weathered da storms. We showed kuleana for dis homestead, and it kept us alive.

"You say we nevah deserve dis lease. Maybe according to US law. But I tell you, when Prince Kūhiō spoke to da US Congress as Hawai'i's delegate, he intended for all kānaka maoli, with even one thirty-second Hawaiian blood, to regain our land. Congress set da blood quantum at fifty percent. Can you imagine da trouble and resentment dis has caused Hawaiian families like ours? Not only did we lose our sovereignty, da government tells us who is Hawaiian enough."

Tūtū trembled with rage. "It takes twenty-five percent Hawaiian blood to inherit a lease. Even before you dropped dis bomb on us, dat means none of Maile's children or grandchildren could inherit dis homestead." She nodded toward Linda. "Dey suffah from dis injustice every single day. Now none of us are Hawaiian enough, not even me."

Alexa looked ready to cry from the onslaught of anger directed at her.

"Auwē," Tūtū said. "Now I have committed a transgression against you. I let my anger get out of control. I apologize fo' upsetting you. E kala mai ia'u."

Alexa nodded nervously but didn't respond.

"I won't ask you not to publish your genealogy chart or share it wit' Bishop Museum. I only ask you to wait until I can pass dis homestead to da only eligible relative I have. DHHL may fight me on dis, but it stay da only solution dat will show respect fo' your work and still preserve our home."

Makalani interrupted. "If you're only three-eighths Hawaiian, who has enough?"

Tūtū turned to her sister. "I will transfer the homestead to Kēhau."

CHAPTER SEVENTY-SIX

Kay stared at her sister in shock. "But this is your home."

Ka'ahumanu shrugged. "I hope you will allow us to stay and mālama da land."

Douglas squeezed Kay's hand in support. The flood of emotions made it hard for her to breathe. All those years ago, she had shunned her Hawaiian heritage because she had believed her grandmother, mother, and newly discovered sister had shunned her.

She scoffed at the irony.

I pretended I wasn't Hawaiian because I had never felt Hawaiian enough.

Ka'ahumanu smiled at Cynthia and Alexa, then continued speaking to Kay. "A representative introduced a bill that would reduce the succession-inheritance quantum to Prince Kūhiō's original intent. This would give Alexa more than enough Hawaiian blood to inherit from you when the time comes. If she wants to return to her roots, you could pass this homestead to her."

Alexa started to cry.

"I know, dear one," Ka'ahumanu said. "One moment I bite off your head, now I offah you all dis. I am truly sorry fo' causing you such pain. I needed your grandmaddah to understand da situation clearly before I explained. I'm sorry, Alexa. Please forgive me. Mahalo. Aloha wau iā 'oe."

Cynthia and Thad hugged their daughter as she cried while the rest of the family waited patiently for their response. As the seconds passed, Kay considered how she might accept her sister's apology on Alexa's behalf. Finally, her granddaughter pulled herself together and pushed her parents firmly away.

"I won't do it," she said. "I cannot cause this much pain."

Ka'ahumanu looked confused. She gestured to her children and grandchildren. "We all understan'."

"No, Aunty. This was never my intent. I'll submit the genealogy to my professor, confidentially, and then I'll send it to you. I'll find other examples from other families to support the sociocultural study I will eventually publish to pursue my career. I will not disclose your parentage. I will not give the government ammunition to kick you off this land." She looked at every relative in the room. "Your concerns are mine. I accept kuleana for you."

Ka'ahumanu rose, tears rolling freely down her face. She enveloped Alexa in a hug. When Cynthia and Thad joined in, the entire family piled on.

Kay stood apart and watched. Not because she felt disconnected. Because she wanted to imprint this moment in her mind so she would never forget.

CHAPTER SEVENTY-SEVEN

"I no can believe you stay go today," Tūtū said to Makalani in that seemingly contradictory yet ubiquitous phrase.

Stay go.

As if the Pahukula in her begged to remain while the Oregon ranger was obligated to leave.

"Moʻopuna, your head's in da clouds. What you t'inking 'bout so serious li'dat?"

Makalani scoffed. "Pretty sure serious is my default mood."

"Nah. You get plenny kine joy in dat heart of yours. You jus' forget to let um out and run."

"Like a puppy?"

Tūtū winked. "Exactly li'dat. Stay and date Pupule. He lighten you up." She cackled to herself. "I only joke 'bout him. But have you considered moving back home to us?"

Makalani paused, surprised that her grandmother had actually voiced the question instead of hinting the way she normally did.

"I've worked so hard for my career. I don't want to quit."

"Who say you gotta quit? You one cop and a ranger. Move back here. Take your pick. You can dig your feet in da mud and pull kalo from da earth." She fixed Makalani with a penetrating gaze. "Manō Nui Punahele nevah visited any family member except fo' you. Why you t'ink dat is?"

"I don't know."

Tūtū nodded as if her case had been made. "How you find out if you not living hea?"

"You think she's calling me back?"

"I only know dat you, above all oddahs, are special to her." Tūtū took Makalani's hands. "I stay so moved when Alexa finally understood and accepted kuleana for her genealogy and our 'ohana."

"You think I need to do the same."

Tūtū laughed. "Oh, Makalani. You always have."

"Your grandmaddah's right," Pāpā said, walking into the semidark room. "You always da first to help, first to care, first to work. What would have happened to Solomon if you not been hea?"

Makalani shuddered.

Pāpā nodded, as if reading her mind. "We woulda lost him forevah. Dat kine grief would have crushed Kaulana and Eric. Our whole 'ohana. Solomon's friends. And Becky? Auwē. Da guilt would have killed her. Dat is, if da mainland drug dealers you stopped didn't take her out wit' Kalei's gang."

He held out his hand to welcome Māmā as she crossed the main room.

"What's going on?" she said.

"Same old story," Pāpā said. "Reminding our daughter of all her good works."

Māmā bypassed his hand and hugged Makalani instead. "You were supposed to let go of all those bad feelings."

"I did."

"Then what?"

"Tūtū wants me to stay."

"We all do," Māmā said. "But you have to do what's right for you."

"What about my responsibility to our family and this homestead? The three of you work so hard. I can't let you shoulder all of this alone."

Māmā rose on her toes and kissed Makalani's cheek. "Oh, daughter. You show kuleana in everything you do. But don't forget, we also have kuleana for you."

Makalani soaked in her mother's love while her luggage waited at the front door.

Stay go.

"I can't stay any longer, but I don't want to leave."

"Pololei kou makuahine," Tūtū said. "Your māmā is right. We will feel your aloha and kōkua from wherevah you live. Now, hele on befo' you miss da flight."

Makalani had almost reached the door when her pajama-clad sister crashed into her arms.

"Why didn't you wake me?" Pua said.

"Are you kidding? I tried."

"Not hard enough."

"Fine. Next time, I'll dump ice water on your head."

Pua fake-shivered. "I'm not the one the snow goddess touched. Go back to your cold and rainy state. I'll see you the next time you crave sun."

Makalani hugged everyone a final time and walked out the door. Her aunties, uncles, and Solomon were waiting on the front lānai.

"Why are you guys up so early?"

"Why you t'ink?" Aunty Maile said. "To say a hui hou aku to you."

Until we meet again.

Never had this farewell resonated so deeply in her heart.

"I'll see you soon, Aunty Maile. I promise."

She hugged Uncle Sanji as well.

Aunty Kaulana opened her arms and crushed Makalani in her embrace.

"Mahalo fo' you everyt'ing you did. Not jus' wit' Solomon. I saw all da work you did fo' da lūʻau. We nevah could have done it wit'out you."

Uncle Eric gave her a thumbs-up, still groggy with sleep.

Solomon, on the other hand, looked clearheaded and awake.

"When you come back, we should paddle out," he said. "Go fishing. Maybe swim wit' a shark."

"That's one way to get in shape," she teased.

He smacked his belly. "Yeah. Dis gotta go."

"No worry beef curry," Pāpā said, shaking his chest like Pupule. "We goin' work it off quick."

Everybody laughed.

They waved from the steps as Makalani drove up the hill, past the grassy lanes where the macadamia nuts and mountain apples grew. Past the mango and ʻulu trees heavy with fruit. Past the majestic banyan at the entrance, where Uncle Eric liked to drink beer. When she turned onto Anahola Road, a gold-caped rooster stretched its neck and crowed for the sun.

She paused at the highway that would lead her down the coast. It had been named for Prince Kūhiō, who had fought the US Congress to make sure kānaka maoli like her grandmother could work and raise their families on the land. Makalani had never felt her gratitude or kuleana so keenly before.

Stay go.

Her heart would remain until she returned.

KAUAI'I STORM CHARACTERS

Main Characters

Makalani Pahukula (28)—Native Hawaiian law enforcement national park ranger

Ka'ahumanu (Tūtū) Pahukula (85)—Makalani's grandmother

Kawika (Pāpā) Pahukula (58)—Makalani's father

Julia (Māmā) Manu Pahukula (56)—Makalani's mother

Pua Pahukula (25)—Makalani's sister

Maile Pahukula Muramoto (56)—Makalani's elder aunt

Sanji Muramoto (58)—Makalani's uncle-in-law

James Muramoto (37)—Makalani's cousin

Linda Smith Muramoto (37)—Makalani's cousin-in-law

Becky Muramoto (17)—Makalani's missing cousin

Emma Muramoto (15)—Makalani's younger cousin

Kaulana Pahukula Ching (53)—Makalani's younger aunt

Eric Ching (56)—Makalani's uncle-in-law

Solomon Ching (22)—Makalani's missing cousin

Kēhau (Kay) Kealoha Ornelas (83)—Tūtū's eldest niece in Honolulu

Douglas Ornelas (83)—Kay's husband

Cynthia Ornelas Worthington (54)—Kay's daughter in San Francisco

Thad Worthington (54)—Cynthia's husband

Alexa Worthington (24)—Cynthia and Thad's daughter, graduate student

Kimo Tagaloa (22)—Kaua'i police officer and Solomon's high school frenemy

Boy (22)—One of Solomon's old football buddies known as "Da Braddahs"

Pupule (22)—One of Solomon's old football buddies known as "Da Braddahs"

Malosi (22)—One of Solomon's old football buddies known as "Da Braddahs"

Sandy Hall (28)—Kapa'a firefighter, Makalani's high school friend

Ikaika ʻŌpūnui (40s)—Hawaiian man homesteading off the grid in Keālia Forest Reserve

Detective Shaw (40s)—Male detective

Detective Lee (40s)—Female detective

Kalei (20s)—Scowling Filipino leader of the paka lōlō gang

Gabe (20s)—Kalei's brother in paka lōlō gang

Chip (20)—Scraggly blond guy in paka lōlō gang

Russell (20s)—Chinese guy with buzz-cut hair in paka lōlō gang

Inoa (30s)—Kanaka maoli guy in paka lōlō gang

GLOSSARY

This glossary uses the ʻokina [ʻ] or glottal stop and the kahakō [ō] as found in the *Nā Puke Wehewehe ʻŌlelo Hawaiʻi* dictionary to recognize the importance of preserving the indigenous language and the culture of Hawaiʻi. Since the ʻokina is considered a unicameral consonant letter, these words are grouped together at the start. The glossary is arranged by ʻōlelo Hawaiʻi words, Pidgin English and common non-Hawaiian words, ʻōlelo Hawaiʻi phrases, ʻōlelo noʻeau (traditional proverbs), locations, and historical and mythological figures. The definitions coincide with their usage in this novel and are not intended to be comprehensive in meaning. Please note that although Hawaiian Pidgin English has been declared an official creole language, it is not to be confused with ʻōlelo Hawaiʻi, the native language of the Hawaiian people.

- ʻOkina that precedes vowel words creates a glottal stop when used in a sentence.
- ʻOkina between vowels designates a glottal stop in the word.
- Vowels without ʻokina between them glide together in one elongated sound.
- A kahakō over a vowel lengthens the sound and increases the stress. For example, the word kahakō stresses the final syllable slightly with an elongated Ō. The word Kālā stresses both elongated vowels equally. Words without kahakō are *usually* stressed in the first syllable for short words, second syllable

for medium-length words, and the second and second-to-last syllables in long words.

- Diphthongs in the Hawaiian language create subtle differences in sound and placement than a simple glide from one vowel to the next. Since this is difficult (if not impossible) to explain in text, vowel combinations are not addressed here, except to note that *au* has a more closed and forward sound than *ow*. Note: If an ʻokina is not present, vowels will glide within and between words in a sentence.

Vowels (nā woela)

A—(ʻā) ah

E—(ʻē) eh

I—(ʻī) ee

O—(ʻō) oh

U—(ʻū) oo

Consonants (nā koneka)

H (hē)—similar to English

K (kē)—similar to English with less air

L (ʻlā)—similar to English

M (mū)—similar to English

N (nū)—similar to English

P (pī)—similar to English with less air

W (wē)—can be pronounced as English *w* or softer *v*

' ('okina)—glottal stop (as in "uh-oh")

'Ōlelo Hawai'i Words

'a'ali'i—Native hardwood shrub so steadfast in the wind that the people from Kā'u—and Makalani—compare themselves to it when they need to stand firm

'ae—yes, agree, approve

'ai—food

'āina—the land

'ama'u—type of fern

'apapane—type of honeycreeper with red males

'aumakua—deified ancestors who become family or personal gods

'aumākua—plural

'elepaio—rare brown birds

'i'i—vibration in voice while chanting

'ike—see or recognize

'ilima—delicate orange flower used in lei-making

'ino—wicked, immoral, sinful, criminal type of transgression

'ohā—starchy corm of the kalo (taro) plant

'ohana—family

'ohe hano ihu—bamboo nose flute

'ōhi'a 'ai—mountain apple tree

'ōhi'a lehua—lehua tree

'ōkole—bottom

'ōkolehao—(iron bottom) liquor distilled from tī root in a still of the same name

'ole—without

'ōlelo—language, speech

'ōlelo Hawai'i—Hawaiian language

'ōlelo no'eau—wise or entertaining proverb

'ono—delicious

'o'opu—fish (general)

'ōpū—belly

'ukulele—four-string musical instrument brought over by Portuguese immigrants 'ulī'ulī—feathered rattling gourd used as a percussion instrument in Hawaiian dance

'ulu—breadfruit

ahu—stone

ahupua'a—land division from mountains to sea

akamai—intelligent

ali'i—monarch, chief, chiefess, ruler

aloha—love, greeting, farewell

auwē—an expression of love, grief, disappointment

hākā moa—ancient Hawaiian arm wrestling game played while standing on one leg

haku—to braid or plait, braided or plaited (as in haku lei)

haole—white person

hala—pandanus tree; transgression (general), type of transgression during ho'oponopono when harm is done by omission or delay

hālau—long house, meeting house (as in for hula instruction)

hale—house

hale pule—house of worship

hapa—part or portion as in hapa-Hawaiian, hapa-haole, hapa-Pākē

hāpai—pregnant

hāpuʻu—type of fern

hau—type of hibiscus tree

heiau—place of worship, often a stone platform or earth terrace

hele—to go, come, walk, move

hewa—transgression of doing things to excess or going overboard; mistake, fault

hoʻomaikaʻi—very good (see maikaʻi)

honi—to kiss, traditionally the act of touching foreheads and noses while exchanging breath

honu—turtle

hoʻoponopono—to correct; the Hawaiian practice of forgiveness and conflict resolution

hoʻoweliweli—threatening clouds

huakaʻi pō—a procession of ghost warriors who roam the night and enforce Hawaiian law

hūi—an interjection or way of calling "hello"

hula—Hawaiian dance, to dance the hula

huli—to turn, rotate, flip over as in hulihuli chicken that is turned over on the grill

i'a lomi—massage, rub, squeeze, knead (i'a lomi salmon)

imu—cooking pit, underground oven

ipu heke—polished double-gourd percussion instrument used in Hawaiian chants

kāhili—feather standard, symbol of royalty

kāhili ginger—type of yellow ginger that grows from a column

kaikaina—younger sibling or cousin of the same sex

kalo—taro

kālua—to bake or cook in the ground, as in kālua pig

kama'āina—native born, born in a place (not necessarily of Hawaiian blood)

kānaka—people

kanaka—person

kānaka maoli—Native (true) Hawaiian people

kanaka maoli—Native (true) Hawaiian person

kāne—man

kapu—taboo, forbidden, no trespassing

keiki—child, children

koa—largest of Hawai'i's native forest trees, valuable wood, brave, bold, fearless, warrior

kōkua—help, helper, assistant, relief

konohiki—subchief overseer of an ahupua'a land division

kuhina nui—regent or coregent

kukui—candlenut tree or nut, commonly polished and strung into a lei

kuleana—reciprocal responsibility, right, privilege, concern

kulikuli—noise; Be quiet!

kūlolo—rich coconut cream and kalo dessert

kumu—teacher

Kumulipo—creation chant

kupuna—respected elder, grandparent, relative, or close friend of that generation

kūpuna—plural

kupuna wahine—old woman

lānai—patio, porch, veranda, balcony

lauhala—hala leaf woven into lauhala mats

laulau—bundles of tī or banana leaves usually containing pork or salted fish

liliko'i—passion fruit

lo'i—irrigated paddy, field, terrace for kalo or rice

lōlō—feebleminded, crazy, numb

lū'au—feast; tender kalo leaves, especially when baked (squid lū'au); slang for flat feet

lua—bathroom

mahalo—thank you

māhele—division, portion, as in the Great Māhele when King Kamehameha III redistributed the land

maika'i—good (see ho'omaika'i)

maile—fragrant green vine used for lei-making

mālie—calm

maka'āinana—commoner in ancient Hawai'i, general citizen

Makahiki—ancient four-month lunar festival in honor of Lono, god of agriculture, with games, rest, and a taboo on war

makai—ocean, often used to indicate a direction toward the ocean

makua—parent, as in makua kāne (father) or makua wahine (mother)

mākua—plural

makuahine (makua wahine)—mother

mālama—to take care of, tend, preserve, protect

mālie—calm

malihini—visitor, stranger, foreigner, tourist, guest

māmā—mama, mother

mana—supernatural or divine power or authority

manamana pili—little finger

manō—shark

mauka—mountain, often used to indicate a direction toward the mountains

mele—song or chant

moa pāhe'e—ancient Hawaiian game where competitors slide heavy darts between stakes

mo'opuna—grandchild

moloā—lazy

mu'umu'u—loose gown, shift

nēnē—Hawaiian goose

nō ka 'oi—the best

nui—grand, large, magnitude, importance; e.g., mahalo nui (big thanks) or manō nui (shark god)

pa'i 'ai—dense kalo paste, eaten alone or diluted quickly into poi

paka lōlō—(numbing or crazy weed) local word for marijuana

Pākē—Chinese, China

paniolo—Hawaiian cowboy

pāpā—papa, father

papa ku'i poi—poi pounding board

pāpale—hat, head covering

pāpio—reef fish (pressed down flat)

pau—done, finished (also pau hana)

pīkake—jasmine flower used for lei-making

piko—navel, crown of head, crown of hat

piko'ole—crownless, without crown; as in piko'ole pāpale (crownless hat)

pilau—stink, rot, spoiled, foul

pili—wild grass commonly used for thatch

pōhaku—rock stone

pōhaku kuʻi—stone pounder with traditional knobbed shape

pōhaku kuʻi ʻai puka—stone ring-shaped pounder, usually used by ancient Hawaiian women

poi—starchy paste made from pounding kalo, a staple in the Hawaiian diet

poke—to slice or cut into pieces (as in fish)

pono—righteous, moral, correct

pūʻili—split bamboo sticks used as a percussion instrument in Hawaiian dance

puʻu—peak or promontory

puʻuhonua—place of sanctuary and peace, designation awarded to Queen Kaʻahumanu by her husband, King Kamehameha I

puaʻa—pig

pua kenikeni—(ten-cent flower) a fragrant yellow flower once sold for ten cents per lei

puka—hole, entrance

pūneʻe—moveable bed-like couch

pūpū—appetizer, shells

tī—(kī) ti plants

Tuahine—more common spelling of Kuahine, the famous misty rain in Mānoa, Oʻahu, named for the mother who turned into rain after her daughter was murdered. (*Kuahine* also means *sister*)

tūtū—(kūkū) grandparent, commonly used for grandmother

tūtū nui—great-grandmother

wahine—woman

wili poepoe—feather-lei-making method that's fluffy instead of flat

wiliwili—blossoming leguminous tree with lightweight wood

Pidgin English and Common Non-Hawaiian Words as Used/Spelled in the Book

befo' time—back in the day, before

bettah—better

bolo head—bald head

boom kanani—exuberant expression of approval

boy—affectionate nickname

braddah/bruddah—friendly term for guy or brother

broke—break

buggah—a person (especially male) or sometimes a thing (especially when causing trouble)

bumbai—later on, eventually, or else

can / no can—it's possible, it's not possible

chance um—take the chance

char siu—Chinese barbecue pork

choke—plenty, a lot

crushing on—has a crush on

cuz—cousin

da—the

dakine—pronoun used in place of or preceding a noun (as in get dakine or get dakine car)

dan—than

dass—that's

dass why—that's the reason

dat—that

dea—there or their

dem—them, follows a name to signify that person and everyone else (Where Kay dem stay?)

dey—they

eh—hey

evah—ever (as in whatevah)

FBI—from the Big Island

fo'—for

fo' real—truly, are you serious, you've got to be kidding

geev'um—go for it, don't give up

goin'—going to

good fun—enjoyable, fun

grind—eat

hamajang—messed up

Hawaiian time—slowly, running late

hea—here

hele on—get going, move it (*hele* is Hawaiian for go, walk, move)

high maka maka—full of one's self

howzit—greeting like hello, how is it, how are you?

Japanee—Japanese

junk—things of no value

jus'—just

kakimochi—Japanese rice crackers, also called mochi crunch

kaukau—slang for food

konnichiwa—Japanese word for good afternoon

latahz—later, see you later

leftovahs—leftovers

li hing mui—salty, sweet, sour Chinese plum preserved or dried with
    licorice, salt, and sugar, sometimes ground into powder to flavor
    other foods

li'—like

li'dat—like that

li'dis—like this

malasadas—Portuguese doughnut

mo'—more

moke—(rhymes with choke) describes a local who is big, tough

monkeypod—wide-canopied (saman) tree introduced to Hawai'i in 1850s

musubi—Japanese rice ball that is mixed, filled, or topped with another ingredient, typically nori (dried seaweed), umeboshi (pickled plum), Spam, egg, meats, or vegetables

nah—no, no way, just kidding, really?

nevah—never, don't, didn't

nevah mind—don't pay attention to

no need—not necessary

no worry beef curry—don't worry

not'ing—nothing

obāsan—Japanese word for grandmother or older woman

oddah—other

ohajiki—Japanese flicking marble game using flat glass discs

okoshi—Japanese puffed rice

one—number used as an article in place of "a" (e.g., catch one wave)

or what—phrase tacked on at the end of a question

pissed off—angry

plate lunch—take-out meal usually served with two scoops rice and one scoop macaroni salad

Podagee—Portuguese

primo—number one, the best

remembah—remember

saimin—a mixed-cultural noodle soup originating in Hawai'i with a simple shrimp soup base whose name is drawn from the Chinese words sai (thin) min (noodles)

shaka—hand signal for hello, thanks, howzit, formed with thumb and pinkie extended from a fist

shoots—right, yeah, I agree, let's do it

sistah—sister or affectionate word for or way to call a woman

slippahs—slippers, known as flip-flops on the mainland (not in Hawai'i)

Spam—salty processed pork made by Hormel brought to Hawai'i during World War II

stay—used at the end of a question to ask where someone is (Where she stay?) or thrown in front of a verb, as in stay come ovah hea, stay go already (see also *try*)

stink eye—mean look

t'ank/s—thank or thanks

t'ink—think

talk story—gossiping, passing the time, chatting, having a conversation

tita—sister or a tough woman

togeddah—together

try—show me, or thrown in front of verbs as in try come, try eat, try go, try wait

ube—Tagalog word for purple yam

wit'—with

yups—I agree

zori—slippers usually made of rubber

'Ōlelo Hawai'i Phrases

'Ai ā mā'ona.—Eat all you want.

'O ia mau nō.—Always the same.

A hui hou.—Until we unite again. (Way of saying goodbye.)

Aloha e.—Greetings to you. (As in Aloha e, Makalani.)

Aloha wau iā 'oe.—I love you.

E kala mai ia'u.—Please forgive me.

E komo mai.—Come inside.

E mālie.—Be calm.

Hana hou.—Do again. Repeat.

Hauʻoli lā hānau.—Happy birthday.

He ʻōpū halau.—Implying a person's heart is as big as a house.

Kulikuli!—Be quiet!

Mahalo iā ʻoe mai kākou a pau.—Gratitude from all of us.

Mahalo e ke Akua.—Thanks to God.

Mahalo me ke aloha.—Gratitude and thanks with love.

Mahalo no kou hele ʻana mai.—Thank you for coming.

Mahalo nui loa.—Thank you very much.

Mākaukau ʻoe e kōkua?—Are you ready to help?

Mālama i ka ʻāina.—Care for the land.

Naʻu ka hauʻoli.—The happiness belongs to me. My pleasure.

Nō ka ʻoi.—The best.

Onaona i ka hala me ka lehua. He hale lehua no ia na ka noe.—Fragrant
with the breath of hala and lehua, this is the sight I long to see.
Lyric from *Oli Aloha* ancient Hawaiian chant.

Pa'a ka waha.—Close your mouth.

Pololei kou makuahine.—Your mother is right.

Uoki!—Stop! Quit! Don't touch!

'Ōlelo No'eau (Hawaiian Proverbs) as Described in the Book.

(Find a comprehensive collection of Hawaiian words of wisdom with beautiful translations in *Ōlelo No'eau: Hawaiian Proverbs and Poetical Sayings* by Mary Kawena Pukui, Bishop Museum Press.)

'A'ohe hana nui ke alu 'ia.—No task is too big when we all work together.

'A'ohe mea koe ma kū'ono.—Nothing is left in the corner. (Said of someone who gives without reservation.)

'Ike aku, 'ike mai. Kōkua aku, kōkua mai. Pēlā iho lā ka noho 'ana 'ohana.—Recognize others, be recognized. Help others, be helped. This is how the family lives.

Aloha mai nō, aloha aku; o ka hūhū ka mea e ola 'ole ai.—When love is given, love should be returned. Anger cannot sustain life.

E hume i ka malo, e ho'okala i ka ihe.—Tighten the loin cloth, sharpen the spear.

He ali'i ka 'āina; he kauwā ke kanaka.—The land is a chief; the person is a servant.

Locations on Kaua'i

'Olokele Plateau

Alaka'i Swamp

Anahola (town, bay, beach, stream/river)

Coco Palms Resort

Fern Grotto Cave

Grand Hyatt on Po'ipū Beach

Hanalei

Hanalei Bay

Hanapēpē

Hikinaakalā Heiau

Hōkū'alele Peak

Ka'apuni Road

Kalāheo

Kalalau Valley

Kalalea Juice Hale

Kamokila Village

Kanepo'onui Road

Kapa'a (town, fire station, marina, high school)

Kaua'i

Kaumuali'i Highway

Kawaikōī campground

Kawaikōī Stream

Keālia Beach and Forest Reserve

Kekaha Beach

Kilohana Lookout

Ko'olau Hui'ia Protestant Church

Kōke'e State Park

Kuaehu Point

Kuamo'o Road

Kūhiō Highway

Līhu'e

Lumiha'i Valley

Makaleha Peak

Makaleha Trail

Manō Mountain (a.k.a. King Kong Mountain)

Moalepe Trail

Moloaʻa trail

Mount Waiʻaleʻale

Nā Pali Coast

Nounou Forest Reserve

Olohena Road (State Highway 581)

Pihea Trail and Vista

Poʻipū

Princeville

Puʻu o Kila Lookout

Shipwreck Beach

Smith's Fern Grotto Marina (a.k.a. Kapaʻa Marina)

Sugi Grove campground

Uluwehi Falls

Wailua Game Management Area

Wailua Homesteads

Wailua River

Waimea

Waimea Canyon

Wainiha Valley

Historical and Mythological Figures

'Ōhi'a—noble warrior from legend

Hāloa—second son of Wākea and Ho'ohōkūkalani, his daughter by
Papahānaumoku

Hi'iaka—patron goddess of hula, Pele's youngest and favored sister

King Kamehameha I (Kamehameha the Great)—ruler of Kingdom of
Hawai'i 1795–1819

King Kamehameha II—ruler of Kingdom of Hawai'i 1819–1824

King Kamehameha III—ruler of Kingdom of Hawai'i 1825–1854

Kūlanihāko'i—mythical lake in the sky from which rain falls

Lehua—maiden from legend

Lono—god of agriculture; associated with fertility, clouds, storms, rain,
and thunder

Papahānaumoku (Earth Mother)—first mother of Hawaiian people

Pele (Madame Pele, Tūtū Pele)—goddess of volcanos

Poliʻahu—goddess of snow, known for compassion

Prince Kūhiō (Jonah Kūhiō Kalanianaʻole)—prince of the Kingdom of Hawaiʻi until it was overthrown in 1893, became a US Congress delegate for the Territory of Hawaiʻi

Queen Kaʻahumanu—queen consort to Kamehameha I and served as kuhina nui (coregent) of the Kingdom of Hawaiʻi, 1819–1838

Queen Kamakahelei—queen regent of Kauaʻi, 1770–1794

Wākea (Sky Father)—god of the light and heavens, first father of Hawaiian people

ACKNOWLEDGMENTS

It's always so challenging to write the acknowledgments for a book, especially one as personal as this. Although I can trace my Hawaiian ancestry from Hawai'i Island 1783 to Moloka'i to Maui and to O'ahu, where I was born and raised, it took me five published novels before I felt confident enough to write a novel set in my home. As with many Hawaiian diaspora, I worried I might be out of touch. After living on the mainland for decades, what could I write that would ring true and show the proper respect? Little did I know that my mixed-race heritage, deep love of family, and broad life experiences would be the key to writing a hopefully entertaining and relatable work of commercial fiction that also honored my people and addressed some of the issues facing kānaka maoli today. Little did I know how the process of researching and writing *Kaua'i Storm* would enrich my life.

I want to begin by thanking Kaulana Fraiser, a Punahou classmate who grew up on Kaua'i and talked story with me for hours on end. Her knowledge, experience, and understanding of Hawaiian history, this island, and the struggles facing local kānaka maoli enriched this book and my life. Thanks as well to my cousin Wayde Ching and Punahou classmates John Kolivas, Melinda Walker, and Mealani Evensen for reading all or sections of my early drafts. I'm so grateful for their feedback and encouragement.

Mahalo to my Hawaiian language teacher, Kumu Maile Naehu on Moloka'i, for properly introducing me to our language through her immersive online course—although I sang and chanted Hawaiian mele in my youth, my understanding was limited to key words and phrases. Kumu Maile was also gracious enough to fact-check my use of ʻōlelo Hawaiʻi in this novel. Any mistakes that slipped in are entirely my own. Find her at kahalehoaka.com.

Mahalo to my artist sister, Vonnie Brenno Cameron, for introducing me to Kumu Maile. Our ʻohanaʻs ancestral connection to Molokaʻi inspired Vonnie to interview the kūpuna and paint an exquisite portrait series she later gifted to them. You can view the paintings on her website mixed in with her other stunning portraits at vonniebrennocameron.com.

As with all my books, *Kauaʻi Storm* began with research and then evolved into characters and genealogies. My story emerged from there. Since so much my research is done online from hundreds of locations—historical accounts, interviews, videos, articles, blogs, maps, resources—it would be impossible to list them all. However, I do want to mention the Nā Puke Wehewehe ʻŌlelo Hawaiʻi online dictionary. I continue to rely on wehewehe.org for the most comprehensive definitions that include variations, phrases, and cultural information.

Eternal thanks to the late Mary Kawena Pukui, whose life works have preserved our Hawaiian culture, language, and traditions. Her translations of our ancient wisdoms have become an integral part of Native Hawaiian life. For readers interested in learning more, I recommend Mary Kawena Pukuiʻs beautiful and comprehensive collection, *ʻŌlelo Noʻeau: Hawaiian Proverbs and Poetical Sayings* from Bishop Museum Press.

Mahalo nui loa to my brilliant editor and dear friend, Chantelle Aimée Osman, for her mālama and kōkua. Her insightful questions and suggestions encourage me to stretch and grow while always making me feel valued for the author I am. Chantelle edited my first three Lily Wong mystery thrillers, which included my debut, *The Ninja Daughter*. Working with her again at a new publishing house feels like coming home. And with Thomas & Mercer, that home is *spectacular*.

Special thanks to Ploy Siripant for the stunning book cover—I put it on my phoneʻs lock screen so I can look at it a hundred times a day. Thanks as well to Wendy and all the other editors who put eyes on this manuscript, with a special shout-out to Sarah E. for the most remarkably comprehensive and caring copyediting I have ever received. Although I may never learn all their names, I am beyond grateful to all of the consummate and caring professionals at Amazon Publishing who have and continue to work on my behalf. I also want to extend my deep gratitude to the Cultural Research Read reader they hired. It meant so much to have my work truly seen, analyzed, and commended by a Native Hawaiian as culturally and critically astute as her.

Mahalo to my agents, Nicole Resciniti and Lesley Sabga of the Seymour Agency, for believing in me and this book. Writing is the most emotional and personal career I have ever undertaken. I am so fortunate to have these ladies in my corner.

A special mahalo to my dear friend and Thomas & Mercer author-sistah Lyn Liao Butler for putting me up in her peaceful condo in Kaua'i. I'm listening to the ever-present roosters crow from the forest outside her backyard as I write.

Thanks as well to all the wonderful booksellers who have supported me through the years: Book Soup, Vroman's, Flyleaf Books, Mysterious Galaxy, Murder by the Book, Doylestown Bookshop, Tattered Cover, and so many more. I especially want to thank Barbara Peters, John Charles, Patrick Millikin, and Pat King at The Poisoned Pen for handselling all my titles and giving me a literary home.

And last but never least, my beloved 'ohana for their love, support, and constant encouragement. They are there when I falter and when I succeed. They listen to my babbling until I make sense. They cuddle and value me when the words will not come. They pick me up when I'm down and motivate me to keep writing and create. As with Makalani Pahukula, 'ohana means everything to me. I treasure my relationships as a mother, grandmother, wife, daughter, sister, aunty, niece, and cousin.

Me ke aloha iā 'oukou a pau e ku'u 'ohana aloha!

With love to all of you my dear family!

ABOUT THE AUTHOR

Photo © 2024 JLyn Portraits

Tori Eldridge is the Hawaiian, Chinese, and Norwegian author of the Lily Wong mysteries, *Dance Among the Flames*, and numerous short stories. Born in Honolulu, she graduated from Punahou School with classmate Barack Obama before performing as an actress, singer, and dancer on Broadway, television, and film, and earning a fifth-degree black belt in To-Shin Do ninja martial arts. Her literary works have garnered Anthony, Lefty, and Macavity Award nominations and the 2021 Crimson Scribe for Best Book of the Year. Tori lives in Portland, Oregon, with her husband, near her precious moʻopuna (grandchildren). For more information about Tori, her book club extras, and her reading ʻohana, visit www.torieldridge.com.